PRAISE FOR
YESTERDAY & FOREVER!

SWEET TEMPTATION

Adam lifted an eyebrow, an amused smile on his lips, daring Maggie to dive in. "You think I don't enjoy romance? That perhaps there is no romance in my soul?"

"I'm sorry," she said quickly, trying not to laugh this time. "It's just you're so dramatically different from anyone I've ever known. I'm just not used to the sort of, oh, formal way things are here." She aimed for an apologetic look but couldn't quite hide the twinkle in her eye.

"Do you like Shakespeare?" He looked at her sharply.

"I do. What could be more romantic than *'a pair of star-crossed lovers?'*"

Surprised, Adam nodded appreciation at the quote. Maggie smiled smugly. The first point to her, and the game had barely begun.

Adam flipped open the book and paged through it, quickly finding the passage he wanted.

"'...Arise, fair sun, and kill the envious moon, who is already sick and pale with grief that thou her maid art more fair than she....'"

Maggie studied his expressive face, quelling an impulse to run her hands through his already tousled, thick blond hair. She could almost feel the silky texture of his cravat and yearned to pull it free, releasing his throat to her caressing lips.

Yesterday & Forever

Victoria Alexander

LOVE SPELL NEW YORK CITY

LOVE SPELL®

October 1995

Published by

Dorchester Publishing Co., Inc.
276 Fifth Avenue
New York, NY 10001

The name "Love Spell" and its logo are trademarks of Dorchester Publishing Co., Inc.

Printed in the United States of America.

This book is dedicated with thanks:
To co-workers, for not laughing.
To family and friends, for unwavering confidence.
To the FNOB Alliance, for friendship and support.
To Tory and Alex, for unquestioned love.
And to Chuck, who never, ever doubted.

Prologue

The swans glided silently by the daffodils, the regal bearing of the birds a complementary contrast to the sunny flowers nodding enthusiastically in the breeze. It was a scene to delight an impressionist . . . Monet or Renoir. A setting bucolic and serene.

"Too damn serene, if you ask me," Maggie Masterson muttered under her breath, and surveyed her surroundings through narrowed eyes hidden by dark glasses. She slumped lower on the wood-slatted garden bench and closed her eyes against the tranquil sight.

Zing!
An arrow flashed by her cheek.
Zing! Zing!
A flurry of arrows shrieked past her, scattering the

11

hapless swans. Tourists screamed and scrambled in their panicked efforts to escape the sudden onslaught. Maggie bolted upright and whirled to face the scene behind her.

An army of archers advanced from the dark shelter of the trees, the sea of bodies broken only by men on horseback clad in shining armor. Maggie clambered to stand on the bench and boldly faced the oncoming hordes.

From nowhere, an ebony stallion charged, reared, and pawed the air. Sunlight glinted off the silvered armor of the knight astride the magnificent beast. She shielded her eyes against the glare. A crimson plume thrust jauntily above his helmet was bent double from the force of the wind of his charge. The black steed thundered toward her, halting mere inches from where she stood. Maggie refused to so much as flinch.

The knight tore his helmet from his head and flung it to the ground. His tousled blond hair fell in joyous abandon around a strong, bronzed face. Mahogany eyes gleamed above a roguish smile.

"Lady Margaret, it has been a long time."

She raised a curt brow. "Indeed it has, Sir Cedric."

He quirked an amused brow. "Have you been waiting long?"

"Practically forever." She crossed her arms over her chest. "What kept you?"

He shrugged as best he could in the rigid armor. "Oh, this and that. Slaying dragons, rescuing damsels, and of course there were the Crusades."

"Of course." She nodded, mollified by his response. "Well, at least you're here now." She reached her arms out to him. With one powerful motion he swept her

*up and set her before him on the charger. "Cedric!" She
shivered. "Your armor's so cold!"*

*His eyes twinkled down at her. "Indeed, my lady, but
beneath this frigid steel beats a heart aflame with desire
for you."*

*"Oh, good line, Cedric." She gave him an admiring
glance.*

"Thank you," he said modestly.

*Maggie snuggled closer to the unyielding armor,
hard and cold beneath her head. She shifted with discomfort. Her head slipped lower. Abruptly, she jerked
upright.*

The swans floated undisturbed, their surroundings
still placid and peaceful. Maggie brushed her dark
hair away from her face and sighed. That was some
daydream, complete with a knight in shining armor,
no less. She'd never had a fantasy like that before.
Her lips curled in a rueful grin. But Sir Cedric was
definitely something to dream about.

She gathered up the assorted traveling parapher-
nalia that had fallen out of her tote bag and hoisted
herself to her feet. Her gaze fell once again on the
innocent swans and she studied the birds thoughtfully. Why did the beautiful creatures irritate her so
much? They were completely inoffensive, harming
no one, simply drifting with whatever current came
along. . . .

That was it, she realized with a mental snap of her
fingers. The birds simply drifted aimlessly, with no
purpose. Exactly how her sister, Kiki, described
Maggie when she'd insisted her younger sibling accompany her to London.

Kiki. Petite, pretty, and damn near perfect, she was a free-lance photographer with an international reputation and little patience for a sister with no particular direction in life and no apparent ambition to change.

"Come on, Maggs," Kiki had said a short month ago. "You don't have any real focus in your life. You're twenty-six, and you still don't know what you want to do when you grow up. Take that job of yours. I thought it was going to be temporary."

"It was." Maggie shrugged. "But it kind of grew on me."

"I'll say. You've been doing it now for three years. Maggs, you majored in art. You have a real gift for oils and watercolor. You're wasting all that talent in a job designing labels for canned fruit."

"I'll have you know it takes a lot of skill to make sliced peaches look good enough to eat," Maggie said in halfhearted defense. She grinned sheepishly at her sister's concerned expression. "Maybe I'm just not cut out for a career. Maybe I just want to find Mr. Right and be a stay-at-home wife and mother."

Kiki sighed. "Fine. Whatever makes you happy. Anything would be better than nothing. You're just—"

"I know, I know," Maggie said. "Drifting, I'm just drifting. I appreciate the concern, really I do, but I have to run my own life." She threw up her hands helplessly. "Even if I'm not exactly sure how."

Kiki shook her head in a vague gesture of resignation. "Well, at least come with me to London. You can get away and do some serious thinking. We'll spend two weeks there, then I have a job a few hours away. We can stay together or split up. What do you say?"

Maggie knew from the beginning she didn't have a choice. If Kiki wanted her to go to London, she'd surely be on the next plane. Their relationship was that simple. Kiki had been mother and father to her since their parents died in a car accident ten years ago.

Still, it annoyed her that her sister, a mere six years older, insisted on controlling her life. But Maggie loved her too much to put up more than a token fight and hated to let her down. She suspected the way she lived her life did just that. Worst of all, Kiki was right. Maggie knew it long before her sister made it an issue.

Maggie kicked the pebbles at the water's edge. All her life she'd sensed something missing. But what? That was the big question. What did she want? A home and family? A solid career? Success? Love? Maggie had never even championed a cause. A heavy sigh slid from her heart and escaped through her lips. She just didn't know; she only hoped she'd recognize it when she found it. Whatever "it" turned out to be.

"Maggie." Kiki's voice intruded on her soul-searching. Maggie turned toward the tiny, energetic blonde approaching at full speed. "I've seen enough botanical gardens for one day. How about you?"

"Oh yeah. I've pretty much had my fill."

Kiki grinned at the sarcasm in Maggie's tone. "Great. We've got to get going if we want to catch the next train back to London. If we don't make it, we'll lose our dinner reservations."

"Reservations." Maggie groaned. "Can't we just get takeout pizza or something? I'm beat, exhausted, ready to drop. Why can't we do something that requires less effort than a restaurant? I'm not even hungry." She turned her best give-me-mercy expression to her lively sister.

Kiki ignored the familiar look and propelled Maggie to the garden's main gate. "Has your big sister worn you out?"

"Yes, yes, I give up."

"Sorry, sweetie, I promised some friends we'd meet them. After dinner, you can go right back to the hotel and collapse. I promise. But right now get your rear in gear and get going. I don't want to miss that train."

"Great." Maggie heaved a heartfelt sigh and dragged after her sister.

Maggie had to admit, once again, Kiki was right. The food was wonderful and the restaurant had the kind of atmosphere and old-world charm you could have featured on a postcard. Even Kiki's sophisticated friends were fun. Still, Maggie passed on plans to sample London's nightlife in favor of returning to her hotel room and bed.

Outside the restaurant, she glanced up and down the quiet, almost residential street. If the restaurant was the epitome of London, so, too, was this night. Mist swirled around her ankles in damp clouds. Mysterious, romantic, and more than a little lonely.

"Never a cab around when you need one," she said with resignation.

"Beggin' your pardon, miss." A quiet, scratchy

voice intruded on her thoughts. Startled, Maggie swiveled around. A horse and antique carriage was parked on the street nearly beside her.

"Where the hell did that come from?" She could have sworn the carriage wasn't there a minute ago.

"Sorry if'n I startled you, miss." The owner of the voice was poised on a leather-covered bench high behind the horse, looking much as he sounded: elderly, wizened, and tiny, more gnome than man. Maggie shook her head at the fanciful idea. But what better addition to a foggy night in London than an ancient, slightly mystical old man who looked as if he possessed the wisdom of the ages?

"That's okay, I just didn't see you. I must be more tired than I thought. Have you been here long?"

"A long time, miss, a very long time. This be my route, ye see. And you're lookin' like ye need a ride." Nimbly, the gnome jumped from his perch, landing lightly by Maggie's side. Minuscule and weathered, he seemed more like a wooden carving than a living, breathing being.

Vivid blue eyes guarded by bushy, white eyebrows surfaced amid a sea of leathered wrinkles, all crowned by a wreath of snowy curls. His clothes were old-fashioned and well worn, pants sewn from some kind of homespun material, shirt loose and flowing, covered by a soft leather vest. To Maggie's not so critical eye he looked authentic, although she had no idea what period of British history he was made up for. History never was one of her strong suits.

"I was looking for a cab. I want to go back to my hotel."

"Need a rest, do ye? Ain't nothin' more restful than a ride in me carriage." The gnome offered his hand in a gallant gesture.

Maggie hesitated a moment. "Why not?" She smiled, accepting his warm and surprisingly steady hand. "After all, I'm in London. It's a Sherlock Holmes kind of night. I might as well take advantage of it and get the full effect."

The gnome helped her step into the carriage. She snuggled into the worn, tufted seats, the sharp smell of leather and the pungent scent of horse tickling her nose.

"Besides," she said as the gnome climbed up to his post in front of her, "you just don't know when a chance like this will come your way again, do you?"

"No, miss." He clicked his tongue. The horse pricked up his ears and the carriage started off. "Ye never know with chances and choices." He paused as if considering his words. "I hear folks say destiny is a matter o' choice, not chance. But mebee it's a little bit o' both. Ye never know what might be ahead when ye hit a fork in the road. Take the safe choice and mebee ye'd be passin' up somethin' special, somethin' ye cain't name, but somethin' ye know is missin'. Then mebee that's the time to take a chance. Take a path ye wouldn't take otherwise and mebee, just mebee, that's destiny. But ye see," he said with a chuckle, "I'm jist talkin' about a carriage ride, o' course."

"Of course." His words mulled though her mind and the setting spurred her imagination: the soupy London night, a carriage ride, and an ageless philosopher.

Something was definitely missing in her life, and this gnome spoke about that very thing. Weird. But more than likely his speech was a standard spiel to enthrall unsuspecting tourists. Still . . . it was a little spooky, and a little thrilling, and more than enough to make Maggie glad she hadn't passed up this particular fork.

She smiled and relaxed against the carriage seat. The fog drifted closer, deeper, a blanket around her. The carriage rattled slowly through the shrouded streets, the moist, heavy cloud growing thicker, growing closer.

Maggie frowned, a twinge of unease trickling through her. "Is the weather getting worse? Is it always this bad?"

"It's typical, miss, jist typical. It's always like this . . . every time. . . . "

His voice faded in the mist, his soothing tones reassuring. The gentle rocking of the carriage lulled her, and her eyes slipped closed. Without warning, a sudden jerk brought her fully to her senses.

"What's going on?" Had they been hit by a car? Panic gripped her stomach and she tried to pull herself to her feet. She screamed but couldn't hear the sound of her own voice. A rushing roar, like an approaching train, filled her ears. Wasn't that the same kind of noise tornado victims reported hearing? Was this some kind of freak storm? An accident? She could see nothing through the white, swirling clouds.

A jarring wrench tossed her off balance and propelled Maggie helplessly through the air. She barreled into a firm, solid object. The sharp impact

19

knocked her breath away. Her head smacked a hard surface. Searing pain ripped a scream from her throat.

Then . . . nothing.

Chapter One

April 12, 1818

Adam Coleridge, Seventh Earl of Ridgefield, struggled to contain his anger and pressed deeper into the plush velvet seat of his chaise coach. He steadily massaged a painfully throbbing spot just above his left temple. His right hand lay clenched in a fist in his lap. Through narrowed eyes he glared at the source of his pain.

The lovely blonde occupying the seat opposite him was a picture of composure and self-confidence. Only her hands, twisting the ties of her reticule, betrayed the fact that Lady Lydia Coleridge was not as assured as she seemed. Adam's gaze never left his sister's face. He took perverse pleasure in catching those moments when she would forget her perusal of the fog-shrouded, passing scenery and steal a glance at him from beneath lowered lashes.

"Did you have a good time, Lydia?" he said through tightly clenched teeth.

"Oh my, yes, Adam." Lydia laughed. "It was lovely. Such a crush."

"Would you care to explain to me just what you thought you were doing tonight?"

"Why, Adam." She avoided his eyes, her tone suspiciously innocent. "Whatever do you mean?"

"Don't play that game with me." Adam leaned forward, his face looming within inches of hers, forcing her to look at him. "That game of pretending there's absolutely nothing wrong with flouting convention, leaving scandal and disruption in your wake. And tonight I find you exposing your lower leg in front of some of the most disreputable rakes in London!"

"It was a wager." She sighed in obvious anticipation of his response.

"You were betting? Good lord." He groaned and sank back in his seat. "I am almost afraid to ask. What kind of a wager?"

"Oh . . ." Eyes downcast, she struggled diligently with her now tangled reticule strings. "It had something to do with the shape of a horse's leg and its speed. It doesn't signify."

"And were you planning to run a race as well?"

"Possibly." She shrugged, returning her attention to the passing scenery.

"Lydia." He groaned again, the pain in his temple now throbbing at a furious pace. "It's not bad enough that since your coming-out I've caught you dressing as a boy to sneak into places where decent women, or any women for that matter, are not permitted; you've dampened your dresses in a shocking display

22

of indecency, run off to Gretna Green—"

"Just that once," she said under her breath.

"Once is enough, I should think."

"My dear brother." Lydia finally raised her gaze to his. "I had no intention of actually marrying Connor. It was a lark. At any rate, you caught us before we were scarcely gone more than a few hours."

"That is beside the point. You do not seem to understand you are destroying any chance at a good marriage. As much as I have tried to divert any breath of scandal, there is still talk.

"Lydia." He drew a steadying breath in an effort to achieve a calmer and completely rational tone. "I want only your happiness. When Father died it fell to me to look after you. I have done my best, but you have thwarted me at every turn. You have turned down any number of respectable matches."

"Most men are interested primarily in my fortune, followed by my face." She shrugged. "I expect more of the man I wed."

Adam ignored her. "You are three and twenty now, practically on the shelf."

"Thank you for noticing, dear brother." Her words dripped with sarcasm.

Adam sighed again. "I don't mean to offend, but your behavior is intolerable. I admit, I am partly to blame. I have let you have your way far too often. However, if things do not change . . ." He paused. "I shall be forced to do something we will both regret."

"What?"

"I shall be forced to make a suitable marriage arrangement for you." He addressed her in a formal, lofty tone. "Under the terms of Father's will, I am your guardian and have such authority until you reach the age of thirty."

For one stunned moment, Lydia stared, obviously aghast; then she abruptly burst into peals of laughter. "Oh, fustian, brother. You would never make me wed a man I do not want or love. Yours is an idle threat. And I do not know if marriage is what I want." Her voice grew thoughtful. "I'm well aware that I have reached an age where most women are already long wed and producing a brood of children. And while that is not unappealing, perhaps it's simply not meant to be."

"No, Lydia." Adam's voice was firm. "To make a good match is your duty and responsibility. I have made my decision." He ignored a twinge of conscience. "If you do not select a proper husband, I shall choose one for you. You have one month."

Lydia's eyes widened with disbelief. "Oh, Adam, you wouldn't!"

"I would and I will, my dear. There are several eligible parties who have spoken to me about you in the past. I'm sure one of them can be brought up to scratch." Noting her genuine dismay, his tone softened. "It's not my wish to see you unhappy, but you leave me no other option. I am sure whomever I select will be someone you can share your life with, and in time, even grow to love."

"Adam, I will not allow this." Lydia's eyes flashed. "You cannot force me into marriage against my will."

"No." He considered his words and braced himself for the effect they would have on her. "You're right. What I can do is move you to one of the country estates and place you on limited funds. With your penchant for shopping and your love of social engagements I imagine it would not be nearly so pleasant a life as the one I propose. However, it is entirely up to you."

"You give me little choice, brother." Anger and resentment thickened her voice. Lydia glared and snapped her head away, staring blankly at the vague shadows outside the window, hands clenched tight in her lap.

Adam eyed her cautiously. The journey home continued in silence. He had not expected to feel quite so much like an overbearing, unreasonable cad, but he believed his decision was in Lydia's best interest. He had to do what was necessary to secure her future. In Adam's mind, he had as little choice as the one he just gave his sister.

Reassured somewhat by her silent demeanor, Adam closed his eyes and noted the pain in his head had eased. The unpleasant duty attended to, he relaxed and succumbed to a newfound sense of peace and satisfaction. Perhaps he would give her more than a month to settle on a husband. He could afford to be gracious. He had won the battle and victory in the war loomed ahead. Not until they arrived at their Grosvenor Square home did Lydia speak again. She descended the carriage and turned toward her brother.

"You say I have a month." Her voice rang cool and controlled. "And I must find a husband to meet your requirements?"

"Yes . . ." He cautiously drew the single syllable out. He noted the look in her eye and the sense of victory and peace he'd relished so briefly faded.

"Well then, my love, I will accept your challenge."

Peace and victory vanished altogether.

"It isn't a challenge. It isn't some game, some foolish wager. I am completely serious."

"So am I, dear brother." She looked him squarely in the eyes. "So am I." Lydia turned on her heel and marched toward the steps.

"Bloody hell." Adam groaned under his breath and walked after her, the throbbing in his head returning in full force.

Preoccupied with the latest twist in his quest to assure his sister's happiness, Adam barely noticed the sounds of an approaching coach. He glanced absently at the shrouded streets but saw nothing beyond the glowing halo cast by the gaslight. Dismissing the distant clatter as a figment of the night, he turned his attention back to his sister. Two steps later, the sound of the coach grew louder, sharper, the unmistakable noise of a carriage out of control.

"Lydia, look out!" Adam lunged toward his sister, shoving her out of harm's way. A bare second later an object smacked into him at full speed. He staggered with the impact.

"Adam, are you hurt?" Lydia said, her voice rising with concern.

"Yes, but what—"

"Good God, Adam." Lydia gasped. "It's a woman."

Adam knelt by the crumpled figure at his feet, illuminated by the dim light of the street lamp. Although dressed in outrageous clothes, it was indeed a woman.

A lovely woman.

Adam noted the fragile curve of her chin, the pale, nearly translucent skin under a dusting of powder, a slight blush on her cheek. Relieved to find she breathed, Adam gathered the unconscious woman into his arms, strode up the steps and into the house.

"Send for a physician." He barked commands to the servants clustered curiously at the doorway. Carrying her up the broad marble stairway took little effort. Light, tiny, delicate, she fit naturally into his arms. He shifted her weight, drawing her tighter into his embrace. A spicy fragrance wafted around her. Her hair, more red than brown, reached to her shoulders and brushed his face with every step. A gold filigree heart on a slender chain nestled in the hollow at the base of her throat. Matching bobs dangled from her ears. Thick lashes left dark smudges where they rested on her cheeks. Full, wine-red lips parted slightly with each breath. A thought came to him unbidden. Would the color rub off if he pressed his lips to hers, let her breath mingle with his own?

Adam laid his burden gently on the bed in the nearest vacant chamber, surprisingly reluctant to release her. He paused by her bedside, momentarily mesmerized by the rise and fall of full, ripe breasts barely concealed under a scandalously thin yellow garment. Over that, she wore what appeared to be a type of man's leather coat. Flung open, the coat revealed a figure tapering seductively from firm breasts to small waist, the undergarment tucked into heavy blue cotton trousers. Adam's gaze lingered appreciatively on the swell of her hip, the curves and valleys displayed by the close cut of the odd breeches. He fought a momentary impulse to reach his hand out and run it down the sleek length of her shapely leg. Desire for this stranger surged through him.

Abruptly Adam stepped away, a puzzled frown furrowing his brow. What was he doing? He was not given to the seduction of helpless women. He examined his feelings objectively. Why this immediate attraction, this shocking, almost irresistible pull to a complete stranger? To a woman he'd never met and not yet spoken to? Not normally an impulsive man, he, in fact, prided himself on keeping his emotions locked firmly under control. Except, of course, where his sister was concerned. And now this bit of baggage as well.

His gaze caressed her, the mahogany curls fanning across the pillow, the delightful figure deliciously displayed in the scandalous clothing . . . the shoes.

"What manner of footwear are these?" He leaned over the bed for a closer look. With a tentative finger, he poked the odd-looking soles, the letters N-I-K-E emblazoned on the side.

A servant called from the doorway, interrupting Adam's examination. "Milord, the doctor is on his way."

"Excellent, Wilson." He turned to the butler. "Have her changed into more appropriate attire, perhaps one of Lydia's night rails, and bring her clothes to me in the library. Be quick about it. I would prefer not to have to deal with a doctor's questions. I have enough of my own." With one last, speculative glance at the bed, he strode from the room.

Adam threw open the doors of the library. Lydia perched on the edge of the desk studying some kind of large, leather pouch.

"Adam, look, I found this outside, next to the woman. I believe it must be hers."

"Odd-looking thing for a woman to carry." He accepted it from his sister's outstretched hands. "Perhaps it will give us some clue as to who she is and where she's from." He emptied the contents on the desk, spreading the unfamiliar objects over the surface.

"Good lord!" He gasped. "What kind of hoax is this?"

Lydia stared curiously at the display. "What are these things?"

"I have no idea." Adam picked up a leather wallet and, peering inside, pulled out several notes. It appeared to be some kind of currency but it was smaller than anything he'd seen before, the monarch pictured on the bill unknown. He withdrew several cards, somewhat larger than calling cards, made of a hard, thin, smooth, shiny board. All had raised numbers and one had the letters V-I-S-A.

He handed the cards to Lydia. "What do you make of these?"

Her pretty forehead furrowed in a thoughtful frown. "Calling cards, do you think?"

"I rather doubt it. But what purpose they might have escapes me."

Adam arranged them carefully on the desk and next selected a small blue book. Very thin, with a silver coat of arms featuring an eagle and the words *Passport* and *United States of America*. Opening it, he found the name Margaret Melissa Masterson, and a likeness of the woman upstairs.

"A very good likeness." He showed it to Lydia. "An

excellent artist's work, very lifelike."

Almost too lifelike.

"I would assume this is her name. Here. Margaret Melissa Masterson. And here it says birth date." He tapped a finger on the line and frowned. "But this cannot be accurate. It says—"

"January 12, 1969." Lydia gasped and turned astonished eyes toward her brother. "Can this be true?"

"Of course not. It must be some kind of ruse. Although to what purpose I cannot fathom." He surveyed the hodgepodge of items on the desk with a wary eye. "Perhaps you should retire and I will deal with all this."

Lydia's eyes flashed with indignation. "I most certainly will not. This is fascinating. Even if it is a hoax it is obviously quite well done. I refuse to go to bed until you and I, together, get to the bottom of it all."

"Fine." Resigned to the inevitable, he picked up a black box, roughly the size and shape of a small brick. Words were printed on it here and there, but there was little that made any sense.

Lydia pointed to printing on the box. "I know that's spelled incorrectly but could it be cannon? Could this be some kind of firearm or weapon?"

"I hardly think so." Adam turned the thing over, inspecting each side. "However, it would be wise to set this aside for now."

Some items scattered on the desk were easily identified: a pair of dark glasses, sketch pads, and peculiar, although recognizable, writing instruments. There were two magazines, one entitled *Time*, the other *Cosmopolitan*.

Lydia stared, transfixed by the cover of the magazine she held. "Bloody hell!"

"Lydia!" Adam snatched the periodical from her hands. "Good Lord."

It was his turn to be shocked. The cover featured the likeness of a woman dressed, or rather undressed, in the most revealing of costumes. Neckline plunging to navel, fabric clinging like a second skin, one leg exposed nearly to the hip.

"I believe I shall need some time to study this." Adam flipped through the pages quickly and shot his sister a pointed glance. "I don't think this is the proper sort of thing for you to look at, however."

"Don't be stuffy, Adam. It's obviously a magazine for women."

She snatched the publication from him and pointed to the cover. Lydia cast a smug look at her brother. "Right here it says "How to Catch Mr. Right in the Nineties." The phrasing is odd but there's no doubt as to its meaning, and that is definitely a subject for females."

He retrieved the magazine once again. "Nonetheless, respect my wishes and leave this alone."

Even as the words left his lips he knew his sister would get her hands on the journal as soon as he turned his back. He made a mental note to remember to store it in a safe place.

He paged through the second magazine and set it aside for further review later. Adam marveled at the glossy covers, the vivid, lifelike images. Both magazines were dated May 1995.

While the periodicals were at least easily identifiable, other items were quite frankly amazing,

31

stretching the boundaries of imagination and belief. They discovered a small, thin, rectangular box with raised square buttons, each marked with a number. When pressed, the numbers appeared in a type of window on the box. Adam played with the device, and finally determined it was intended to do mathematical calculations.

"Remarkable." Adam vowed privately to investigate more thoroughly later.

Lydia, too, found some of the bag's treasures delightful. She unfolded a cloth pouch and cried out with glee.

"Cosmetics. Oh, do look, Adam. It simply can't be anything else." She selected a small, flat box with a transparent cover and flicked it open. "It's rouge, I'm sure of it. And look, it has its own brush. How wonderfully convenient!"

She examined each object in turn, deciding the tubes of colored wax were probably for lips, the bottle of flesh-colored liquid and matching powder for skin. She toyed with a metallic tube, finally unscrewing it and withdrawing a wand with a circular brush at its tip. "I wonder what this is for? It looks terribly interesting."

"Put it back, Lydia."

She wrinkled her nose in a petulant expression and replaced the cosmetics in the pouch.

While the items on the desk were fascinating, no less intriguing were the woman's clothes. Wilson brought them to the library shortly before the doctor came and went. Their guest would be fine, the doctor announced. She had a slight bump on the head and should be allowed to rest as long as possible.

Lydia fingered the yellow undergarment. Adam inspected the blue trousers.

"Her garments are definitely odd but well made and of good quality," he said, examining the seams. "Excellent work here. Lydia, have you ever seen anything like this?" He showed her the trousers' fastenings. Rows of tiny metal teeth locked together with the passage of a small pull. Adam yanked and found it extraordinarily tight.

He shook his head. "Unbelievable."

"Adam, don't you think this is, well, some kind of corset?" Lydia held a sheer, white, cupped strip of material in front of her.

"I think that is obvious, my dear. And I think you know it."

Lydia had the good grace to blush and avoid her brother's gaze. She placed the corset back on the desk and reached for the next garment, so sheer it was transparent and resembling stockings stretching from toe to waist, all in one piece.

"Oh, Adam." She sighed with envy. "Isn't this lovely? It's obviously some type of stockings but so very delicate."

"Very nice." He mumbled absently and concentrated on the curious shoes, made of fabric and a material hard yet flexible. Not leather, nothing Adam had ever seen. These, too, he set aside for more intense perusal later.

Much of what they examined was unique, even remarkable, but Adam was not prepared for the contents of a yellow envelope bearing the words *FAST PHOTO, 24-hour processing*. He unfolded the packet and pulled out a stack of thin, glossy papers.

"Good lord." His gasp drew Lydia quickly to his side. They stared at the papers, seeing likenesses so realistic they could scarce be called paintings. But what on earth were they?

"Do look, Adam," Lydia cried, watching her brother flip through the papers. "Here's the Tower of London. And this one is the British Museum. And here—" Her voice rang with recognition.

"Yes, yes, Westminster Abbey." Adam shook with excitement. "This is incredible. What accuracy, what amazing detail. They cannot be mere paintings." The stack totaled 36, each depicting a different London scene, some familiar, others completely unknown.

"Adam?" Lydia pointed to one likeness. "Isn't that the woman upstairs? And here, and here, too?" She rifled through the papers.

"I believe so. And look, in several others there is the image of another woman."

"What on earth do you think these things all over the streets are?"

"I don't know." Adam squinted, trying to get a better look. "They appear to be some kind of vehicles. But isn't this odd? I haven't seen a horse in any of these street scenes. Why are there no horses?"

He wondered about more than that. Even when he recognized a particular building or a certain street, it appeared much different from what he was accustomed to seeing. Wires hung everywhere. Lamps and signs appeared strange and unfamiliar. The depictions seemed to be London, but a London somehow changed.

Brother and sister stood side by side, contemplating the items arrayed on the desk before them.

"What does it all mean, Adam?" Lydia said quietly.

He ran a hand across weary eyes and sighed deeply. "I don't know. I wish I did."

"It's almost as though—" Lydia turned wide eyes to her brother. "As if she comes from another place. Not just America, but somewhere else altogether, somewhere much farther. Almost from . . . a completely different world."

Hours later, Adam stood outside the guest chamber door. Lydia retired some time earlier but too many thoughts churned through his head for sleep; too many unanswered questions remained. He hesitated a moment, then gripped the knob and stepped into the room.

Silver moonlight filtered through the window. Curtains billowed gently. A soft moan drew him to the bed. He approached silently and leaned above the woman, close enough to make out her face in the scant light, light reflected in the necklace and ear bobs she still wore.

"Who are you, Margaret Melissa Masterson? Where do you come from?" An intensity underlaid his soft whisper.

As if in response, she moaned again and tossed on the bed, incoherent words mixed with sobs. He bent closer, straining to understand.

"No . . . Kiki . . . where are you . . . no." Her thrashing increased. Adam reached out to calm her. She struggled and he stared into open, unseeing eyes. His strong arms enfolded her, pulling her close. Adam groaned, acutely aware of the feel of her breasts pressing against his chest through the thin

Victoria Alexander

fabric of her gown. Desire overwhelmed him. He
tilted back her chin and brushed his lips lightly
against hers. The tension eased from her body.
Slowly, reluctantly, Adam pulled away. She lay limp
in his arms, her eyes closed once again.

So much for not seducing helpless females.

The lack of self-control annoyed him, and Adam
laid her gently back on the bed. Drawing the bedclothes around her, he spied an odd-looking bracelet
on her left wrist. Curious, he picked up her hand and
carefully slipped the bracelet off her arm. The wide
gold band had an attached glass case. Inside the
numbers 12:00 flashed.

"How very odd," he said. "It could be some type of
watch or clock but there are no hands, no numbers,
no even a face. Still, it appears to be a kind of time-
piece. A device to track time perhaps. Time . . ."
Adam's voice trailed off and he stared at the now
serene figure on the bed.

"Of course, that's it!" The pieces of the puzzle
clicked neatly into place. "That's the answer!" With
a last quick glance at the bed, he turned and raced
back to the library.

He searched impatiently among the items on the
desk and muttered to himself, "Where was that? I
know I saw something here."

He scattered the pile of shiny cards until he found
the one he had noticed earlier but put off examining
in the wake of so many other fascinating discoveries.
A small, stiff card with some type of transparent material encasing it, it had the words *Driver's License* at
the top and another one of those remarkable likenesses. This one, too, was of the woman upstairs.

"Where is it? Here!" he seized the card triumphantly and laid it on a cleared spot on the desk. "And this." He grabbed the blue book marked *Passport* and placed it next to the card. "And these." He snatched up the magazines and added them to the arrangement.

His gaze flew from one to the next to the next; he could scarcely believe his eyes. On the card marked *Driver's License* the birth date was January 12, 1969. On the passport booklet, the birth date was the same, January 12, 1969. And the magazines bore the date May 1995. But of course they would. She wouldn't be reading periodicals written when she was born.

"Bloody hell."

Stunned, Adam stared at the evidence before him. Too fantastic to believe, yet too logical to deny. The answer to the questions raised by the images too lifelike to be paintings, the unreal quality of the magazines, the mathematical device, the clothes, and those blasted shoes.

"Good lord." Adam gripped the edge of the desk. "Can it be? Is this possible? Is she not merely from another place? Is she from . . . another time?"

Morning came and went before Lydia made her way back to the library. She slipped through the doors and silently observed her brother. Adam sat behind the desk, oblivious to everything but the magazine in front of him. He appeared crumpled, disheveled, as though he'd spent the night in his clothes. Surprising for a man who prided himself on his appearance almost as much as he did his skill with the reins or his competency in handling estate business.

This was scarcely the look of a man who would force his own sister into an arranged marriage. In the excitement of their discoveries, Lydia had nearly forgotten her brother's ultimatum; nearly, but not quite. It wasn't that she didn't want to be married. On the contrary, a husband and children were her most heartfelt desire. But Lydia watched friends marry for wealth, position, and family, and others marry for love. Some of those in arranged matches eventually seemed to find wedded bliss. Others took their pleasure outside the marriage bed. Lydia vowed she would be an ape leader, and dwell in solitude in the country before submitting to such a marriage.

Her eyes narrowed in speculation. Adam was a man thoroughly up-to-date on scientific inventions and discoveries. Had his position in society been different, she was certain he would have spent his life as a scholar. Of course, he would have had to overcome his now nearly forgotten wild streak. Nonetheless, his fascination with this Miss Masterson's possessions could be turned to Lydia's advantage. If he found the woman as interesting as her belongings, perhaps he would forget this nonsense about finding his sister a husband. Or at the very least, give her more time.

"Adam, did you retire at all last night?" She walked briskly across the room.

"What? Oh, yes, of course." He appeared haggard and nowhere near rested. "I simply couldn't sleep, that's all. Sit down; I have something to discuss with you."

He hesitated, then gestured to the items on the desk. "So, what do you make of all this?"

"I have no idea what to make of it." She shrugged. "It's all very peculiar."

"If it is not a hoax, some well-devised ruse," he said cautiously, "then it may well be we have a visitor, and I say this reluctantly, from another time."

Lydia stared, eyes wide with disbelief. "Oh, Adam, that's ridiculous."

"I know, believe me, I know." He leaned back in the chair and absently ran his fingers through his hair.

"I have been pondering this all night. Reading these magazines, studying these items and, ridiculous as it may well sound, this is the only answer. Our Miss Masterson comes from another time. I believe a time approximately one hundred and seventy-seven years in the future."

"You're serious, aren't you?" Lydia could not remember ever seeing her brother draw a rash conclusion. On the contrary, he gave careful consideration to all matters before him. If he believed this, it simply must be true.

"Quite serious. Look." He picked up one of the magazines and waved it at her. "This shows me a world so totally foreign from our own it is hardly recognizable. There are many things here that are appalling. Poverty, famine, and war still rage. Moral values appear virtually nonexistent. But there are wonders here, too."

He rose and paced the floor, gesturing with the

journal in his hand. Excitement shone in his eyes as his words spilled out faster and faster.

"There are forms of communication and transportation never imagined in my wildest dreams. Illnesses that would kill us are referred to here in passing as mere childhood annoyances. Goods and services are provided by mechanical methods in numbers beyond measure. Good lord, Lydia, people can actually fly."

Lydia stared at him, stunned. "Are you certain?"

"As certain as I can be. It is the only logical answer. The only thing that explains all of this." He waved the magazine at the articles on the desk.

Lydia's gaze traveled from her brother to the desk and back to Adam.

"It does make sense, more or less." Her voice was quiet, thoughtful. "I had wondered about the birth date, of course, and those wonderful little paintings, or whatever they are."

She glanced again at the stacked items on the desk, then turned back to her brother. Caught up in his excitement, she realized the possibilities of his discovery.

"But how marvelous, how terribly exciting! What fun it shall be. We can take her around. She can tell the future. Maybe show some of these remarkable things. She'll be the darling of the ton, the hit of the season."

"Damnation, Lydia!" Adam exploded. "You will not speak of this to anyone. We don't know for certain if this insane conclusion is correct. And even if it is true, who would ever believe it? For our sakes, and possibly for her safety, we must keep this to ourselves." He leveled a stern gaze at his sister. "I am deadly serious. Do you understand?"

"Oh, all right." Lydia's lower lip jutted out in the pout she'd perfected in childhood. "But we can't keep her a prisoner. Once she wakes up, if of course this isn't some kind of prank, I daresay she won't be at all happy to find out she isn't even born yet. I certainly wouldn't be."

"Very well." Adam sighed in resignation. "What do you propose?"

"Well, first she's going to need suitable clothes."

"Clothes?"

"Clothes." He apparently failed to grasp her meaning. With a sigh of her own Lydia replied, "Yes, my darling brother, clothes. You cannot expect her to go around in those things she was wearing. As interesting as they appear, they simply will not do. She needs to be properly dressed."

"But we have no idea how long she will be here."

"Adam," she said, as though addressing a small boy, "how long she will remain with us simply doesn't signify. If she is not dressed properly, at the very least the servants will comment. And our servants will talk to other servants, and so on and so forth. If you really want to keep where she came from a secret, the best thing for all concerned is to make sure there is no gossip."

"Of course." He returned to his chair. "How quickly can it be done?"

Lydia smiled triumphantly. Shopping for someone else was the next best thing to shopping for herself. "If I plead and cajole and offer to pay far more than I would under ordinary circumstances, I believe my modiste can provide an appropriate wardrobe by say, day after tomorrow. In the meantime Jane can shorten some of my things."

His gaze wandered back to the items on his desk, and Lydia could see she'd already lost his attention. "I'll be going then?"

"Fine." His eyes focused once again on the magazine in his hands.

Lydia smiled and strolled out of the room, her basic belief in men confirmed. In spite of their posturing and condescending attitudes, manipulating them was so very easy for Lydia she sometimes wondered if she should feel at least a little guilty. But guilt never entered her thoughts. Her mind was too full with the seeds of plans and plots to make Miss Margaret Melissa Masterson as appealing to Adam as her magazines and other trappings. Meddling in this mystery woman's far more intriguing life would surely keep her brother out of hers. A smug smile firmly in place, Lydia called for a carriage, grabbed her hat, and sailed out the door.

Afternoon drifted into evening and still Adam remained at his desk. He read and reread the magazines. He examined Miss Masterson's possessions over and over. Some of what he read and what he saw remained incomprehensible, too far removed from the scope of his knowledge and imagination to understand. But he could grasp most of it and his spirits soared with the awesome evidence of man's advancement.

Immersed in the wonders of a future time, he barely noticed the light of day fade. He never saw a discreet Wilson silently light the gas lamps. Vaguely, he was aware of Lydia coming in and saying something about a card party. An untouched supper tray sat on a table near the door.

At midnight, he finally pushed his chair away from the desk. With a weary step, he moved toward a crystal decanter and the amber liquid it held. He poured the brandy and swirled it in the glass.

"What is a woman from a world like that like?" he said. "What does she think? What does she want? What does she need?"

Surrendering to an irresistible urge, he left the library and climbed the stairs to her bedchamber. He pushed the door open and moved silently over the carpeted floor to the bed. Extremely improper, his uninvited presence in a lady's bedroom. He didn't have the excuse of exhaustion or excitement as he'd had last night. Yet, inexplicably, he needed to be here.

She lay sleeping quietly tonight. Peaceful. Serene. Beautiful. Adam stood over her, contemplating the tousled hair, slightly flushed cheeks, barely parted lips. The tangled bedclothes left one nearly naked leg exposed. He sipped the brandy still in his hand.

"I need answers, Margaret Melissa Masterson," he said softly.

Pulling a chair to the side of the bed, he sat and swung his legs up to rest on the bed, one crossed over the other. For minutes, or perhaps hours, he stayed. Watching her sleep. Waiting for her to awaken. And wondering . . . what would happen then?

Chapter Two

Maggie opened her eyes slowly and gazed at her surroundings. It was a charming room: high, ornately plastered ceiling, four-poster bed, beautiful antique furniture, and just the right blend of old-fashioned style and natural warmth. A room lived in and used every day. A room pretty yet comfortable. A room totally and completely unfamiliar.

"Where the hell am I?" She jolted upright and cringed, every muscle in her body screaming. Her head throbbed and she ached all over as if she'd been beaten, or worse, enrolled in an aerobics class. But the physical battering was nothing compared to her emotional turmoil. Maggie loved a good party and a good time, but absolutely never in her life had she awakened in an unfamiliar room.

"What is going on here?" Maggie threw her feet over the side of the bed and gingerly stood. "Where are my clothes?" She glared around the room as if it were somehow responsible for her predicament and hobbled toward a huge wardrobe, muscles protesting every movement. Maggie pulled open the doors and rummaged through the clothes inside.

"Beautiful things. Really neat stuff." But nothing was even remotely familiar. None of the clothes were hers, and Maggie stifled a rising sense of unease. The garments in the wardrobe were terribly elegant and very formal, at least to someone whose preferred style was jeans and a sweater.

"Okay," she said. "Calm down. Let's just go over the basics. I know my name. I'm Maggie Masterson. When last I checked, I was in London. So far so good. Now for the trick question. How did I get here?" She gazed at the engaging chamber. "And where is here, anyway?"

The door to the room creaked open and Maggie turned sharply.

"Where are my clothes?" she said.

The young woman at the door jumped but quickly recovered to drop a quaint curtsy.

"Begging your pardon, miss. I don't know about your things. But the master said to bring you these." She held out an armful of clothes.

Barely noticing the girl's long dress and starched apron, Maggie strode toward her. She seized the clothes and held them out for appraisal.

"No, no, these aren't mine." Her voice rang with impatience. "I want my stuff back. I just want to get my things and get out of here. How do I do that?"

"I don't know, miss." The girl stared wide-eyed at Maggie. "I only know the master said to give you these."

Maggie cast a disgusted glance toward the delicate, floor-length dress she held in her hands. "Look, I can't wear this.

"Here." She thrust the dress at the girl. "Take it back and tell me where to find this master of yours."

"Milord is in the library, but you cannot disturb him."

"Oh, you bet I can. Now, where is this library?"

"The bottom of the main stairs to the right, but you cannot go down there." The girl appeared positively shocked. "Not in your night rail!"

The unfamiliar word confused Maggie. "My what?" The girl stared at her nightgown. It wasn't until then that Maggie paid any attention to what she wore. A beautiful white gown fell long enough to cover her bare feet and trail slightly behind. Lots of material, but fairly sheer.

"This?" She plucked at the delicate material. "Oh, don't worry about this. Look, I know we're from different countries and all, but I can't believe anyone's going to be shocked by seeing me in anything with as much material as this getup. Besides, I wear less than this for grocery shopping and from what I've seen of London so far, I'm fairly conservative. Of course"—she eyed the girl speculatively—"nothing is as conservative as what you're wearing."

Abrupt realization dawned and Maggie thought she understood.

"Oh, I get it. This is some kind of period hotel or bed and breakfast, right? You know, where everyone wears costumes and pretends to be Henry the Eighth or Queen Victoria or something. That's cool, that's really neat." Maggie inched toward the door. "But

46

you see, this is all some kind of weird mistake. I'm not supposed to be here. So I'll go downstairs and see the master, or head honcho, or whoever and get this straightened out. Thanks, so long."

Maggie shot out the door and raced down the hall in what she hoped was the right direction. Other costumed employees stared and she ignored a wave of self-consciousness.

A prim and proper–looking butler-type dropped his jaw at her approach and she grimaced to herself. *Maybe I should have changed.*

"Excuse me," she said sweetly. "The main stairs?"

"That way," he croaked and pointed ten feet down the hall.

"Thanks." Maggie dashed past him. Easily finding the stairway, she flew down the stairs and pulled up short at the bottom. No less than four massive double doors to the right of the stairs confronted her.

"Oh, this is swell."

She eyed the doors and tried to decide which was the best bet for a library.

"Okay." Maggie paced back and forth and considered the options. "In old mansions like this there was usually some kind of front parlor, and maybe sitting rooms, and of course dining rooms and breakfast rooms.

"As for the library, well, this looks like as good a bet as any. I just hope I don't end up in some kind of conference or meeting or something."

Maggie swung open the second set of doors and gasped.

Before her in a magnificent, elegant, almost unreal setting were high, ornate ceilings, a glittering chandelier, and damask draperies. The room shimmered in green and gold.

"What a gorgeous restoration." Maggie stared in appreciation at the delicate striped settees, Louis XIV chairs, and Aubusson carpet. "This looks practically new and totally authentic. Someone did a great job."

She backed out of the room, closing the doors behind her, and glanced curiously down the hall.

Why there aren't more guests? All the people I've seen so far are obviously employees. That's really weird; this place is neat. You'd think it would be busier.

Feeling a bit like Alice in Wonderland, Maggie considered her choices. Which way to turn next? What door to try now? Alice, at least, had the guidance of a rabbit and wasn't dressed in a ridiculous nightgown.

Maggie turned to the next set of doors.

"One more time." She grasped the doorknob, pushed firmly, and, taking a deep breath, stepped inside.

"Wow!" Awestruck, she faced a classic British library straight out of "Masterpiece Theater." Endless mahogany shelves reached to the lofty ceiling. Each shelf was crammed with leather-bound books.

"Pardon me," a soft voice interrupted.

Maggie screamed and jumped. "Yow! Oh, jeez! You scared the hell out of me!"

Maggie glared into a pair of brown eyes so dark they could have been black, set in a face that just missed being classically handsome. His skin had a natural, light bronze tone; his features were strong and firm, topped off with dark blond hair. A killing combination and Maggie's main weakness in men. This one stood cool and collected behind a massive mahogany desk. She stared and immediately categorized him as . . . a hunk.

"Sorry, but you really startled me. I'm not usually so jumpy." Good God, she was babbling. She never babbled. "It's just that I'm looking for the library, and I really have no idea what's going on, and I can't find my clothes and—Hey!"

Maggie caught sight of her tote bag on the desk. Neatly lined up next to it were the various bits and pieces she deemed necessary for traveling.

"That's my stuff!" Maggie rushed to the desk. "That's my wallet, and passport"—her hand flitted over the objects—"my camera, traveler's checks, and my credit cards, and hey!"

She glared at the hunk. "My clothes! What gives you the right to go through my stuff? Who are you anyway? I want to get out of here right now. I want the American Embassy!" Her earlier unease threatened to return as full-fledged panic.

"My dear woman." The hunk strode around the desk to her side. "I'm afraid you really must sit down before we discuss this further." He put his arm around her shoulders and tried to lead her to a chair.

Maggie wrenched out of his grasp and glared up at him, a small part of her reluctantly noting his broad shoulders and how he towered above her.

"Don't treat me like a child. I'm an adult, an American citizen. I want some answers and I want them right now."

"As you wish." He sighed. "I really did not want to break this to you like this, but it does seem the quickest way to answer at least some of your questions. And I might add"—he lifted an eyebrow—"recover your composure."

Panic now mingled with indignation and anger. Maggie narrowed her eyes at his superior expression and couldn't resist a quick comeback.

"My composure is just fine, thank you." After all, he certainly didn't look like a serial killer.

The hunk strode to the window and pulled the curtains aside.

"Come here." It was a voice obviously used to issuing commands and being obeyed. Maggie continued her mutinous glare.

"Come here, if you please," he added in a gentler tone. "Now, look out the window and tell me what you see."

Maggie lifted her chin and marched to the window. Nothing looked particularly surprising. It was a typical London street. Perhaps a little cleaner than most. Definitely quieter. Maggie had no idea what she was supposed to look for or at. She glanced quizzically at the man who, in turn, appeared to study her anxiously.

"Simply give me your observations, your impressions."

She concentrated on the scene before her. It was really quite charming. Across the cobblestone street was a square of some sort. A horse-drawn carriage passed by, adding to the picturesque atmosphere.

"That's strange," she said. "There's absolutely no traffic out there. No parked cars either. Is it some kind of a holiday?"

The hunk ignored her question. "What else don't you see?"

"I don't get it? What do you mean?"

He frowned. "Miss Masterson, I believe you to be fairly intelligent. Now please, look out and tell me what is missing here."

"Fine." Arms crossed over her chest, she stared out the window. "I don't see cars. I said that already." She gave him a pointed glare. "I don't see, oh, I don't know, telephone wires, electric wires. I don't see any streetlights, no wait, there are lamps, gas, I think. I don't see stop signs, stoplights."

She spun to face him. "So far, all I do see is that you live on a quaint, old-fashioned street. I like the street lamps; it's a cute touch. But every picture I've ever seen of London is quaint and old-fashioned. What's your point?"

"Miss Masterson," he said, impatience now obvious in his tone, "don't you notice anything that strikes you as out of the ordinary? Anything on the street or in the house?"

"Everything strikes me as out of the ordinary," she said. "I'm not from here. Everything is different from what I'm used to and where I live. Even in this house, it's a little weird. Everybody, including you, is wearing bizarre, old-fashioned costumes. You also seem to have a passion for antiques."

She glanced around with grudging respect for his taste. "But lots of people love antiques. My own sister has dragged me to auctions and through historic houses for years. I still don't get what you're driving at."

"I'm afraid this could be something of a shock." He

51

gazed at her with concern evident in his ebony eyes. In spite of her annoyance, a shiver of warmth thrilled through her at his look. "I am fairly certain the question is not so much where are you as when are you."

"What?"

"As farfetched and totally unbelievable as this may seem . . ." He paused as though considering his next words. "I have come to the unmistakable conclusion that you have very possibly . . ." Again he hesitated as if weighing the effect his words would have on her. "Traveled through time."

Stunned, Maggie stared at him.

"Bull," she said flatly. "What a crock. That's the craziest thing I've ever heard of. Nobody travels through time. You can't do that. People travel to places, not times. Oh sure, there are time zones and time shares and time off for good behavior. You can be on time, or out of time, or not in time, or playing for time—" She was babbling again but she didn't care. This guy, cute as he might be, was obviously nuts. Living in an antique world, he now apparently believed he was part of it.

"I don't know what kind of a scam you're running, but you're not going to get away with it. If you've kidnapped me for money, I don't have any." Another, more morbid thought struck her. "Oh, jeez, you're not some kind of white slaver or something, are you? I thought that kind of thing only happened in old books, or the *National Enquirer*, or *True Confessions* or something."

The words bubbled through her lips without thought or warning and she frantically considered ways of escape. Slowly, hoping he wouldn't notice, she inched her way around the wall, aiming for the door.

"Miss Masterson," he said. "I know this is a shock and I am sorry to be so abrupt. I had hoped to explain in a somewhat less startling fashion. I understand you need time to take all this in. The very idea of time travel is ludicrous. However, I have had since the night before last to try to comprehend this."

"Night before last?" Maggie continued her subtle movement, a fraction of an inch at a time. If she could keep him talking, with any luck, she could make a break for it.

"Yes, that's how long you have been unconscious. I will explain everything, but first I really think"—he approached her—"you need to be properly dressed."

"Don't come near me!" She desperately surveyed the room for something to use as a weapon. A crystal decanter, half-filled with amber liquid, stood on a nearby table. Perfect. She lunged for it. Maggie grabbed the decanter and hefted it like a softball, the heavy weight comforting in her hand. "Don't touch me!"

"Good lord, woman. I have no intention of harming you. I simply want to get to the bottom of this. And I would prefer you put that down. That brandy is one of the few remaining bottles my father stored before the war. It is still far superior to anything currently available. If you feel the need for protection . . ." He strode toward the fireplace and grabbed a poker. "This would far better suit your purpose." He held the implement out to her.

Maggie's gaze locked with his, the realization of how ridiculous the scene was dawning on her.

Threatening him with brandy? What was she going to do? Force it down his throat?

She fought the urge to give in to hysterical laughter, and cautiously reached for the poker. She'd play along with him for now. Besides, she couldn't go anywhere dressed like this.

She gently replaced the decanter on the table and accepted the poker. Now this was a real weapon. She relaxed just a bit.

He sighed with obvious relief. "Thank you."

"That brandy must be pretty good stuff." She suppressed a smile. "Now what?"

"Well, Miss Masterson, I really think—"

"Hey, how do you know my name?"

"It was not difficult to determine." He waved a hand toward the desk. "It's on many of the items we found in your satchel."

"And just who are you, anyway?"

His face broke into a smile. In spite of herself, Maggie grudgingly acknowledged, she liked it. A lot. A single dimple in his cheek made him approachable and, God help her, sexy. Too bad. Great-looking men always seemed to be either married or gay, or like Sir Cedric, a figment of an overactive imagination. And this one was very probably a deranged kidnapper.

"I believe that is the only question I can answer without hesitation. I am Adam Coleridge." He grew serious. "And I, too, have questions I want answered. Now, if you please." He opened the library door and called to a servant. "Go with Jane. She will help you dress properly. I find it rather distracting to hold serious discussions with beautiful women who are practically naked. Although under other circumstances . . ."

His voice trailed off and Maggie noted a dangerous gleam in his eye. A thrill raced through her at the look and the compliment, followed by annoyance at her involuntary response. She had to keep in mind her firm conviction: the man was nuts.

He gestured graciously toward the weapon in her hand. "And please, by all means keep the poker if you wish."

The beginnings of that killer smile played around the corners of his lips. Maggie steeled herself to ignore it and its effect on her.

A servant appeared in the doorway. Poker clutched to her chest, Maggie raised her chin and stalked out of the room.

"Believe me, pal, I intend to."

Chapter Three

She marched off, an indignant figure. Adam noted with appreciation the way the light silhouetted her voluptuous form in the sheer white gown.

What a cunning little chit that one is.

Most women of his acquaintance would have fainted dead away at the very thought of being alone and helpless, faced with the unknown. This bit of baggage not only had the courage to face up to him and the spirit to attempt to protect herself, she quite obviously did not believe him.

He chuckled and turned back to the desk. This woman might turn out to be even more interesting than her time. Dealing with her could well be an enjoyable endeavor, possibly a challenge. It had been quite some time since a woman, any woman, provided a challenge for him. Still, it was a challenge from which Adam had no doubt he would emerge the victor. After all, regardless of where she came from, or rather, when she came from, some things never changed. When all was said and done she was still only a mere woman.

And no match for a man.

Maggie studied herself critically in the full-length mirror. It had taken nearly an hour to change, partly due to what she thought of as delaying tactics. First, she sent Jane for her underwear. Regardless of where—or maybe when—she was, if that was what the Looney-Tune downstairs wanted her to believe, she insisted on her own underwear. It was weird though, the way Jane examined her bra, almost as if she had never seen one. A ridiculous thought Maggie shrugged off and credited to nerves. That man and this house must be getting to her.

Reluctantly she allowed the girl to help her dress, an annoying and irritating process, but, as Maggie discovered, necessary given the large number of tiny buttons and loops. Didn't the British know about zippers, for God's sake?

Next, she'd sent the girl for food. Hunger always took her mind off everything. If she had to deal with crazy men, even really great-looking ones who oozed charm and sensuality, she needed to keep up her strength.

With the maid gone, she searched the room. All she wanted was one little electric outlet, one insignificant light switch; even a single, solitary crummy old ordinary light bulb would do.

Nothing.

No obvious electricity, no overhead lighting, no cords, no plugs, no outlets, no appliances of any kind, only candles and some type of gas lamps. Absolutely nothing to prove or disprove the date.

Looking out the window didn't help either. People passed by on horseback and in carriages. Some vehicles seemed familiar in a historic way, but most were very strange in appearance, definitely antique. Everyone, absolutely everyone, wore costumes. But outside the window, as in the room, she saw nothing to prove she had or had not traveled through time.

A queasy, sinking feeling lodged in the pit of her stomach. Crazy as it seemed, bit by bit evidence piled up. Evidence she simply was not prepared to accept. Maggie racked her brain for answers. Okay, maybe this wasn't a period hotel; maybe she'd stumbled into an entire re-created neighborhood or village—like Williamsburg back home.

A desperate idea with no real foundation, but she clung to it like a lifeline. She pushed away the nagging thought that some of her London guidebooks would have mentioned such a place. The unsubstantiated theory helped suppress the ever-present threat of panic. Funny how much more the thought of traveling through time terrified her than the idea of being kidnapped by an antique-loving lunatic. Only to herself would she admit fear.

"The best defense is a good offense," she said to the image in the mirror. An image she thought looked pretty damn good.

The dress was lightweight, some kind of muslin, in a becoming lime green. Short, slightly puffed sleeves and a high waistline emphasized her full breasts. The skirt fell to her feet, gently clinging and molding in all the right places.

"Well, at least whatever scam I've stumbled into has the good sense to pick an attractive time period for fashion. I could be standing here in a hoop skirt and crinolines.

"Now." She sighed and nodded at her reflection. "Stay mad and you won't have a chance to be scared."

She grabbed the poker off the table and in her best Fred-Astaire-with-a-walking-cane imitation, saluted the image in the mirror. "Good luck. You're going to need it."

With a deep breath, she headed back to the library.

Maggie threw open the doors and firmly stepped inside. The handsome, crazy man behind the desk stood at her approach. This time she stared directly at him. And he stared directly back. Maybe too directly. An assessing gaze that traveled from her head to her toes, followed by a complimentary smile. Or was that a leer? Heat rose in her face. She clenched her teeth, refusing to give him the upper hand.

"You look delightful, Miss Masterson."

"Thanks, you don't look half bad yourself." Smugly, she noticed his eyebrow lift in response. A little bravado, a little anger, if she could just hang in there.

He gestured at the poker in her hand. "I see you still have your protection with you."

"I've grown very attached to it." Maggie breezed into the room and selected a chair near the desk. She perched on its edge, placed the poker across her lap, and directed a level gaze at Adam. "It's Coleridge, isn't it?"

"Adam Coleridge, actually." There was a distinct twinkle in his eye. "Seventh Earl of Ridgefield, to be exact."

"Congratulations." She hoped he recognized sarcasm when he heard it. "So, what year did you say this is anyway?"

There went the eyebrow again. "It's not merely what I say. It's what happens to be accurate at this particular moment. It is the year of our Lord eighteen hundred and eighteen."

"Eighteen eighteen! I don't know anything about 1818! That would be somewhere between . . . what? Napoleon and . . . Queen Victoria, right?"

"Queen whom?" Didn't that eyebrow ever stay still?

"Oh, come off it." Exasperation tinged her words. "You know, Queen Victoria? Ruled for, like, fifty plus years? Gave her name to a whole time period? Women wore long dresses and things called bustles, I think." She paused, trying to recall everything she could remember about the Victorian age. "Oh yeah, they made really great furniture. My sister loves it. Let's see, what else? Oh, I know. It was very, very stuffy."

He frowned, obviously confused. "The furniture?"

"Of course not," she said. "The queen was stuffy. Straitlaced, morally upright, you know, stuffy. Just the word *Victorian* meant anything very old-fashioned or prudish." She eyed him sharply. "You expect me to believe you don't know this? That this really is 1818?"

"That's correct."

"That would be what? Two hundred years? One

hundred and fifty? What?" She jumped to her feet and circled the desk, searching for her calculator, brushing close to him in the process. Grabbing the instrument, she punched in the numbers. "Okay, 1995 minus . . ." she muttered under her breath, "equals . . . one hundred and seventy-seven years."

Maggie turned wide eyes to Adam.

"You're telling me I traveled one hundred and seventy-seven years into the past? Are you kidding?"

"That's the only answer that seems to make sense."

"Great. Swell." Maggie could tell he really believed this. She had to get out of here. "You know, this is all coming as quite a shock."

He actually looked sympathetic. "I daresay."

"Could I possibly have a glass of that brandy you were raving about earlier? It couldn't hurt."

"Brandy?" He seemed surprised. "Perhaps you would prefer something else. Ratafia or sherry?"

Maggie sighed with impatience. "I don't know what ratafia is and I can't stand sherry, so brandy would be great."

"Very well."

Maggie followed Adam to the table bearing the brandy decanter. He poured a snifter and offered it to her. Reaching out, Maggie saw her hands tremble. Adam placed the glass in her grasp, covering her hand with his own. An almost physical shock shot through her at his touch. She raised startled eyes to him, forgetting for a moment to hide the fear and confusion revealed there. She stared into the dark, smoldering depths of his eyes and read compassion and curiosity and . . . desire.

61

"Are you quite all right?" His voice was quiet and concerned.

"Fine." She pulled her hands free from his and drew a long drink of the liquor. The burn cascaded down her throat, steadied her nerves. She couldn't— no, wouldn't—let him see her fear. Maggie squared her shoulders and returned Adam's concerned gaze with one more than a little defiant.

"Now what, Coleridge? What's next?"

"Well, I don't really know." Frowning, he poured himself a glass. "I suppose the first thing would be to determine precisely how—"

"Adam, I have everything arranged." A pretty young blonde blew into the room like a whirlwind. "I have spent a scandalous amount of money, but our guest should be properly attired by tomorrow. And then I—" She caught sight of Maggie and stopped short. "Oh, you're awake. How wonderful. I have been so looking forward to meeting you."

The newcomer descended on her, catching Maggie's hands in her own. "I know we are going to be good friends."

"And you are?" Maggie said.

"Miss Masterson." Adam sighed. "Allow me to introduce this hoyden. As much as I am sometimes reluctant to admit the connection, this is my sister, Lady Lydia Coleridge."

"Of course," Maggie said. How could she have missed it? The distinct resemblance between the two was obvious. A paler, smaller version of her brother, Lydia had hair that tended toward silver where her brother's resembled burnished gold. In the feminine member of the family, the rich, dark, velvety brown of Adam's eyes changed to a lighter shade, more amber than brown. Lydia stood just short of her brother's chin, still a good four inches taller than Maggie. The differences were minor, the similarities striking.

Lydia arched an eyebrow at her brother, dropping Maggie's hands. "I gather Adam hasn't mentioned me?"

"I have scarce had time, Lydia. Miss Masterson woke only a few hours ago. I have been attempting to explain the situation to her."

"Oh, you mean about the time travel?" Lydia said blithely.

Good God, she's as crazy as her brother.

Maggie chose her words carefully. "You think I've traveled through time, too, right? You agree with him." She nodded toward Adam. "That the year, this year, is 1818?"

"Of course, my dear. There is absolutely no doubt about that. I can't imagine what a shock this must be for you. Oh, dear." Concern and perception shone in her eyes. "You aren't doing at all well, are you?"

"I'm fine, really."

Ignoring Maggie's protests, Lydia led her to a sofa and urged her to sit.

"This must be terribly confusing and upsetting. I know in your place I would surely—"

"She doesn't believe me," Adam said.

"Not believe you?" Lydia turned eyes wide with amazement to Maggie. "Whyever not?"

"Are you kidding?" Maggie leapt to her feet. "Where are you people coming from anyway? No, wait, don't answer. I know. 1818. Look, I don't know anything about 1818, but I do know about 1995. And

I know there's no such thing as time travel. What I don't know is what kind of a scam I've fallen into and what you people want from me."

Maggie glared at Adam and Lydia. Lydia appeared amazed at the outburst and possibly a little impressed. Adam looked resigned. He'd seen Maggie in this state before.

"Adam, you're going to have to do something," Lydia said.

"Bloody hell, Lydia. I don't know what to do. I wish I did." He sipped his brandy thoughtfully. "If we knew how she got here . . ."

"Adam, that doesn't signify at the moment." Impatience colored Lydia's words. "It seems to me the first thing you must do is convince her as to the truth of what has happened."

"Yeah," Maggie said. "Prove it!"

"Prove it?" he said.

"Of course, Adam. You must convince her." Buoyant with obvious excitement, Lydia turned to Maggie. "You need proof and you shall have it."

"Really?" Adam's voice weighed heavy with sarcasm. "And how do you propose I provide such proof?"

"It's very simple, Adam. I saw those likenesses she had. Our world is quite different from hers. Differences that are very easy to see." Triumphantly Lydia laid her trump card. "All we have to do is show her the town."

"No!" Adam said.

"Yes!" Maggie cried.

"It's the perfect answer," Lydia explained patiently. "She will be able to see the truth for herself.

And since it's nearly five o'clock, we shall simply take a ride in the park."

"Good lord, Lydia, we can't take her to the park. Even though she is properly dressed now, and looks quite charming—" He cast an admiring glance in Maggie's direction.

"Thanks."

"—once she opens her mouth, there will be no possibility of avoiding attention. Have you been listening to her?"

"Hey! What's the matter with the way I talk?" Indignantly, Maggie crossed her arms over her chest and glared. This English snob had a hell of a lot of nerve.

"I'm sure there is nothing whatsoever wrong with how you speak when you are in familiar surroundings. I apologize if I've insulted you."

She narrowed her eyes and nodded grudgingly. "Okay."

"But," he said, "to my ears, your language is atrocious. I can generally understand your meaning, but it takes a great deal of effort. And, Miss Masterson, forgive me for saying it, you have a nasty temper and a somewhat vulgar vocabulary."

Sharp silence fell like a slap.

Lydia turned shocked eyes first toward her brother, then toward Maggie.

Adam's challenging gaze remained riveted on his guest.

Maggie fought to keep herself under control. She refused to give this pompous, overbearing, dictatorial, stuffed-shirt bite in the shorts the satisfaction of watching her blow up. Mentally counting to ten, she took a deep breath and smiled.

"I think, Coleridge, if I put every bit of effort and self-control that I possess into it, I can get through a simple ride in a park without disgracing you."

She fluttered her eyelashes in what she could only imagine was genuine southern-belle fashion. Disgusting, blatant, but effective.

"Well, of course," Adam stammered, obviously expecting a more outraged response. "I didn't mean to imply—I just thought—Good lord." He groaned.

Lydia threw Maggie a conspiratorial smile.

"Adam, we shall tell everyone that she is a distant relation from America. I daresay no one will expect terribly much from her and any problems can be easily explained away."

"You don't think much of Americans, do you?" Maggie said dryly.

Lydia's smile turned apologetic. "It's just that it's so terribly far away and very, well, rustic and uncivilized. Then, of course, there was the war. Although a lot of people really didn't seem to have much interest in that, being far more concerned with the French at the time."

"Oh yeah. Right." What war? Which war? Revolutionary? Eighteen twelve?

"I don't like this. I don't like this at all." Adam's brows pulled together in a disturbed frown. "But you may very well be right if our guest is to be convinced we are not villainous kidnappers."

Maggie winced. After all, for villainous kidnappers, they were turning out to be charming and gracious.

"And if we are going to attempt this rash, not to

66

mention dangerous escapade, we had best begin. The sooner we leave, the sooner it will be done with. I shall call for a carriage." He strode from the room, issuing orders to waiting servants.

The two women watched him depart.

"Is he always like this?" Maggie asked, curiosity laced with sarcasm.

"Oh my, yes." Lydia sighed. "What he really needs is a wife to take him in hand. But he won't marry before he sees me settled. And I have no intention of marrying just to satisfy his sense of responsibility."

Lydia rose and offered her hand to Maggie. "Now then, since we are going to be together for a while at least, may I call you Margaret? Miss Masterson is so very formal, and since we are to be relations, no matter how distant—"

"Oh, please, call me Maggie." Genuine liking for this pretty blonde flooded her. If she wasn't careful, she'd start believing all this 1818 bull.

"Maggie it is, and you must call me Lydia. Now then, we have to find you a hat and, let's see, perhaps. a shawl. Adam will be waiting and he can be so impatient.

"You'll love driving in the park." Lydia stepped briskly out of the room, Maggie trailing in her wake. "It's usually quite delightful and there's always such a good chance to meet someone interesting or hear the latest on-dit."

And a chance to escape.

Minutes later, Maggie sat in a small open coach next to Lydia. Adam faced them from the opposite seat. Grim-faced and silent, he glared in turn at Maggie, Lydia, and the passing scenery.

Lydia kept up a steady stream of chatter, but Maggie paid no attention, concentrating instead on the streets rolling by. Caught up in a crowded procession of coaches and carriages, Maggie hoped fruitlessly for even a glimpse of a car, a bus, a cab. Everyone appeared in costume, right down to the plentiful beggars in the streets.

Where were the cops when you really needed them? In her experience they always seemed to be right there to catch you zipping a little too fast along a country road, but when you wanted them, try to find one.

The carriage passed through the park gate. Maggie noted nothing familiar, nothing modern, nothing that said 1995. Her gaze moved restlessly, trying not to miss a single clue that could provide answers. The queasy, sinking feeling in her stomach returned.

Maggie's eyes told her what her mind simply could not accept. Even in a historical park there would be tourists, people not in costume. Where were they? Where were the Americans in their tacky shorts with their guidebooks and their loudmouthed teenagers? Where were the Japanese with their high-tech cameras? Where were the perpetual college students backpacking their way through Europe?

Once, briefly, Maggie met Adam's searching gaze. He seemed to study her every move, her slightest reaction. She refused to let him see the fear building, the panic growing with every turn of the carriage wheel.

She had to get away. But how? Commandeering a carriage was out of the question. The only horse

power she knew how to control remained firmly under the hood of a car. And she hadn't ridden a horse
since childhood. That eliminated the possibility of
"borrowing" a beast to make her escape. Besides—

"Good God, they're riding sidesaddle." Maggie
stared at the women on horseback.

"Of course, my dear." Lydia surveyed her curiously. "Don't women ride sidesaddle in your day?"

"No. Women in my day wouldn't put up with it.
We are equal to men up to and including riding a
horse." Maggie glared at Adam, who simply raised
an eyebrow as if to question the sanity of such a society.

While the park was packed with people in carriages and on horseback, Maggie noticed many others strolling though the grounds. That was it. She
couldn't ride or handle a carriage but she could
damn well walk.

"Wait. Hold it. Stop." She interrupted Lydia's comments on some fashion faux pas in another carriage.
"Sorry, but I'm really not used to riding in carriages,
and it's making me . . . oh . . . kind of . . . well, sick to
my stomach. I'm going to be ill if I don't get out of
this thing. You know, lose my lunch. Could we walk
a bit? Please?"

Adam studied her for a moment as if debating her
sincerity, and Maggie did her best to look as green
as possible. But Lydia jumped right in.

"How inconsiderate we've been not to have
thought of that. Walking will do us all a world of
good. Adam?"

"Fine." He called to the driver. Jumping out of the
carriage, he extended his hand to Lydia, helping her

descend. He turned to Maggie and she offered her hand for his assistance. Ignoring her, he placed his steady hands on either side of her waist and gently lifted her to the ground. For a fraction of a second she stared up at him, her gaze locked with his. Acutely aware of the heat emanating between them, the nearness of his hard, strong body, she caught her breath. Was it panic that still fluttered in her stomach or something else?

"Th-thanks," she whispered.

"My pleasure," he said softly, holding her a shade longer than necessary.

"Shall we?" Lydia interrupted, oblivious to the charged moment.

The trio strolled down the shady walkway. Lydia greeted acquaintances; Maggie and Adam were silent, at least one of them more than a little confused.

When pressed to introduce her, the brother and sister explained she was a distant connection from America. Lydia did most of the talking; Adam remained noticeably quiet. Maggie kept her mouth shut, trying to reconcile her reactions to Adam with her need to escape. Didn't hostages often come to like, even love, their captors?

"Ridgewood. Ridgewood. I say, old man, we haven't seen you in ages. Where have you been hiding?"

Adam turned toward the call. Two men on horseback greeted him with the enthusiasm of old friends. Glancing quickly at Maggie, he appeared satisfied at her behavior and, with a genuine smile, approached the newcomers.

"My dear Lady Lydia," a shrill voice trumpeted.

"How are you?" An immense, older woman with two girls in tow bore down on them like a tornado on a trailer court.

"Good lord." Lydia turned away from the overbearing matron and groaned at Maggie. "It's Lady Wentworth. She's a dreadful bore and a horrible gossip, but obviously inevitable."

Lydia pivoted to face her fate, a falsely sincere smile plastered securely on her face. "Lady Wentworth," she gushed graciously. "How delightful. I don't believe you have met my cousin from America, Miss Margaret Masterson?"

Maggie smiled slightly and nodded. Regardless of Lydia's opinion of Lady Wentworth, within moments the three women captured her attention with animated conversation.

Maggie checked out Adam. He still spoke with his friends, paying no attention to her or his sister. Immersed in her own conversation, apparently consisting of the latest gossip, Lydia could be counted on not to notice if Maggie stayed by her side. Or not.

This was it. The chance she'd waited for.

Casually, hoping not to attract attention, Maggie took a few slow steps. She glanced at Adam, then Lydia. No one noticed. A few steps more. Again, no one noticed. The inching continued, slowly, sedately. Still no notice. At a distance of a good ten feet, she gave up all pretense at discretion. She turned and strode against the flow of carriages, hoping to get out of the park. Conscious of the stares of the people she passed, she ignored them and stepped up her pace until she reached a measured jog. A pretty good trick in the long dress. Adrenaline, triggered by increasing

71

apprehension and alarm, spurred her on.

She burst out of the park gate, finding herself on a vaguely familiar street. Maggie slowed and scanned the area in a desperate search for a cop or, at this point, anyone who looked like they hadn't just stepped out of the nineteenth century.

Nothing.

Maggie hiked up her skirts and ran. Full-fledged terror pushed her feet faster and faster. She flew past astonished onlookers but barely noticed and didn't care. Abruptly she pulled up short. Directly in front of her was the Wellington Museum.

Gasping to catch her breath, she stared at the familiar landmark with relief. She'd toured the former home of the great military leader a few days ago. London's version of a subway system, the Underground, was nearby. It was right about—she whirled around—here!

Nothing.

No Underground.

No signs.

No indication of anything missing, anything out of place.

Everything looked untouched. As if nothing had ever been here. As if all she remembered didn't exist. As if it hadn't been built yet!

Maggie denied the dawning realization. "It can't be. It just can't be."

The truth crashed in on her, overloaded her senses. All she'd seen, heard, even smelled since she woke up assailed her and pointed to one inevitable conclusion. If Coleridge was telling the truth, if she had traveled through time, then everything made sense. It was the only answer that did make sense. The only thing that didn't make any sense at all, that didn't fit, that was completely out of place, was Maggie.

The world spun beneath her. An overwhelming sense of exhaustion slammed into her with as much force as her revelation. Her mind refused to accept what she knew to be true. Her body seemed to shut down. Blackness closed in. Knees buckling, she collapsed as if in slow motion.

An iron grasp swept her up mere inches above the ground.

"I hope you now have your proof," a voice muttered grimly.

Maggie struggled to focus on the man carrying her. His face swam in and out of her vision.

Coleridge, of course. The thought gave her a warm sense of safety and security. Weird to like a kidnapper this much. She sighed and nestled closer, her mind drifting off.

Uncomfortably aware of her movements and cognizant of the impropriety of their positions, Adam nonetheless gripped her tightly. The feelings she aroused did little to temper his anger. He stalked through the streets, returning to the park, muttering all the way.

"Bloody hell. The woman has absolutely no sense. Why on earth would I, of all people, or anyone for that matter, make up a story as ridiculous as time travel? Absurd! And now look at what's happened. I knew this was a mistake, all this 'prove it' nonsense."

Adam nodded curtly to shocked observers, knowing full well this escapade would be fuel for every gossip in the ton by morning. At least no one knew the real truth. That was the lone saving grace in the entire fiasco.

"I say, Ridgewood, is she all right?" an acquaintance called as Adam strode briskly by.

"Quite." Adam responded in clipped tones designed to discourage further conversation. "She still has not fully recovered from her long voyage from America."

"Jet lag," Maggie murmured.

Never breaking his determined stride toward the carriage, Adam pulled her closer and whispered sharply in her ear, "Keep that mouth of yours closed."

He drew his head back and groaned in irritation. She had already drifted off.

He watched Ridgewood stride across the park, a beautiful woman cradled in his arms. The earl seemed to hold her a shade too closely, a bit too intimately. His eyes narrowed and he considered the possibilities. This would bear watching. A grim smile creased his lips. Perhaps, finally, the opportunity he'd waited and watched for had arrived. He would bide his time to make sure. He could be patient. It scarcely mattered anymore; he'd already waited a very long time.

For the third time in as many nights, Adam again lingered at Maggie's bedside, watching her sleep. He no longer worried about the impropriety of his presence. Lord knew, she probably would not care. Last night she had been an intrigue, a mystery. Tonight she was infuriating, annoying, irritating, and, he had to admit, at least to himself, irresistible.

"Good lord, woman." He glared at the peaceful, sleeping figure. "What in God's name am I going to do with you?"

Chapter Four

In those fragile first moments of awareness, in a place somewhere between deep sleep and consciousness, Maggie mulled over the strange things she dreamed. Dreams of a handsome, arrogant man and a visit to a far-distant time. Wait till Kiki heard about this one. Maggie smiled and her eyes fluttered open. She gazed around the room. A charming room with a high, ornately plastered ceiling, a four-poster bed, and beautiful antique furniture. Just the right blend—

"No!" Maggie bolted upright.

Her gaze flew around the room. This was no dream; this was real. All of it. The period costumes that weren't costumes at all, the missing cars, street signs, phone and electric wires, the lack of outlets in the house. All the things so familiar through her entire life she barely paid them any attention, now took on a significance far beyond their everyday role in

76

the twentieth century. They all pointed to the truth. Somehow she had actually traveled through time.

"Oh, damn." She groaned and flung herself back on the bed, pulling the blankets over her head. How could something like this happen?

She took a deep breath and in one last grasping at straws, peeked out from under the covers. Nothing had changed. Reluctantly, she accepted what she could no longer deny.

Fear and panic subsided under a wave of anger and indignation. Who the hell did this to her?

With a muttered curse, Maggie tossed the bedclothes aside and tumbled out of bed. She stalked to the wardrobe and hastily flipped through the clothes. Realistically, she'd need help to get into any of these things and she didn't want to waste time finding a maid.

"Waste time? Ha, that's a laugh."

Impatient to get going, she caught sight of a robe lying on a nearby chair. Maggie threw it on, raced out of her chamber and downstairs to the library.

She flung open the doors and burst into the room, spotting Adam again at the desk where she'd first met him.

"Okay, Coleridge," she said in her most demanding tone. "What the hell are we supposed to do now?"

Adam quirked an eyebrow, his gaze drifting over her in an infuriating but definitely sexy, calm, and thorough manner.

"Do you ever feel it necessary to be properly dressed?"

"Clothes," she said, "are the very least of my worries right now. In case you haven't noticed, we have a major-league problem on our hands. Or"—she gave him a challenging look—"should I say I?"

Maggie glared, her defiance a shield hiding the fear inside. What if he said she was on her own? She was an intelligent, independent twentieth-century woman but could she function in an early nineteenth-century world?

Alone?

Maggie didn't particularly want to find out.

The beginnings of a smile played across his lips. "I rather think 'we' is appropriate."

Relief flooded through her, followed by annoyance. She resented being dependent on anyone—correction—any man, especially this arrogant, self-righteous snob. But as much as she hated to admit it, she really couldn't go this one alone.

"Great. Thanks," she said, a hint of embarrassment in her voice. "I just needed to know where I stood. I mean, after all, I guess I kind of fell into your life here. And I'd understand if you wanted to dump me and this whole mess."

Throughout her rambling speech, Adam stared from behind the desk. Leaning back, elbows resting on the arms of his chair, he steepled his long fingers lightly at chest level. His face, however, betrayed his feelings, astonishment mingling with more than a little indignation.

"My dear Miss Masterson." He leapt from his chair and circled the desk to approach her. "I know not how things are done in your day, but here and now when a gentleman finds a lady in serious distress he is honor bound to provide assistance. I could not possibly let you cope with this ordeal alone. Why, even if I found a man in this unique situation I would feel compelled to help."

"But," Maggie said slowly, choosing her words carefully, "you don't think a man would need as much help as, oh, say, a woman. Women being so . . . oh, let's see, helpless?"

He smiled warmly, obviously pleased she understood his rationale and completely oblivious to the sparks Maggie couldn't keep from her eyes. "Precisely."

"Why you—" She struggled for the right words, grasping a phrase from her sister's feminist past. "Male chauvinist pig!"

Adam's smile faltered.

"You have the nerve, the audacity to think a man could handle this situation better than a woman? I'll have you know in my time, women do everything men do. We have careers. We manage our own money. We own property. We've been voting for more than seventy years. In my day, some men even work for women. Your country's even had a woman prime minister."

Adam paled. "Are you quite through?" She nodded smugly. He continued, his voice controlled, his words clipped and curt. "Then do me the courtesy of listening."

Maggie opened her mouth.

"Keep still," he said. "It is my turn."

Maggie stared at him, a towering pillar of barely controlled rage. Maybe she had misjudged him.

"I am well aware of the many accomplishments of women in your time. I have thoroughly read your magazines and while I do not understand everything, the status of women in your society cannot be denied. I do not know if women go through some remarkable change in the next one hundred and seventy-seven years or if we have given them less than their due today, but know this, Miss Masterson." He stood within inches of her, glaring down at her upturned face. "I do not mean to insult you and tender my apology if I have done so. Your manner of behavior and way of speaking are foreign to me. Women I know do not act as you do, and I cannot think of one who could cope with the dilemma you find yourself in. I have certain expectations about women that you simply do not fit. It is not easy for me to reconcile long-held beliefs with the reality of you. I would that you show the same sort of patience with me that I will attempt to show to you.

"Although,"—he fixed her face with a steady glare—"you make it extremely difficult."

He stalked to his chair. Once seated, he leaned forward, his elbows on the desk, hands clasped together. "I don't know what a male chauvinist pig is, although it is not hard to determine that the phrase is not a compliment. I suggest you bear in mind the differing standards of our respective societies before making further pronouncements about my character."

He looked so stern sitting there, Maggie almost thought she was 12 years old and in the principal's office again. Funny, but his obvious anger didn't increase her fear. Instead, it calmed her down. This head-on clash of two distinctly different cultures might turn out to be pretty funny. Maggie could use all the laughter she could get. Until she figured out how to get out of this mess, anyway.

"Okay." She pulled a chair up to the desk and smiled sweetly. "Your apology is accepted."

Adam sputtered and Maggie held up a hand to silence him.

"If we're going to survive this relationship without killing each other, I think we need to drop this particular discussion right here and now. What do ya say? Okay?"

She gave him a questioning look. He sighed and Maggie thought he rolled his eyes a bit.

"Agreed." His tone signaled agreement and resignation to the terms of the cease-fire.

"Great." She grinned and plopped into the chair she'd positioned by the desk. "So, as I was saying, what the hell are we supposed to do now?"

"Miss Masterson." He shot to his feet. "You simply cannot continue to use such unseemly language. It is not acceptable for well-bred young ladies to curse."

"Oh, sit down, Coleridge." She waved him to his chair with an impatient flick of her hand. "You're right, of course." She wrinkled her nose at his look of shock that she actually agreed with him. "While I'm here I need to act like a native and I promise to try. Okay? Good enough?"

He nodded.

"Great, but you need to keep some things in mind, too. First of all, I'm not a young lady. I'm an adult."

"I assumed you to be at least one and twenty."

"Actually, I'm twenty-six." She noted his surprised look. "Is that a problem?"

"No, of course not." He seemed uncomfortable,

possibly even disappointed. "I had simply assumed you were unmarried."

"I am unmarried. I mean single."

"Well then, surely you have been widowed?"

"No," she said slowly. "What's the matter?"

"The matter, Miss Masterson, is very probably with me." He ran his fingers absently through his hair. "Regardless of what I say I have certain preconceived notions about women and what is and is not expected of them. In this world, a twenty-six-year-old unmarried woman is generally considered on the shelf, too old to make a good match." His gaze probed deeply into hers. "Therefore, I naturally assumed you were much younger or had been married. You are so very lovely."

The compliment lingered in the air. Heat flamed in Maggie's face. Aware of her own churning feelings, she marveled at his brown eyes growing darker with . . . what? Passion? Desire? The look they shared, the charged moment, was more than enough to turn Maggie's legs to rubber. She didn't get it. Even when this man drove her up a wall there was something about him that made her want to melt into his arms, and more.

"Why have you not wed?" His quiet voice was thick with barely controlled emotion.

"I don't know," she replied just as softly. Was it getting hard to breathe in here? Her gaze was still locked with his. What had she been saying? Oh, yeah. Marriage.

"I guess I never found the right person." Her response was barely a whisper. For a moment, Maggie ached to throw caution to the winds and fling herself into his arms. What would it feel like to share his embrace? His kiss? His bed? And looking in his eyes she knew the same thoughts, desires, and possibilities surged through him as well.

"Well. Ah." Adam cleared his throat, destroying the moment that had grown too intimate for comfort.

"Yeah. Right." Maggie sighed, torn between relief and disappointment. She'd have plenty of time to sort through her feelings later. And she really didn't need to complicate an already complex situation with a relationship. Even if the man in question made her senses reel and her knees grow mushy.

"Shall we start at the beginning, Miss Masterson?" He was abruptly all business.

Not quite sure why she found that more than a little annoying, Maggie interrupted. "Before we get going, please don't call me Miss Masterson. It makes me feel like an old lady schoolteacher. And since my age is already going to be a problem here, let's not compound it."

"It shan't be a problem. You certainly do not look your age, and if anyone is so rude as to ask, we shall simply lie."

"Great," she said under her breath, "lying about a birth date that hasn't happened yet."

He waved aside her words. "It doesn't signify, Miss—Margaret?"

"Maggie."

"Fine then, Maggie. Now, how did you arrive here?"

"If I knew that we wouldn't have a problem, would we?" Sarcasm dripped off her words.

"Miss Mas—Maggie," Adam said crisply. "We shall

not accomplish a thing if you do not cooperate."

"I know, I know, I'm sorry. It's just that . . . Well. Damn it." Maggie ignored Adam's wince. "I'm scared. I am really, really scared."

Maggie pushed out of her chair and, wrapping her arms around herself, paced the room. She tried to put her confusing thoughts into words, for Adam and, even more, for herself.

"I don't understand what's happened. Why I'm here. It feels like some kind of joke, a giant cosmic mistake. I'm a displaced person. A temporal refugee. I'm not supposed to be here!"

Her voice suspiciously close to a scream, Maggie took a deep breath, fighting to regain control. And losing.

"Don't you get it?" She whirled to face Adam. "Do you realize technically I'm not even born yet! Do you have any idea how that feels? I have no past. No history. Everything I know, everything I grew up with, everything I'm familiar with, doesn't exist! I don't know anybody. I have no one here, no friends, no family. Oh my God, Kiki!" Her eyes widened with horror. "My sister. She'll be frantic with worry. She must have the cops combing London by now. And I don't even have a way to let her know I'm okay!"

On the edge of full-fledged hysteria, Maggie's vision blurred with tears, her breath coming fast and choppy.

Immediately, Adam was at her side, grasping her shoulders, looking down into her face. "Miss Masterson. Maggie. Please calm yourself. I have every confidence this will all be resolved."

She stared up at him, battling to maintain control,

struggling to keep a lid on the panic threatening to explode within her. She blinked back hot tears. Adam pulled her closer. Her head lay on his chest and he stroked her hair.

Wrapped in his arms, without thinking she matched her breathing to the stroke of his hand. Maggie's fear and panic ebbed away, replaced by the now familiar feeling of safety and security. And a growing need for this man to do more than simply hold her.

She turned her head toward his, a single tear slipping down her cheek. "Adam?"

The desire they'd suppressed from the moment they met could no longer be denied.

"Maggie." With a groan he swiftly brought his lips down to meet hers. Her welcoming mouth opened under the pressure of his and his tongue swept inside. Only the light robe and night rail separated her straining body from his hard, strong length. Their mouths explored each other's in a mating ritual as old as man, as eternal as time itself. Never had Maggie been kissed like this. He ripped the breath out of her, replacing it with his own. His tongue teased and fenced and danced, leaving her knees again unable to support her. She dissolved in his arms, reveling in an awakening passion she never dreamed possible.

Dimly she struggled to think. This was getting them nowhere. Or maybe they were headed someplace she'd rather not go, at least not now.

"Adam." She gasped, dragging her lips from his. Her head dropped back and tilted to the side, giving his mouth access to a particularly sensitive spot just below her ear. He ran a flurry of devastatingly light kisses down to the point where her neck met her shoulder. A tremor of passion shivered through her and she wanted nothing more than to release herself to him completely.

But this had to stop. Marshaling her last ounce of control, she pulled away.

"Adam, stop." Her breath rasped through her lips.

"Why?" He bent back to feather another shower of kisses on her now achingly sensitive neck.

"Because." She wrenched out of his grasp and fought for breath.

"Coleridge, this isn't the time or the place. I don't even know you. I don't know what impression you got from those magazines of mine but I don't make love with men I don't know. Granted, the moral standards of my time aren't as strict or uptight as yours, but I am not promiscuous."

Adam stared at her a long second, unfulfilled passion still smoldering in his eyes. Only his fists clenched by his side gave any real indication as to his true feelings.

"Of course. Once again, I apologize if my actions have insulted you." His voice was so cold and controlled she wanted to smack him. He wanted her as much as she wanted him, but it wasn't right. Not yet. Even so, she resented his treating her like a stranger.

"Now then, Miss Masterson . . ."

Maggie ignored his deliberate reversion to the formal title. Adam took his place behind the desk and, dipping a pen in an inkwell, sat poised to write. He leveled a cool gaze at her.

"What do you remember?"

"You're going to take notes?" She ignored the faint

trembling in her hands and, trying to appear firmly under control, dropped back in her chair.

"Indeed." He nodded. "It may help."

"Okay." She sighed. If he wanted to be all stuffy and businesslike, she could deal with that. It wasn't what she wanted in their relationship, but at this point she wasn't sure what she did want so she'd play it his way. For now.

"What do I remember? I was visiting London with my sister, Kiki. She's a free-lance photographer."

"A what?" Adam asked.

"A photographer," Maggie said impatiently. "You know, she takes pictures?"

Realization of where—and more importantly, when—she was dawned on her. "Sorry, I forgot. All this hasn't been invented yet. Pictures, photographs, how to explain . . ."

Maggie jumped up from her chair and leaned over the desk. The items from her bag were still neatly arranged in precise piles.

"Here." Triumphantly she found the photo envelope and pulled out the pictures. "These are photographs, images captured on film." She searched for the right words. "That's a special kind of, well, I guess paper is the best way to describe it. It's very sensitive to light. You put the film, the paper, in this."

Maggie grabbed the camera and handed it to him. "This is a camera. The film goes here. The lens opens for just a fraction of a second, letting in the light and recording the image on film."

She smiled with satisfaction at her explanation until she noticed Adam's frown of concentration. Complete and utter confusion was scrawled across his face.

"Oh jeez, I'm sorry. I'm not explaining this well. I've lived with this stuff all my life and never really thought about how it worked and never really cared. I just take it for granted that it will work when I need it." She drew a deep breath and wondered how best to explain.

She moved to Adam's side of the desk and took the camera from his hands. "See this window?" She pointed to the viewfinder. "Look through it."

He held it up to his right eye.

"Whatever you see in the viewfinder will be recorded on film when you press the button. Get it? Do you understand?"

"Amazing." Adam looked around the room, the camera still glued to his eyes. "We speculated it might be a weapon of some sort."

"Weapon?"

"Well," he said sheepishly, "it says cannon."

"Cannon?" Puzzled, she frowned, then realized the truth and laughed.

"That's the manufacturer, the company that makes it. Let me have it."

Reluctantly he did so and Maggie took it halfway across the room.

"Stand up."

He frowned suspiciously, his eyes narrowed. "Why?"

Maggie laughed. "I'm going to take your picture. Now stand up."

Adam rose to his feet.

"Say cheese." She laughed again at his puzzled

look. "Just smile. It doesn't hurt. Although I have heard of primitive tribes who feel taking their picture can capture their souls."

He seemed startled and she grinned, shaking her head. "Don't worry about it. I wouldn't dare capture your soul. Now smile, Coleridge."

Through the viewfinder, Maggie watched a devastating killer smile put a sexy twinkle in his eyes and reveal that lone dimple in his chiseled cheeks. Her heart skipped a beat. No doubt about it, the man was a certified hunk. She stared a shade longer than absolutely necessary to make sure of the focus, a lame excuse in an autofocus camera. Maggie hit the button, took the picture, and set off the flash.

"Bloody hell, what was that?" Adam rubbed his eyes frantically. "You've blinded me! I can't see anything!"

"Oh damn, I'm sorry. I forgot about the flash." Guilt propelled Maggie to his side.

"It'll be okay in a second or two. I'm really sorry." Genuine concern battled with amusement at his plight. After all, he'd never run into anything like this before. Maggie bit her lip to keep from smiling. With a sympathetic expression, she stared up at him.

"It's like looking into the bloody sun." Adam blinked his eyes experimentally. But you are correct. I seem to be quite recovered now. What was that light?" Curiously, he took the camera from her. "There's no candle here, no gas that I can see. Where did it come from?"

"It's just a little battery-powered electric light." At his questioning look, she groaned. "I can't explain electric power and batteries." She glanced at the camera. "But I can show you how this works and you can take a picture of me."

She stood inches from him, explaining the various parts of the camera and what to do to take the picture. Adam breathed in her heady, spicy scent, listening to her words with only partial attention. How could he concentrate on anything she said when she stood there barely covered by the light wrapper and nightclothes?

She thought she had angered him by cutting short their embrace. In fact, Adam was angry at himself. No matter what concessions he made aloud about twentieth-century women, he firmly believed this creature to be as helpless as the women of his time.

She might well have courage and spirit that led her to speak her own mind in a deuced irritating and even infuriating manner. Adam would have dismissed any woman of his time with those qualities from his consideration without a backward glance. But with Maggie, the things that made her so annoying strengthened, in some perverse way, the irresistible attraction she held for him. An attraction made all the greater by their kiss.

He could not remember a mere kiss affecting him that deeply before. Ever. A kiss that seemed to reach to his very soul, closing his mind to everything but the sensation of her lips against his. The feel of her in his arms. The way her body fit in perfect complement to his. No novice to kissing, or what followed, for that matter, Adam nonetheless had a difficult time controlling himself when she pulled away. Loss of control was a unique experience and it shook him in a way no woman ever had.

In spite of her air of independence, she had let him see her vulnerability and fear, confirming a lifetime of beliefs about the fairer sex. No matter how much he wanted her, no matter how much her responses showed she wanted him as well, he would not take advantage of her. He would temper his passions and concentrate on helping her return to her own time. If, of course, that could even be done.

"So, do you think you can do it?" Maggie's question brought Adam's attention back to the matter at hand. The so-called camera device.

"Certainly," He accepted the camera from her with confident enthusiasm. "Stand over there." He gestured to the door. Gazing at her through the viewfinder, he paid less thought to Maggie's instructions than to the way her nightclothes clung to her voluptuous figure. The way her hair flowed freely to a cloud of misty curls at her shoulders. The way that even in the black-and-white tones of this viewfinding-thing, sparks shot from eyes he already knew were a brighter green when angered, a deep, almost forest color when aroused.

"Are you going to take a picture or what?"

"Sorry." He prepared to activate the device. If he wanted to keep his intentions toward her honorable he needed to pay more attention to her twentieth-century marvels and less to her timeless attributes.

Adam pushed the button and the flash went off. This time he was prepared.

Pride at his accomplishment shone in his eyes. "How was that?"

"It was fine." She grinned in amusement at his satisfied expression.

"When do we see this picture?" he asked eagerly.

"Oh, Coleridge, I'm sorry. It has to be developed."

Sympathetically, Maggie noted his disappointment. He looked like a little boy who had just been given a toy without batteries. "I don't have the skills to process the pictures. Even if I did, I'm sure the chemicals involved haven't been invented yet. I'll get them developed when I get home. But . . ." A surprising sense of dismay shot through her at the thought. "I guess you won't get to see them."

She wondered at the vague feeling of loss but shook it off.

"How do you propose to go home?" Adam returned to his chair.

"I don't know." She sighed and sank back into her own chair. "I'm not even sure how I got here. All I know is I took a carriage ride with a little old man for a driver." She strained to remember and tried to ignore Adam's intense scrutiny.

"He was quite a philosopher, going on about chances and choices and destiny. It was a foggy night. And all of a sudden, it felt like something hit the carriage. Maybe a car." She glanced at Adam. "Do you understand cars?"

"The vehicles in the pictures?"

She nodded.

"Go on then." He observed her as intently as if she were a bug under a microscope.

"Well, that's about it. It was like I was thrown through the air. I remember hitting some-thing . . . and . . ." Her gaze met Adam's. "The next thing I remember is waking up here. Pretty nuts, isn't it?"

A frown of concentration creased his brow. "It is most unusual."

"I still can't believe this." She shook her head in wonder. "I mean I wake up one morning and it's May 1995, and the next morning I wake up it's 1818."

"What was the date in 1995?" Adam said thoughtfully.

"Let's see." She paused, pulling her thoughts together. "We arrived in London on the seventh and we'd been there for five days so it was . . . the twelfth, I think."

"Please be precise."

She fought to remember, drawing her brows together in a puzzled frown.

"Okay, let me think. We have—had—tickets to a show on the thirteenth. I remember because they were so hard to get. And that was the next night so . . . yes, it was the twelfth. Definitely May twelfth." She nodded firmly, more than a little pleased with herself.

Adam leaned back and eyed her cautiously. He seemed to choose his words with care. "I do not want to put too much importance on this," he said slowly. "But the night we found you was April twelfth. Disregarding the years, of course, that's a discrepancy of a month."

"A month," she echoed.

"Lydia and I were arriving home after concluding a particularly unpleasant discussion about her future. I had nearly forgotten that," he said. "I mustn't let that business slip; however, it doesn't signify at the moment. We were walking to the door when we heard a carriage out of control. There was a great deal of fog so we never actually saw the vehicle."

He leaned forward and gazed into her eyes. "The object you hit was me."

They stared at each other for a long moment, realization hitting simultaneously.

"The carriage," they said in unison.

"That's it!" Maggie shouted with excitement. "That's the answer."

"It does appear so." Adam smiled at her enthusiasm.

"And if the carriage brought me here"—Maggie's mind raced—"it can take me back."

She jumped up and leaned over the desk.

"With that month difference maybe I can go back when it's May twelfth here. Oh, Adam, I know it, I feel it. The carriage will come a month from now and I can go home!"

Chapter Five

Adam stared at her green eyes glittering with excitement. Could they have found the answer? Could it possibly be that simple? Merely wait for the right day and a carriage would appear to spirit her back to her own time?

The thought of Maggie vanishing from his life as abruptly as she'd appeared caught Adam by surprise. Not until this moment had he realized how very much he wanted to know this visitor from another time. He wanted to learn more about her world and teach her about his. He wanted to share her thoughts, her feelings, and more. Much more.

But if indeed she would only be with him for less than a month, his desires were not only unwise, they could destroy them both. His resolve to keep his distance strengthened.

"It is certainly plausible," he said lightly, concealing the conflicting emotions. "It seems your stay with us shan't be long after all, if indeed this theory is correct."

"Guess not. Less than a month now, if we're right. And it really feels right." Excitement rang in her voice.

Then it hit her. Less than a month until she returned to 1995. Less than a month to be with this man who affected her like no man ever had. If she returned, and confidence filled her now that she would, he'd be long dead and buried before she was ever born. As strong as the pull between them, involvement with Adam would only break her heart. A weird quirk of fate had brought them together but gave only a tantalizing glimpse of what might have been.

Maggie and Adam fell silent, each deep in their own thoughts. Lydia swept into the room unnoticed. Far more astute than most gave her credit for, she immediately sensed the tension in the air and assumed it had more to do with their obvious attraction to each other than the overwhelming problem of time travel.

Lydia had already noted the sparks between her brother and their houseguest, even while giving the well-practiced appearance of being oblivious to the goings-on around her. She'd developed the skill years ago when she first realized young ladies were not often in demand for their intelligence or perception. She eyed her brother and their guest speculatively. This was going far better than she'd dreamed. Adam had not mentioned that ridiculous husband nonsense once since Maggie's arrival.

"Here you are." Her announced presence startled

both Maggie and Adam. "Maggie, you're not dressed yet?"

"Oh I—" She glanced at Adam. "I had other things on my mind."

"Hurry off to your room then," Lydia said in the manner of a beneficent general ordering his troops. "I'll send Jane up to help you dress and . . . have you eaten?"

Maggie shook her head.

"Then I'll have a tray sent up as well. Do try to be quick, we must be off. My modiste has sent word that she needs a final fitting as soon as possible. With luck, we shall have your clothes, or many of them anyway, completed by tomorrow."

Flushed with triumph, she turned to Adam. "I told you I could accomplish this. Nearly an entire wardrobe in a matter of a few days."

"What wardrobe?" Maggie asked.

"Why, a wardrobe for you, of course."

"Lydia," Adam said quietly, "she's not going to be here long."

Lydia frowned. "Whatever do you mean?"

Adam glanced at Maggie and she signaled for him to explain.

"We believe Maggie came here, to our time, by way of a mysterious carriage on the night of May twelfth. We think she is to return on that same day in our time. Less than a month from now."

"Oh, dear." Lydia's mind raced. This new development could hamper her plans to distract Adam with Maggie. "Are you positive?"

"No," Maggie said quickly. "But it makes sense. I guess we just have to wait and find out."

"I see." It sounded as if this theory had more basis in fancy than fact. And that meant if it was convenient to ignore it, Lydia would.

Brightening, she pointed out what to her was far more obvious. "Regardless of the length of time you'll be with us, you will need to be attired in the latest stare of fashion." She smiled impishly. "After all, you are a distant relation of the Earl of Ridgewood, remember? Now go along. I'll see you in the foyer when you're ready."

With one last glance at Adam, Maggie left the library.

Lydia turned to her brother, who seemed distant, lost in his own thoughts. "Adam, whatever is the matter?"

"What? Oh, nothing, nothing to concern you. Just pondering this whole confounded situation." He bestowed a tolerant smile on his sister. "Take care of this wardrobe business and I will deal with the rest."

She stared at him for a long moment. That condescending attitude he adopted whenever anything of extreme importance came along had irritated her since childhood. Very often, she refused to put up with it. But this time perhaps it was wiser not to distract him from Maggie's problems by doing battle head-on. His words dissolved the twinge of guilt she might have felt by playing with the lives of two people who might not possibly have any future together.

The trip to the dressmaker occupied Maggie and Lydia for most of the day. Maggie never appreciated the ease and convenience of mass-produced, off-the-rack clothing until forced to act as a human mannequin for some French-accented seamstress. But she had to admit, the woman was a genius. The clothes she whipped up were absolutely gorgeous. Maggie chastised Lydia more than once for the vast amount of money being spent and the wide array of clothing Lydia insisted she needed.

"Really, Maggie." Lydia sighed after one particularly heated debate when the modiste and her assistants left them alone. "I'm sure I know what you require far better than you."

Maggie tried to interrupt but Lydia quieted her with a stern glance and continued. "The clothes you arrived in and the ones I've seen displayed in your magazines may very well be suited for the life you are used to leading. But in my life they simply will not do. So, please, allow me to deal with what I know best."

"But ball gowns?" Maggie shuddered. "Do I really need ball gowns?"

"Of course." Lydia sounded surprised that she would even ask such a question. "Maggie, it's the height of the season. Adam has ignored invitations since you've arrived, not that he accepts many anyway, but there are obligations he—and I—are committed to. It would hardly do to leave you home alone. Besides"—a twinkle shimmered in her eye—"you shall have a wonderful time. There is nothing like a soiree or, better still, a ball with a huge crush of people and, of course, the waltz to make you feel just the thing."

"Waltz?" Maggie groaned. "I don't know how to waltz."

Lydia frowned. "Well, I know it is still not considered acceptable everywhere, but I assumed everyone knew how to waltz by now. Surely in your time . . . ?"

"We don't waltz," Maggie said miserably.

"What do you do? Country dances or quadrilles perhaps?"

"Not exactly." Maggie searched for the right words. "Dancing is a kind of freestyle thing."

"Freestyle?" Lydia frowned in confusion. "I fear I have no idea what you mean. At any rate, it doesn't signify because here we waltz. We will have to teach you. Or rather, Adam will. He's quite wonderful and very sought after as a partner when he deigns to make an appearance."

"Really? How nice," Maggie said coolly, surprised how annoying she found that bit of information.

"Oh, my, yes." Lydia continued, apparently oblivious to Maggie's attempt at nonchalance. "Adam is considered quite a catch on the marriage mart. He has a significant fortune, a well-respected name and title, and, even though he is my brother, I have to admit he is an extremely handsome figure of a man. I have lost count of the number of eager girls and ambitious mamas who have set their caps at him in the past."

"So how has he escaped?" Maggie pretended more interest in the piece of silk she fingered than in the answer to her question.

"I daresay I don't know," Lydia replied just as lightly. "Before Father died, Adam was considered quite a rake. Gambling and wenching and such. He had a rather unsavory reputation with a wide variety of women. In fact, at the time, I'm not sure a decent family would have had him for their daughter in

100

spite of his wealth and position. Although there were some who still insisted on throwing their daughters at him.

"He came close to marriage once, but I always thought it more a matter of convenience than any genuine affection on his part. I'm not sure Adam ever realized how taken the young woman was with him. I've always thought she read far more into his attentions than was called for. Adam always considered the marriage mart something of a game. He broke a fair number of hearts."

"Adam Colcridge? The same stuffy, uptight Adam Coleridge I've met?" Maggie scoffed. "That's really hard to believe."

"Nonetheless, it's true. Adam flirted with proper young ladies from the best families but gave his full attention to those who were, well, rather less than proper. I'm not supposed to know about such things, but people, especially servants, do talk. And if one is simply observant . . ." Lydia shrugged.

"At any rate, when Father died, seven years ago this summer, Adam changed dramatically. After the funeral he locked himself away for nearly two months. Refused to come out of the library, Father's library, at Ridgefield Manor. It was quite frightening. He would not talk to anyone and barely ate enough to live. The servants muttered that he had gone quite mad.

"When he finally came out, he made no mention of exactly what he did during that time and quite honestly I was afraid to ask. I was barely sixteen. Adam was all the family I had left and"—she sighed deeply—"I was concerned about his health and his

101

mind. And he seemed fine, just extremely different. Much more sedate and controlled. Reformed, if you will.

"He threw himself into handling family matters and estate business. Became the very model of propriety. He practically eliminated his social life. Oh, he kept his club memberships and made sure he was there to accompany me after my coming-out, but the wild nights and the women that went with them ended. As if now that he was the head of the family, he needed to behave accordingly. Of course, he felt compelled to look after me. It was very much as if he was trying to make amends to Father for the scandalous life he led."

Lydia tilted her head thoughtfully. "But you know, I don't believe Adam's scandals and escapades really bothered Father. I always thought he was rather proud of his son. Father was a bit of a rake himself in his day, you know. And it always seemed to me that he thought Adam would grow out of it, take after him perhaps. Father did not marry Mother and settle down until well into his thirties. Adam was twenty-five when Father died."

"You notice a lot more than you let on, don't you?" Maggie said.

Lydia cast Maggie a long, pensive look, as if carefully considering both her words and whether she could trust Maggie to hear them.

"Yes, I believe I do. But I have learned through the years what is and is not expected of a woman. I am to be pretty and decorative. My accomplishments should include music in some form. I play the pianoforte because I have no voice for singing. I am able to embroider and sew a fine stitch. I speak French passably and can manage a household, both in town and in the country. I have mastered all that is expected of a young lady in my position except finding a husband."

Lydia sighed heavily. "And now Adam is threatening to take that out of my hands."

Maggie stared, shocked. "Do you mean he could make you marry someone you don't want to?"

"It's not uncommon." Lydia quickly jumped to her brother's defense. "He is acting in what he believes is my best interest for my future. And in spite of my accomplishments, in the past my behavior has not always been as acceptable as it should have been."

Sudden insight struck Maggie. "You break the rules, don't you?"

"Well, I don't break them so much as merely bend them a bit. I find the rules, as you call them, so"—Lydia searched for the right word—"so confining." She added with a surge of anger, "And bloody unfair, too!"

Maggie nodded, encouraging her to continue.

"Adam had his opportunity to do whatever he wanted and has suffered no lasting consequences. If I, however, even dance with a man more than twice, my reputation will be a shambles. I cannot ride a horse or go for a walk without a servant in attendance. And heaven forbid I should ever be alone with a man. There are even streets in London where women are not to be seen."

"You're kidding!" Maggie knew 1818 was long before women's lib but this was ridiculous. "That's crazy. Why don't you just do what you want?"

"Quite simple, really." Lydia shrugged with resignation. "I don't have that kind of courage. Oh, I enjoy pushing the limits of acceptable behavior, but I'm afraid complete revolution isn't in me. To be totally ostracized from society is a fate even I shudder to contemplate."

She smiled, a gleam returning to her eye. "Besides, I do tend to get my own way far more often than many unmarried women I know. It may well be the biggest benefit of having a doting brother, even if his current well-meaning intentions are a bit tyrannical."

"What are you going to do about that husband business?" Maggie figured Lydia wouldn't take Adam's finding her a husband lying down.

"Oh, I have some ideas," Lydia said vaguely.

Maggie started to ask what kind of ideas but the modiste and her staff bustled into the room in a flurry of silks and laces. She made a mental note to learn more about Lydia's plans later. Maggie didn't know why, but somehow Lydia's cryptic comment left her with an indistinct sense of approaching doom.

It was late afternoon before they finally returned home. Maggie would never have believed a simple session with a dressmaker would be so exhausting, but she was dead on her feet. Of course, she'd spent all day being the object of Lydia's attention, as well as that of the modiste and what seemed like a flock of twittering assistants. All Maggie wanted to do was head straight to her room and her bed. Even dinner held no appeal.

Almost too tired to keep her eyes open, she feared she was too keyed-up to sleep. Maggie worried if she lay down now she'd toss and turn for hours. She needed something to help her get to sleep. Brandy? That would do it. She headed for the library.

Maggie breezed into the room, headed straight for the crystal decanter, and poured herself a glass. She took a sip. The warmth of the liquor flowed through her and she sighed.

"I told you it was quite good, didn't I?"

Maggie whirled toward the unexpected voice. Adam lounged in a chair near the fireplace.

"Is this becoming a habit or what?" she said, her voice sharp with surprise. "Every time I turn around you're sneaking up on me."

He raised an eyebrow and saluted her with the glass in his hand. "I believe I was here first."

"You're right." She sighed. "Sorry." She crossed to the sofa and collapsed. She laid her head on the armrest, swung her legs up, and stretched her body out along the sofa's length. In the extremely comfortable, semireclined position, Maggie observed Adam over the edge of her glass.

"I've really been a bite in the shorts since I've been here. I know that. And you and Lydia have been the greatest. Letting me stay with you, getting me clothes. And I honestly do appreciate it."

"Yes?"

"Remember I told you this morning I was scared?" He nodded and she continued. "Well, what if this whole thing isn't temporary? What if I can't go home in a month? What if I'm stuck here forever?"

"Would that be so bad?" His eyes gleamed intently.

"Would it be so terrible to spend your life here?"

"Yes!" She caught herself at the look of regret that passed through Adam's eyes so quickly she could have been mistaken.

"No. I guess not. Maybe. I don't know! I'm a creature of my environment, my history, my society. Can I exist without all that? It's like starting over on a desert island. I don't know."

She shook her head slowly, then gazed at him. "And what about you and your sister? How long can you pass me off as a weird, distant relative from America? What do you do if I can't go back?"

"I daresay we shouldn't worry about that unless it happens. In the meantime, is this truly so awful?"

"It's just so complicated here. So many dos and don'ts, rules and regulations. There's a lot to keep track of."

A light of sympathy shone in his eyes. "I imagine it must be difficult for one not used to it."

She took another sip of the brandy. "No shit, Sherlock."

"Miss Masterson!" Adam lurched upright in his chair. "I thought you understood. I thought you were beginning to grasp what is and what is not acceptable language. I don't know who Sherlock is but it is not difficult to understand the meaning of that particularly salty phrase. And 'no shit Sherlock' definitely does not fall within the boundaries of well-bred behavior. Do you comprehend what I'm saying at all?"

Maggie widened her eyes and had the good grace to blush. Warmth spread across her cheeks, and for a moment embarrassment kept her silent.

"I'm sorry," she said after a long pause. "I know I promised to act like I belong here and I really am trying. Honestly. But you have to remember one thing." She sat up and leaned forward, gazing into his dark eyes. "You, and Lydia of course, are all I have right now. If I can't let my guard down with you, I'll go crazy. I'm living a total lie here and that's hard enough. But if I can't get a break when I'm with you, I don't think I can do it." She paused and took a deep breath.

"So please don't get mad at me when I forget all the little details about behavior and decorum here. I need to be able to be myself sometimes. As tacky as it may seem, this is who I am. I'm sorry if I disappoint you."

"Oh," he said softly and reached to push an errant lock of her hair behind her ear. "I'm not at all disappointed." His hand traveled down to cup her chin. His bottomless brown eyes locked with hers. "So far I have been confused and confounded as well as infuriated and annoyed." His thumb lightly caressed her lower lip and she resisted the impulse to respond. "But I have also been intrigued beyond measure and lured by a mysterious attraction even I cannot fail to respond to."

"Oh . . . yeah. Right," she breathed. Wow! This guy was good.

Really good.

Abruptly he removed his hand and she nearly fell forward. Struggling to maintain her dignity and pretend nothing happened, she wondered at the look of . . . what? Satisfaction in his eye? Surely she was mistaken. Maggie downed the last of her brandy and stood.

"Well, I'm wiped out, so I'm going to bed. Thanks for everything."

"It is distinctly my pleasure." He picked up her hand and brushed his lips against it lightly. "And one more thing."

His gaze bored into hers and she wondered if he would kiss her again. Would she have the strength or the desire to pull away this time?

"Yes?" She tilted her face toward him in expectation.

"I was curious." The underlying currents in his soft words matched her own. "I have replaced all the items from your satchel and thought perhaps you would like to keep them with you." He dropped her hand and strode behind the desk. He bent down and disappeared, only to rise with her tote bag in one hand, her folded clothes, shoes balanced on top, in the other.

"I would suggest hiding them somewhere out of the obvious sight and reach of the servants. Or would you prefer I keep them?" His eyebrow raised with the question.

"Oh, no." She reached for her things, glad for the breathing space the action provided to pull herself together. The man had an irritatingly powerful effect on her. "I'll take them. Thanks. See you tomorrow."

She crossed the room and managed to open the door in spite of the burdens in her arms. A vague disappointment that he had not attempted to kiss her, not pursued their mutual desire of that morning, annoyed her. She really had to stop drooling over him.

She closed the door. A low, self-satisfied chuckle trailed in her wake. She shook her head. Her mind must be playing tricks on her. After all, she was very tired and the only person behind her was Adam. What on earth did he have to feel smug about?

Chapter Six

Maggie sailed down the stairs the next morning far more refreshed than she'd been since her arrival in London, in either century. Maybe her sister was right. Maybe what she really needed was a chance to get away and think about her life. Maggie laughed to herself. Kiki had no idea just how far away from her 1990s life she'd gotten.

Overnight Maggie had reached a decision. This was her vacation and she was going to enjoy it. If she had to spend it in 1818 London instead of 1995 London, so be it. It would definitely be different and might even be fun. Now that she had come to grips with where and when she was, she was determined to enjoy every minute of the month allotted her.

At the bottom of the stairs she ran into Adam in the foyer. Far more casually dressed than she'd seen him before, he wore some kind of buff-colored pants, dark jacket, and polished boots. The look flattered him but she couldn't help wondering idly what he'd look like in a pair of jeans and a T-shirt, both a shade too small.

"Good morning." He smiled with apparent pleasure at her approach. His gaze traveled appreciatively over her, spreading heat wherever it lingered. "Those clothes suit you admirably."

"Thanks." A shiver scampered through her and a blush warmed her cheeks at the compliment. "This is one of Lydia's. Mine aren't quite ready." She nodded at his clothes. "Where have you been?"

"Riding. I try to ride as often as I can. Usually every morning. Unfortunately there's not always time."

"Too bad," Maggie said lightly. "I guess that means you can't go with me today."

He frowned suspiciously. "Where are you going?"

"Well." She took a deep breath and let the air and the words rush out. Somehow she didn't think he'd approve of her plans. "I've decided to do some sightseeing while I'm here. You know, take advantage of the situation. Have some fun. Enjoy myself."

"And where precisely do you plan on doing this sightseeing?" He quirked an eyebrow.

"I don't know for sure." She furrowed her brow in thought, sank onto the stairs, and patted the step beside her, indicating that he sit. He joined her, leaning his back against the banister.

"My sister made all our sightseeing plans. I didn't want to come to London in the first place. She pushed me into it."

"Why didn't you want to come to London?" Curiosity shone in his eyes. "It is a magnificent city."

"I didn't see the need for it, I guess. My sister

111

thought it would do me good to get away." She wrinkled her nose at the thought. "Kiki, that's my sister, thought I had no direction in my life. She feels I'm basically going nowhere. Kiki's pretty much of an overachiever. She figured this was a good chance to put some perspective on my life. You know, from a distance."

"You most definitely have achieved distance and, I suspect, a rather unique perspective." Irony colored his words.

She laughed. "No kidding. But I don't think this is exactly what she had in mind. Anyway, Kiki made up lists of things we were going to do. She's very organized and makes up lists for everything." Maggie paused and smiled, remembering her sister's habit.

"The lists?" he prompted.

"Oh, sorry." She thought for a moment. "Let's see. We were going to visit some of the spots Charles Dickens wrote about. And the mythical Twenty-two Baker Street, home of Sherlock Holmes. And the haunts of Jack the Ripper."

Adam frowned in puzzlement. "I'm afraid none of that sounds even vaguely familiar."

She stared, then realized what she had done. "I know." She sighed. "I keep forgetting that what seems ancient to me hasn't even happened yet. Maybe I should explain."

Maggie ticked the points off on her fingers. "Charles Dickens was, or rather will be, one of the greatest British writers of all time. He'll be read and studied for generations. Dickens wrote the most wonderful Christmas story ever. Most people probably know it by heart. Then there's Sherlock Holmes."

"Sherlock?" A teasing smile crossed his lips.

"Never mind." She ignored the gleam in his eye. "Sherlock Holmes was a fictitious detective. He was brilliant and could solve almost any mystery simply by his powers of observation and deduction. The Holmes stories are among the best mysteries ever written."

"And this Jack the Ripper is a literary figure as well?"

"Oh, no." She leaned toward him and widened her eyes. "He was very real. He was a murderer here in London. Killed four or five women, prostitutes mostly, I think, in the 1870s or maybe 1880s. I don't remember for sure."

"And your time reveres such a man?" His shocked expression surprised her.

"No, of course not." Indignantly she glared at him. "You really do have the wrong impression of my time. He isn't revered. It all happened over a century ago and they never discovered who he was. It's one of the great criminal mysteries of all time. Who was Jack the Ripper? It's a question that even in my day researchers, criminologists, and even plain old armchair detectives are still trying to solve."

She cast him a sidelong glance. "There was even speculation at the time that he was a member of the royal family."

"I wouldn't be at all surprised." Adam smiled wryly. "Between insanity, philandering, and other scurrilous activities, I would not put murder out of the realm of possibility."

"Well, don't worry about it." She shrugged matter-of-factly. "It won't happen for years yet."

"No, I suppose not."

He seemed to ponder the idea momentarily, then apparently shook it off. "This still leaves us at our original point. Where do you want to go? Were there not any places in London that you, not your sister, wanted to see?"

"Sure. I wanted to go see the impressionists at the Courtauld Institute. But you know what? They aren't painting yet. They won't be painting for another, oh, fifty or sixty years."

She bent toward him. "I'd love to see the National Portrait Gallery, too. Does that exist yet?" He shook his head. "Great. Terrific." She sank back against the stairs.

He regarded her with his annoying amused smile and raised that infuriating eyebrow again.

"I'm truly sorry my city can't offer you all you came here expecting. But I assure you there are many delights in London for visitors."

She narrowed her eyes in suspicion. "Yeah, right. Like what?"

"Well, there's Westminster Abbey, and the Tower, and, of course, the British Museum."

"Don't they have a lot of ancient Greek and Egyptian stuff?"

"An excellent collection."

"Great. Sounds like fun." She bounced to her feet. "Now if I were at home I'd just go there by myself; but I assume I can't do that here, right?"

He nodded. "That's correct."

"So are you going to come with me?" She stretched out her hand to him.

Adam unfolded himself from the stairs and took her hand. An almost electric current shot through her at his touch.

"I would be delighted to accompany you." He smiled and again she was struck by what a wonderful smile it really was.

"Terrific. Now, where can we get something to eat in this house? I'm starving."

They strolled through the galleries of the British Museum at a leisurely pace. Maggie linked her arm through Adam's and savored the feel of his warm, hard body next to hers, his hand covering hers. He'd occasionally remove it to point out some treasure or other and she was surprised to note how impatient she was for its return.

They spent long minutes examining the Elgin marbles, huge chunks of Grecian carvings torn from the Parthenon and brought to England by Lord Elgin. Adam had seen them before. Maggie had only seen photographs.

"They're magnificent," she breathed.

"You like them?" Surprise colored his words. "I was under the impression you weren't particularly interested in history."

"I'm not much on history," she said ruefully. "All those names and dates drive me nuts. But this"—she gestured toward the marble reliefs—"this is art. I'm an artist. Pretty basic stuff, commercial work, but it's how I make my living."

Adam shook his head skeptically. "I still do not understand why your society permits women to work like men."

The pleasure of their day together so far took the sting out of his words. Maggie wondered if she was developing some tolerance for his sexist attitudes. It wasn't as if the man knew any better.

"Coleridge." She laughed. "How am I ever going to get through to you?"

He raised an eyebrow. "I have had the exact same thoughts about you."

She laughed again and this time he joined her. In easy companionship they continued their tour until they paused in front of the Rosetta stone.

"Amazing, isn't it?" she murmured softly, awed by the huge tablet. "How one discovery like this can unlock so many ancient secrets?"

"I don't understand." Puzzlement spread across his face.

"Well, see how it's divided into three sections?" She waved her hand at the black basalt rock. "The top is Egyptian hieroglyphics, the middle I think is a different form of Egyptian, and the bottom is Greek. It's the same information written in all three languages."

"Good God!" He gasped, obviously shocked by her casual comment.

Maggie widened her eyes and stared at him. "You didn't know that? No one's figured that out yet?"

"Not to my knowledge. And I do try to keep abreast of the latest discoveries."

"Oh, Adam, this is a terrible mistake. I shouldn't have said anything. Please don't tell anyone!"

"Why on earth not? This information should be acted on at once."

"No." How could she make him understand? "Don't you see? If you told anyone it could change history. It could be really minor, just a change in a date. But it could have serious repercussions."

"I'm sorry." He shook his head in confusion. "I don't see what possible effect this could have."

She struggled to find the right words. "I don't either, but it seems to me there are dangers involved in time travel. Things like paradoxes. You know, how you can't go back in time and stop your grandfather from marrying your grandmother because then you'd never be born? Which means you couldn't go back in the first place and so on and so forth."

Maggie shook her head. "I don't think you're supposed to change history. Even something that seems relatively minor and insignificant could ultimately have a big impact." She stared helplessly up at him. "Am I making any sense?"

"I believe so," Adam said. "Perhaps you're right. How very intriguing." He spoke thoughtfully, as if considering the idea. "You mean to say that anything you do here could have long-range effects. The smallest thing could change the future and your world. Is that what you mean?"

She breathed a sigh of relief. "That's it exactly."

"So have you come to any other conclusions about traveling through the ages?" Maggie noted the twinkle in his eye and her mood lightened.

"As a matter of fact I have." She smirked. "I've read a lot of science fiction and watched a lot of *Star Trek* and *Terminator* stuff." She groaned at his look of complete confusion. "I'll explain another time, Coleridge. Trust me on this one." Explaining photography was nothing compared to space travel and Comdr. Data.

"Anyway, it seems to me there are probably, or at least there should be, rules about time travel. Laws of nature maybe, like gravity. Rule number one, what we just talked about: Don't change history."

A quizzical frown creased his forehead. "But how can there be rules or laws if no one has ever done this before? If no one knows what these rules are?"

"That's exactly it. We don't know that no one has ever traveled through time. For all we know, people could be doing it every day."

"That's extremely farfetched. I sincerely doubt there are travelers romping through the centuries." He lifted a skeptical eyebrow. "But for the sake of argument, I'll grant you that. We don't know for sure. So;"—an amused light glimmered in his eye and Maggie ignored the thought that he was humoring her—"what are these rules?"

"Well, it seems to me right now there's one more person in this world, in this time, than there's supposed to be. There's an imbalance. So it only makes sense that I'm going back. That will put everything back the way it's supposed to be."

"You still believe your carriage will come back for you on the twelfth?"

She considered his question carefully. "I'm not certain. It's just something I feel. I can't explain."

Maggie paused, then nodded toward the stone.

"It all seems so relative, doesn't it?" she said. "Time, I mean. Ancient Egyptians probably thought

118

they had all the time in the world, yet now their incredible civilization is just a memory. The amazing art they created is relegated to a measly display in a museum." Her words drifted into silence and she gazed at the massive black rock, its secrets still shrouded in the shadows of time.

Adam seized the opportunity to study her unobserved. He had never encountered such a woman as this before. She was spirited, stubborn, unruly, yet courageous and undaunted. He found her language both puzzling and atrocious, but she obviously had intelligence and depth he had not encountered in a female before.

Intelligence was not an attribute he would have thought attractive and definitely not one he had sought before. But in Maggie, her mind was as compelling as the lovely package it came wrapped in. Add to that the immediate physical attraction between them and Adam would be hard-pressed to keep his resolve firm to stay away. Right now he was not entirely certain he still wished to.

"Coleridge, are you listening?"

"What? Oh sorry." He struggled to regain his composure, but her brilliant green eyes bored into his accusingly.

"I said, what's next?"

"Classical sculpture?"

"Great, let's go." She took his arm once more and they resumed their tour of the best the British Museum had to offer a visitor to London in 1818.

Maggie wandered aimlessly through the Coleridge mansion alone. She and Adam had spent the better part of the day at the museum, but tonight he and Lydia had a party to attend. A soiree, whatever that was. They'd invited her along but Maggie begged off. She wasn't ready to face a lot of people yet and was grateful Adam and Lydia didn't push her.

Maggie had a tray brought to her room for dinner and thought she would enjoy being alone with time to think. But as the evening wore on, she grew bored and lonely. Her solitary, impromptu exploration of the house filled the hours, but even as she prowled the halls, the frustrating restlessness continued.

Her self-guided tour did take her mind off her problems. She discovered several more parlors or salons. None quite as large as the green-and-gold room she'd stumbled into her first morning, but all equally elegant. She found what she assumed was a ballroom, with a huge chandelier covered with sheets hanging like a forlorn ghost in the center. She made her way through an enormous formal dining room and the smaller breakfast room she'd seen this morning. She checked out the location of each of the mansion's several water closets, those up-to-date conveniences of which the staff was extremely proud. Maggie found one on her first day and with relief vowed never to use the chamber pot in her room.

Eventually, her meandering led her to the library. She was growing to love this room. Warm and inviting, it reeked of furniture polish and old books. A distinctly masculine room. Adam's sanctuary. Maybe that was why she felt so comfortable and secure there. Say what she would about the man, he did give her a feeling of safety and protection.

Maggie wandered over to a bookshelf and perused the titles, some familiar, many unknown. She noticed a great number of scientific books standing side by side with classics, including Chaucer, Milton, Dante. Maggie conceded the respect due the great authors but in terms of actual reading had always found them ponderous and frankly boring.

She moved to another shelf and discovered Shakespeare. Maggie ran her fingers over the assorted collection and decided to pass. She enjoyed the Bard but preferred his works onstage rather than on paper.

Roaming around the room, she caught sight of a copy of *Pride and Prejudice*. She hadn't read Jane Austen since college and grabbed the book with delight. She was never all that wild about Austen but the book represented something familiar in this completely foreign place.

She snuggled down in a corner of the library sofa and within minutes, lost herself in the lighthearted tale of love and misunderstanding. Maggie found the book far more enjoyable now than when she first read it. Perhaps because then the characters were part of a world she could not relate to. Now, at least for a while, their world was hers.

"So you like the writings of Miss Austen?"

His now familiar voice interrupted her. Maggie glanced up from the volume and her heart skipped a beat. Adam leaned lazily against the door frame, arms crossed, regarding her with interest. She hadn't seen him dressed formally before now and he not only looked fantastic, he exuded an aura of controlled power and sensuality.

121

Staring at him, Maggie wondered why men ever gave up cravats and ruffled shirts, form-fitting jackets that emphasized broad shoulders and trim waists and skin-tight pants that left little to the imagination and had hers working overtime. With his blond good looks, dark, velvet eyes and dimpled cheek, it was easy to see why women were attracted to him. She could well imagine how he acquired the now forgotten reputation of rake. Excitement quivered within her.

Her best interests lay in avoiding Adam. Logically that made sense. But her decision to settle in the library was based as much on a suppressed desire to see him as it was on the need for a good book. Logic had little to do with it. She was tempting fate, dangerously and deliciously.

She smiled. "I find I like her more than I used to. Do you?"

"She is extremely popular."

"In my time this work is considered a classic example of the British novel."

He shrugged, expressing his opinion of the questionable taste of her time. "I find her writings too . . . sentimental for my taste."

"And too romantic?" Maggie's tone teased but she treaded dangerous waters. Wasn't it only this morning she swore not to get involved with him?

He lifted an eyebrow, an amused smile on his lips, daring her to dive in. "You think I don't enjoy romance? That perhaps there is no romance in my soul?"

Plunging ahead, Maggie took a deep breath and laughed. "Well, you just don't strike me as the romantic type. You're so businesslike and, well . . ."

"Controlled, perhaps? Precise?"

She laughed again. "I was going to say stuffy."

The eyebrow shot up once more and she noted a genuine look of surprise in his eyes.

"I'm sorry," she said quickly, trying not to laugh this time. "I really don't think you're stuffy. It's just that you're so dramatically different from anyone I've ever known. I'm just not used to the sort of, oh, formal way things are here." She aimed for an apologetic look but couldn't quite hide the twinkle in her eye.

"Stuffy!" He snorted, and strolled casually across the room to the shelves.

Not romantic? Adam Coleridge? Earl of Ridgewood?

Adam had never received a single complaint about either his manner or his attentions to women. Especially not from women. In his hell-raising days he'd considered himself a charming and accomplished lover. And since then he had not lacked for female companionship when he chose to pursue it.

He surveyed the books on the shelves. "I suppose you find Lord Byron or Sir Walter Scott romantic?"

"Not particularly." Adam heard the amusement in her voice. If he looked her way, he would surely see a challenge light her eyes. Not romantic? Ha! He'd see about that.

A nagging thought in the back of Adam's mind reminded him of the necessity of keeping his distance from this woman. But what harm could an innocent flirtation do? He was a man and men could control their emotions. And after all, she was the one who had issued the challenge.

Hadn't she?

He plucked a volume from the shelves and pulled a chair close to Maggie.

"Do you like Shakespeare?" He looked at her sharply. "Do you even know Shakespeare?"

"Give me a break." She laughed. "Yes, I know Shakespeare. Not personally, of course." She paused at his look of confusion.

"It's a joke. See, that's what I mean about you. You have absolutely no sense of humor. You're too uptight, too severe, too straitlaced, too—"

"Stuffy?" he asked.

"There you go again. You take everything way too seriously."

"Miss Masterson, you have maligned my character and personality and you expect me to simply wave it away. I have grave responsibilities which account for the serious aspects of my nature. However, I do enjoy humor when I see it. And as for romance, I may consider it silly and uninspired in the work of Miss Austen but I recognize and appreciate it in the hands of a master."

"In what?" A teasing tone sounded in her voice. *"The Taming of the Shrew?"*

"That may well be appropriate under the circumstances." The amused smile returned. He had the look of a man who had just gained the upper hand and knew it.

"However, in terms of romance, my first choice would be *Romeo and Juliet*. Do you not agree?" He stared deeply into her eyes.

Yep, dangerous waters all right. How long would she be able to stay afloat? Unfortunately, the danger added to the thrill. Upped the stakes. Maggie had no qualms about playing this little game. As long as they played only with words.

"I do. What could be more romantic than 'a pair of star-crossed lovers.' "

Surprised, Adam nodded appreciation at the quote. Maggie smiled smugly. The first point to her, but the game had barely begun.

Adam flipped open the book and paged through it, quickly finding the passage he wanted. " 'He jests at scars that never felt a wound,' " he read. " 'But soft! What light through yonder window breaks? It is the East, and Juliet is the sun!' "

The balcony scene. The ultimate romantic scene of all time, at least in Maggie's eyes. Had been since the seventh grade when she and Jimmy Bennett were picked to memorize the lines and recite them for a class. The assignment meant a week of after-school study sessions at her house or Jimmy's. But Maggie didn't care. She'd had a silent, hopeless crush on the boy all year. The balcony scene always brought back the poignant pangs and passions of first love.

Jimmy moved away at the end of the school year and as time passed, Maggie rarely, if ever, thought of him. But *Romeo and Juliet* never failed to leave her with a flutter in her stomach and a longing in her heart.

Still, if a man of her own time had pulled this, Maggie would have laughed out loud. To call reading *Romeo and Juliet* hokey and cliched was an understatement. Although, to be honest, it had never happened before. At least not in her adult life. Somehow, from Adam, it seemed not merely right but . . . perfect.

" 'Arise, fair sun, and kill the envious moon, who is already sick and pale with grief that thou her maid art far more fair than she.' "

As much as she enjoyed Shakespeare on the stage, the best performances, even Jimmy's, paled next to the impact of Adam reading the immortal words.

His rich, strong voice swept through every corner of the book-lined room. The mellow, honeyed tones wrapped her in a cocoon of sensual imagery. Even the look of him in the elegant, formal evening clothes added to the rich texture enveloping her. The library shimmered in the gaslight, the atmosphere rich with the possibility of magic.

" 'See how she leans her cheek upon her hand! O that I were a glove upon that hand, that I might touch that cheek!' "

Maggie studied his expressive face, quelling an impulse to run her finger along the line of his chiseled jaw, feel the shadowed stubble there. The temptation lingered to run her hands through his already tousled thick blond hair. She could almost feel the silky texture of his cravat and yearned to pull it free, releasing his throat to her caressing lips.

It would take so little to fall in love with this man. Possibly she was already a bit in love. Thoughts of him certainly seemed to be on her mind every waking moment and she'd only known him for what? Two days? But on the other hand, time had taken on whole new possibilities.

What was it about him that drew her to him like

a compass needle to magnetic north? Would this irresistible pull be as strong if she were on familiar ground, or was her growing desire more a result of time and place than anything else? Maggie didn't think so. Deep inside she instinctively sensed that with this man it would be the same regardless of where or when.

" 'Lady, by yonder blessed moon I vow, that tips with silver all these fruit-tree tops—O, swear not by the moon, th' inconstant moon.' "

Adam's hands cradled the book gently, almost reverently. His strong, steady fingers stretched occasionally to turn a page. She longed to reach out, entwine her fingers with his, revel in the touch of his hand.

Her thoughts drifted back to this morning's kiss and she dwelled on what might have happened. What could still happen. She imagined being in his arms again. Imagined what magic those fingers could create, what secrets they could unleash.

Lost in her thoughts and Shakespeare's words, Maggie hardly noticed when Adam closed the book. His hands clasped hers and her startled gaze met his. It took a moment to realize he wasn't reading; he knew these words by heart.

" 'Good night, good night! Parting is such sweet sorrow . . .' "

He picked up her right hand and brought it to his lips. Turning it over, still gazing into her eyes, he kissed her palm lightly. A surge of sensual delight shot through her.

" '. . . That I shall say good night till it be morrow.' "

Victoria Alexander

He kissed the other palm. His eyes never left hers. A yearning for more washed over Maggie. Her head swam. Her body ached.

"It's very late." His gentle voice abruptly jolted her back to reality.

"What? Oh, yeah. Right," she stammered, trying to regain whatever shred of composure she had left, but he still held her hands. She snatched them away and looked up to see him regarding her with an amused expression. Too flustered to do battle, Maggie wisely held back. She stood and headed for the door, then turned back to Adam.

"I believe I owe you an apology." She smiled. "You definitely have a romantic soul. And you may not be nearly as stuffy as I thought."

"Thank you, Miss Masterson . . . Maggie." He returned her smile and bowed elegantly.

Maggie closed the library doors and collapsed against them. She needed to catch her breath. A good general knew when to retreat as well as advance and this skirmish was lost. Those last few moments alone were a major battle in self-control. Now desire and frustrated passion left her weak and trembling.

A relationship with Adam would end in disaster. She didn't want to go home and leave her heart behind. But then, a small voice nagged, maybe she should stop fighting because maybe it was already too late. And, the voice continued relentlessly, maybe what she'd find with Adam, even for a short time, would be worth the price.

Another line from Shakespeare flashed through her mind. Not from *Romeo and Juliet* but tailor-

128

made for this situation. She muttered under her breath and headed for the stairs.

" 'Lord, what fools these mortals be.' "

Adam swirled the brandy in his glass and contemplated the door Maggie had walked through moments before. He imagined she stood on the other side of that door, trying to regain control. Adam chuckled softly and sipped the liquor. She tried so very hard to conceal the effect he had on her but it was clearly a charade. He grinned with satisfaction. Not romantic? Stuffy? Ha.

Adam had enjoyed tonight, enjoyed the game, the challenge, and especially the triumph. There were no doubts that he indeed came out the winner. And winners did not give up their prize.

He knew not when it happened, but somewhere between this morning and the moment Maggie walked out tonight, his feelings crystallized, evolved from simple passion and desire to . . . what?

Love?

Adam didn't know and didn't care. He had vast experience with women, but love?

Never.

He only knew a woman had never enchanted him like this. Miss Margaret Masterson suited him and he would not give her up.

Adam wanted Maggie in his bed and in his life, permanently. He merely had to wait until she realized she wanted it as well. Then he would move heaven and earth, and old men in carriages, and time itself to keep her by his side and in his world.

Forever.

Chapter Seven

Maggie breezed into the breakfast room with an air of serenity that belied her conflicting emotions. All night she'd tossed and turned, her mind replaying vivid images of Adam's touch, Adam's kiss. The feelings he aroused confused her. Men in her life were few and far between, but it wasn't as if she was an innocent, blushing virgin. She'd known desire before, even imagined herself in love.

But for whatever reason, this seemed different. Adam affected her senses far more intensely than any man.

Ever.

One look from him melted something at the very core of her being. One touch of his hand left her trembling. One kiss . . .

Her heart told her to go for it. Enjoy what she could and if she fell in love, well, she'd deal with that when it happened.

But a highly protective, annoyingly sensible voice inside screamed any involvement with Adam, physical or emotional, carried a real risk of heartbreak. Through the long, sleepless night Maggie had debated the question.

Was it a risk worth taking?

She peered around the room, disappointed not to find Adam. Only Lydia sat at the table, going through a stack of what looked like mail. She glanced up with a welcoming smile.

"Good morning."

"Hi." Maggie took a plate from the sideboard, selecting from the vast array of breakfast fare. The food here tasted far better than she was used to, richer somehow. Of course these people had never heard of cholesterol or calories. If she didn't watch out, she'd go home the size of a small elephant. She reluctantly passed on the more tempting—and fattening—items.

Carrying her meagerly filled plate, Maggie settled in the chair next to Lydia. Curiously she glanced at the correspondence. "What are you doing?"

Lydia leaned back with a sigh. "Invitations are coming in from everywhere for balls, soirees, card parties, dinner parties. I am having a difficult time deciding which we shall attend."

"We?" Caution tinged Maggie's tone.

"Of course." Lydia arched an eyebrow in a manner suspiciously like Adam's. Was that some kind of irritating family trait?

"It is past time you began accompanying us. You simply cannot remain hidden here. Most of the clothes we ordered have been delivered and you no

131

longer have any excuse for begging off. Besides, the entire ton is buzzing with questions about the beautiful American relation Adam carried through the park the other day."

"Oh, that's swell." Maggie groaned. "You mean I'm already the subject of gossip?"

Lydia nodded serenely.

"But I thought the idea was to keep my presence low-key. How can I do that if all these society types are watching me?"

"You shall do fine," Lydia said confidently. "It's not as if you will be alone. Adam and I will be at your side every minute."

"I don't think I'm ready for this," Maggie said. "You told me there are all the ridiculous rules you people have. I'll never be able to keep them straight."

Lydia brushed aside her objections. "It's not that complicated." Her eyes twinkled. "Besides, there are so many things one can't do it's fairly easy to remember the few one can."

Maggie stared, too horrified to realize Lydia was joking. How could she possibly get through the kind of formal affairs people in this era attended routinely?

"Adam will be meeting us shortly in the ballroom to teach you to waltz." Lydia turned her attention back to the stack of invitations.

Maggie sighed, her moment of panic giving way to reluctant acceptance. Maybe she could handle it with the right help and the right teacher. It didn't look as if she had much of a choice.

* * *

Maggie faced Adam in the center of the modest ballroom. Lydia sat off to one side at what she called a pianoforte. To Maggie, it looked pretty much like the pianos of her time, maybe a bit smaller. It was reassuring to note music was one thing that transcended time.

Maggie gazed up at Adam with delight. He really was tall. She'd noticed his height earlier, how he always seemed to be towering above her. But some flaring emotion usually prevented her from paying any attention to something as mundane as height, at least in their encounters so far. At five feet, four inches, Maggie was used to being on the short side, used to looking up at most men. Adam was a good ten inches taller. And tall men brought out the best—or was it the worst?—in her.

Adam's already familiar smile of amusement played on his lips. "Are you quite ready?"

"I suppose." She drew a deep, nervous breath. "What's first?"

"Do you know nothing at all about dancing?" An eyebrow rose in surprise.

"Of course I do. I'm not stupid." Maggie bristled at his condescending attitude. "I'll have you know my mother made me take ballroom dancing when I was a kid."

"And that was . . . how long ago?" The smile widened into a definite grin.

"Don't be so smug. I'm just not used to this. I'd like to see how you'd do dumped in a totally new environment."

The defense of her lack of social skills seemed a source of incredible amusement to him. Annoyed,

Maggie made a concerted effort to calm down. "But I've always been a fast learner, so let's get going."

"My pleasure."

"I'll bet," she muttered under her breath.

The infuriating grin still plastered on his face, Adam nodded to Lydia to begin playing. He took Maggie's right hand in his left. Placing his other hand firmly on the small of her back, he pulled her tight.

Very tight.

"Are we supposed to be this close?" She gasped, knowing full well her shortness of breath had little to do with his tight grasp, and everything to do with the pressure of his hard, firm body against hers.

"Yes." He gazed into her eyes and she lost herself in the excitement they promised, the desire they revealed. Swept away on a tide of nerve-tingling anticipation, Maggie barely noticed Adam sweeping her off her feet literally as well.

"You are doing far better than I expected," he said, a note of approval in his voice.

"What?" Jerked back to reality, Maggie promptly stumbled, stopping them both in their tracks. "Sorry."

What was wrong with her? Every time she looked into this man's eyes, every time he touched her, she turned positively worthless. If this kept up she wouldn't need to worry about any kind of involvement with him. She'd simply melt into a small puddle at his feet and that would be that.

Squaring her shoulders and taking another deep breath, she glared up at him. The amused, vaguely superior expression she found so irritating remained on his face, almost as if . . .

He couldn't possibly know what she was thinking. Or what happened to her when he came within 20 feet.

Could he?

"Shall we continue?" He drew her into his arms once again.

Maggie nodded and concentrated on following his lead and listening to Lydia's music. She caught on quickly and in no time waltzed with Adam as easily as if they'd danced together all their lives.

Her confidence grew and she relaxed, turning her attention toward the man holding her securely in his arms. She promised herself that this time he wouldn't get the upper hand.

"So how am I doing?" She tilted her face toward his.

"Excellent." Adam smiled and tightened his already firm grip.

He had not held her like this before, and he found the feel of her supple body against his delicious beyond all expectation. Hard-pressed to continue the lesson, he reveled in the scent of her hair, the delicate placement of her hand in his, the remarkable sensation of her breasts brushing against his chest.

He longed to reach down and nuzzle the sensitive point on her neck, savor the taste of her skin beneath his lips. Beyond all reason, he wanted to sweep her into his arms and carry her to the nearest secluded spot. To hell with waiting for her to burn as hotly for him as he wanted—no—needed her. As he whirled her around the dance floor, her eyes darkened, their emerald tone deepening to the color of a forest glade.

He had seen that color before. He would not have to wait long.

Maggie tossed her head back and laughed with the sheer exhilaration of flying across the room in Adam's arms. In the grip of a sensation nearly as powerful as his touch, Maggie marveled that women ever let the art of waltzing escape them. Granted, the dance was not really suited to social functions of the late twentieth century. But, oh, what a glorious feeling. Her dress swirled around her ankles. Her feet barely skimmed the floor.

Adam executed a particularly intricate move and Maggie followed his lead effortlessly.

"Very good," he murmured, appreciation glowing in his eyes.

"Thanks." Satisfaction rang in her voice. "I told you I was a fast learner. I'm a natural at stuff like this."

"A natural?"

Laughter bubbled from her lips. "Some things just come easy, naturally, like dancing."

"What else comes naturally?" Adam stared down at her, his face the picture of innocence.

"All kinds of things." Maggie tossed off the words lightly, but her glance dared him to go on.

"Indeed," he responded softly, his voice a caress, sending chills of anticipation up her spine. "Can you be more explicit?"

Her eyes locked with his. Drawn into their velvety depths, she read acknowledgment of her dare, and acceptance. She laughed with delight and confidence.

Maggie conceded last night's defeat but she

wouldn't lose round two. She wouldn't let her emotions carry her away. She wouldn't fall in love. And as much fun as verbally fencing with him was, right now perhaps discretion really was the better part of valor and a change of subject was in order.

"Have you thought any more about my little problem?"

"Problem?" He looked perplexed.

"You remember? I'm not from around here."

"Oh, of course." Comprehension dawned on his face. "I have thought of little else but you. And of course your problem."

Was it her or did everything he said have a double meaning?

"And . . ."

"I have considered your conclusions." An amused smile played on his lips and he looked down at her. "But let us take your assumptions a little further, shall we? For the sake of argument, say the reason you came here in the first place was because this is where you ultimately belong. You were fated, destined, to come here. This is, if you'll forgive the expression, your future."

Startled by his suggestion, she stared. "I hadn't thought of that."

"Well, perhaps it is something you should think about." He abruptly seemed far more serious and intense. His eyes darkened with meaning that sent desire rippling through her. Once again she abandoned herself to the music and the movement and the man.

If not for the circumstances, if this were her own time and place, she might not ignore the tiny voice inside whispering that perhaps this was indeed her fate. That Adam, perhaps, in all the world, in all of time itself, was the one man right for her.

But it wasn't different.

In spite of their discussion of rules and her future, Maggie's belief that she didn't belong here and would be leaving stayed firm. She was a twentieth-century woman with all the baggage that entailed, including independence and a sense of equality as well as a definite need for panty hose, television, and micro-waves. There was no way she was fated to live her life in a place where indoor plumbing was consid-ered up-to-date.

As for Adam, she wanted him and didn't doubt he wanted her as well. There wasn't anything wrong with that. Not for a woman of the 1990s. But in spite of her thoroughly modern ideas could she really have Adam on those terms? No emotions, no commit-ments, just enjoy the moment? Could she handle it?

This wouldn't be an easy game to play. The stakes were high.

For Maggie, defeat meant losing her heart.

Forever.

Lydia's gaze followed the couple as they twirled upon the polished floor. They danced for nearly an hour and Lydia was pleased with how quickly Mag-gie mastered the steps. Always in excellent form, Adam never failed to make his partners look good. But even Lydia had to admit, not quite this good. Adam and Maggie danced as one, as if halves of the same whole.

Lydia frowned. She did not want her brother heartbroken, merely distracted, and she certainly did not believe Maggie's nonsense about leaving in a month. Whatever unexplained force tossed her here in the first place could not possibly be relied on to snatch her back.

When most people looked at Lydia they never saw past the blond curls, pert nose, and amber eyes. They never suspected that hidden within the willowy body beat a heart of pure logic. It simply did not make sense that Maggie's arrival was without purpose. As no other purpose presented itself, Lydia reasonably assumed that, since she had, after all, come on the night of Adam's ultimatum, Maggie's purpose was to help Lydia avoid a forced, arranged marriage.

Perfectly logical.

Lydia's touch lightened on the keys and the notes drifted to a close. Maggie and Adam continued to dance, never noticing the music had stopped. A satisfied smile crossed her lips.

"Very good!" Lydia clapped her hands and flitted across the floor. The dancers drew apart; only their eyes still met.

"Maggie, you have done beautifully," Lydia said. "Hasn't she, Adam?"

"Beautifully." Adam's gaze lingered on Maggie.

"Thanks." Maggie addressed Lydia but her attention remained on Adam.

Lydia studied them critically. She could easily take her time. Neither seemed to notice her presence. Her plan was working quite nicely. "Really excellent, Maggie. You should have no problems tonight."

"Tonight?" Maggie gasped, her focus now firmly fixed on Lydia.

"Of course tonight. We're going to the Duke and

139

Duchess of Broadmore's ball." Lydia strove for a look of innocence. "Didn't I mention it?"

"No, you didn't mention it." Maggie turned a pleading expression to Adam. "Not tonight. I'm not ready. I can't."

Lydia sniffed. "You will simply refuse all dances except the waltz, which you obviously have a gift for, and follow my example. You shall not only be fine, you shall have a delightful evening."

"Coleridge," Maggie said.

"I'm afraid, my dear, Lydia is very probably right," Adam agreed, a sympathetic note underlying his words. "The incident in the park has brought you to the attention of the ton. Many are beginning to wonder why they have not seen you publicly. I believe it is time. You can dance and beyond that—"

"I know, I know." Maggie sighed. "Keep my mouth shut. I have—what was it? Oh yeah, a 'nasty temper' and a 'vulgar vocabulary.'"

"But," Adam leaned over and whispered softly in her ear, "you aren't at all stuffy and there definitely is romance in your soul."

Chapter Eight

Maggie surveyed the Duke's grand ballroom with curiosity. Her hand crept up to touch the filigree heart nestled in the hollow of her throat. The metal warmed by her skin boosted her courage and confidence. So did Adam. The look of stunned amazement on his face when she appeared dressed for the ball confirmed what her mirror already told her. She looked fantastic, like a princess from a storybook. Maggie's build and height were as much made for the style of the times as this dress had been made for her.

The delicate green ball gown highlighted her eyes, emphasized the red tones in her hair, accented her creamy skin. The dress molded to her curves, the high waist complementing her well-endowed figure. At first the extremely low-cut neckline seemed far too revealing and she wondered if she looked as naked as she felt. But Adam's gaze lingered appreciatively on the exposed swell of her breasts and her reservations vanished.

Maggie sailed through the receiving line with ease, thanks to the subtle guidance of Adam and Lydia. The introduction to her hosts, the Duke and Duchess of Whatsit, went without a hitch. Of course, only Maggie thought of them as Whatsit. Remembering names was not her forte, and since they insisted on tacking titles on everyone, well, she might as well give up right now. Maggie barely had time to take in the spectacle around her before she and Lydia were surrounded by men clamoring for their attention.

"Maggie, I'd like to introduce you to Lord Crofton and Lord Wells. This is Lord Handley and this is Mr. Ainsworth. Gentlemen, may I present Miss Margaret Masterson, visiting from America."

Lydia introduced her with a skill and speed that left Maggie struggling with a severe case of sensory overload.

"And you must meet Lord So and So, and of course here is the ever so charming Lord Such and Such."

In the whirl of introductions, names and faces blurred into a kaleidoscope of confusion. But within moments Maggie understood two basic facts about life in 1818 that lifted her confidence yet again. One, these men were all extremely charming and obviously interested in her. And two, regardless of whether it was the nineteenth century or the twentieth century or very probably the thirty-second century, flirting in any time was pretty much the same. Maggie was a master of that fine art.

Fortunately it wasn't especially difficult to maintain the "keep your mouth shut" advice and still disarm the gentlemen around her. After all, they didn't expect brains in a pretty woman, or any woman, according to Lydia. And while Maggie didn't flaunt her intelligence, she did use it to her advantage.

"Delighted to meet you, Miss Masterson." One of the crowd grasped her gloved hand in his and lifted it to his lips. "How long will you be gracing our fair city?"

"My plans are indefinite at the moment." She hedged and gave the man before her a teasing smile. He wasn't quite as tall as Adam but she still had to look up at pale blue eyes set in a pleasant face, surrounded by sandy brown hair. His stocky build conveyed a sense of power, and Maggie thought him quite attractive. In fact, all the men she met were attractive. Had men lost something through the centuries or did the formal black-and-white attire make any man look great?

"I'm afraid I didn't quite catch your name."

"Maggie," Lydia cut in, "this is Lord Lindley."

"Miss Masterson, I hope I shall have the pleasure of a dance?"

His request threw Maggie momentarily and panic surged in her chest. She wasn't sure how to explain, what exactly to say. Before she could, Adam appeared at her elbow.

"Miss Masterson is regrettably sorry, but since she is recently arrived from America, she is not familiar with our dances. She does waltz, but as her relative I'm afraid I cannot possibly allow her to partner anyone outside the family."

Maggie struggled to contain a relieved giggle.

"Extremely sorry, but I'm certain you understand."

He steered her toward the dance floor, leaving Lord Lindley with a strange, considering expression on his face that said he didn't understand at all.

Adam and Maggie took their positions, one of his hands holding hers, the other on the small of her back. A loop around her free wrist held up her skirt, and a fan dangled from her hand.

"I thought it was against the rules to dance with any man more than twice?" A teasing lilt lightened her tone.

"It is perfectly acceptable," he said loftily. "I am your relation."

"But you aren't, really."

"But I could be." His eyes darkened and he swept her into the dance at the start of the music. Taken aback, Maggie nearly stumbled. What the hell was he trying to say? She stared at him but he avoided her gaze, and she reluctantly turned her attention to the dance and the dancers.

Like a setting out of an epic movie, the huge ballroom glittered in gold and crystal. Elaborately dressed women in rainbow hues shimmered with jewels. Men, some in radiant colors but most in black-and-white formal dress, radiated wealth and power. It was all so wonderfully British. Maggie had to remind herself this was no scene from a PBS drama. This was real. And for now she was part of it.

The music died, and Maggie and Adam swayed to a stop at the edge of the dance floor. She opened her mouth to ask what Adam meant by his earlier cryptic comment.

"Ridgewood! Adam!" A rich, masculine voice interrupted her thoughts.

"Richard!" Adam's face shone with pleasure.

Maggie turned toward the voice. A tall, ruggedly handsome man with a wide grin approached them, accompanied by a lovely blonde nearly as tall.

"Adam, it has been far too long." The two men slapped each other on the back exuberantly. Maggie wondered if this was male bonding nineteenth-century style and noted how their action had the same feel of men giving each other a high five, or football players patting each other on the butt. Some things really didn't ever change.

"I know. I've been remiss in not keeping up with old friends." Adam cast an admiring glance at the blonde. "But since your marriage I assumed you to have more important things on your mind."

The woman smiled knowingly.

Adam turned to Maggie. "Maggie, this is Lord and Lady Westbrooke, Richard and Amanda. This is Miss Margaret Masterson, a distant relation of ours from America."

"America, how wonderful!" Amanda exclaimed with delight. "I, too, am from America. Philadelphia. Where precisely are you from?"

"Denver," Maggie said without thinking. "Colorado."

At Amanda's blank look, Maggie realized her mistake. She searched her mind, frantically looking for a way out of this dilemma. Where the hell was she from?

"Colorado . . . County. That's it! Denver in Colorado County. In . . . oh . . ."

145

What states were there in 1818? She glared in desperation at Adam. He shrugged helplessly and . . . Good God, she was in trouble now! He raised both eyebrows!

"Oh . . ." Tottering on the brink of panic, Maggie struggled to think. "Oh . . ."

Come on! Name a state!

"Oh . . . hio?"

Recognition registered on Amanda's face and she frowned. "I'm afraid I am not very familiar with Ohio. Much is still frontier, is it not?"

"Oh, yeah." Maggie sighed with relief and felt as if she'd just won Final Jeopardy. "It's very rustic, rural, very rural. Lots of frontier. Trees, too. Lots and lots of big, big trees. And, um, bears. There are bears. . . . "

"I believe you mentioned a breath of fresh air earlier?" Adam finally came to her rescue and took her arm. "Richard, we shall speak later." He nodded to Amanda and directed Maggie away.

"Very nice to meet you," she said over her shoulder.

Richard watched the retreating figures hurry into the garden and noted his wife staring intently.

"How very odd," Amanda said, speculation in her voice. "She appears to be hiding something."

"I hope not, my dear." Richard gave her a lazy smile. "It may have escaped your notice, but he is in love with her."

Adam ushered Maggie quickly down the terrace steps to a fairly private corner of the garden. The effort to keep up with his long strides kept Maggie quiet. Until now.

"I don't believe this. What a disaster," she said. "I don't know anything about Ohio."

"That was painfully apparent." Adam crossed his arms and leaned casually against a tree, not bothering to hide his amusement at her tirade. "I believe you mentioned something about trees and bears? It sounded delightful."

Too wrought up to give him the scathing answer his comment deserved, she ignored him. "It's like I'm being punished for something. That's it. I'm being paid back for every time I ever said 'What do I need to study history for? I'm going to be an artist.' And the answer was always 'You need to be a well-rounded person.' Ha. The real answer is because someday you'll be casually traveling through time and discover you need to know this stuff so you won't look like a total and complete idiot."

She paced back and forth, gesturing wildly. "I never liked history. It was boring. And now here I am living it. What a laugh. What a joke. What a bite in the shorts. And you." She whirled toward him and leveled a blistering look. "You were absolutely no help whatsoever."

He shrugged nonchalantly, obviously trying to stifle a smile. "What would you have me do?"

"What? Oh, I don't know." Her mind raced. "You could have let me know how many states there are in the Union. In America."

"How many are there in your time?" He raised an inquiring eyebrow.

"Fifty."

147

"Good lord," he said. "I would not have dreamed it possible. Does the country now stretch over the whole of the continent? How did such states develop? Are they autonomous or dependent? Is the republic system of government still functioning?"

Incredulous, Maggie stared at the genuine curiosity on his face. "What are you? Nuts? I can't believe you want to discuss the geopolitical evolution of the United States. Here. Now. I think we have—"

"Twenty," Adam said calmly.

"Twenty what?" She was completely confused. "What are you talking about?"

"Twenty states. The answer to your question." Apparently giving up all pretense at hiding his amusement, he broke into a broad grin.

Too upset for its usual infuriating effect, Maggie simply aimed her best drop-dead look at him. "You have absolutely no idea what I'm trying to deal with here. I feel like I'm in one of those dreams, you know."

He shook his head in obvious fascination.

"Where you're naked and everybody else has clothes on, only you don't know you're naked until it's too late? Haven't you ever had a dream like that? That's how I felt in there. By the time I realized what was wrong it was too late."

A voice inside warned her about overreacting. But she'd developed a good head of steam and wasn't about to let it go. "It's all so mind-boggling." She collapsed onto a garden bench. "And I am so damned confused."

She glared at him for a long moment. Adam seemed to be carefully considering his words.

"You are confused," he said slowly. "I barely understand a word you say. Listening to you is like listening to a foreign language, colorful and exciting, but one needs an interpreter. The words and phrases that pour out of your mouth at breakneck speed make absolutely no sense whatsoever."

"Like what?" Sincerely curious, Maggie didn't grasp his problem.

"Like what? Like that, although that expression is not too difficult to grasp. Neither is 'get it?' But others . . ." He glanced at her sharply. "Are 'kids' children?"

She nodded.

"I thought so," he said with satisfaction. "But what is a 'major-league problem'? Or a 'bite in the shorts'? How does one 'boggle one's mind'? Can you actually 'drive someone up a wall' in your time? And what in God's name is an 'oh kay'?"

Throughout Maggie's life she had had a natural, well-developed sense of the absurd that saved her from embarrassing tight spots more than once. Her temper flared fast and burned hot but usually extinguished just as quickly, often replaced by a recognition of the ridiculous.

Maggie stared at Adam and her frustration slipped away. At the definite spark of amusement in his eyes, she laughed and couldn't seem to stop. Within moments Adam joined her, his rich, clear laughter surrounding them. He reached down, clasped her hands in his, and pulled her to her feet. They faced each other, bodies shaking with mirth until a tear danced down her cheek.

"So what do we do now?" She sniffed and smiled up at him.

"Now?" He released her hands and let his slide around her waist.

"Now." Her hands slipped up his shoulders.

His lips descended on hers gently. A kiss light, ethereal. Her lips parted beneath his and his tongue lazily traced the inner edge of her mouth. Desire surged through her. Her fingers crept to his neck and pulled him closer. The pressure of his lips on hers increased. He drew her tongue into his mouth, and any possibility of coherent thought disappeared.

Their lips still joined, he picked her up and swung her around to rest against a tree. The rough bark pressed into her back. She didn't care. Her body molded to his and she felt his hard arousal through the layers of fabric separating them. Lost in a sea of sensation, she moaned, her head falling back. His tongue followed the line of her jaw to her ear and he nibbled on the sensitive lobe, his faint breath sending chills shivering through the very core of her being. Featherlike kisses trailed the line from ear to shoulder, his tongue flicking the heated surface of her skin. He found the pulse point at the base of her throat and his tongue played across the throbbing he discovered there.

One hand was splayed on her back; his other traced the edge of the dress's neckline. Fingertips, playful and tantalizing, brushed the tender mounds of flesh. His hand slipped under the silken fabric, pushing the material down and releasing her breasts to him. He cupped one in his hand, his exploring tongue trailing lower, agonizingly slowly. She strained toward him, nipples erect and hard. Gently his tongue outlined the flushed circle, the sensitive skin taut with anticipation. He drew the hardened bud into his mouth, trapping it lightly with his teeth, his tongue teasing it into mind-numbing arousal. Maggie gasped, her grip tightening around his neck, her breath coming quick and fast. Fire flashed through her veins; passion surged in her blood.

Adam's mouth continued to plunder her breasts, suckling, caressing. His hand dropped and he gathered the fabric of her skirt, raising it slowly an inch at a time until he reached her leg. Delighted, he recognized the odd, one-piece stockings she wore on her arrival. He ran a hand slowly up the silken fabric pausing at the curve of her hip. His fingers found the waistband and dipped inside. Maggie shuddered at his touch.

He withdrew his fingers and trailed them lightly over the flat of her stomach, drifting ever lower. His hand cupped the round curve at the apex of her thighs and she squirmed slightly, increasing the pressure of his fingertips. Through the thin material he could feel her heat, feel her moisture. She was his for the taking but he wanted more from her than mere lovemaking.

Much more.

Reluctantly, Adam removed his hand and smoothed down her skirt. He readjusted the bodice of her dress and gently pulled her back to reality.

"Maggie," he whispered against her ear.

"Hmmm?" She sighed, her eyes still half closed.

"Maggie." He caressed the edge of her ear with his tongue. "We have to go back."

She moaned softly. "Then stop doing that."

He cupped her chin in his hand and looked deeply into her eyes. They seemed finally to focus, the color a satisfying deep forest green.

"Later," he said quietly.

"Later," she said with a tremulous breath.

For a long moment their gazes locked. And Maggie knew in the charged silence agreements were reached, vows traded, promises exchanged.

Lydia thought only she noticed their absence and only she was aware of their return. From across the room she noted the high color in Maggie's face, the possessive way Adam held her arm. She smiled at her success and turned her attention back to her current partner. All was going very well indeed.

He stood a distance away and noticed Lydia Coleridge's attention turn toward the entry to the garden. His gaze followed hers and he, too, watched the couple's return. He, too, noticed the woman's flushed face, the obvious ownership in the man's touch.

The woman intrigued him. He did not think she was as insipid as most females of his acquaintance. His sharp observations indicated a rare intelligence she apparently did not want discovered. He sensed she hid something more. Perhaps this venture would be far more enjoyable than he'd anticipated.

Grim satisfaction flowed through him. He no longer doubted that this was indeed what he'd been watching for. His long wait was finally nearing an end.

*   *   *

It was an evening out of a fairy tale, and Maggie its Cinderella. The glittering ballroom, the beautiful, elegant women, the handsome, stately men. To Maggie's eyes it was a fantasy come true.

With Adam by her side, she reveled in the scene around her. Her sheer enjoyment of the evening had much to do with the shared passion in the garden. She quivered every time he turned his sensual, caressing gaze toward her.

Later.

Maggie met what seemed like vast numbers of people and handled the conversations as best she could. She kept her mouth shut. Many of Adam's friends commented on how long it had been since he'd seen them. Surprised, she meant to ask him about it.

Later.

Lydia joined them occasionally. She danced every dance with a new partner and rarely gave any man the benefit of a second dance. But she was never without partners, never without a crowd of men avidly pursuing her favors. If she wanted to get married, she obviously had her pick of eager candidates.

Waltzes seemed few and far between and Maggie used the breaks to quiz Adam about people or customs she didn't understand. Her biggest confusion of the night had a lot to do with her own problem remembering names. Here, everyone apparently had at least two.

"I don't get it," she said after they'd finished a conversation with an acquaintance of Adam's. "I thought your name was Coleridge."

"It is."

153

"Then why does everybody call you Ridgewood?"

"Ridgewood is my title."

"But Coleridge is your name. Why don't they call you Coleridge?"

Adam stared at her with an expression of mild amusement. "I don't know. That's simply the way it is."

"Humph." She snorted in derision. "Well, I'm going to keep calling you Coleridge. We don't have titles in America."

He leaned over and whispered in her ear, "Perhaps that is what's wrong with your country." The twinkle in his eyes took any sting out of his words and Maggie wrinkled her nose at him.

They stood side by side, watching the dancers. An invisible current of desire and anticipation and growing need arced between them. Maggie did her best to keep the conversation light, not easy when Adam turned his rich, simmering eyes on her. Taut expectation inside her heightened the excitement of the night and sharpened her senses beyond measure.

Later.

They idly sipped champagne, lost in each other's eyes. A stunning woman swooped down on Adam.

"Adam, my darling, it has been such a very, very long time."

Maggie blinked in surprise at one of the most beautiful women she'd ever seen. About her own height with ebony hair and eyes nearly as dark, she had porcelain skin and a perfect figure.

"Caroline." He raised her hand to his lips. "Allow

154

me to present a relation of mine from America, Miss Margaret Masterson."

She nodded slightly and flicked her eyes over Maggie with disinterest before returning her attention to Adam.

"I had no idea you would be here tonight. I had heard you no longer come to functions like this as often as you once did."

She cocked her exquisite head to one side and gazed at him inquisitively. Maggie instinctively disliked her. She looked too much like a predatory animal contemplating the next meal. Maggie recognized a killer when she saw one.

Adam shrugged nonchalantly, amusement in his eyes. "It's simply not necessary to accept every invitation. I value my time too highly to waste it."

"But Adam," she said with an obviously practiced pout, "we used to have such a grand time. Although . . ." She sighed prettily. "Now that I am married again I assume it would not be quite the same."

"Regretfully so, I'm afraid." Adam smiled. "So you are now Lady Hargreave?"

"Yes, but Adam"—she crinkled her perfect nose and tapped him on the shoulder with her fan—"you of all people should know how unimportant names are. You remember, 'What's in a name? That which we call a rose by any other name would smell as sweet.'"

Shakespeare.

Caroline trailed the fan slowly down his arm and cast him a wistful look. "Do you still know it by heart, Adam?"

Shakespeare?

155

By heart?

Was this woman saying what Maggie thought she was saying?

Speechless, Maggie turned to Adam. He had the unmistakable look of a child caught with his hand in the cookie jar.

"Maggie," he said cautiously, as though reading her thoughts.

A huge, heavy knot sank in the pit of Adam's stomach as Maggie's eyes lightened to a vivid green. He well knew that color and braced himself for her outburst. "Maggie, I think we should—"

"Lady Hargreave." Maggie's voice took on a cool, authoritarian tone. "We have some pressing family business to discuss. I hope you understand, but we need to speak privately now."

Caroline turned toward Adam indignantly. "Adam?"

Adam never took his eyes off Maggie. "Delightful to see you again, Caroline, but we really must say good evening."

Caroline threw him a petulant glare and flounced off. Adam paid no attention and concentrated on Maggie.

Why wasn't she screaming? Why wasn't she making a scene? It was what he expected, how she'd reacted every other time she'd been angered. Why was she so calm?

So controlled?

So cold?

"Maggie, I can explain." He regarded her anxiously. Her demeanor was unsettling. Almost frightening. She turned icy green eyes toward him.

"I don't think an explanation is necessary. I think it's all perfectly clear." She spoke with a quiet, crisp precision that chilled Adam's blood.

"You used a well-rehearsed routine to get what you wanted. And I admit it was extremely effective. *Romeo and Juliet*, gazing deeply into my eyes, kissing my hands. Oh, it was good, it was very good. Your technique is impeccable. But I have a few questions."

"Maggie, I . . ." Adam stared at her helplessly. He could take her ranting and raving but he didn't know how to deal with this quiet, cold manner she'd adopted.

"About tonight? The scene outside? Was that step two? Another part of your highly refined seduction? If I asked Lady What's-her-name over there, will I find out you typically have women half-naked in the garden?"

Her eyes flashed icy bolts and he winced, her accusation perhaps more true than he wanted to admit.

"I trusted you, Coleridge. You and Lydia are the only people here, literally in this entire world who know who, and I guess, what I am. You alone know what I'm going through, how damned confused and scared I am. And yet you tried to take advantage of that.

"I know how you and your entire world see women: as objects, as possessions. But I thought something special was happening between us. I thought I had your friendship, maybe even your respect, and fool that I am, I thought you cared about me. Instead it turns out I'm just next in line on your list of conquests. Was that the idea? See if you can get the woman from the future into bed? Find out if there are any new developments in the next one hundred and seventy-seven years? Well, let me tell you something pal, tab A still fits into slot B."

She flung a disgusted look at him. "Where I'm from, if a woman wants to sleep with a man, she has that freedom. I admit, moral standards are different than they are here. But I don't care what century it is, I don't like being used. I don't like to be tricked."

Maggie started to leave but turned back to Adam. "The thing that really annoys me is how I almost fell for it."

Maggie marched off, her step measured and sedate, her head high. A casual observer would have thought nothing wrong. Part of Adam admired how firmly she kept herself under control in spite of her anger. And there was no doubt she was angry. Her eyes told him that.

If she'd only let him explain. It wasn't as if he'd planned the night in the library or anything that happened afterward either. Oh, he admitted that particular scene from Shakespeare had come in handy in the past. But it had nothing whatsoever to do with her. Didn't she realize this was different from any of his past liaisons? Surely she would understand if she would only listen to him. He refused to lose her over something as insignificant as this.

"Bloody hell," he muttered.

"Whatever did you do, Adam?" A fan tapped him lightly on the arm. Lydia stood beside him, pinning him with a perplexed expression. Another woman making his life difficult. At least he still had some control over this one.

Lydia observed Adam carefully. A sinking feeling warned her she'd just made a mistake. Obviously all was not going as well as she'd assumed. Lydia's gaze caught her brother's, the sudden gleam there increasing her unease.

"You are coming with me." He grabbed her arm and propelled her across the room.

"What are you doing?" Lydia gasped.

Both brother and sister were far too familiar with the ways of the ton to let anyone know there was anything amiss. To outward appearances they looked as if they were simply taking a pleasant stroll together, if somewhat more quickly than normal.

"Adam," Lydia said through clenched teeth, "answer me. What is wrong?"

Adam pulled up in front of a tall, handsome, dark-haired man and thrust his sister forward roughly. "Here," he said. "You wanted her once; she's yours now. Marry her, Connor."

Lydia and a startled Connor stared. Adam turned on his heel and stalked off.

"Well, my dear, what was that all about?"

Still gazing after her brother, Lydia shook her head.

"I really don't know what's come over him. I think—" Abruptly noticing who she spoke to, Lydia turned with smile of real pleasure.

"Connor. In the midst of all this I hadn't even realized it was you. When did you get back to London?"

An amused smile drifted across his handsome face. "Several weeks ago."

"And you have not called on us? Connor, I am heartbroken." Lydia threw him a pouting glance.

Connor laughed. "I doubt that you have ever been heartbroken, my dear. I am confident the heart-breaking is all on your side. Now what was all that with Adam about?"

"Dance with me and I'll explain."

He gave her a quizzical glance. "If I remember correctly, your dances were always spoken for."

She waved his objections away with a flick of her fan. "It doesn't signify."

Connor took her arm and escorted her onto the floor. "Ah, Lydia, it's good to know some things never change. You still do exactly what suits you."

"And what of you, Connor?" Lydia raised an inquiring eyebrow. "You, too, have always done precisely what you wanted. I understand you made your fortune in India?"

"Quite," Connor said with a sigh. "I would have stayed there, too, had it not been for this blasted inheritance nonsense."

"That's right, I had forgotten. You are now the Viscount St. Clair." Lydia cast him a sympathetic look. "I was sorry to hear about the death of your cousin."

"I wasn't," he said bluntly. "I never particularly cared about the title. My cousin was a mean, vicious man who only wanted to make everyone else as miserable as he was."

"Oh, my."

"Now, my dear, enough of that. What's all this marriage business about?"

Lydia crinkled her nose in distaste. "Adam has decided it's past time for me to wed. If I do not select a husband, he will choose one for me."

"He's right, you know. You should have a husband."

"Connor." Lydia stared, shocked that he would side with Adam.

"Calm yourself." Connor chuckled. "I agree that you should be married. However, I do not necessarily condone Adam's methods."

"That's better." Lydia sniffed, somewhat mollified.

He started, as if an unpleasant thought had just struck him. "He has not selected me for this human sacrifice, has he?"

"Connor," Lydia said, an offended tone in her voice. She rapped him sharply with her fan. "Do you not wish to marry me?"

He ignored the attack, the amused smile again returning to his lips. "Lydia, my darling, I know you too well and love you far too much to marry you. We have known each other since I tagged along behind your brother and you were still in leading strings. I fear we are far too much alike to suit."

"But you did want to marry me once. Surely you have not forgotten the ill-fated attempt to spirit me away to Gretna Green." She peeked at him under lowered lids and flashed an impish smile. He returned it fondly.

"If memory serves, my funds had all but vanished and under the terms of my grandfather's will, I had to marry to inherit the portion he set aside for me. And I further remember"—he gazed down at her, eyes twinkling—"I was quite in my cups at the time."

"Indeed." Lydia nodded.

"And," he continued, the twinkle growing more pronounced, "you were rather foxed yourself."

"Perhaps."

"I will never understand," he said thoughtfully, "how you managed to convince a man as intelligent as Adam that it was a kidnapping. According to my recollection—"

"Connor"—she quickly jumped in—"it was a very long time ago and better forgotten. Don't you agree?" She gave him her most appealing look, eyes wide, lips slightly pouting. Connor laughed with delight.

"Enough. I give up. It was indeed a long time ago." He gazed deeply into her eyes. "But perhaps I should marry you."

"No, Connor." She laughed lightly. "I shall not give you a second chance. Besides, I fear you're right. We are far too alike to suit."

"Ah." He gazed heavenward dramatically, the agonized expression on his face made unconvincing by the smile in his eyes. "Now you have done it again, broken yet another heart. I shall have to pull myself together and attempt to carry on bravely."

"Connor." She laughed once again. "I have truly missed you."

"And I you." His expression sobered. "You know that I shall be there if you ever need anything." The twinkle returned to his eye. "Excluding a husband, of course."

"Of course." Lydia smiled up at him. Connor was not the answer to her husband dilemma. Maggie was. But the memories he triggered might help in that respect. Lydia would have to do some long, hard thinking and careful planning. But it might work. And with Connor's help . . .

Lydia flashed him a well-practiced, dazzling smile guaranteed to make every other man in the room green with envy. This evening was turning out better than she'd hoped after all.

Chapter Nine

Maggie had no desire to talk to Adam and absolutely no wish to hear any of his so-called explanations. Perhaps women didn't abandon social functions on their own here, but she wasn't from here and those weren't her rules. Maggie did not hesitate to make her way home. Alone. She simply asked a servant for Adam's carriage and sent the driver back for Adam and Lydia. It was, she thought, a piece of cake.

The brief ride gave her time to think. Time wasted. She couldn't concentrate on the problem at hand, couldn't focus her thoughts or feelings. A surreal detachment gripped her, as if she were watching someone else.

Odd. She wondered almost analytically why she wasn't seething with rage. Why hadn't she ripped his head off?

Maybe she just didn't care.

Maybe she cared too much.

Distancing herself let Maggie examine that idea objectively, carefully, emotionlessly. If Adam's actions affected her to the point that her emotions needed to shut down, it would mean he meant far more to her than she was willing to admit or accept. She pushed the thought away firmly. No, the numbness inside probably had more to do with some kind of time travel jet lag than any real or imagined feelings for Adam.

Maggie went to bed before Adam and Lydia returned home and slept fitfully. Once, she thought she heard footsteps pause outside her door, as if someone debated coming in. But eventually the footsteps continued on their way.

It wasn't particularly difficult for Maggie to avoid Adam, especially with Lydia's unwitting help. She stayed by Lydia's side, accompanying her wherever she went. And Lydia was constantly going somewhere.

The vivacious blonde took her on what seemed like an endless shopping trip. It was the 1818 version of "shop till you drop." And Lydia had it down pat. They stopped at milliners', and bootmakers', and fabric shops, and a variety of other places Maggie couldn't possibly name. While fascinating and fun, it also made Maggie homesick for a good old American shopping mall. And just like modern shoppers, Lydia never seemed to actually have any cash.

"But we have accounts," Lydia told her, expressing surprise that such an explanation was even necessary. "They simply send the bills to Adam. Don't you have accounts?"

"Well," Maggie said thoughtfully, "we have credit

cards. I suppose that's pretty much the same thing."

Maggie filled her in on the use and misuse of credit cards and Lydia agreed, the basic principle was indeed the same.

Lydia spent money like water. But when Maggie commented on it, Lydia brushed the question aside, saying simply they could well afford it. From what Maggie had seen so far of the Coleridge life-style she could well believe it. Still, she hesitated to buy anything herself. Only when Lydia insisted did she make any purchases.

Maggie wasn't the only one asking questions. Mesmerized by tales of the future, Lydia pumped Maggie for answers about everything from cars to careers. Much of what she heard was so far removed from her own world, she accused Maggie of making it all up. But Maggie assured her the wonders of the twentieth century were all very real, or at least, they would be someday.

Once Maggie realized just how limited Lydia's life really was, she tried hard to answer her questions as thoroughly as possible. While Lydia's intense curiosity encompassed virtually every subject Maggie touched on, one of her greatest interests lay in the clothes of Maggie's time, especially the scandalous yet intriguing clothes pictured in the pages of Maggie's *Cosmopolitan*. In spite of Adam's objections, Maggie loaned the magazine to Lydia and she read it thoroughly.

"For the most part, I believe I understand the clothing you wear." Lydia seemed to choose her words carefully.

They sat in the carriage returning home, and Maggie thought it more than a little bizarre to be discussing 1990s style as dictated by *Cosmo* while riding through a distinctly 1800s world.

"They seem extremely well suited for comfort. Although to be completely honest . . ." She turned a worried expression to Maggie, as if concerned about offending her, and looked her straight in the eye. "They're not especially pretty, are they? I haven't seen anything that's particularly elegant. It's all so, well . . . dull."

Maggie stared at her for a long moment, then broke into a grin. "I've been trying to explain, life is very different. Women in my time have to work for a living. I have a job I go to every day, except weekends. A big evening out is maybe pizza and a movie. Oh, sure, I'll go to bars or parties with friends, but that's usually just jeans and sweaters. There are no balls or soirees. There isn't even a season."

Maggie laughed at Lydia's look of sheer horror. "It's not that bad. I wouldn't have time for all that even if we had a season. And there are all kinds of compensations. I make my own money. I go where I want when I want. I don't have to have a servant chaperon me every minute. In fact, I don't have servants at all. And I don't have to get married if I don't want to," she said with a triumphant flourish.

Lydia looked awestruck by the possibilities and maybe even a little uncomfortable. She appeared to give thoughtful consideration to Maggie's description of her world.

Her eyes narrowed. "Is it acceptable, however, to have servants if one wants them?"

"Of course." Maggie laughed again. "But they are

very expensive and only people who are terribly rich have them."

Lydia brightened. "Well, it's fine then. I am terribly rich."

Maggie kept grinning and shook her head.

"Now." Lydia settled herself more comfortably in the carriage. "Tell me what a bar, a movie, and a pizza are."

For a split second Maggie thought how very much like Adam Lydia was. He, too, had seemed fascinated by the future. She sighed in resignation, rolled her eyes toward the heavens, and begged silently for help on how best to explain the mystery of pizza.

Bouquets of flowers filled the foyer, greeting Maggie and Lydia on their return. Most were for Lydia and she gave them the matter-of-fact perusal shown only by someone used to such offerings. But two dozen magnificent yellow roses carried a card with Maggie's name. She regarded the gift with suspicion. If Adam thought he could follow one tried-and-true scenario with something as cliched as flowers, he'd just have to think again.

"Maggie, they're lovely." Lydia's attention turned from the bouquets addressed to her. "Aren't you going to read the card?"

"No," she said bluntly.

"Then I will." Lydia snatched the card from its resting place among the blooms. "It says 'Regretfully, you left before our dance. Another time perhaps?' " Lydia looked up in surprise. "It's signed Edward Lindley."

"Who in the world is Edward Lindley?" Maggie

plucked the card from Lydia's fingers, examining it curiously.

"You remember, you met him last night. Lord Lindley? He asked you to dance right before Adam swept you away?" Lydia wrinkled her brow thoughtfully. "I don't know him very well but he's always seemed quite charming. I believe he has a sizable fortune and is in line for a title. His grandfather is a viscount or baron or something, I forget which." Lydia's eyes twinkled with mischief. "I believe you have made an impressive conquest."

"Great." Maggie groaned. "What I don't need right now is a conquest."

Lydia threw her a sharp look. "No, my dear, a conquest may be the very thing you do need right now."

Startled, Maggie wondered if maybe Lydia was right.

Maggie agreed to go to a party that night with Lydia. Descending the stairs to the foyer, she discovered Adam, formally dressed and ready to accompany them. Lydia kept her busy all day but Adam lingered always in the back of her mind. And he was the last person she wanted to see now. She steeled herself against the pounding leap of her pulse and refused to let his presence disturb her.

"Maggie, I would very much like to speak with you," he said quietly.

Maggie stared for a long moment. "I don't think so."

She turned to retreat up the stairs and he grabbed her arm, swinging her around to face him.

"Maggie, please listen to me."

"Don't touch me." She jerked her arm away. "Don't touch me again. Look, I know that women here have no rights whatsoever, but I'm not one of them. I appreciate your hospitality, especially since I have nowhere else to go, but that's where it ends. Just because I'm living here does not make me your property. So don't put your hands on me again. Ever."

"Maggie, please." His eyes pleaded, tempting her, for a second, to give in. She sensed pleading in any way, shape, or form was foreign to this proud, arrogant man, and it took all her self-control to resist his request.

"Can it, Coleridge." She started up the stairs, then turned back. "Please tell your sister I'm not going tonight. All of a sudden I don't feel like partying."

Adam's gaze followed her up the stairs. Why in God's name was she being so stubborn? This misunderstanding with Maggie haunted him all day until he could think of little else. He wanted her back in his arms, melting under his practiced touch. He missed the sound of her voice, missed how she teased him with her unpredictable ways and her incomprehensible phrases. He would rather have her threatening him with pokers or raving about her confusion with his world than this cold, hard disdain.

A sense of annoyance grew. He honestly could not understand why she would not even listen. Why she would not let him tell her how much she now meant to him. Why she would not let him admit, perhaps, the use of Shakespeare was a mistake. But a mistake made years ago when he'd cultivated it merely to suit his purposes, not a mistake with her.

Her reactions were exactly what he'd hoped for when he pulled the volume of Shakespeare off the shelf. Initially, all he thought of was victory, savoring her surrender to the poetic phrases and timeless passages. But afterward, his mind returned again and again to those moments in the library, when he sensed her gaze upon him, caught a hint of her intoxicating scent in the air, felt the almost palpable warmth emanating from her beckoning body. This had never happened to him before.

With Maggie, everything was different.

With Maggie, old words exchanged between young lovers took on a new meaning. Never before had he glimpsed what it must have been like to be in the throes of a first love. A love threatened by forces beyond control. A love doomed from the very start. Never before had he understood why, ultimately, the pair chose death over separation.

Without Maggie, would his life be worth living?

Adam shook the thought off, annoyance rapidly turning to irritation and anger. Damn the chit, anyway. He might not be willing to die for her but he might very well kill her. What was she but a nuisance and a bother? Even with all her astounding revelations about the twentieth century she remained as irrational and incomprehensible as any other woman. If this was what the future held, she could bloody well keep it, as far as he was concerned.

"Adam." Lydia broke into his thoughts. "Have you seen Maggie? I would like to—"

"She isn't coming," Adam said harshly. "And I'm not going either. I'll accompany you and find someone to escort you home, but I find my plans have changed. I will be spending the evening at my club."

"Adam, whatever have you done to her?" Lydia glared at him.

Would no one give him any credit in this house? His own home? That damned woman had turned his life upside down and now even his sister was questioning him.

"I have done nothing." Words clipped and precise, he directed his annoyance at Lydia. He certainly did not owe his sister any explanation.

Adam ushered her toward the door, shooting her a cool gaze. "And, my dear, how is your search for a husband coming? I believe you have barely three weeks left."

Lydia's startled look gave Adam a certain amount of satisfaction. Triumphing over at least one woman lifted his spirits somewhat. A pity, though.

It was the wrong woman.

Maggie stalked into her room and slammed the door behind her. Too furious to keep still, she paced back and forth, muttering under her breath.

"He's got a hell of a lot of nerve. Thinking he can explain this away and I'll fall panting into his arms. Ha! I can't believe I trusted him. He's like every other man in every other place and probably every other time. They're all interested in one thing and don't care what they have to do to get it."

Maggie paced and muttered, muttered and paced for a good 10 minutes, eventually working the rage out of her system. Anger replaced the numbness of last night. Slowly she calmed and her wrath faded.

Only the pain remained. Sinking onto the edge of the bed, realization stunned her. That was why she was so mad.

His calculated actions hurt.

Really hurt.

Almost from their first meeting, Adam had given her a feeling of safety and protection in this strange new world. Now he'd shattered her trust.

Painful as that was, it was insignificant compared to knowing he didn't think any differently of her than he did any other woman. She was merely one of a crowd of what? Dozens? Hundreds? She didn't begrudge him his past any more than hers should make a difference to him.

But that magical night in the library had an impact on her she would never get over, and never forget. The immortal words of Shakespeare, the warm and intimate setting, the primeval, magnetic pull of the man all made an indelible mark on her soul she could never erase.

It all made her love him.

Maggie groaned and threw herself backward on the bed. That was it, wasn't it? Even as she had debated the pros and cons of a relationship with him, it was already too late. She'd been fooling herself all along. He'd claimed her in the library that night as surely as if he had actually taken her to his bed.

And she would never be the same.

In love with a man there could be no possible future with. In a few weeks he would be as remote as if on another planet. They were separated by nearly 200 years, and there was absolutely nothing she could do about it.

A tear trickled down her cheek. Maggie wasn't much for tears and disliked women who gave in to their emotions, but she couldn't seem to stop herself and didn't seem to care. Tears rolled down her face and she lay curled up on the bed.

She wanted to go home.

She wanted her sister.

And more than anything, she wanted Adam.

All things considered, it was best to avoid Adam altogether. The action was almost too easy and Maggie wondered if he wasn't avoiding her as well. A subtle quizzing of Lydia confirmed her suspicions, more or less. Even though, with Lydia, Maggie was never quite sure if she received a straight answer or simply Lydia's oddly convoluted, strangely logical way of interpreting the world. Lydia said her brother typically occupied his days with family business, or at a boxing saloon, or involved with his stables. In the evening, if he wasn't at home, he occasionally served as her escort but more often spent time at his club. In short, Lydia had no idea where he was but implied he appeared far busier than usual and definitely was nowhere to be seen.

Several times Maggie hovered on the verge of going to the library. She told herself she needed something to read, but in reality she hoped to run into Adam. Accidentally, of course. Drawn as irresistibly as a moth to a flame, and just as dangerously, she was forced to call upon every inch of willpower she possessed to stay away.

Staying away completely seemed the best course. If she came face-to-face with Adam her resolve would be swept away in a tumultuous wave of passion and desire. Sex was one thing, but love was another matter altogether. The sooner Maggie got over Adam, the better. She still had a few weeks left here and, with luck, would be over this love business before she returned to the future. Maybe the pain would be gone by then, too.

She already missed him, already yearned for a glimpse of his face, the touch of his hands, the caress of his lips. If she didn't get over it now, how much worse would it be when she went back home?

Would she look for his face on every street? Look for a resemblance in every passing stranger, wondering if this was a great-great-grandchild? Would she spend long hours in libraries, trying to find out what became of him, trying to discover what woman he eventually chose to spend his life with? Play Juliet to his Romeo? Would she want to know when he died? If his life was happy without her?

She knew what he meant to her, but did she mean anything to him? Would he even remember her as the years went by? Would a month spent with a crazy, unconventional woman from a future too far away to even imagine simply fade into an amusing bedtime story for his children and grandchildren? Would there come a time when the stories became more real than the memories? When even he began to doubt that someday men would fly and lifelike pictures would be captured on paper and a woman with volatile green eyes and hair more red than brown had briefly touched his life? And would it all happen long before she'd taken her first breath?

Painful, depressing thoughts and images crowded

175

Maggie's mind, increasing her restlessness. Inactivity only heightened her heartache, and an almost frenetic, defensive energy gripped her. She had to keep moving.

Lydia helped, setting an impressive pace. She and Maggie made calls during the afternoon. Their first stop, much to Maggie's surprise, was Lady Wentworth's.

"Lydia, I thought you didn't like her?"

"Oh, I don't. But she is such a horrible gossip that if I don't put in an appearance every now and again, I feel certain I would be her next target. Besides," Lydia whispered behind the starched back of the butler showing them in, "I always learn such fascinating things."

The servant ushered the women to a large salon and it was all Maggie could do to keep from gasping out loud. She'd never seen anything like this room in her life, never imagined it in her wildest dreams. It was an oriental theme gone berserk. The wallpaper glowed a vivid red. Black lacquered chests fought for dominance with end tables and chairs carved to resemble bamboo.

The dragons nearly took Maggie's breath away. Carved dragons, gilded dragons, dragons as the arms of chairs, as the bases of tables, on the walls, on the carpets, they seemed to serve every conceivable purpose and cover every available space. It was a Chinese nightmare.

"Lydia." Maggie grabbed her arm, needing support from the almost physical effect of the overwhelming chamber. "What is this?"

"Shh." Lydia hissed. "It's the first stare in furnishings. Extremely fashionable. Although my own personal taste runs to something less likely to breathe fire."

Maggie choked back a laugh. A few flames in this room might be an improvement. She pulled herself together in time to join Lydia in greeting Lady Wentworth's daughters and the grand dame herself. In this setting the overbearing matron looked positively subdued compared with the other dragons competing for attention. Again, Maggie nearly lost it but a sharp glance from Lydia helped her smother a threatening giggle. Maggie spotted a particularly obnoxious knickknack and fought to keep her expression serene, hoping she could hide the amazement and amusement the room triggered.

Not until then did Maggie notice other visitors. They didn't exactly blend in: it was just difficult to sort out people from mythical beasts. Lydia turned to greet someone emerging from the reptilian menagerie.

"Quite amazing, is it not?" a voice asked from behind Maggie's shoulder.

"What?" She turned to find Lord Lindley and smiled in recognition. "Oh, hello. What's amazing?"

His blue eyes sparkled. "Why, the room, of course. Surely it has not escaped your notice?"

"I don't see how it possibly could," she said wryly. "I don't mean to be rude. I'm not wild about this particular style."

He chuckled and shook his head. "Tactful as well as beautiful. I must say America is producing impressive representatives these days."

"Thank you." She suppressed an almost instinctive

urge to drop a curtsy. This time period was definitely getting to her. "And thank you for the flowers. They were lovely."

"I thought yellow would be appropriate with your hair and eyes. Although now that I see you again I must say even roses don't do you justice."

His frankly admiring gaze threw her. She wasn't used to elaborate compliments, but after a moment, embarrassment turned to gratification and surprise. She liked this kind of treatment far more than the offhand comments offered back home.

"Well, thank you again. Your words are every bit as extravagant as your flowers."

He grinned in obvious appreciation. "I shall have to remember American women are not as retiring as our English ladies."

She laughed, warming to the verbal repartee. "Now that *is* a compliment and something I, for one, am proud of."

"Now then, when do you think we could have that dance?"

"Dance?" She laughed self-consciously. "I hate to admit this, but I really don't dance. I waltz a little but that's about it."

"A waltz, then." His eager expression turned to a considering frown. "But will Coleridge allow it? He seemed rather protective as your only relation here."

At Adam's name Maggie bristled. "Relation or not, he doesn't have much to say about it." Impulsively she added, "I would love to dance with you, but Lydia is planning our social activities, so I have no idea when we might have that chance." She gave him a regretful smile.

"I see. In that case would you do me the honor of accompanying me for a drive in the park? Tomorrow perhaps?"

A dance was one thing. Being alone in a carriage with this guy, no matter how cute or how nice, was something else altogether.

"Oh, I don't think so. Thanks."

"The day after then?"

His persistence flattered her but still she hesitated. It didn't seem like a very smart idea. Lydia's attention turned back to Maggie at that moment and she caught the end of Lord Lindley's request.

"Oh do go, Maggie. It will do you good."

"Yes, Maggie," he echoed. His eyes sparkled and he brought her hand to his lips. "It will do you good."

"I give up." She laughed. What the hell. She'd have to pay attention and think before every single word but how hard could that be anyway?

"I'd be delighted to ride with you on the day after tomorrow. Okay?"

His eyes narrowed and his brow creased in a perplexed frown. Maggie sighed. She really had to watch her mouth. "I mean, if that's all right with you?"

His expression cleared and he smiled down at her. "Until then." With a slight bow he turned away. Lydia and Maggie made their good-byes and headed for their next visit.

Aside from an occasional slip of the tongue, Maggie adapted quickly to the social rules of these brief visits. It was pretty basic. Typically, Lydia and Maggie would not be the only guests. If no men were present, the women talked about fashion, and after

Maggie's session with the dressmaker she could generally wing that. Since women were, in any place or time, still women, the topic typically turned to men. Who was available? Who was actively seeking a wife? Who was interested in whom?

Surprised, Maggie noticed how often a man's attractiveness seemed measured in the height of his title and the depth of his wallet. Virtually every eligible man discussed faced a critical analysis on the basis of those questions. What was his annual income? How many country places did he own? If not titled now, was he in line for one? And who would have to die for him to get it? It all seemed very cavalier and downright greedy in Maggie's eyes.

Maggie also noted that whenever Adam's name came up, speculative looks were sent her way. She ignored them but questioned Lydia in the carriage between visits.

"Adam is extremely eligible," Lydia said patiently. "He is two and thirty years now and it is past time for him to choose a wife and start a nursery."

"Start a nursery?" Confused, Maggie's eyes widened. "What do you mean? He's going to be a florist or grow trees or something?" The women exchanged puzzled looks, neither quite comprehending what the other attempted to say.

"Maggie, I have absolutely no idea what you're talking about." Understanding broke on Lydia's face and she laughed. "Not that kind of nursery. A nursery for children."

"You mean he'd get married just to have children?"

"Not just children. An heir, a boy. Only boys can inherit a title and much property is entailed."

"I don't understand."

"I'm not sure I thoroughly understand it myself but entailed property goes along with the title and if there is no male heir, the title and the property goes back to the Crown." Lydia shrugged. "That's why it is imperative for Adam and others in his position to marry, have a son, and ensure the succession. It's his responsibility to his family."

"So . . . why hasn't he?" Maggie's words were slow and measured.

"I suspect for the same reason I haven't. He has never found someone he wanted to spend the rest of his life with."

Lydia sighed. "I believe my dear brother, for all his brisk, efficient ways and precise, controlled life is a romantic somewhere deep inside. Our parents' marriage was a love match. I was very young when Mama died but Adam was twelve. And I think that influenced him greatly."

She stared moodily at the passing scenery. "I think he wants what our parents had, as do I."

"I see," Maggie said quietly, and the two women sat silent for a few moments, each thinking her own thoughts.

Lydia abruptly returned to the subject. "You are not the only one asking about Adam's marital prospects these days. There is some talk that Adam has finally settled on a match."

"Oh, how nice." Maggie's words echoed hollowly. She struggled to suppress an almost physical pain.

Lydia glanced at her sharply. "The talk, my dear, is centered around you."

"What?" Maggie bolted upright in the carriage.

"Naturally." Lydia ticked off points on her gloved fingers. "There was the incident in the park, when everyone noticed how Adam held you far more firmly than necessary as he carried you. Then there was the ball. The way the two of you waltzed as if you were meant for each other. And, of course, neither of you danced with anyone else."

Lydia leaned back in the carriage seat and pinned Maggie with a direct look. "The latest on-dit is that you are here from America for the sole purpose of marrying Adam."

Stunned, for once Maggie had absolutely nothing to say. She simply stared at Lydia and wondered if Adam had heard the gossip. If he had, what did he think? Did he care?

"Maggie, don't be so surprised. I could have told you this would happen. Although it really didn't occur to me until it was too late." She smiled sympathetically. "It doesn't signify. When you leave we shall simply say you went home to America. It will be the subject of talk for a few days; then something else will come along and it will be forgotten. And with you gone, there will be dozens of willing girls ready and eager to take your place."

"Oh, yeah, right," Maggie said quietly. A lump in her throat burned at the thought of someone taking her place with Adam. A place, she told herself firmly, she had already relinquished and had no claim to anyway. The reminder didn't help. Maggie fell silent, her stare fastened unseeingly on the world passing by the carriage.

Lydia observed her critically. Maggie obviously cared for Adam. Why else would she try so hard to avoid him? Lydia noted that Maggie's preference for her company had an almost compulsive air about it. Maggie and Adam might well be the two most stubborn people she had ever seen.

Lydia drew a deep breath. The plans formulating in her head the past few days were taking a definite shape, and none too soon. Every time Adam grew cross with Maggie, he'd take it out on her and bring up that nasty marriage business. No closer to selecting a husband now than when he first issued his threat and more resolved than ever not to bend to his ultimatum, she had to get his attention back on Maggie. In the meantime, Lord Lindley could possibly be a great help.

Lydia smiled to herself. A dose of jealousy might be just the tonic her dear brother deserved.

That evening, Lydia dragged Maggie to some type of recital in a mansion even more lavish than the Coleridges'. An easy function to get through; Maggie simply appeared as if she listened to the frequently off-key soprano, apparently the daughter of the house. Again, she and Lydia were the subject of attention for numerous young men, and again she found flirting to be timeless as well as easy. She could handle it as long as she displayed more bosom than brains and no one asked specific questions about her background. Those that came up, she and Lydia deflected lightly.

The musical interludes, such as they were, provided Maggie with breathing space. Gratefully she realized that was why Lydia accepted this invitation. Would Adam be here as well? Periodically she scanned the packed room, but she never saw him and berated herself when relief that she did not have to face him battled with disappointment at his absence.

Edward Lindley joined Maggie and Lydia briefly. Maggie actually enjoyed the comfortable conversation and wondered if there might be the makings of a friendship here. She'd always had good male friends. Maybe that was why she'd never fallen seriously in love. God knew she could use all the friends she could get now. Friendship with Lindley was a pleasant thought, but reluctantly she had to face reality. The rules and structure of Regency England probably didn't allow for platonic friendship.

Adam came late and stayed only a few moments. He wanted to force Maggie to talk to him, make her listen to what he had to say. From the back of the room, he stared at her, watching her laugh and chat with . . . who was that? Edward Lindley? Adam didn't know the man but immediately disliked him intensely. He turned abruptly and walked out. It was a first. Adam had never backed down from a fight in his life.

Did he leave because he had too much pride? After all, he had done nothing that truly warranted this extreme reaction from her, so why should he be the one to apologize?

Or did he have too little courage?

What if he told her of his feelings? How important she had become to him and how very much he missed her. And what if after he told her all that, what if she simply didn't care? Did he have enough courage to face that?

The next day took on the same characteristics as the day before. Boredom stalked Maggie. All these people ever seemed to do was shop and gossip and party.

"Isn't there anything else here?" Maggie complained to Lydia. They'd put in a full day of calls and now were taking a leisurely carriage ride in the park. It filled the time but did nothing to cure Maggie's continued restlessness. Lydia suggested a drive and, at this point, Maggie was game for anything. Even so, it surprised her when Lydia took the reins herself.

"I didn't know you were allowed to drive." Maggie stared with surprise and admiration.

"Well, not all that many women handle the reins themselves," Lydia said. "But it's not unheard of. I simply badgered Adam for years and eventually he grudgingly taught me." She gave a sharp flick of the reins and smiled confidently. "Even he admits I am quite good."

Eagerly she turned to Maggie. "Would you like to learn? It really can be wonderfully exciting."

Maggie laughed ruefully. "I don't think so, thanks. But some kind of exercise would be great. Although I'm sure you don't have health clubs or swimming pools or Richard Simmons."

Lydia ignored the unfamiliar activities and considered the question. "Well, we could ride. Do you ride?"

"Not since I was a kid at summer camp. I used to go every year and I really liked riding. If I remember, I was pretty good, but it's been a long time." Maggie

185

nodded toward a couple on horseback. "And there's no way I could ride with one of those. In my time a sidesaddle is pretty much a thing of the past."

Lydia's eyes narrowed and she watched the riders file by.

"You know," she said slowly, "I haven't bent any rules lately."

Startled, Maggie stared, intrigued by a gleam in Lydia's eye. "What do you mean?"

"Only that I have never ridden astride," Lydia replied innocently.

"Never?" Given Lydia's admitted pursuit of her so-called adventures, Maggie found her admission hard to believe.

"Never," Lydia said solemnly. "The perfect opportunity never presented itself. Until now."

Maggie observed her closely for a long moment, then grinned. "Adam won't like it."

Lydia shrugged. "Adam won't know."

"All right!" Maggie whooped with excitement. "When can we go? Where?"

"Let me think." Lydia's eyes narrowed and she thought for a moment. "The park is really the only place in town. We'll have to go very early, even before the earliest riders are out. So it will have to be before dawn. And we'll have to saddle our own horses to avoid the grooms and stableboys."

"Great. Can you get some pants?"

"Pants?" Lydia's face registered shock.

"Yeah, pants. Britches, pantaloons, whatever you call them." Maggie nodded at a woman on horseback. "You're not going to ride in one of those getups. You'll kill yourself. My jeans are hidden in the back of my wardrobe, so I'll be fine, but if we do this, you have to have pants."

"Very well." Lydia sighed. "And I have such a lovely new habit, too." She sighed again. "I'll simply have to steal something from one of the servants."

Maggie leaned toward her eagerly. "Do you need help?"

"Oh, my, no." Lydia smiled sweetly. "It's been a while since I have, shall we say, borrowed men's clothing but I'm reasonably sure I remember how. Now then, which of the servants would have clothes to fit me?"

The women laughed and giggled their way back home as they worked out the details of their illicit ride. Maggie didn't want to get Lydia in trouble, but, after all, it was her idea. She suspected this would be a big deal if they were caught. So they simply could not get caught.

Maggie and Lydia went to bed early. They wanted to be up and gone before dawn. They didn't have to explain why they decided not to go after all to a party they'd accepted an invitation to. This was yet another night Adam didn't put in an appearance.

For the first time in days, Maggie slept soundly. She never heard the footsteps again stop at her door in the middle of the night. She never noticed how long they hesitated there. And she never woke to the lonely echo of the sound as it finally retreated down the dark hallway.

Adam absently swirled the brandy in his glass and stared unseeing at the flames in the fireplace before him. It was his fourth brandy, or perhaps his seventh. He no longer counted. He was not, however, in his cups. On the contrary, while each sip darkened his mood, each glass brought his thoughts into sharper focus. And they focused on only one thing.

Maggie.

He could not get her out of his head in spite of his best efforts. Except for the moment last night, he had not seen her for two days. Deliberately. He filled those days with business and strenuous exercise, boxing and riding. His evenings were spent here at his club where his obviously glum demeanor did not encourage company.

Adam had not behaved like this in years. Not since his father died. In those days his drinking and carousing and gambling were his ways of striking back at the loving but domineering father who could not understand why his only son wanted to go to war or why his son believed it was his duty to king and country to join the fight against Napoleon. Adam never could explain to his father why he considered it a question of honor. His honor and his family's. His father not only forbade his involvement, but his influence in government and military circles was such that when Adam tried to circumvent him, it was to no avail. And Adam resented it.

Resentment that manifested itself in wild behavior. For years Adam lived with reckless abandon, following his emotions, giving in to impulse, pushing strength and courage far beyond the pale of acceptable behavior. Never quite crossing the line into the unforgivable yet never quite completely respectable either.

When his father died, grief and guilt paralyzed

him. Even vast amounts of very fine liquor did not ease his pain. Alone, he struggled to come to terms with the relationship he could no longer change. Gradually, through the long days locked away in his father's private refuge, he began to comprehend, began to see that, as strong as his father always appeared, he could not face the possible loss of his son in battle. He remembered his father's face when Adam was involved in some particularly difficult scrape or scandal. Behind the anger, there was always a glimmer of amusement, a touch of pride, a hint of paternal love. Too stubborn and defiant to recognize it at the time, Adam didn't realize what he'd had until his father's death. What he'd lost.

The impetuous youth came out of his father's library a mature man, setting aside emotion and vowing to turn his life around, to make the estates profitable and carry his name honorably, to make his father proud. He succeeded admirably, harnessing the same intensity he had once used in the pursuit of pleasure. If somewhere along the way he had gone too far, become too ruthless in business, too cold and self-controlled in his personal life, too . . . well, stuffy . . . so be it.

And now, for the first time in years, he sat around swilling brandy after brandy. And why? For a woman? Even in his rakehell days he had not acted like this over a mere woman. The Cyprians and demimondes he associated with knew what to expect from him and he from them.

In younger days he'd partaken of all the acceptable—and many of the unacceptable—pleasures London had to offer. In spite of his unsavory reputation, he was still considered a prize, if somewhat tarnished, on the marriage mart and much sought after as a guest. When he deigned to make an appearance, he had few qualms about flirting and charming innocents and near innocents in their first seasons. He was typically careful to make clear his intentions, to make sure no young miss or her family expected more from him than he was willing to give. Adam's sense of honor always remained stronger than his rebellion.

Why was Maggie so very different from the women he knew? A normal woman would have let him explain. A normal woman would have welcomed him back with open arms. After all, he was still an extremely eligible catch. A normal woman would have understood previous encounters.

He ignored the nagging question in the back of his mind. Why on earth was he wasting his time? Why did he even care? He wanted her, of course, wanted her in his bed and by his side. But what exactly did that mean? Would he offer her carte blanche? Would she even consider that? Was that what he wanted?

No. He sighed. He had never offered to keep a woman before and would not start with Maggie. Then what did he want?

"You are a sorry sight."

"What?" Adam glanced up into the amused eyes of Richard Westbrooke. "Oh, Richard." He returned his sulking attention to the flames flickering in the hearth. "What are you doing here?"

Richard settled in the chair beside him and signaled a waiter for a brandy. "Amanda and I were at a particularly boring soiree and she was having much too good a time to drag herself away, so I left. I shall return for her later. I might ask you the same question."

"I am thinking," Adam mumbled.

"I see." Adam heard the amused note in his friend's voice. "And how is she?"

Startled, Adam turned toward him. "She?"

"Yes, the intriguing creature you were with the other night."

"Maggie," he said darkly.

"Yes, Maggie. She is an original. What are you going to do about her?"

Adam growled. "What makes you think I am going to do anything about her?"

Richard chuckled. "Adam, I have known you for many years and I have never seen you quite this bad. Even in the old days when at any given moment either of us could have been found foxed and ready to do battle at the slightest provocation. It's been my experience when any man looks like you do there is very probably a woman behind it."

"Maggie."

"Yes, Maggie."

"She is impossible," Adam grumbled.

Richard smiled knowingly. "Amanda was impossible, too, until I married her." He chuckled again. "Still is, in fact. Why don't you marry her?"

"Marry Maggie?" Surprised, Adam noted the idea did not sound at all farfetched.

"She would make a delightful countess."

"Ha." Adam snorted. "Delightful isn't the word I'd use. Stubborn, intractable, annoying, impulsive—those are some of the words I'd use."

"Very well." Richard laughed. "She would make an interesting countess."

"She would, wouldn't she?" Marry Maggie? Adam agreed reluctantly. It might well be the perfect answer. If he married her she certainly couldn't leave him. She would be his always.

Maggie was the only woman he had ever met to affect him this deeply. For the first time in years, he was alive again because of her. The intensity of the attraction between them shocked him but he could not deny it. Maybe this was why she had come to his time. Maybe the gods had brought them together. Maybe this was, indeed, their fate. The thought lifted his spirits, only to have them plunge again.

"She won't even talk to me," he said glumly.

"Adam." Richard scoffed. "I have seen you work your way back into the good graces of many an angry woman. Remember that dancer back . . . when was it?"

"Years ago." Adam waved the question aside, then brightened. "That was a good job, wasn't it?"

Richard nodded. "No man could have done better."

Again Adam's spirits fell. "But I couldn't do the same with Maggie. No, she'd find out. Think it was part of a well-rehearsed plan."

"Well, I have confidence in you. You will come up with something. I must be leaving." Richard stood to go. "By the way, did you hear about the robberies in the neighborhood? Thieves breaking into houses? I hear they've hit a few near you. Amanda is quite alarmed and had me put extra men on."

"Yes, I've heard," Adam said absently, his mind

still on his more pressing problem. "I've alerted my staff."

"Very well, then." Richard shook his head, a smile of amusement again on his lips. "I can see you have more, ah, thinking to do, and I must collect my wife." He stared to leave, then turned back. "Oh, and, Adam."

His sharp tone captured Adam's attention and he wondered at the serious note now in his friend's voice.

"One more thing. Originals are very difficult but well worth the trouble. Amanda has made my life happier than I could have ever imagined. Your Maggie may well do the same for you. But . . ." He hesitated as if uncertain how to proceed. "There is something very different about her. I don't think she is quite what she appears to be."

Adam groaned and slumped further into his chair. He stared once again at the flames, pulled a long drag of his brandy, and cursed under his breath. "No shit, Sherlock."

Chapter Ten

"Maggie. Maggie." A voice called in the dark.

Her mind still fogged with sleep, her thoughts failing to focus in the blackened room, Maggie's eyes drifted open.

"Maggie!" The voice grew more insistent.

"What?"

"Shh! It's me."

Maggie's eyes adjusted to the dark. The ghostly figure leaning over her bed took shape. Lydia? What was she . . . ? Of course, they were going riding. How could she have forgotten?

"Damn." Maggie tumbled out of bed. "I must have overslept. Sorry."

She scrambled into the jeans she'd placed on the foot of the bed the night before. "It's not too late, is it?"

"No," Lydia whispered. "But we really must hurry.

Here." She thrust a wadded-up piece of fabric at her. "Put this on."

Maggie grabbed the material and shook it out. It looked like a shirt. "What is it?"

"It's Adam's linen. I'm wearing one as well."

"I was going to wear my T-shirt."

Lydia shook her head. "The yellow garment? No, that's too scandalous even to consider and not nearly warm enough for this morning. Besides, if anyone sees us in these, we might pass for boys. I brought this, too."

In the gloom, Maggie squinted to make out what appeared to be a blanket.

"Here, take it. It's a cloak."

Maggie grabbed the heavy wool garment and dropped it on the bed. She pulled the shirt over her head and struggled with the buttons, eventually leaving it open at the neck. Soft and full, it smelled faintly of Adam.

"Okay, let me just get my shoes." Maggie stumbled to the wardrobe and grabbed the Nikes from their hiding place. Leaning against the massive piece of furniture, she pulled on the shoes and bounced lightly on the balls of her feet, enjoying the pleasant, familiar spring. It was great to be back in her own clothes again. Even though the flowing dresses and lightweight slippers here were growing on her.

She grabbed a brush and ran it through her hair, then tossed it on the bed and snatched up the cloak. She threw the oversize garment around her shoulders. "Ready?"

"Ready." Lydia nodded, pulling up the hood of her

own cloak to cover her blond curls. She carefully opened the door and peered cautiously into the hall. "Follow me."

The women silently crept along the darkened passageway, trying not to alert any of the mansion's sleeping residents. Lydia led the way down a servants' stairway that ended near what Maggie assumed must be the kitchen. Here was a corridor and what appeared to be a back door or maybe a servants' entrance.

Lydia flipped back her hood and pulled a key from an invisible pocket. Carefully she fit the key in the lock and turned it. The door creaked open slowly and they slipped through, closing it silently behind them. Within moments they were at the stables.

Two horses stood saddled and ready.

"I thought you didn't want anybody to know about this," Maggie hissed.

Lydia shrugged. "I didn't, but I was not at all sure if we could saddle the horses ourselves, so I asked George to help. Don't worry. He'll keep our secret, won't you, George?"

The silent George nodded somberly.

"Besides, I paid him to be still."

"You actually had real money? Cash?" Maggie's voice dripped with sarcasm.

"Of course," Lydia said loftily. "Now shall we?"

It had been a long time since Maggie last mounted a horse, but the skill came back to her quickly. She sat astride within seconds and waited for Lydia to do likewise. But Lydia remained standing, eyeing the horse with more than a little skepticism. "Perhaps this idea was not well thought out after all."

"Oh, come on. Where's your spirit of adventure? We've come way too far to give up now." Maggie turned to the stableboy. "Is there something she can stand on to get into the saddle?"

George brought a stool and eventually Lydia sat astride the animal, which looked nearly as unsure as she.

"This is odd, isn't it? Sitting like this." Lydia adjusted herself in the saddle. "But really quite comfortable and one doesn't feel as if they're about to slide right off. I could become quite used to this." She turned to Maggie. "Ready?"

"After you."

Lydia took the lead and Maggie followed her out of the stable and into the street to the park.

The pair passed through the park gates in that uncertain time of morning between the total black of night and the rosy glow of dawn, with much of the world shadowed gray and indistinguishable. Wisps of mist swirled and hugged the ground, scattered only by their passage. The *clop-clop* of the horses' hooves echoed through the lonely streets. The air hung heavy with early morning dew. Tendrils of hair curled around Maggie's face. The furtive nature of their ride, the quasidisguises, even the still of the predawn hour stimulated Maggie. Excitement coursed through her veins.

They passed few people on the street, only a carriage here and there apparently returning home from a late night out. In the park they rode alone, the hour still too early for even the most avid rider. They trotted through deserted, tree-lined lanes. Maggie grew confident both in the saddle and in their ability to pull the whole thing off without incident.

They rode deeper into the park and Maggie turned to Lydia. "Is there someplace where we can let loose? You know, really have a good run? Maybe a race?"

"Oh, one does not race in the park. It's simply not permitted." Lydia shook her head firmly.

"Come on," Maggie said. "You're riding astride. You're wearing pants. And you're worried about a little thing like speeding? Relax and let's enjoy it."

"Your point is well taken," Lydia said ruefully. "I accept your challenge." She laughed and dug her heels into the horse's flanks. He lunged forward and took off, leaving Maggie gaping after them.

"What challenge?" She urged her horse into a canter. "What's with this family and their challenges anyway? Damn. If I lose her I'm in big trouble."

Her horse picked up speed and they raced in the direction Lydia disappeared. Maggie's body moved with the rhythm of the beast and, after a moment, she lost herself in the sheer enjoyment of the ride, of being one with the broad, handsome animal. Exhilaration, primal and primitive, surged through her and she felt every inch as much a creature of nature as the one beneath her. This was the release she sought, the answer to her restlessness. She kept an eye open for Lydia but reveled in the sheer ecstasy of her powerful flight.

She slowed her horse to a walk and continued to search for Lydia. It had been a while since she'd seen her and an uneasy feeling crept over Maggie. It wasn't quite daylight yet, although it was much lighter than when they'd arrived. She had absolutely no idea where she was in the park. Maggie thought the area seemed a bit off the beaten path but she'd only been to Hyde Park twice, three times if a visit in another century counted.

Maggie's first thoughts were for Lydia's safety. She didn't want anything to happen to her. Guilt swept through Maggie. If Lydia was harmed, regardless of whose idea this outing was, it would be Maggie's fault. Lydia wouldn't be here if it wasn't for her.

Maggie wasn't confident of her own safety, either. This was downright spooky. Her horse steadily pushed forward and her earlier unease gradually turned to real fear. In the dim light surrounding trees took on strange and frightening shapes. The crackle of twigs in the faint breeze seemed somehow sinister. The occasional branch brushing her hair startled her and she jerked in the saddle, her heart in her throat.

"Don't be paranoid," she muttered softly, taking comfort in the sound of her own voice. "You don't know exactly where you are but you're still in a city park. You can't get too lost. Just chill out."

She took a deep breath and continued her monologue. "Granted, this is a scary place, but think how charming it is in the daylight with all those people parading around. Don't think about muggings in Central Park or Jack the Ripper or anything like that. That's decades and decades from now. This is the original kinder and gentler place. Right?"

She glanced around as if expecting an answer and afraid she might hear one. "Stay calm. Don't get freaked out."

A faint sound in the distance caught her attention

and she reined her horse to a stop. The noise from somewhere behind her grew steadily louder. It sounded like something crashing through the trees. Something big. Something nasty. Heading toward her.

"Oh, damn. Come on." She spurred her horse and they shot off in no particular direction, just away from whomever or whatever was behind her. Maggie's heart thudded wildly in her chest. Terror lodged in her mind. She could think of nothing but escape. Her horse flew past the trees and Maggie clung to his neck tightly. The racket of her pursuer grew louder and louder until she almost felt the hot breath of a demon beast behind her. She refused to spare a single, precious moment to glance back and strained ahead, urging her horse forward. Blind, numbing fear clogged her mind at the thought of what she might see.

Without warning a hand reached out and grabbed her reins, expertly pulling her horse to a stop. Acting only on instinct, she slipped to the ground and took flight, running as fast and as hard as she could. Her blood pounded through her veins; her breath rasped through her lips. Adrenaline pumped her legs faster and faster. Branches clawed at the heavy cloak over and over like grasping hands, impeding her progress.

A hand grabbed Maggie's arm, jerking her to a halt, ripping a scream from her throat. Frantic with terror, she struck out blindly. Breaking every self-defense rule she'd ever learned, Maggie doubled up her fist and swung indiscriminately with all the power she possessed.

"Yow! Bloody hell!" an incensed but extremely familiar voice yelled.

"Adam? Oh, jeez." Shock widened Maggie's eyes and slowly she focused on Adam's grim, furious face. Her legs suddenly too weak to support her, she sank to her knees and buried her face in her hands. For a long moment she fought to get her breathing under control. Terror ebbed away and relief filled her. She wanted to laugh and cry at the same time. Finally she uncovered her face and glared up at him.

"You scared the hell out of me." She scrambled to her feet. "I had no idea who was chasing me. I thought you were going to kill me."

Adam's eyes narrowed. He had the look of a man struggling to contain himself. How much trouble was she in?

His hands knotted into fists by his sides and he spoke through clenched teeth. "I am going to kill you."

He grabbed her arm and dragged her toward his horse standing patiently a few feet away.

She struggled against him. "Where are we going?"

"Home."

"What about my horse?" She scanned the woods around her, hoping the missing horse would provide an excuse to delay what was coming. Anything to put off facing Adam's wrath struck her as a very good idea.

He tossed her up on his saddle as if she were a sack of potatoes and leapt behind her. "He shall be taken care of."

She sat flattened against him. His arm around her

waist held her securely, his free hand holding the reins.

"But Lydia, I've lost her." Informing him of his missing sister, while dangerous, seemed like another good delaying tactic.

"She should be home by now." His tones were clipped and crisp.

She twisted around to face him. "But what—?"

"Miss Masterson!" Obviously any patience Adam had up to this moment had now evaporated as rapidly as the early morning mist. "We shall discuss this later. My purpose at this point is to get you home unobserved. The task will be made much easier if you will simply keep your mouth shut."

She started to speak.

"Shut up."

"Fine." She settled in for the brief ride home. Her position pinned against him would have been pleasurable at any other time, but at this moment, even though she knew according to the rules of his life she was in the wrong, anger replaced remorse. Her fighting spirit was up. She was looking forward to having it out with him.

Maggie marched into the library two steps ahead of Adam and pulled up short at the sight of Lydia looking anxious and more than a little chagrined.

"Are you all right?" Lydia said.

"How did you get here?" Maggie said at the same time.

Lydia nodded toward Adam. "He had a carriage and a driver."

"He got me on horseback," Maggie said wryly.

Adam closed the doors firmly behind him. "I think an explanation is in order." His voice sounded calm and controlled but his eyes flashed dangerously.

"Me, too." Maggie whirled to face him. "Go ahead, explain."

"What?"

"Explain why you chased me through the park, scaring me half to death. Explain what gave you the right to haul me back here like a bag of groceries. Explain how you knew where we were in the first place. Explain—"

"George told me."

"Damn," Maggie swore under her breath.

"George?" Lydia said. "But I paid him!"

Adam turned stormy eyes on Lydia. "But I pay him more. George knows where his loyalties lie. And it's a bloody good thing, too. Imagine my surprise when he greeted me with the news that you two had taken horses and gone God knows where. And dressed like that, no less." He spit the words out as if they were somehow distasteful.

"What's wrong with the way we're dressed?" Defiance drenched Maggie's words.

"You know full well what's wrong. Maybe there is, after all, an excuse for you, for the way you think and act." He turned to Lydia. "But what in the hell was in your mind? You know the irreparable damage this little stunt could do to your reputation. I am grateful no one was around to witness your disgraceful behavior."

"My behavior?" The anger in Lydia's eyes now mirrored her brother's. Facing off against each other, the two had never looked more alike.

203

"What about you? What about your behavior? It was nearly dawn and you were just getting home!"

For the first time Maggie noticed Adam's evening clothes: ruffled silk shirt, elaborately tied white cravat, black jacket. The elegant clothes, the fury in his eyes, and the stony set of his jaw created an impressive and intimidating figure.

"I had been home. You had both retired. I went out again." He sighed angrily. "My behavior is not in question here."

Adam forced himself to calm down. His initial panic and fear when he learned the women were missing gave way to relief when he found them safe, followed quickly by anger. Neither Maggie nor Lydia had any real notion of the dangers facing unescorted young women in the dim recesses of the predawn day.

"Since I obviously cannot trust you two alone and I am not about to play nursemaid to you every minute, I have made a decision."

He paused to let his words sink in. Maggie and Lydia exchanged anxious looks. Adam directed his next comments to his sister.

"There are far and away too many temptations in town. I can see that Maggie makes a more dangerous companion for you than any of your previous cohorts. I had hoped you'd grown out of escapades like this but I was mistaken. I am sending both of you to the country as soon as I can make arrangements."

Maggie stared in disbelief. If she left she might blow her only chance at getting home. She shook her head vehemently. "No way, pal. Not on your life. I'm staying right here."

"What?" Adam's stunned expression was almost comical. He'd apparently never faced outright defiance from a woman, any woman, before.

"I am not going either," Lydia said in the calmest voice she'd used so far.

He whirled toward her, fists clenched by his sides, eyes flashing, every line of his body tight with rage. "You will!"

Lydia returned his glare with a serene, almost amused expression. "No, I most certainly will not. This is the second time in recent weeks you have made one of your decisions regarding my life and I will no longer put up with it. Under the terms of Father's will you are my guardian and I accept that. But I am not a child and I refuse to be treated like one."

Maggie stared at the scene played out between brother and sister, impressed at the self-assured, somewhat regal way Lydia acted. Adam, on the other hand, looked like he'd burst a blood vessel any moment. Maggie wanted to cheer Lydia on but tactfully, and probably wisely, decided to stay out of it.

"You gave me a month to find a husband. I have no intention of leaving before the allotted time. I plan on enjoying every minute of it right here." Her eyes shot daggers at him. "If at the end of that time I am not betrothed, I will retire to the country as per your threat, because I absolutely refuse to marry anyone that meets your qualifications and not mine."

"You'll bloody well do as I say."

Ignoring him completely, Lydia stepped to the door, opened it, and turned back to her brother.

"She's right, you know. You are a bite in the

shorts." She sailed out the door and closed it firmly behind her.

Lydia floated up the stairs, hoping there were no servants around to notice the self-satisfied grin she could not keep off her face. Poor, dear Adam. She'd never openly defied him. Ever. She'd never had to. Lydia always did exactly as she wished and paid whatever price came due later. Adam typically raged at her over the minor crises she created but he always protected her, too. Protection that in recent years saved her from any potential slur on her honor or good name.

Of course her escapades weren't truly terrible. She'd never been seduced, for example. Lydia preferred to think of them as larks, minor adventures. As she'd told Maggie, she didn't have the courage to totally flout convention. She liked the social whirl of the ton far too much to be forced to give it all up simply because of scandalous behavior, no matter how enjoyable such behavior might be.

She wasn't exactly sure why she'd blatantly defied Adam this morning. Usually she worked her own subtle form of manipulation on the dear man. Perhaps it was Maggie's influence. Perhaps it was just time.

Poor Adam. She had absolutely no intention of accepting an arranged marriage or making a desperate match herself in the next few weeks. Regardless of what she said in the library, she would not spend the years until she turned 30 banished to the country.

Maggie was still her best chance at getting Adam off this ridiculous marriage business. He obviously cared for the woman. She could tell by the way he turned so surly whenever he was at cross purposes with her. He merely needed to learn how much he cared. The time had come for her to put her plan into motion. She would need help but could probably make the arrangements easily. For now, she would return to bed. Nothing exhausted her more than an early morning ride.

Maggie and Adam stared at the door, sharing a stunned silence, Adam's face a mask of conflicting emotions. Maggie read outrage in the angry tilt of his jaw and tension in his powerful body. But confusion was there as well, a hint around his dark, stormy eyes, a suspicion on his furrowed brow. His expression triggered a surge of compassion. Poor guy. He'd probably never faced a situation where things were totally out of his control before.

Adam turned dark, flashing eyes toward her and any feelings of sympathy vanished. Her heart dropped to her stomach at the fury rampant on his face, the controlled rage of his stance. "And as for you . . ." He started toward her.

"Hold it right there." She shoved her hand in front of her and lifted her chin defiantly. "You may have the right to run your sister's life but, as far as I'm concerned, you have absolutely no right to run mine."

"As long as you are in this house you are my responsibility." Adam glared and turned abruptly. He strode to the table and poured a glass of brandy. Obviously trying to regain his self-control he downed the liquor in one swallow and splashed out a second glass.

Maggie stalked past him and poured a glass of her own. Following his lead, she, too, downed it greedily. Her eyes watered and she choked back a cough, but she refused to let him see the effects of the drink. Within moments, the warmth of the brandy spread through her and she poured another.

"You are corrupting my sister."

"What?" She slammed the glass down on the table, amber drops splattering on the polished surface. "I'll have you know this wasn't my idea."

"It wasn't?" He raised an eyebrow in an expression that clearly said he didn't believe her. "Riding astride was not your idea?"

"No." She stifled a glimmer of guilt. "Not really."

"Oh?" There went the eyebrow again. "And I suppose it wasn't your idea to wear trousers and—" He peered at her sharply and recognition washed over his face. "My good linen. You're wearing my good linen."

"Well," she said, evasion in her voice, "okay, maybe that part was my idea." Anger at his attitude sparked within her. Who did he think he was, anyway? "Ultimately, this whole thing is your fault."

"My fault." Adam gasped, looking genuinely surprised. "How in the name of all that's holy is this my fault?"

"It just is." Maggie wasn't making a whole lot of sense but she was too mad to care.

"Why is it my fault?"

"Because." *Because what? Because he broke your heart?*

208

"Because you used me," she said. "You used a line on me like you've probably used on every other woman who's passed through your life."

"I did not." Righteous indignation stamped his face and accompanied his words. "Not every woman."

"What? Oh great, that makes it much better."

"I didn't mean it that way." Adam ran his hand through his hair in an anxious gesture. "You would not let me explain."

"You didn't try very hard."

"You refused to listen!"

"You should have made me listen. You're the big, macho nineteenth-century lord of the manor. You're used to everyone obeying your every whim. What's the matter? Was it a little intimidating to find a woman who didn't fall at your feet in awe of your money and your title? A woman willing to stand up to you and not take the kind of bull you dish out? Was dealing with me just too much of a challenge?"

"A challenge? What challenge? Every time I came near you, you melted in my arms. If I had wanted you in my bed you bloody well would have been there by now. But why would I want someone with absolutely no inkling of proper behavior, no apparent consideration for anyone's problems but her own, and the social manners and mouth of a guttersnipe?"

"A guttersnipe?" Maggie gasped.

A firestorm of fury swept through her, and without thinking she did what she had never done before in her life. She drew back her hand and let it fly.

Chapter Eleven

Adam caught her open hand in midair and the resounding slap reverberated through the library. The very air seemed charged, shimmering with barely concealed tension and emotion.

Shocked by her actions, Maggie's eyes widened and she stared at Adam. Their gazes locked for a long, electric moment. Slowly Adam brought her hand to his lips, turned it, and kissed her palm. His eyes never left hers.

"Damn," she breathed.

"Bloody hell." He groaned and pulled her unresistingly into his arms.

Their lips met and all Maggie's bottled-up emotions burst free like a swollen river breaching a weakened dike. She twined her hands in his hair and his lips crushed hers. His tongue invaded her mouth and she received it greedily, desperate for the intoxicating sensation. She wanted to devour him, wanted him to devour her in return.

His hands cupped her jeans, and he ran his fingers over the curve of her buttocks. He slipped his hands under her loose shirt, his touch searing her bare skin. She gasped at his heat and he pulled her tighter against him. Her hands slid down his neck and she fumbled with the knotted cravat at his throat, finally wrenching it away to open the neck of his shirt. Breaking the seal of their kiss, she let her lips find the sensitive skin at the base of his throat. His head fell back and he groaned at the feel of her exploring tongue. Her mouth traveled lower, desperate for the taste of him. She pushed his jacket over his shoulders and he shrugged it off, letting it fall forgotten.

Frantic with a too long buried need, she struggled with his shirt, opening it to the waist. Her fingers ran over his exposed chest and she reveled in the firmly muscled expanse and the texture of crisply matted hair beneath her fingertips.

With one quick movement, he grasped the hem of her shirt and pulled it over her head. She wore the odd, white corsetlike undergarment she had had on when she'd arrived, and he drank in the sight of the creamy flesh rising above the filmy fabric, heaving beneath. He pulled her closer and his mouth traveled the valley between her breasts. A breathless moan escaped her and she clutched his head to her chest. His tongue traced the edge of the garment and she quivered beneath his lips.

"Here," she whispered and deftly unfastened the front closure of her bra, releasing her breasts to his plundering mouth. He lavished attention on each one in turn, taking one, then the other. He pulled, suckled, and teased until she thought she couldn't endure the exquisite pleasure another moment. Her hands grasped the shirt stretched taut across his back and her head fell forward.

Abruptly, he drew back and claimed her lips with his, hungry and demanding. She clung to him, her legs liquid, no longer able to provide support. He pulled her closer and she gasped at the sensation of his bare chest against her naked, sensitive breasts. His manhood beckoned through the fabric separating them. She strained her hips forward to meet his. Lost in a fog of sensual anticipation, she existed only in the touch of his hands, the taste of his skin, the heat of his body pressed to hers.

Together they sank to their knees, mouths still engaged in a frenzy of taste and touch. Her arms wrapped around his neck. His hands traveled across her hips and stomach, finding the juncture of her thighs. She groaned at the pressure of his touch through the denim of her jeans and moved rhythmically against his hand. He stopped and she shuddered, grasping him convulsively. He found the waistband of her jeans and struggled with the button, finally ripping it off in a haze of unrelenting desire. Impatiently, he pushed the zipper open and slid the pants down her hips.

His hand circled the tender flesh of her stomach and trailed to the curls between her thighs. He explored the soft, moist folds of skin beyond and found the point of her passion. His fingers toyed and played until she nearly wept from wanting him.

"Oh, Adam, now, please," she cried, frantically clutching him closer.

He eased her back on the plush carpet and stood, tearing off his clothes. She wiggled out of her jeans and waited impatiently. He towered above her and for a moment she thought how very much she loved him. Then he was there, filling her with the essence of his being.

"Maggie," he said with a groan. Her warm, moist body enveloped him, and Adam thought he had never known such intensity, such pleasure, such perfection. The fire, the fury, and the passion of this woman were his and he wanted nothing more than to take her to heights he had never suspected possible. Until now.

She wrapped her legs around his and strained against his thrusting strength. They moved in the rhythm of the ages, faster and higher to a place she never dreamed existed, never imagined could be reached. Together they climbed where surely no one had been before until ultimately he shuddered convulsively against her and she screamed softly as the world exploded around them.

Adam propped himself on one elbow. His gaze drifted lazily over the naked woman beside him. A smile played across his lips and he drank in the sight of her. Disheveled hair framed her flushed face, her lips parting slightly as she breathed. Her eyes were closed and long dark lashes delicately brushed her cheek.

When had he lost control of his life? Was it when Maggie had tried to strike him? When Lydia openly defied him? Or was it much sooner? The night he found Maggie crumpled at his feet perhaps? Somehow the answers no longer interested him. The only thing interesting him at all was her.

The intensity of their lovemaking shocked him. He never knew it could be quite so remarkable, quite so consuming. She unleashed passions in him he never dreamed existed. And now, lying here, studying her, tenderness and peace filled him. He wanted to take her in his arms and hold her close, always. He wanted to protect her, care for her. Before today, he thought she merely suited him. But it was far more than that. With her he was complete. Fulfilled. Whole.

He had asked himself once before if this was love. Now he knew.

Desire rose once again within him. He trailed his fingers lightly down the valley between her breasts and traced a circle on her stomach. Her eyes fluttered open and she gave him a contented smile. Pleased, he noted her eyes were still a deep, forest green.

"Do you really think I have the manners and mouth of a guttersnipe?"

He reached over and brushed his lips against hers. "You have a lovely mouth." His lips moved to her ear. "And wonderful ears." His mouth traveled to her neck. "And a truly superb throat."

His tongue drifted lower and delight shivered through her. "You realize we're lying here on the rug stark naked?" She struggled to keep her thoughts together. He shifted to a position over her, his tongue now teasing her breasts.

"I had noticed that," he murmured and continued his exploration.

"What about the servants?" Breathing grew difficult.

His mouth caressed her stomach, his tongue tracing intricate patterns. "They won't come in if the door is closed." His words fluttered against her bare body.

"But what . . . ?" Her voice was barely a whisper.

"Don't you ever stop talking?" He growled out the words softly, his mouth still nuzzling her belly. She willingly gave up and lost herself to the exquisite sensations he created.

He lifted his head and gazed up at her. "You do realize this changes everything?"

She sighed in agreement and he returned to the task at hand.

His hands gently caressed her inner thighs and her legs fell open. His fingers stroked the quivering folds of flesh and she moaned with the sheer enjoyment of his knowledgeable touch. A throbbing built deep within her and she wondered vaguely if he could feel it, too.

His tongue flicked the focal point of her pleasure and she gasped at the amazing sensation. She tensed at the new intimacy. A glimmer of apprehension tore her mind from the remarkable feeling.

"Adam." She gasped out the words cautiously. "I don't know . . ."

"Hush, my love."

She surrendered completely. All possibility of coherent thought fled and she spiraled in a whirlpool of erotic indulgence. She writhed uncontrollably, her nails digging into the carpet beneath her, des-

Victoria Alexander

perate to escape the sweet, sinful torture. More desperate not to.

Flashes of blinding, hot pleasure surged into every crevice of her being until she wept with desire and whimpered for release. Adam's hands, lips, tongue explored every surface of her body, and every nerve screamed with the flaring heat.

Over and over he brought her to the brink of mindless ecstasy. Over and over he held her back. She grasped his shoulders. Primordial pressure built deeper, higher, and she moaned in mindless wonder.

Sensing her complete arousal, Adam could no longer contain his own rampaging need. His throbbing, pulsating manhood bored into the hot, wet oblivion of her. He groaned, submersed in the sensation of their joining and swept away once again on a timeless wave of passion.

She wrapped her legs around his hips and instinctively matched her movements to his, countered his thrusts with hers, molded her body to his own. She arched her back, frantic for every contact, every movement a new pinnacle of excitement. His lips crushed hers and their hard, rasping breaths crashed and collided. She demanded and devoured. He filled her insistent body with a fierce intensity he never dreamed existed.

Together they soared to unbelievable heights where their very souls joined. Bonded. Merged into one. Where they crossed the border that separated one life from another. Where neither knew where one left off and the other began. Until finally, forged by flames of passion and fired by blazing desire, an inferno of ecstasy erupted within them. Their bodies shuddered and shook and they clung desperately to each other.

And Maggie knew no matter what else might happen, this was meant to be. Fated as surely as night follows day. As certain as the seasons.

As inevitable as time itself.

Maggie lay on her side, Adam's body molded around hers. She marveled at the way they seemed to fit together so perfectly, as if one body was made with the other in mind. She sighed in lethargic contentment and snuggled deeper into his arms. A kiss tickled her ear.

"I could stay like this always," Adam said.

Twisting, she turned to face him and snaked her arms around his neck. "Really?" She brushed her lips across his. "I was under the distinct impression I drove you crazy."

"You do." His eyes twinkled. "But I find I am beginning to enjoy the ride."

She laughed with delight and her gaze locked with his. Almost imperceptibly, his eyes sobered.

"Maggie." He pronounced her name slowly as if choosing his words carefully. "Tell me about him. About the man you loved."

"What man?" She stared, puzzled. "What are you talking about?"

"The man who took . . . the man you gave—damnation, I don't know how to ask this." In his eyes she read frustration and something she couldn't quite define.

Realization struck her and she wasn't sure if she should be amused or annoyed. Embarrassment min-

gled with concern on the face of the normally un-
flappable Earl of Ridgewood and warned her to take
his question seriously. The tender way he held her
took the edge off any conclusions he might make
about her character.

"Coleridge," she began gently, "are you saying you
noticed I'm not a virgin?"

He nodded silently. She studied his face for a moment. "Does it matter?"

Maggie held her breath, surprised to find his answer would matter quite a bit. Her gaze probed his
and the pause before he spoke seemed to last a lifetime.

"No." He answered with the firmness of a man who
had come to a decision and found it correct. "I understand the standards of your time are different
from the standards of mine. And I accept that." The
look in his eyes softened and his voice was gentle. "It
is jealousy, I fear. I find myself in a rage that any
other man has known you like this."

She stared and thought surely he could see her
love for him shining in her eyes. "Adam," she whispered, "no one has ever been with me like this before."

Propping herself up on one elbow, Maggie locked
her gaze with his. She studied him a moment, then
plunged ahead. "I've slept with two other men. One
in college, one a couple of years ago. Both times I
thought I was in love." She shrugged awkwardly.
"Both times I was wrong. In my day, it's very unusual
for a woman of my age to be a virgin. In fact," she
said wryly, "it's unusual for any adult woman to be
a virgin."

"And men do not mind?"

"I don't think so." She reflected for a moment, then grinned. "If they did, I think they could easily prevent the problem. Don't you?" She gazed at him innocently. He laughed aloud at her expression and tried to pull her close.

"Your turn."

"As you wish." He sighed solemnly. "I am not a virgin, either."

"Adam!" She laughed and swatted playfully at him. "Knock it off, I'm being serious." He plastered a somber expression on his face but the twinkle in his eye gave him away. She pretended not to notice. "Lydia told me you almost got married once. What happened?"

Adam shrugged, his demeanor now serious. Had she struck a nerve? Maybe this was a question better off not asked.

"In my youth, I was not quite as . . ." He hesitated as if searching for a word.

"Stuffy?" she said, smiling impishly.

He gave her a quelling glare. "I would prefer self-controlled. At any rate, I gave my affections quite freely—"

"So I've heard," she said wryly.

He ignored the interruption. "There was a young woman whose family took my flirtations far more seriously than intended. I never thought she did, although sometimes I wonder. . . ." He paused as if remembering. "I do not think I singled her out particularly. I was no more attentive to her than to anyone else. Nonetheless, there was speculation that we would wed, gossip I paid no heed to."

219

Maggie gazed at him curiously. "So what happened?"

A shadow crossed Adam's eyes. "My father died. I needed time to myself. To sort out my life. Afterward I learned she, too, had died. A carriage accident, I believe."

He shrugged matter-of-factly. "I was sorry, of course. But I had no serious feelings or intentions toward her. I don't believe she had any toward me. Our marrying was a mere figment of gossip and rumor."

Maggie reached out to lightly trace the line of his jaw with her fingers. "I'm glad you aren't married now."

He caught her hand and drew it to his lips. Adam gazed into her eyes and whispered against her palm, "So am I, Maggie, so am I."

The clock in the hall sounded the hour.

"Bloody hell!" Adam leapt to his feet. He reached his hand down, grasped hers, and pulled her up to join him.

"What is it?" she said breathlessly.

"Six o'clock." He found her jeans and shirt and tossed them to her. He muttered and pulled his own clothes on. "Six o'clock. Servants will be throughout the house within minutes if they aren't already. Here we are, stark naked." He stopped his tirade abruptly and glared at her.

She stood where he had pulled her to her feet, making no attempt to dress and grinning at his panicked expression.

"I thought you said the servants wouldn't come in here if the door was closed."

It was his turn to grin. "I lied."

She realized the implication of his words and her mouth dropped open. Then she, too, frantically dressed, wiggling into her jeans. "Damn," she muttered. "My button is missing."

"I must apologize for that," he said formally, then seemed to take notice of just how ridiculous such formality was, given the circumstances. It resembled a scene from a bad sitcom. Adam wore a shirt but his pants were little more than halfway on. Maggie had pulled her jeans up but the waist gaped where the button was missing and she had no shirt on at all. The absurdity of the situation struck them both at the same time. Adam's deep, rich tones matched the laughter bubbling through Maggie's lips. Within moments, they were once again in each other's arms, finding refuge from their uncontrollable mirth.

Adam kissed the tears of laughter from her cheeks and spoke with regret. "I wish we could stay here together all day. But we should both get some rest and I do have business to attend to today."

"I know." She sighed, pulled away from him, and pulled her shirt over her head. "Besides, I have a date this afternoon."

"A date?" A perplexed expression crossed his handsome face.

"Yeah, a date," she said lightly, looking under furniture for the mate to the tennis shoe in her hand. "You know. An appointment, an engagement."

"What kind of engagement?"

"A ride in the park." Intent on her search, Maggie paid no attention to the steely tone in Adam's voice. Her muffled voice came from a direction about halfway under the sofa. "With Edward Lindley. Here, gotcha." Triumphantly holding the errant shoe high, she stopped short at Adam's cold, hard expression.

"What is it? What's wrong?" Concerned, her gaze searched his face.

"You will not drive in the park with Lindley today or any other day."

"What?" Amazement rang in her voice. "Why on earth not?"

Adam stared at her, a dozen reasons running through his mind. *Because I love you. Because I want to marry you. Because the thought of another man anywhere near you drives me insane.* But he had not yet declared himself and hesitated to do so now. She reacted to him with unbridled passion, but was it love on her part? Adam Coleridge had little to fear from any man, but the answer to that question from this slip of a woman tightened a vise of apprehension around his heart.

"Because." His tones were hardened steel, what Maggie called his lord-of-the-manor voice. "I said you will not, that's why."

Astonished, Maggie stared. Was this the same funny, loving man she'd been with all morning? Indignation swept aside her tender feelings.

"That's a load of bull, Coleridge." She threw her shoulders back and looked him directly in the eyes, her gaze as icy as she could make it. "We've gone over this before. Read my lips."

She ticked off the points on her fingers. "One, I am not a woman of your time and I refuse to be treated like one. Two, I am not a possession, not an object. Three, I do not belong to you or any man and I do

222

not need to be taken care of. Four, I am not your responsibility and five and six and seven and eight— I do not take orders from you. I'll see anyone I damn well please!"

Her glare tangled with his, and her eyes flared a challenge he'd be hard-pressed to miss. "Give me one good reason why I shouldn't go on an innocent little carriage ride."

Say something. Tell me this meant more to you than a one-night stand. Tell me you care about me. I love you. Say something to make me stay.

"I . . . am . . . ordering you . . . not to go."

Her heart plummeted. If he had only asked instead of ordered. If he cared about her even a little, he would have taken her feelings into consideration. Wouldn't he? He knew full well she wouldn't respond to his ridiculous order. It was obvious that any illusions she harbored about what she meant to him were just that. Illusions. Illusions fostered when he seemed to meld with her inner being, touch her very soul. Illusions she now knew were as evasive as gossamer and just as unsubstantial.

"Wrong answer, pal." She snatched up her cloak and, shoes in her hand, marched to the door. She managed to fling it open and glanced back at him. He loomed in the center of the room, fists clenched by his sides. A muscle in his tightly clamped jaw twitched, and fury smoldered in his dark, bottomless eyes. He'd never looked so angry or so magnificent. A golden god of war.

Her throat ached unbearably. If she didn't get out of there now she'd run back into his arms, willing to give up her principles and her pride to be with him.

She marshaled every ounce of self-control she possessed to resist the temptation, but surrendered to the impulse to let him know exactly what he'd thrown away.

"I told you every other time I've slept with someone, I thought I was in love. I thought so this time, too. Obviously I was wrong. Again."

She swept out of the room without a backward glance.

Adam stared at the closed door and tried to digest her parting shot. *I thought so this time, too.* The words echoed in his mind. *I thought I was in love.*

She thought she was in love? With him? She loved him?

She loved him.

A broad grin split his face and he wanted to yell for the sheer joy of it. Of course she loved him. How could she not? Granted, they clashed at every turn, but when they meshed it was magnificent. He had never been so alive and vibrant in his life as when he was with her. Surely her passionate responses, not just while lovemaking but in every other encounter as well, indicated she had the same reactions to him.

She loved him!

He continued to dress, grinning like an ass, but he didn't care. Nothing mattered but that one unbelievable fact. Certainly Maggie was angry with him now, but they could resolve their differences. He truly believed love could indeed conquer all. The admission surprised him. His soul had far more romance in it than even he had ever suspected.

He would allow Maggie her little jaunt in the park with Lindley. After all, he had nothing to fear.

She was his, body and soul.

She loved him.

He cast a quick glance around the library and noticed her odd undergarments lying halfway beneath the desk. In one deft movement, he swept them up and discreetly stuffed them under his jacket. With a jaunty step, he swaggered out of the library, through the foyer, and up the stairs. A voice inside warned him to wipe that silly grin off his face before the servants noticed but right now Adam didn't care if a houseful of hirelings or the entire world knew.

Miss Margaret Melissa Masterson loved him, and at this moment in the year of our Lord eighteen hundred and eighteen, that made him the happiest man on the face of the earth.

Maggie was miserable.

She lay curled in a ball on her bed, tears rolling down her cheeks. Disgusted, she swiped at them. She'd cried more here than she had in her entire adult life. What was the matter with her anyway? She wasn't usually such a wimp.

Okay, so she'd been flung through time for some unknown reason. So she ended up in an era she knew practically nothing about and had to watch every word she said. So she had to lie about who she really was and where she came from. And then to top it off, she went and fell in love with a nineteenth-century sexist. Was that any reason to cry?

Damn straight.

This was turning out to be a pretty crummy vacation after all. It was April twenty-first, her ninth day here. If her theory was correct, and she'd leave on the twelfth of May—21 days left. Three full weeks to deal with Adam or avoid him. Three long weeks to continue this weird charade. Three brief weeks to get over loving a man who saw her only as a possession and a problem.

She sniffed and wiped her nose impatiently with the back of her hand. Damn! When did they invent Kleenex anyway? Wallowing in self-pity would get her nowhere fast. There was nothing she could do about being here and nothing she could do about Adam.

Her unhappiness was as much her fault as his. He was only interested in getting her into bed, or in this case, on the floor. The session with Shakespeare told her that. She had no one to blame but herself for reading too much into making love this morning. The facts were there. She had to face them and deal with them. Period.

She tried to attribute her tears to exhaustion. The predawn ride and the session in the library had taken their toll. What she really needed now was sleep. Later she'd consider how to survive the upcoming few weeks. For the moment she'd escape her problems in blissful slumber. After all, in a few hours she had a date. One she'd very likely paid a big price for. And there was no way in hell she was going to miss it.

Chapter Twelve

A bouquet of wilted posies had more life than Maggie, at least by the looks of her. She definitely drooped.

Lydia sighed with exasperation and eyed Maggie trooping languidly down the stairs. She did not appear at all like someone about to go off for a drive with an eager suitor. Lydia narrowed her eyes in speculation. What happened after she left the library? Did Maggie and Adam do battle? And if they did, who won? By the looks of her, not Maggie.

Oh, she was as pretty as ever. Her deep blue dress set off her reddish hair nicely, the style complementing her figure. But in an unguarded moment Lydia caught a glimpse of sheer misery in Maggie's eyes.

Lydia greeted her at the door to the green-and-gold salon with a barrage of questions. "What on earth happened this morning? What did Adam say?" Lydia's brow arched in inquiry. "What did you do?"

"Nothing." Maggie walked to a settee and settled herself gracefully. "Absolutely nothing."

Lydia's mouth dropped open in disbelief. "He didn't lecture you? He didn't renew his threat to send us off to the country? He didn't do anything?"

"Nothing worth mentioning." Maggie calmly pulled on a pair of gloves. "I don't want to talk about Adam anymore."

"But surely he—"

"No more." Maggie's sharp tone and firm, direct look took Lydia by surprise. She sank into a chair, nodding in stunned resignation.

"Thank you." Maggie's voice softened. She picked up her hat and tied it over her hair. "Is Edward here yet?"

"I don't believe so." Lydia wondered at Maggie's strange behavior. What had happened in the library? What on earth did Adam do to her? And why did she refuse to discuss it?"

"Lady Lydia, Miss Masterson." Wilson interrupted her musings. "Lord Lindley has arrived." The butler stepped aside to allow Lord Lindley to enter the room.

He looked at Maggie and his eyes lit up. Maggie at once became gracious and charming, any problems either forgotten or at least well hidden. He was at Maggie's side in an instant, bowing over her hand. She actually seemed to encourage him. Considering her understandable reluctance to go in the first place, it was all very odd.

"Lydia, you remember Lord Lindley?" Maggie turned to her friend.

"Of course. How are you?" Lydia extended her hand. She, too, could be gracious and charming when the need arose.

"Lady Lydia." Lindley's lips brushed her hand. His surprised gaze met hers. "You are not driving today? Would you care to accompany us?"

"How very kind of you to ask, but I have other matters to attend to." She tilted her head and glanced up at him in a practiced pose. "Will we see you tomorrow at Lord and Lady Ainsworth's soiree?"

"It's highly probable." His eyes twinkled at her, then searched out Maggie. "If you and your cousin will be there, then surely I will be in attendance as well."

"I see," Lydia murmured and withdrew her hand.

"Miss Masterson, shall we?" Lindley offered Maggie his arm and she accepted.

"See you later, Lydia," Maggie tossed over her shoulder. She and Lindley walked through the foyer and Lydia listened to her light banter and Lindley's appreciative chuckle.

Lydia folded her arms over her chest and leaned against the salon doorway, eyeing the departing couple. It was not a proper pose for a young woman but Lydia's thoughts were not confined to those of a proper young woman anyway.

Lindley was charming and handsome, all any woman could ask for. Lydia's standards were high and discriminating, and even she could see his undeniable appeal. If Adam didn't take care he would lose Maggie. And it would serve him right.

Annoyed, Lydia shook her head. She no longer understood either her brother or Maggie. For two people so obviously attracted to each other, they seemed to be doing all they could to make each other miserable. It was Adam's fault, no doubt. Her lips compressed in a firm line. This situation was ridiculous and it was past time she took matters in hand. Connor would help. Connor would do anything for her. After all, they were better than lovers.

They were friends.

It was no longer a question of using Maggie to help avoid marriage. Now it was a matter of her brother's happiness. The more he and Maggie raged at each other, the more it convinced Lydia that his happiness did indeed lie with her. She had not seen Adam alive in years. Now if she could just get through to him. Where was he anyway?

"Adam," she called imperiously and headed for the library. She wanted to know what happened last night and she wanted to know immediately. More important, she wanted to know what he planned to do about it. If she were clever, maybe she could get him to admit he saw Maggie as more than just an intrusion on his well-ordered life. If Lydia's plans worked out, she would be.

Maggie glanced around curiously from the rather impressive height of Lord Lindley's carriage. He drove with a natural ease. Growing confident in his skill and ability with the reins, she relaxed her death grip on the seat beneath her. She still preferred a nice Mustang convertible, but right here and now, an open-topped carriage was obviously the next best thing.

"Miss Masterson," Lindley said, "I am extremely

pleased you decided to join me. I feared when I arrived you would have begged off."

"Please call me Maggie. Miss Masterson is way too formal." She gave him an encouraging smile and noted with satisfaction the light in his eyes. "Why did you think I wouldn't show up?"

He shrugged. "Ridgewood has seemed extremely protective and I thought perhaps he might forbid you to accompany me."

"Who?" Puzzled, Maggie stared; then understanding dawned. "Oh, you mean Coleridge. I never will get used to how everyone uses titles here instead of names. I call him Coleridge." She narrowed her eyes. "And he has nothing to say about what I do or do not do." A cold note sounded in her voice. "I'm not his responsibility, and I don't have to ask his permission to go for a ride in the park or anything else."

"But he is your only male relation here." Lindley's face expressed his surprise. "As head of your family, it is only natural he make decisions regarding your activities. You are under his protection."

"That's not how it's done in my ti—" Maggie caught herself "—in my country. And I'm not about to put up with that attitude here." She looked straight in his eyes. "Lord Lindley—"

"Edward," he said.

"Edward. I'm used to having a great deal of freedom and to making my own decisions about every aspect of my life. Up to and including who I dance with and who I ride in the park with. If Adam Coleridge doesn't like it, that's his problem. Do I make myself clear?"

He stared at her with obvious admiration. "Perfectly."

She threw him an impish grin. "I gather women in England aren't as outspoken as I am?"

His smile warmed his eyes. "I was going to use the words free-spirited and independent." His attention turned briefly to a passing carriage and he nodded a quick greeting. "I daresay Ridgewood doesn't seem like the type of man to take your attitudes in stride," he said casually. "I don't know him well, but he has always struck me as a man in control of his life. He seems very precise and demanding, even cold and somewhat aloof."

Maggie mulled over his words and chose her response carefully. She owed a certain amount of loyalty to Adam despite their problems. "When I first arrived, that's exactly how he struck me. But to be honest, he's been very kind, thoughtful, and generous. He's shown me a great deal of hospitality. He's made me feel at home as much as possible and I appreciate it."

Edward frowned, obviously puzzled. "But you are family."

She laughed lightly. "Distant, very distant. And I showed up without any advance warning. So"—she shrugged—"I'm really lucky he welcomed me as warmly as he has.

"Now, I'm sure there are far more interesting things to talk about than Adam Coleridge." She aimed her most provocative smile at him. "Tell me what I should see in this fascinating city of yours while I'm here."

Maggie forced a look of rapt attention to her face

and tried to focus on Edward's conversation, but thoughts of Adam kept creeping into her mind. Firmly she pushed him away, determined to give Edward her complete attention. He really was extremely nice and quite handsome as well as charming company. The only thing wrong was that he wasn't the man she longed for.

He wasn't Adam.

The scene looked much the same as at the first ball Maggie attended. This ballroom glittered as brilliantly. The dancers sweeping over the floor were as skilled. The women were as beautifully attired, the men as impeccably dressed. But it all seemed somehow tarnished. Maybe she was growing immune to the spectacle that once captured her imagination.

At the last ball she'd entered on Adam's arm, filled with the excitement of his presence and anticipation of the evening to come. Tonight she forced herself simply to be here.

She squared her shoulders and, taking a deep breath, surveyed the room spread before her. Yesterday's drive with Edward bolstered her confidence. Even without Adam she could probably hold her own. Her appearance in the deeply low-cut gown added an extra measure of courage.

After a night of little sleep interrupted by turbulent dreams, she decided once again to make the best of her stay here. With Lydia's encouragement, this party seemed like the most appropriate place to start.

Maggie hadn't seen Adam since she stalked out of

the library yesterday morning. When she returned from her drive with Edward, Lydia told her Adam had been called away unexpectedly to one of the estates and wouldn't return home until tomorrow morning.

If he got bent out of shape over a simple carriage ride, how much more irritated would he be to discover she was not only attending this soiree, but planned to waltz with anyone and everyone who asked? He didn't have the right to run her life or issue orders. The sooner he figured it out, the better.

Maggie's anger over his tyrannical attitude steadily gained ground on her heartache. She was determined to ignore the knot in her chest and the lump in her throat and have a good time. No . . . make that a great time.

"I have been counting the moments until your arrival."

A smiling Edward stood at her elbow with an offering of champagne in his hand. His sky-blue eyes sparkled in his handsome face and her spirits lifted.

"Why, thank you. This"—she accepted the champagne and lifted the glass in a mock salute—"and you are exactly what I need right now."

"Ah, Maggie." He placed his hand over his heart and sighed dramatically. "I fear you shall break my heart before this evening is over."

His declaration threw her for a moment. He wasn't serious, was he? Sure, Edward could help her get over Adam, but she had no desire to hurt him. A twinkle danced in his eyes and she laughed in relief.

"Edward, you're a terrific actor."

"Am I?" He caught her gloved hand with his, and

swiftly lifted it to his mouth. Brushing his lips across the back, he gazed deeply into her eyes. "Are you certain of that?"

She let a smile linger on her lips and glanced at him in her most flirtatious manner. As long as her heart wasn't involved, she could play this game of verbal fencing. Play it and win.

"Where I'm from, there's an old saying: Never say never. Frankly, here I'm certain of nothing, but it's a risk I'm willing to take." She tossed her head back and caught his gaze with hers. "Are you?"

His eyebrows lifted in an expression of mild surprise and appreciation. "You are definitely an original. I wonder, are your actions as intriguing as your manner?"

"Edward." She laughed. "That's for me to know and you to find out."

A startled expression flashed across his face at the unfamiliar phrase and he stared at her curiously. She sipped her champagne and returned his gaze over the edge of her glass with her best innocent air. Abruptly he grinned.

"What a delightful proposition." He nodded toward the dance floor. "They are playing a waltz. I believe this is our dance."

"You bet." She downed the last of her drink and handed the empty glass to a passing waiter. Maggie offered Edward her hand. "I'm all yours."

He led her to the floor. "Not yet, my dear," he murmured softly under his breath. "Not yet."

Her startled gaze flew to his and she noted a fair amount of satisfaction on his face. Her flirting hadn't gone too far, had it? That was silly. She brushed the thought away. This was harmless party talk. It meant nothing and Edward wouldn't take it seriously. Besides, she wouldn't be here long enough to really break any hearts.

Flying across the floor in Edward's arms, losing herself in the sensation of the dance, she agreed with Lydia. Tonight was exactly what she needed. There was nothing like a good party and an interesting man to heal a broken heart.

Maggie danced off with Edward, and Lydia nodded with approval. That should keep her guest occupied for a while. Now if she could just find Connor . . . She scanned the crowded ballroom. Lydia tapped her foot impatiently. She had sent him a note requesting he meet her here. It would be just like Connor to ignore her summons, to go blithely about his business at the very moment she needed him most. If she wasn't quite certain he was the only one who would consider helping her, she would simply find someone else. But there was no one in the world she trusted as completely as she did Connor. Even though he was never as prompt as she wished.

"Have you given up on me yet?" Busy searching one side of the ballroom Lydia didn't notice his approach from the other direction. Surprised, she found him standing right next to her.

"Well, it's high time you put in an appearance," she snapped. "Where on earth have you been?"

Connor raised an eyebrow condescendingly. "Lydia, my love. Do not chastise me if you want to secure my help. Now apologize."

She threw him a withering glare. "Fine. I apologize."

He lifted her chin with one bronzed finger and smiled into her eyes. "Say it like you truly mean it, Lydia."

She glared at him for a moment, then burst into laughter. "I give up, you win." She gave him an apologetic smile. "I am sorry, but I am counting on your help. And I must admit, I am a bit nervous about pulling it all off."

"Pulling what off?" His brows drew together in a cautious frown. He had been involved in Lydia's escapades before, but it had been years since the last fiasco. "What devilish plot have you concocted this time?"

"It's really not all that devilish," she said defensively. "And it's for a very good purpose. Actually"— she grinned with pride—"it's extremely clever."

"Lydia." Connor groaned. "Through our entire lives, from the time we were children together, whenever you have gotten that look in your eye, inevitably you escaped with a mild reprimand and I was flogged. Aren't we too old for your schemes?"

"Connor." She chastised him with a glance. "I shall never be too old. But if, however, you are not up to helping me . . ." Her voice drifted off, leaving an unspoken threat in the air.

"If I refuse to help you"—his words were sharp— "will you give up this plan, whatever it is?"

Lydia gazed up at him with all the sweetness and innocence she could muster and answered softly, "Absolutely not."

He groaned again. "We are no longer children,

Lydia. Your schemes are not as harmless and charming as they once were."

"I agree." She sighed. "The stakes are much higher now."

Connor stared for a moment, then threw his hands in the air in a gesture of defeat. "I am at your mercy. What fiendish plot have you come up with this time?"

"Connor," she chided gently. "Don't raise your voice. Let's go out and find a nice quiet spot in the garden where we can talk privately."

She took his arm and ushered him across the room. Connor would help her. He always had. She only wished he would get that grim look off his face, that look of a condemned man being led to his own execution. With Connor's help nothing could go wrong. Lydia absolutely refused to consider the repercussions if, just possibly, something did.

Connor's mouth dropped open in obvious disbelief. If he wasn't so attractive, he would surely resemble nothing so much as a startled goldfish. Lydia returned his gaze with all the natural serenity at her disposal.

"You know what you are proposing borders on the insane and is most probably criminal?" He leaned forward on the garden bench beside her.

"Very likely," Lydia said lightly.

"Does that not concern you?" He was plainly astounded by her plan and she suspected it was not the cleverness that impressed him.

She gazed directly into his eyes and favored him with a Madonna-like smile. "Not at all."

"Bloody hell, Lydia." Connor leapt to his feet and paced to and fro before her in the secluded garden alcove. "Let me be certain I understand this grand scheme of yours. You propose to have Maggie, this woman you are convinced is perfect for Adam, kidnapped so that he can save her. During all this, he will realize he loves her and she will realize she loves him. Correct?"

"Exactly." Pleased he caught on so quickly, Lydia nodded. She wished he would sit down, though. She never realized how tall he really was until he towered over her like this. It put her at a distinct disadvantage.

"Lydia." He groaned and granted her unspoken wish by sinking onto the bench next to her. "I don't believe you have thought this through. How is this kidnapping to proceed?"

"That's where you come in."

"Somehow I suspected as much," he said under his breath.

She ignored him and continued her explanation. "You will provide me with two of your men. I will let them in the back way and make sure Maggie is alone in . . . oh . . . let me think, the library will do. Then they simply kidnap her."

"And how precisely do they accomplish that little feat?" He leaned back, pinning her with his direct look, sarcasm in his tone. "I don't imagine your Maggie shall simply go along with all this."

"I have given that a great deal of thought." Lydia leaned forward eagerly. "I considered laudanum or something to render her unconscious but the aftereffects would be too unpleasant."

"Wise decision." The sarcasm lingered. "It would spoil the effect to accidentally kill her."

"Exactly." She nodded in agreement. "Then I thought about having her bashed over the head. But Connor"—she gazed at him innocently—"I don't want to actually cause her any harm."

"You plan on terrifying this woman by kidnapping her, but you don't want to do her any harm?" An incredulous expression stretched across his face.

"Of course not." Mildly annoyed at his lack of understanding of the finer points of her plan, Lydia drew a deep breath and forced herself to pay no mind to his obvious reluctance. "It seems to me the best way is to threaten her with a gun, tie her up, and put her in a bag."

"Tie her up and put her in a bag? Like a trussed-up partridge? This is what you've come up with? What you expect me to help you accomplish?" He glared at her. "And once we get her in this bag, what do you propose to do with her?"

"I've taken care of that." Lydia spoke proudly. "There is a little inn right outside of the city, scarcely one hour from my house. The Lion's Mane, I believe. I have passed it on my way to the country countless times. We simply have her locked in a private room there to await rescue by Adam. Did I mention the kidnappers shall leave a note asking for Adam to bring a ransom?"

Connor shook his head, looking rather dazed as the full impact of her scheme unfolded.

"No? Well, that is an important point. The way I see this, Adam will discover the kidnapping within an hour or so after Maggie is taken. Thereby ensuring she shan't stay at the inn very long. Adam will arrive, frantic with fear that she has come to harm. Maggie shall be eternally grateful to be saved. Both will come to their senses and realize how much they truly mean to each other." Lydia grinned with satisfaction and triumph.

Connor shook his head slowly. "I will not do it. I will not be a part of this ill-fated plot."

"Of course you will, Connor." Lydia gazed at him with utmost confidence.

Suspicion darkened his expressive eyes. "Why are you so certain?"

"Because, my love, if you do not I shall simply hire men to do this for me. That would be far more dangerous, far more likely something would go wrong. We both know I shall do this with or without your help."

Connor had the look of a man trapped, desperate for any means of escape, a man grasping at straws. "I don't have a gun to use for this kind of thing. I only have dueling pistols."

"I have a gun," Lydia said lightly.

"What?" Genuine shock showed in his face. "Where in the name of all that's holy did you get a gun?"

"It scarcely matters." She flicked the question away with a snap of her fan. "I shall make sure it isn't loaded."

"Excellent idea." Sarcasm surfaced again but Lydia overlooked it to get his cooperation.

"So is it all arranged then?" she asked sweetly.

"No! I don't have any rope. And where will I get a bag?"

"Connor." She sighed patiently. "I will be more than happy to procure the rope and the bag. I will provide the gun. I will even write the ransom note. Although"—she paused to consider this detail—"Adam does know my handwriting, so I shall have to disguise it. All you have to do is provide the kidnappers themselves. I will meet them in the garden around . . . oh . . . ten o'clock tomorrow night."

"Lydia." Connor took her hands in his and gazed into her eyes. "Have you thought about her reputation? She could be ruined by this."

"Oh, my." Lydia started with real surprise. "I had not considered that at all." She pulled her brows together thoughtfully, then brightened. "We shall simply have to make sure no one hears about it. Besides, Maggie doesn't care one whit about her reputation." She widened her eyes as a thought struck her. "But that might be the perfect solution. If her reputation was at stake, Adam would feel honor-bound to marry her. Oh, Connor, what a wonderful idea."

Connor sighed heavily, a sure sign of Lydia's success. Not only had Connor failed to thwart her plan, he had provided another good reason to carry it through.

"Adam will call me out if he discovers your little plan, and I can't say I should blame him."

"Then he must not find out the truth." She stood and pulled Connor to his feet. He truly was a wonderful man. Something of a rake but a good, true friend. If she had been smart enough to fall in love with Connor years ago when she probably should have, she'd be married and settled by now. Instead of doing her best to avoid wedded bliss.

"I think, Connor, you should meet Maggie." She cocked her head and gazed up at him with an impish grin. "Just so you will know what to expect."

Connor groaned as she led him back toward the ballroom. "Adam is right, Lydia. You do need a husband."

Chapter Thirteen

"Maggie, this is Lord St. Clair, Connor, a very old, very dear friend of Adam's and mine. Connor, may I present Miss Margaret Masterson, a distant relative."

Maggie pulled her attention from the crowd of admirers she was trying to charm. She looked up at a man at least as tall as Adam and as different physically from him as night from day. Where Adam's hair resembled burnished sunshine, St. Clair's took the appearance of the other end of the clock, black as midnight, and intense blue eyes so deep they appeared almost navy. He had a polished look about him that screamed superiority and a smug, aloof attitude. Adam's attitude. Maggie took an immediate dislike to him.

Until he smiled. It crinkled the edges of his eyes and put a twinkle in their center. Again she wondered if men had lost something in the years between this time and hers or if she was simply lucky enough to meet all the great-looking guys here.

"Connor, please be charming and attentive to Maggie," Lydia commanded. "I believe I see my next partner approaching. Call her Maggie; she's not terribly fond of formality. American, you know." Lydia greeted her partner and with a farewell nod swept off.

Maggie's gaze followed her departure and she leaned toward Connor. "Is she always like this?"

"Always." His gaze, too, fixed on the figure now dancing across the floor. "Lydia has been somewhat irrepressible her entire life. She goes merrily on her way, rarely giving heed to the possible consequences of her actions. And regardless how often those actions have sunk her deeply in trouble, she simply sees no reason to change." He turned toward Maggie with a sigh. "I must admit, most of the time, I, for one, would regret it if she did."

Maggie grinned up at him. "I love her, too."

"So Miss Masterson, Maggie?" She nodded. "You are a distant relation from America? How very odd. I have known the Coleridge family all my life and cannot recall the mention of American relatives."

Maggie maintained her serene expression. Every day it grew easier to deal with her fictional background. Other than the first embarrassing encounter, she hadn't found it necessary to mention Denver in Colorado County, Ohio, mythical haven for trees and bears, again. Her skills at deflecting specific questions had improved, and being American helped. Whenever she tripped up and used a distinctly twentieth-century phrase, she encouraged her listeners to attribute it to yet another odd idiosyncracy of Americans. She worked the superior British attitude regarding her countrymen to her advantage, even though it seemed vaguely unpatriotic.

"Oh, the connection is extremely distant," she said airily. "I suspect it was already half forgotten." It was time to turn the tables. "Lydia said you are very old friends?"

"Yes. My family's land is next to hers and we played together as children. Adam is five years older than I, so I was always tagging along after him. Lydia is four years younger, so she in turn tagged after me." He grinned at the memory. "Until, of course, she was forced into the mold of a proper young lady and learned the rules of proper behavior."

Maggie inclined her head at the dance floor skeptically. "That was years ago, you say?"

He laughed in response and she joined him. "I said learned them, not took them to heart." The shared laughter dissolved any lingering reservations. It wasn't hard to see why Lydia considered him a friend.

Connor raised an eyebrow inquisitively. "Is your next dance spoken for?"

"Unless it's a waltz, I'll have to pass."

"It is a waltz and I believe it's mine." Adam's voice cut in and Maggie whirled around. She ignored the frantic beating of her heart and flashed him her most withering glare. He smiled down at her, apparently quite at ease and more than a little confident.

"I don't think so, Coleridge," she said through clenched teeth.

Adam's head lowered until his nose nearly touched hers. She widened her eyes and smothered the impulse to step back. His dark eyes glittered dangerously. "Yesterday you said I should have made you listen to me. You shall listen now. You may join me on the relative privacy of the dance floor or we can remain here where virtually anyone can overhear us. Or"—he smirked wickedly—"we could go into the garden."

She gritted her teeth. "I would love to dance."

Connor narrowed his eyes appraisingly. Adam swept Maggie onto the dance floor. The scene before him was clear and a slow grin spread across his face. Adam definitely did not look like a man who needed to be convinced of his affection for anyone. In fact, it was apparent that Adam had gone well past the realization Lydia's scheme was expected to bring him to.

Relief flooded him. The idea of crossing Adam held no appeal. In spite of Adam's thoroughly proper and upright behavior in recent years, his reputation as an expert marksman on the dueling field still lingered.

Where was Lydia? Connor scanned the ballroom in a futile effort to locate her, then shrugged in resignation. It would do no harm to let her continue to make her plans. He would set her straight tomorrow night.

His mood considerably lighter, his grin widened. After all, tonight, he had an engagement with a pretty little actress he planned on getting to know quite well. And if he left now, the evening wouldn't be a total waste.

* * *

"Okay, Coleridge. Cut to the chase. What do you have to say?" Maggie glared up at him as they glided across the dance floor. She fit naturally in his arms. That fact was somehow annoying. Almost as much as the smug smile plastered on his face, a smile that widened to a grin whenever he gazed down at her.

"Ah, Maggie." He laughed. "I am beginning to find your language delightful. Even when I have no idea what you are saying, the sheer sound of your outrageous comments charms me."

Brows knit in confusion, Maggie stared. What was he up to? "What do you want?"

"What do I want?" he said. "Why, Maggie, I wish to apologize."

"Right." She snorted. "You're trying to tell me Adam Coleridge, the big deal, earl of something or other is going to admit he was wrong? Ha! Fat chance."

"That's exactly what I am going to admit." His expression sobered.

Sincerity rang in his voice. "I was wrong. I do not have the right to issue you orders, to tell you who you may see and what you may do." He gazed deeply into her eyes and Maggie's heart leapt to her throat at the emotion revealed there. "I can only offer as an excuse my upbringing and the times I live in, the undeniable jealousy I feel when another man is near you, as well as fears that are somewhat new to me. I fear someone else will discover how remarkable and unique you are. I fear you could love another. I fear I would lose you."

Maggie's mouth dropped open. Thoughts and emotions bombarded her. What was he saying?

What did he mean? Did he really care about her? Love her? Could she trust him?

She barely noticed the end of the dance despositing them near the door to the terrace. Adam hurried her outside. Swiftly leading her to a secluded corner, he pulled her into his arms.

"As for Shakespeare." His gaze searched hers. "I will admit I cultivated that talent for the sole purpose of seduction. But, Maggie"—the anxious light in his eyes told her, in spite of his past, right now he meant what he said. And right now she wanted to believe— "never have those words meant anything to me until I said them to you. Never have I known the love of Romeo and Juliet until I spoke their vows to you. It was a ploy years ago. With you it is real."

Maggie stared, stunned. Despite his initial appearance of confidence, an anxious question lingered in his eyes. He was as unsure of her response as she was.

A wry smile touched his lips. "I suspect I have for once left you speechless."

Maggie shook her head in confusion, pulled out of his arms, and backed away. Disbelief battled with hope. Doubt fought with joy. Skepticism clashed with wonder. She struggled to put her rampaging emotions into words.

"You've had me on an emotional roller coaster since the first moment we met." She impatiently waved away his quizzical look. "Roller coaster. It's a ride at an amusement park." She rubbed her forehead, frustrated. "Never mind. It just means I've been up and down, elated, depressed. In short—confused and off balance. I want to be very sure I understand exactly what you're saying."

He nodded encouragement. "Please continue."

"The Shakespeare business is something you came up with to seduce women, but with me you really meant it? Right?"

"Exactly."

Maggie spoke thoughtfully, choosing her words with care. "And unlike women of your time, I'm used to running my own life without interference or assistance from men and you now accept that." She narrowed her eyes in suspicion. "Also right?"

"Precisely." He grinned.

"I don't know, Coleridge." She shook her head slowly. She wanted desperately to believe him, longed to believe him. He offered a major concession here, abandoning much of what he'd accepted without question all his life because of her. But could she trust him? They were from two completely different worlds. Their ingrained values, covering virtually all aspects of their lives and societies, clashed at every turn.

She shrugged in uncertainty. "I just don't know."

Their eyes locked for a long, tense moment.

"I love you, Maggie," Adam said softly.

Astonishment froze Maggie, and her heart thudded in her chest. It took less than a second for Adam's words to strike her soul. Less than a second for her confusion and doubts to dissolve. Less than a second to throw herself into his arms.

"Adam, oh, Adam." She flung her arms around his neck and clung to him.

"Maggie." His lips descended, crushing hers beneath them. The frustration, anger, and pain of the last days broke under the elation of being back in Adam's arms, and Maggie didn't care what else happened.

"Oh, Adam. I love you, too." His lips covered her face, her neck, her throat, and she responded in kind, frantic for the taste of him.

"I know," he whispered.

"What?" She drew back and peered at him indignantly until finding the twinkle in his eye. "How did you know?"

He laughed. "You told me. You said you thought you were in love." He nuzzled her ear. "It was the most remarkable thing I'd ever heard."

Maggie cocked her head and grinned. "If I'd known, I would've said it a lot sooner."

"How much sooner?" He quirked a brow questioningly.

She sighed, resigning herself to complete surrender. "I've known since the night in the library. The one you and I and Shakespeare spent together."

He grinned wickedly. "I gather the technique is still effective then."

"Adam!" She tried to smack him with her fan but he deftly deflected the blow and responded by thoroughly kissing her. She melted against him, any further resistance dissolving on the night air.

"So," Maggie said, and drew a shaky breath when breathing was again possible. "When did you know?"

"Know what?"

"Know you loved me."

He gazed down at her with an expression that set her pulse pounding. "When I could not stay out of an unconscious woman's bedroom, I wondered.

251

When I discovered a new passion in words I knew by heart, I suspected. But when I held you in my arms and found a world I never dreamed possible, I knew." His eyes filled with such tenderness Maggie's senses reeled with the impact. She pulled his head down to meet hers and her lips met his again, gently at first, until greed heightened their demand.

Abruptly she drew back.

"Just tell me one more thing." She hesitated to ask but she had to know. "It's none of my business, really. And you can tell me so, but given your past, rather active love life and the whole Shakespeare business . . ." She paused, held her breath, and blurted the question. "How many other women have you said 'I love you' to?"

His eyes widened and his forehead furrowed in obvious surprise. "Why, none."

"Great." Relief filled her and she grinned. Could her heart really burst from such joy or did it only seem so at this incredible moment? She flung her arms around his neck and slanted him her most enticing glance. "Then take me home, Coleridge."

From his vantage point in a shadowed doorway he observed the tender scene and permitted himself a small smile. His assumptions were correct after all. In recent days, he had wondered if he wasn't mistaken about Ridgewood and the Masterson woman. If perhaps her outspoken ways and independent manner were distasteful to the cold, aloof earl. Now he could see he was right from the beginning, from the moment he first saw them together. This was what he had waited for, what he had planned for. Ridgewood loved this woman.

It was time.

Chapter Fourteen

Adam bounded out of the carriage before the steps were let down. Maggie breathed an unsteady sigh of relief at their arrival home. Locked in Adam's arms, the ride wasn't long but it seemed filled with anticipation and a fair amount of tension. Her head had nestled on his chest, his heart throbbing beneath her ear. Now that they had declared their love, everything should be perfect. So why was she unsure and hesitant, nervous and apprehensive?

Impatiently she tried to smother the feelings. It wasn't as if they hadn't already made love. As if tonight would be their first time. Still, as she reached out her hand for his assistance, it trembled.

Adam turned and her doubts vanished at the love and desire in his eyes. He pulled her into his arms and carried her toward the door.

"Adam!" She laughed.

"Shut up, Maggie." He grinned. At the base of the

steps he stopped and captured her gaze with his. "I want this night to be perfect."

Her breath caught in her throat. "It already is," she whispered.

He lightly kissed her forehead and strode up the steps. The door opened soundlessly and he carried her inside, nodding to a well-trained Wilson, who gave no indication it was at all out of the ordinary for the master to carry women into the house.

"Sprained ankle, Wilson," Adam muttered curtly.

"No doubt, milord." Wilson's composure remained unruffled. Only the gleam in his eye suggested he thought otherwise.

Maggie giggled and hid her face in Adam's jacket. Even with her in his arms, Adam took the stairs easily and continued down the hall to her room. Pushing open the door, he deposited her gently on her bed.

"Why, Adam Coleridge." She laughed up at him. "What about the servants? Is it proper and correct for you to be in here like this with me?"

Adam's expression grew thoughtful. "No, Maggie, you're right. It is most certainly not proper behavior." He turned and walked out of the room, shutting the door firmly behind him.

For a moment Maggie was too stunned to move. What was that all about? Who cared about proper behavior? Certainly not her. She leapt off the bed and raced after him. Grabbing the brass knob, she pulled. A noise sounded behind her and she whirled around. Adam leaned lazily against a doorway on the far side of the room. A door that, up till now, she'd assumed was some kind of closet.

"What's in there?" She gasped.

"My chamber." A grin stretched across his face. His dimple flashed seductively and a wicked gleam settled in his eyes. He sauntered toward her.

She widened her eyes at his approach. "You mean to tell me all this time you've been right next door?"

"Um-hmm." He kept coming.

"My room is connected to yours?"

"That's correct." He hesitated, the grin changing to a puzzled frown. "That upsets you?"

"Yeah, I'm upset. I'm very upset." She tried to keep her voice as serious as possible. "That we've wasted a hell of a lot of time." She gave him an enticing glance and he grinned back, picking her up once more and carrying her into his room.

Wrapped in anticipation, she barely registered the room. She noted a fleeting impression of deep burgundy drapes and bed hangings, of heavy carved furniture, massive and dark. Adam set her on her feet and took her firmly into his arms. His eyes bored into hers and any doubts vanished at the love revealed there.

Gently his lips descended on hers. Slowly her mouth opened beneath his, and she sighed as his tongue slipped inside. He traced the inner edge of her mouth, the erotic exploration suspending time. He drew back and Maggie's wobbly knees threatened to turn to mush. It took all her concentration to remain standing. She'd never been kissed like that before.

"Wow."

"Be quiet, Maggie," he growled softly.

"Okay." The agreement was little more than a sigh. She tilted her lips toward his but he ignored them, turning his attention instead to the sensitive skin at the base of her throat. Her head fell back and she moaned at the heat of his lips and the skill of his touch. His hands cupped her shoulders and he skillfully swung her around. Her world narrowed to the confines of his hands, his breath, his scent; her head rolled limply forward. His lips glided along her neck, circling from front to back, featherlike kisses that teased at the top of her spine.

Almost imperceptibly, his tongue trailed the ridge of her shoulder, stopped only by the sleeve of her gown. He pushed the silken fabric off her shoulder and nibbled at the exposed flesh. His every move was agonizingly slow and Maggie quivered. She quelled the impulse to submit to the throbbing building within her and savored the sensations heightened by the subtle self-denial and Adam's expertise.

He popped open the buttons of her gown, one by one releasing the pressure of her bodice. He slid the dress down until it rested at her waist, then pulled her tight against his chest. Wrapped in a sensual fog she noted dully he was still fully dressed. The feel of her naked back against his clothed chest . . . wicked and exotic. His hands slid around her waist and up to cup her breasts. Knowledgeable fingers played and teased the hardened, sensitive tips until she moaned and melted against him.

He dropped his hands and pushed the gown down past her knees, catching all she wore underneath along with it, to puddle at her feet. The sinful caress of a faint draft on her naked body whispered over her and she ached for the press of his frame to hers. The erotic touch of Adam fully clothed behind her excited and aroused her. Gently he turned her to face him. Far too lost to be embarrassed, she stood before him. Tremors of desire coursed through her at the stark need in his eyes.

He scooped her into his arms and placed her on the bed. His clothes quickly fell to the floor and her gaze followed his every movement. The glow from the fireplace glinted off his golden hair, highlighted the planes and angles of his muscled body, reflected the smoldering depths of his eyes.

He lay beside her and she moved into his embrace, into his heat, her lips meeting his. She opened her mouth and darted her tongue into his mouth. Quick. Demanding. Hungry. He countered with a leisurely, almost lazy exploration that left her trembling and urgently needing more. She arched closer, twining her hands in the silk of his hair, desperate for his flesh against hers, yearning for the feel of his long, hard length.

He refused to be hurried in his controlled, measured dance of discovery. Refused to quicken the pace of his languid, sweet torture. Refused to give in to the insistent, pounding rhythms escalating inside her. He trailed a hand down her body, a whisper across her inflamed skin, a secret caress on her stomach. She shivered with delicious anticipation. His hand drifted lower, finding the curls at the juncture of her thighs. Her legs fell open. Powerful, knowing fingers skillfully sought out the essence of her womanhood and she moaned at the exquisite, mindless ecstasy he drove her to. A coiled spring wound tighter deep inside her, the tension heightening, the need unbearable.

Adam sensed her increasing excitement. His body responded to her demands but he refused to surrender to her. Yet. He would not allow himself to succumb to the skin flushed with overripe desire, the full, firm breasts heaving with each impassioned gasp, the intoxicating body straining toward him. He wanted their love to be more than she had ever known. More than she had ever dreamed. More than she had ever desired. He wanted to mark her as his forever. She whimpered beneath him, convulsively gripping his shoulders and pulling him tighter to her. Adam groaned, and finally he, too, could take no more of the delectable, maddening torture.

He positioned himself above her, his eyes, dark as night, smoldering with passion. With a joyous cry she arched to meet his downward stroke. Singed by his heat, seared by her desire, she welcomed him to her body and her very soul. They moved together with an instinct born of another time, nurtured in another age. Matching thrust to thrust, movement to movement, one body in perfect, sizzling harmony with the other. Faster and higher they danced, straining as if the sheer force of their frantic desire would discover worlds of passion never dreamed of. This one woman made for this one man.

They poised at the brink of madness for a moment or a lifetime until ultimately together they plunged into an eruption of pleasure. His body shook against hers, hers quaked convulsively, and they clung to each other as if life itself were at stake.

And for that one explosive moment, time stood still.

Time.

Their enemy and their master. For this one single second, defeated. No matter how brief, regardless of how fleeting, the memory of this moment, the triumph of this love would stay with them through all time, filling their yesterdays, coloring their tomorrows.

Forever.

She lay in the massive bed, one hand tucked under her chin, resembling a classical statue, peaceful and serene. Adam chuckled silently at the image. Of all the things he could say about "his Maggie," peaceful and serene would not be among them.

His Maggie.

As much as he liked the sound of that, he'd better never let her know he thought of her as his Maggie. It would no doubt launch her into a speech about not being anyone's property and how she wasn't from this time and did not expect to be treated as if she were, closing with declarations of freedom and independence. He grinned at her sleeping form. He could accept that. Difficult as it was to endure at times, her spirit and insistence of what she considered her rights were among the things he loved about her.

Surprised, he realized he also loved sleeping through the night with her cuddled beside him, and waking to find her still there. There would be no separate bedrooms in this marriage. Adam wanted to spend the rest of his life with her by his side like this. They had much to talk about.

He leaned over and nibbled her ear. "Maggie, my love. Wake up."

Her eyes fluttered open. She stretched luxuriously, slanting him a lazy, sensuous smile. "You were right. Last night was . . . perfect."

He grinned and brushed her lips with his. "I know."

She wrapped her arms around his neck and pulled him closer, turning his light kiss into something far more satisfying.

"Maggie." He groaned. "I must get dressed. I cut short matters dealing with the estates yesterday to rush back to town last night. I must return today."

Disappointment shone in her eyes. "When will you be back?"

"Tonight." He raised her hand and brushed a kiss along her palm. "Will you wait up for me?"

She seemed to consider his request thoughtfully, then gave him a teasing smile. "I think I can arrange that."

"You'd better," Adam growled and kissed her thoroughly. He pulled away and noted her eyes darken. His own desire rose and he pushed the thought from his mind, staunchly but reluctantly. He had to take care of this estate problem. Then he could devote himself fully to her.

He flung back the bedclothes, lifted her into his arms, and carried her out of his room and into hers.

"What are you doing?" she said, clutching a sheet to her naked form. Adam dropped her abruptly on the bed and she bounced awkwardly. He sat down beside her and cupped her chin in his hand, gazing firmly into her stormy green eyes.

"You brought up the question of servants last night. And you were right. Finding you in my bed without benefit of marriage would destroy your rep-utation." His look softened. "I do not want you hurt."

"Adam." She laughed. "I don't care about my rep-utation. I can take care of myself."

He smiled in resignation. "I know. But just this once do as I ask."

"Okay." She sighed and threw herself back on the pillows. "You'll definitely be home tonight?"

"Definitely."

"I'll wait for you in, oh, say, the library?" She gazed at him innocently.

He matched it with a wicked look of his own. "One of my favorite rooms."

"Mine, too." Her eyes were a remarkably deep for-est color and he regretted his inability to respond to the depth of her arousal until his return. "Mine, too."

Lydia allowed herself a congratulatory smile. The day had gone exceedingly well. Far better than she had hoped. She did not even have to lure Maggie to the library. Maggie went on her own. Odd for her to venture into Adam's domain when she had obviously been avoiding him for days.

But then Maggie's behavior today, overall, had been extremely unusual. She'd slept quite late, then stayed in her room most of the day, taking a long bath during the afternoon hours. The scandalized servants were still exchanging shocked comments over Maggie's request for a razor. To shave her legs, of all things, according to the gossip. The idea in-trigued Lydia and she vowed to try it herself at the first opportunity.

Now Maggie sat curled up on the library sofa with

a book, and Lydia reasonably assumed she would stay there for a while. A servant sent from the country by Adam arrived hours ago with a message from her brother. He would be home by midnight. The timing could not have been better.

The hall clock chimed the hour. Ten o'clock. Connor's men should be waiting by now. Most of the servants had already retired for the evening. Even so, Lydia crept furtively to the rear door, unlocked it, and pulled it open. She stepped outside quickly, her gaze scanning the dim, deep shadows.

Nothing.

There was no one there.

Vexed, Lydia took a few more steps and looked for any sign of Connor's men. "Bloody hell," she muttered under her breath. "Just like him. Not only is he always late but his men are late, too." She peered once more around the unmoving shapes and vague, indistinct outlines taking on sinister proportions in the pale moonlight.

Lydia shivered and stepped back inside, determined to wait as long as it took for Connor's men to appear. She did not doubt they would come. Connor had never failed her before. He would not fail her now.

On the fourth or perhaps the fifth time she ventured outside Lydia found Connor's men. It was now nearing eleven o'clock. She finally spotted two figures hovering near a wagon in the alley near the mews, beyond the end of the garden. Indignantly she strode toward them.

"It's about time," she said. The couple froze at her

263

approach. "I suppose Connor gave you the wrong time?"

The men stared first at each other, then at Lydia.

"How's that, milady?" The cautious query came from the direction of the shorter of the two shadowy figures.

"It scarce matters now." Lydia sighed and drew closer. Her gaze swept the men in an assessing manner and she nodded with admiration. "I must say, though, you two have certainly dressed the part. I did not expect Connor to get into the spirit of this evening and I think it's quite charming of him to humor me this way. You will serve extremely well."

They appeared wonderfully sinister. The short one inclined toward excess poundage. The other was several inches taller but every bit as wide as his companion. Both wore shabby, apparently cast-off clothing. Lydia sniffed delicately. There seemed to be a distinct odor lingering about them. They were perfect. She beamed at the men. If only they'd get that baffled look off their faces. Oh, well, intelligence was perhaps a little too much to hope for.

"Now that you're here, follow me." Lydia tossed the words over her shoulder and walked to the door. The men traded glances, shrugged, and followed. "I shall go over this once again with you. Did Connor give you all the details?"

"No, milady." This time the answer came from the larger of the pair.

"I suspected as much. Very well." She halted just outside the door, turned, and stepped behind a large shrub. The men exchanged confused looks and jumped when Lydia reappeared.

"Here." She shoved a length of rope and a burlap sack at them. "I told Connor I would get the rope and the bag and here they are." The men took the articles with obvious reluctance. Lydia's brows knitted in an exasperated frown. "I see I truly must go over this. Listen closely."

The pair leaned forward as if mesmerized by her words.

"The woman you are to kidnap is in the library. Down this hall, through the door, third room on the right. Threaten her with this." Lydia disappeared behind the shrub once more and returned brandishing a wicked-looking weapon. Her startled henchmen gasped and even in the faint glow of the moonlight, she saw them pale at the sight of the gun.

"Don't be such ninnies," Lydia said impatiently. Were these two really as dim-witted as they appeared? She sighed in resignation. They would simply have to do. It was far too late to change her plans now. "It isn't loaded."

In perfect harmony, the men released pent-up breaths. Did each do everything in tune with the other? Lydia shook off the fanciful thought and returned to the matter at hand.

"Now go in there, threaten her with the gun—"

"Begging your pardon, milady," the short one said, hesitation in his voice. "But what should we be sayin' to her?"

The question took her by surprise. "Why, say anything you like, I suppose." She paused to think. "No, wait. Don't say too much. Just tell her she's being kidnapped and to keep quiet and she won't be hurt." Pleased with herself, Lydia brightened. "Yes, that

265

will work quite well, I think. Then tie her hands. There's a strip of cloth in the bottom of the bag. Put that in her mouth, the bag over her head, and voila, it's done." Lydia beamed at her obviously impressed audience.

"That's right clever, milady," the taller kidnapper said, admiration evident in his tone.

"Thank you." Lydia smiled modestly. "Now," she said, her words again brisk and efficient, "did Connor at least tell you where you are to take her?"

The pair again traded looks, the short one speaking with a new air of confidence. "That he did, milady. Don't you worry yourself none. We'll take care of it."

"I have the utmost confidence in your abilities. Now one last thing." The men leaned in as though hanging on every word. "You must make absolutely certain she is not harmed in any way. It would defeat my purposes if she were at all injured. Do you understand?" She gave them each her sternest glance and was gratified to note the almost worshipful expression in their eyes.

Regardless of the class of men one dealt with, their responses never differed when it came to an attractive woman. The same instinct that told Lydia when a man was about to attempt to kiss her or, heaven forbid, ask for her hand, now told her these two would follow her instructions to the letter.

Jane Austen's words danced before her eyes. Maggie had read the same page three times. Sighing with frustration, she tossed the book aside. Her mind refused to focus on the written words. Too many thoughts crowded her head. Thoughts she had resisted all day. Thoughts now demanding attention.

Restlessly, she pushed herself off the sofa and, wrapping her arms over her chest, paced the room. She always could think better on her feet. The emotional turmoil gripping her inside refused to let her sit still. How many steps was it to the wall anyway? One . . . two . . . three . . . It was definitely time to sort out her feelings, past time to face the facts.

The love she shared with Adam was nothing short of remarkable. Never in her wildest dreams had she imagined the intensity of such feelings. How her heart leapt at the sight of his strong, handsome face or the touch of his gentle, knowing hands. Even his infuriating sexist attitudes and his annoying habit of lifting one eyebrow in that superior expression now endeared him to her.

"Damn," she muttered. It wasn't fair. Why did she have to come nearly two centuries into the past to find the one man who filled the empty, aching spot in her soul? The one man who gave her what she never even knew she searched for. The one man she didn't have any possibility of a life with.

"I just don't get it," she cried, surprised to find she had spoken out loud. Fine. Maybe the sound of her own voice would help her work out this mess. It sure as hell couldn't hurt. All day it had been easy to push aside reality and pretend she and Adam could share a life, build a future.

"Future. Yeah, that's the problem, isn't it." She sighed and paced off the room again. Twenty-eight steps, pivot . . . turn, 28 steps, pivot . . . turn . . .

The future, her future, did not include Adam. An

unknown force tossed her through time and into his arms and no doubt would snatch her away again in, what? Nineteen days? She and Adam were as star-crossed as Romeo and Juliet, their love just as doomed.

"I can't leave him," she said to the empty room, "but I can't stay." Book-lined shelves towered above her. The literary wisdom of the ages stared. Silent. Accusing.

"Don't you see?" she pleaded with the rows of leather-backed spines, mute jurors in her trial of passion. "Staying, even if I had a choice, could screw up the next two hundred years. I'm not supposed to be here. I'm out of place, out of sync." Maggie fought to find the words, for Shakespeare and Chaucer and Dante. And more, for herself. "I don't belong here. I have to go back."

A nagging thought throbbed the one-word question she'd evaded and denied and refused to face.

Why?

"Why?" Confused, she tried to focus her words into a cohesive argument. "Why? Because of paradoxes and ripple effects and all those things science fiction writers preach about." She shook her head slowly. "None of that stuff has ever been proved, but it makes sense. I have to go home." The firm tone of her voice made her wonder who she was trying to convince.

She resumed pacing, picking up where she left off. Eighteen . . . 19 . . . 20 . . . As she passed the fireplace another persistent thought struck her with the breathtaking impact of a cold blast from a garden hose on a blistering summer day. She pulled up short.

What if I'm wrong?

Maggie stared unseeing at the flames leaping in the marble hearth. "What if I throw away everything, go home, and I don't have to?" She spoke quietly to the fire. "What if Adam was right when he said maybe, just maybe, this is my destiny?"

She whirled to face the faceless leather-bound volumes, reaching toward them in desperate supplication.

"How do I know?" she asked her noncommittal witnesses. Quiet. Condemning. Her voice dropped to a whisper; her hands fell to her sides. "How do I know?"

Maggie lost track of time standing in the middle of the room, staring mesmerized at the dancing flames. The hypnotic effect, the primeval appeal of the fire, calmed her. She would do what she had to do, what she believed was right. No matter how much it hurt. And, she had no doubts, it would hurt.

Somewhere on the fringes of her consciousness, she heard the library door open.

Adam! Marshaling her control, she pulled a smile to her lips and turned to greet him. The smile froze on her face. "Who in the hell are you?"

Two of the most disgusting-looking men she'd ever seen inched toward her. Actually, disgusting gave them too much credit. Grubby and somewhat slimy in appearance, they reminded her of characters from a Charles Dickens novel. Characters who had gone a bit overboard to get that perfect scum-of-the-earth look. They were too exaggerated to be scary. The taller one held a mass of burlap in one hand, rope and a piece of white material in the other.

"What do you want?" she said in her most imperious tone, surprised and a little pleased to note she had picked up some of the lofty superiority of the British upper classes during her stay.

"Jist do as we say, milady, and ye won't get hurt none." The short, fat one pulled his hand from behind his back to reveal an odd-looking gun. Maggie's heart stuck in her throat. She knew next to nothing about weapons, but she could spot a gun, even an antique one, when she saw it. All of a sudden, the Dickens characters seemed a lot less ridiculous and a lot more sinister.

"What do you want?" she repeated firmly, refusing to let any fear show.

"We've come ta take ye with us, miss." The taller, weasel-faced one slowly approached, waving his rope and burlap at her. He looked so much like a dogcatcher trying to lure an errant hound Maggie almost choked, smothering a hysterical laugh. But the nasty gleam in his eye told her no matter how ridiculous the pair looked, they were deadly serious. And she was in real trouble.

Think! Her mind raced, desperate for a way to help herself. The duo inched slowly closer. She backed away just as slowly, matching them move for move. She'd spent a lot of time in this room. Surely there was more than one way out.

The window. That was it! If she could reach the window, she could dive through the glass to the outside. Of course, she'd only seen that done on TV or in the movies. How hard could it be anyway? Sure, in her own experience glass didn't break quite that easily, not when you wanted it to. But right now she didn't see any other choice.

She darted toward the door, hoping to draw them off in the wrong direction, then swiveled and broke toward the long windows, bringing her arms up to shelter her face. She steeled herself for the jump through and lunged at the glass. Unbelievably, hands grabbed her just as her feet left the floor. They were on her, one clutching her arms, the other trying to wrap the gag around her mouth.

Shocked by how much faster they were than she'd imagined, she struggled furiously but without success. Why couldn't she remember anything from all those self-defense lessons? They already had the gag in her mouth but she refused to give up. A well-placed kick hit home and she gained a small measure of satisfaction.

The fat one screamed. "Bloody 'ell, Freddy, she kicked me in me bleeding jewels."

"Hit 'er then," Weasel-face commanded.

Maggie's desperate fight accelerated, spurred on by panic and fear.

"But we ain't supposed to hurt 'er," the fat one whined.

"Don't be a bloody arsehole, hit 'er!" The weasel tried to contain Maggie's violent, frantic thrashing. A sharp pain exploded in her head. Shock registered for a split second. The fat one actually hit her! She didn't think he had the guts. It was her last thought before slumping to the floor and descending into blackness.

* * *

Lydia eyed Connor's henchmen anxiously. They carried Maggie through the back hall and out the door. The tall one had her tossed over his shoulder, well covered by the burlap bag. Obviously Maggie was cooperating fully. There was no indication of movement within the bag. Good. With a sigh of relief, Lydia headed toward the library to place the ransom note on the mantel. She did not want her future sister-in-law hurt.

Chapter Fifteen

Maggie's eyes snapped open to total darkness. Her head throbbed. The world bounced beneath her. Disoriented, she couldn't make sense of her surroundings. She lay on her side. Where was she? Why couldn't she see? A jarring bump shot a stab of pain to her head but jerked her mind into sharp focus.

Those costumed characters had kidnapped her! Why? More to the point, what did she do now? She was confined in some kind of scratchy bag, maybe the burlap Weasel-face was carrying. A sharp, acrid smell clung to the fibers and stung her nose. A scent reminiscent of . . . what? Spoiled onions? Rotten potatoes? A gag bound her mouth, and her hands were tied behind her back. She tested the bonds and to her delight found the knot loose. Ha! What a bunch of idiots. They must have figured if she was unconscious they needn't worry about keeping her tied. She'd show them. She wasn't a graduate of the Rocky

Mountain School of Karate and Martial Arts self-defense course for women for nothing. Granted, it hadn't helped her much back in the library, but this was different. This time the element of surprise was on her side and she had way too much to lose to give up without at least trying to escape.

Quietly, with the barest of movement, she slid the rope off her wrists. Rough-edged voices murmured low behind and at a level slightly above her. Judging by the bumpy ride, she must be in some kind of wagon or cart. Apparently she hadn't been unconscious too long. Her arms and legs hadn't fallen asleep and weren't stiff yet. Hoping not to attract their attention, she slipped her hands up to her face and removed the annoying gag. Great so far, but she was still in the nasty, stinky bag.

The cart hit a chuckhole and she seized advantage of the bounce and rolled over. Now she faced the voices. Maggie edged a fingernail into the loosely woven fabric and pried it apart for a tiny peek hole. Just as she thought. The Dickens gang sat with their backs to her on a bench above where she lay. If she didn't make any sudden movement to alert them, she could simply slide this sack over her head. Cautiously she inched the bag off, then covered herself with it.

Now what? She sized up her captors. Her experience with them in the library proved they were much stronger and faster than they appeared. The tall one had an evil look about him that frankly gave her shivers. The fat one was a major-league whiner, but probably her best bet for escape.

The bare outline of a plan rooted in her mind. If

this didn't work, they might kill her. And nobody in this or any other century would ever know what happened. Dammit! If she had to die she sure as hell wasn't going to take it lying down.

She curled into a crouch position. A scant inch at a time, she edged her way forward until she squatted directly behind the bench. So far so good. She held her breath and rose slowly. Her eyes drew level with the bench. A flash of lightning illuminated the sky. Lying there between them was the gun. Maggie nearly cried out loud with delight.

She sank down again, pulled her hem up, and tied her dress around her waist. There was no way she could do what she planned with 50 pounds of skirts trailing around her ankles. Finally she gathered the edges of the burlap bag together. Maggie took a deep breath in a hopeless attempt to steady her nerves and calm her shaking hands. Okay. On the count of three. One . . . two . . . three.

Maggie sprang to her feet and in one swift move yanked the bag over the head of Weasel-face. With an ear-piercing yell that would have done the entire staff and student body of the Rocky Mountain School of Karate and Martial Arts self-defense course for women proud, she twisted and turned like Master Ti had taught. With a nearly classic form she'd never shown in class, she executed one superb kick that sent the tall, Dickensian thug sailing out of the wagon in a perfect arc to land several yards away with a soft thud and a loud groan.

Maggie and the fat one stared at each other, one in horror, the other in amazement and more than a little pride. She swiveled and grabbed the gun. In her best television cop impersonation, she aimed it with both hands, straight at his head.

"Take me home, pal," she said. "Now!"

He turned shocked eyes toward her, then toward his partner, groaning under the burlap by the side of the road, then back to Maggie.

"Now!" Maggie gestured with the gun. If this gun trick looked as awesome in person as it did on TV, her kidnapper should be pretty damned intimidated by now.

The fat one snapped the reins, and the horse took off with a jerk that nearly threw her to the floor. She recovered her balance and glared at the driver. "You did that on purpose."

She clambered over the bench, untied her skirts, and settled beside him. The cart wasn't moving that quickly. Not nearly fast enough for Maggie, although she realized one horse could only go so fast.

The fat one gave her a sidelong glance. "It ain't loaded."

Startled, Maggie stared. "What do you mean, it ain't loaded?"

He kept his eyes on the road. "The lady what gave us the gun said it weren't loaded." He shrugged and glanced at her. "She said she didn't want you hurt none."

"That's great. Really thoughtful. Damned considerate." Sarcasm dripped off her words. "I don't suppose you call hitting me in the head and knocking me out hurting me?"

"You kicked me in me family jewels," he said indignantly.

"You were kidnapping me. What the hell was I

supposed to do? Go along quietly?"

"Weren't my idea," he said in a lofty tone that seemed to absolve him of all blame in the matter.

She eyed him suspiciously. "What do you mean? Whose idea was it?" Something he'd said earlier now caught her attention. "What lady gave you the gun?"

"The one in the alley. Looked like a bloomin' angel, she did." He sighed and Maggie could have sworn a look of adoration passed over his grubby face. "Said we was to take the gun, snatch you, and take you to someplace some bloke called Connor knew about." He glanced toward her cautiously. "Since we was lookin' to break into a house or two tonight we didn't think it smart to argue with 'er."

She narrowed her eyes and considered his weird explanation. It didn't make a whole lot of sense. Of course, most of her life lately didn't make sense. "Okay, if the damn gun isn't loaded, why are you taking me home?"

He laughed, a rather nice laugh actually. She peered at him sharply. A closer inspection showed him to be fairly young, probably about her age. He wasn't even really fat. His clothes were merely extremely bulky. Just right to hide stolen goods in.

"Bloody 'ell, miss, I ain't no bloomin' kidnapper. I'm jist a housebreak, a common thief." Amusement twinkled in his eyes. Maggie groaned to herself. She was beginning to like this guy. "Besides, I ain't never seen nobody fly through the air like Freddy did. I didn't want to be takin' no trips like that." He chuckled. "Between you with your screamin' and kickin' and that pretty blonde acting like queen of the underworld it sure has been some night." He shook his head, grinning. "Wait till me Margaret hears about this."

"Margaret?"

"Me missus." He shook his head again. "She ain't gonna like it. Ain't none too pleased about my stealing anyways."

"Why do you do it?" Maggie asked, genuinely curious.

He shrugged and looked her straight in the eye. His were a pleasant green color. "Sometimes you ain't got no choice."

She stared back. There was something vaguely familiar about the man. Or maybe it was just the familiar resignation of the truly poor. "Sorry," she said but refused to pull her gaze away. "There's got to be something else you can do."

He continued to stare and she noted a glimmer of hope in his eyes, followed quickly by disdain. Maggie knew without words this man wondered how someone like her could possibly know what his life was like. And she also knew, sadly, he was right.

He turned back toward the horse and the pair sat silently a few moments. "I been thinkin' I might try me luck in America." He glanced at her quickly. "You're from there, ain't ye?"

She laughed and leaned back on the bench. "What gave me away?"

He flashed her an almost wounded look at the sarcasm and she immediately repented. "Sorry," she said again, promising herself to take him seriously. She considered his comment in silence.

"That's not a bad idea," she said slowly. "America has a lot to offer, especially now." She warmed to the subject and realized how much did lie ahead. "There's nearly an entire continent to explore and settle. Natural resources are in abundance. Land. Adventure. A chance for a good future. You could do a lot worse, you know." She stared at him pointedly.

"I hear there's a lot of opportunity in America." He flashed her a grin. "For an honest man."

She caught the gleam in his eye and laughed. They rode the rest of the way forging bonds of an odd friendship. In spite of the kidnapping and the head bashing, he was taking her home and he certainly didn't have to. She told him all about America, as much as she could remember from history, here and there embellishing a bit to make her country sound even more attractive. She wasn't sure why she wanted this thief-turned-kidnapper-turned-reluctant-rescuer to have a better life. Somehow the idea just seemed right.

In turn, he told her about his life. He had eight kids and never enough to eat. His parents were farmers but he was orphaned at an early age and ran away to the city. Still, farming was where his heart lay. Maggie nodded sagely, confident America in 1818 was a great place for farmers, even though the chance of somebody like him coming up with enough money for passage for a family of ten was pretty farfetched.

He reined in the horse and the wagon rolled to a stop. "Beggin' your pardon, miss, but I'll be leavin' ye here."

Maggie glanced around quickly. The area looked somewhat familiar.

"We're still a wee bit aways from the house we

nabbed you in. Right down that street there. But"—
he shrugged and looked apologetic—"I can't be
takin' the risk that someone ain't out lookin' for ye.
And me."

Maggie understood. "Sure, I see what you mean.
No problem." She turned and jumped off the wagon,
then impulsively turned back and gazed up at him.
"Look, you didn't have to bring me this far, and you
haven't gotten anything out of tonight. Aside from
bruises, that is." She grinned. "I think Adam would
be more than willing to pay a reward. Maybe we
could get you that passage to America."

"I ain't takin' charity," he said gruffly.

"No, you'd rather steal." She shot him an impatient
glare. "It's not charity." She took a deep breath and
forced herself to be calm, continuing in a gentle yet
firm voice. "Listen, it's a reward. You helped me out
and you could have dumped me after I kicked your
friend off the wagon. Come and see us next week.
Ask for Adam Coleridge, he's the earl of something
or other. Besides"—she threw him a conspiratorial
grin—"he'll never miss it. He's got tons of money."

"Bless you, miss," he said quietly, the emotion in
his eyes touching something deep within her.

"No sweat." Maggie flashed a quick salute and
turned once more to leave, again quickly turning
back. "I almost forgot. I don't know your name."

He stood in the wagon, pulled off his hat, and executed a rather well done bow. "Me friends call me
Bert."

"Okay, Bert." She laughed, crossed her arms over
her chest, and tilted her head. "Is there a last name?"

"That there is, miss. Masterson. Bert, Bertram

Masterson at your service." Again he bowed gracefully.

"Bertram Masterson," she said, staring in amazement. Her father's name was Bertram. The name had been in the family for generations. Her name, Margaret, was also a family name. Her father had always been fond of telling the story of how the first Mastersons had come to America because his ancestor had done a favor for a nobleman. The tale had grown to mythical proportions through the years. Maggie had never quite fallen for it, never paid that much attention to the details that seemed more spectacular whenever the yarn was spun. But she did remember the part about the reward.

Passage to America.

"Wow!" she breathed. She stared in awe at an actual ancestor, and he stared back. Maggie shook her head and grinned again. "Come and see us, Bert, and good luck."

"Good luck to you, too, miss." He sat back on the bench and clicked to the horse. The wagon slowly moved off.

"Bert," Maggie called after him and he turned toward her. "When you get to America, encourage your kids to keep moving west. It'll be a great life. I promise." He nodded and she waved. The wagon pulled farther away.

"After all, Bert," she said under her breath, watching him drive off, "someday a descendent of yours needs to be born in Colorado."

Was she now the cause of her family coming to America or would it have happened anyway? Was she destined to play a part or was it just a bizarre fluke? Had she interfered in history or simply helped it along?

The implications of her actions, the crazy impact of time travel, and a dozen other questions tumbled through her mind. Questions she wasn't up to facing right now. She had to get back. Turning to start the short walk, a shiver of fear skated through her. Would she be safe by herself? She glanced down and smiled wryly. Tired and filthy, her dress torn, Maggie resembled any other beggar on the street. No one would bother her looking like this.

In spite of everything, the knock on the head, the moments of sheer panic, and the bruises inflicted by the bouncing ride, the encounter with Bert had left her with a warm, fuzzy feeling. Maggie threw one last look at the retreating wagon, then headed toward the house that right now felt very much like home.

Adam strode into the library with an eager step, then pulled up short. Maggie wasn't here. Disappointment surged through him. Surely she would be here waiting for him. He had even sent a message ahead saying he would be home by midnight. Adam had hurried to settle his business, and pushed his horses to the limit to get back. He glanced at the clock. It was still not quite twelve. Why wasn't she here?

Of course. It was late: she had probably grown tired and was upstairs waiting. Adam grinned with anticipation. The day spent away from Maggie strengthened his resolve to marry her. Tonight he would formally ask for her hand, even though he considered the matter settled already. He turned to leave the room and his eye caught sight of a pile of correspondence stacked on his desk. Duty battled with desire and he groaned aloud. It would take only a few moments to go through and then he could turn his complete attention to Maggie. Resigned, he approached the desk, scooped up the sheaf of papers, and quickly shuffled through them.

A discreet knock from Wilson interrupted him. "Milord, Lord St. Clair is here. To see Lady Lydia."

"At this hour?" Why would Connor stop by so late to see his sister? "Very well, Wilson. Show him in and find Lydia."

With a nod, Wilson retreated, returning with Connor moments later.

"Connor." Adam greeted his old friend with genuine affection. "I am sorry we have not had time to get together since your return to London. In fact, I believe we've only seen each other once, at the Broadmore ball." An appalling thought stopped him in his tracks. "Good lord, Connor, you didn't take me seriously, I pray? You're not here to marry Lydia, are you?"

Connor laughed and Adam released a sigh of relief. It wasn't that he didn't like Connor. In fact, he'd always thought of him as something of a younger brother. Lord knew he wanted the best for his sister. But in spite of his sarcastic words the other night, a match between the two of them did not strike him as right somehow. Adam studied him intently. Still . . . the situation might bear another look. Lydia could do far worse.

Abruptly, the laughter died in Connor's throat. "Adam," he said, caution in his voice, "get that look off your face. You know full well I am not about to get myself leg-shackled to Lydia or anyone else. Besides"—he grinned—"Lydia and I know each other far too well to suit. It's been my observation that a successful marriage requires a few mysteries, perhaps even a secret or two."

Adam grinned back. "Well said. So why have you come to see my sister at this late hour?"

Connor shrugged. "She asked me for a favor and I must tell her I shall not go along with her little plot. I had planned to be here earlier but certain . . . er . . ." Connor seemed to have trouble finding the right words and Adam could not resist a slight chuckle at his obvious discomfort. There was wry satisfaction in knowing he could still make Connor feel as if he were 12 and in trouble again.

"Certain what?"

"Blast it, Adam," Connor sputtered. "Certain previous engagements took longer than expected." He glared as if daring Adam to say something.

"Brandy?" Adam said innocently.

"Please," Connor said, still in apparent discomfort.

Adam poured glasses for them both and they stood, sharing the kind of companionable silence only old friends can.

"Connor? What on earth are you doing back here—" Lydia burst through the door, stopping short at the sight of Adam. "Adam. You're home. How . . . nice." A honeyed smile graced her lips and Adam immediately grew suspicious.

"Lydia," he said, "Connor has come to explain he cannot take part in whatever scheme you have attempted to rope him into this time."

Lydia's eyes grew wide. A flash of pure horror crossed her face. She turned toward Connor and grasped his arm, fear evident in her eyes. "What does he mean? What do you mean?"

Connor's dark brows drew together in a questioning frown. "There is no reason to be overset. I simply saw Adam and Maggie together last night and realized there was no need to carry through with your plan." Lydia's face paled. Connor glanced toward Adam. "It was a typical Lydia plot. She thought if Maggie was kidnapped, you and she would realize how much you mean to each other and marriage would result. I was to supply the kidnappers. It was actually quite clever." He turned to Lydia and tensed at the mask of shock on her face. An amused chuckle died on his lips.

She released her grip and sank into a chair, burying her face in her hands.

"Lydia?" Adam struggled to control a growing sense of foreboding.

Tears glimmering in her eyes, Lydia pulled her gaze to search his. "But they came, Connor, they came."

Connor shook his head in apparent confusion. "I never sent anyone."

"Lydia," Adam spoke slowly, measuring his words, "where is Maggie?"

"Oh God, Adam, they took her!" Tears trickled down her face.

"Who took her?" Adam fought back the fear and panic that threatened to overwhelm him. In two long strides, he stood in front of his sister. Grabbing her shoulders he pulled her to her feet.

285

"Who took her, Lydia?" His words rang with anger.

"I don't know. I found them outside, two men. I thought they were Connor's men."

"What happened? How did they get in?" Adam shook her roughly. In all their years, he had never been this harsh with her, never this angry. He could tell by her eyes she was scared. For the first time in his life, he wanted her to be.

"I—" Lydia gasped. "I helped them. I let them in." She sobbed and choked out the words. "I told them what to do. I thought Connor sent them." Her eyes pleaded with her brother.

"Do you know what you've done?" He thrust her away before he completely lost control. "Your childish stunts are no longer mere pranks. You've put Maggie into the hands of God knows who. Men who could kill her or worse. We may never see her again. Your meddling in my life may well have cost Maggie hers."

Lydia stood facing him, a dazed expression on her face. She lifted her chin defiantly and fire flashed from her eyes. "You meddled in my life first."

"You're right, Lydia." His voice grew quiet and controlled. Deadly. Cold. A tone he had not used since the days when he could best an opponent with his chilling manner off the dueling field as easily as with a weapon on, a voice he would not have thought still came as easily as his own breath.

"Your life, whether you like it or not, is my responsibility. You can relieve me of that by marrying. Until then I shall continue to do what I think is best. And in the future, you will trust me to know what is best for me as well. I will not condone anything but model behavior from you from now on or so help me, Lydia, sister or no sister, I will make your life a living hell."

A voice inside chided him for being so harsh. This was, after all, his spoiled, beloved sister. But the thought of losing Maggie forever turned his heart to icy stone and triggered the rigid self-control he'd perfected years ago to prevent his emotions from affecting his actions, adopted now to deal with his sister and keep him from going mad with fear and helpless frustration.

"Adam," Connor said, "perhaps we can find her. They can't have gotten too far."

Adam nodded. Action was better than doing nothing. Activity would help fill this numbness inside. He turned to Lydia. "How long have they been gone?"

"Not more than an hour," she said quietly.

"Let's go." Adam brushed by his sister and strode out the library, Connor close on his heels. The men raced toward the front door, Adam hoping against hope that as futile as it seemed, maybe, just maybe, there was a chance of finding her. And then, by God, he would never let her out of his sight again.

Maggie was less than a block away when the first raindrops hit. She'd been dimly aware of the thunder and lightning but was far too busy with other problems to pay any attention. Until now. "Great. Just what I need. The perfect ending to a perfect evening."

She trudged toward the house, every step increasing her irritation and her questions. Who would want to have her kidnapped anyway? Bert mentioned the name Connor and it sounded vaguely familiar, but she'd met so many people here it was hard to keep them all straight.

And who was this woman Bert described as an angel? Maggie really hadn't met many women at all since her arrival. The chances that she'd made any female enemies were pretty slim. The thought of Lady Hargreave flashed across her mind but she dismissed the idea. The woman didn't strike Maggie as the kind who would expend a lot of effort on something like a kidnapping unless she could gain a great deal in return. No matter what she once had with Adam, she had nothing to gain now. Besides, there was no way anyone would describe that evil woman as an angel.

The gentle rainfall quickly progressed to a full-fledged downpour. Maggie tried to run, but her drenched gown weighed her down and made the attempt impossible. Forced to concentrate on putting one foot in front of the other, Maggie plodded forward until she finally reached the house. She dragged herself up the first steps and the door flew open. Adam rushed past so quickly she got only a glimpse of his face. Her heart stood still at his expression. Cold. Determined. My God, what had happened in her absence? His speeding figure knocked her off balance and she tottered precariously on the stairs.

"Hey!" She flailed her arms, struggling to keep from falling on the rain-slicked step.

Adam halted his headlong rush and whirled toward her.

"Maggie?" He peered at her through the pouring rain. "Maggie!"

His expression of sheer joy sent excitement and pure happiness racing up her spine. He grabbed her, pulled her into his arms, and crushed her to his chest as if he would never let her go.

"Oh God, Maggie." He kissed her lips, her cheeks, her eyes, and held her face between his hands. "I thought I might never see you again." His anxious gaze searched hers. "Are you unharmed? Did they hurt you?"

The concern she read in his face nearly broke her control. "I'm okay," She gave him a teasing smile. "I told you I could take care of myself."

"So you did." He grinned down at her. "But I did not know that extended to foiling kidnappings."

His grin was her undoing. The terror and fear of the last hour swamped over her and tears burst her dam of emotions. "Oh, Adam." She sobbed. "I've never been so scared. I didn't know what was going to happen. Who those people were. If they were going to kill me or what."

He pulled her tight again and murmured in her ear, "You're safe now, my love. That's all that matters. I have you back."

She shuddered. Relief and exhaustion hit simultaneously and her head seemed light, her tired mind fogged. Being in his arms again was like coming home. Maggie's heart warmed in his embrace. Her strength drained away and she sagged against him. At this moment, this was where she belonged. In opposition to everything she believed in, right now she wanted to depend on him, wanted to be taken care of, wanted to be his. She tilted her head up at him and smiled.

"It's good to be back." The smile and her voice grew faint. She was too wet and miserable to keep going. "Now," she said with a sigh, "do you think we could get out of this damn rain? I'm soaked."

Adam whooped with delight and scooped her up in his arms. "Even your atrocious language is music tonight."

He laughed, carried her into the house, and deposited her on the sofa in the library. One of the maids already had blankets, and Wilson provided a hot cup of tea. Adam sat beside her. In front of the fireplace, she snuggled in his arms. Her lids drifted closed, the warmth of the room and the man flowing into her.

Maggie's eyes flew open. Something she'd paid no attention to now registered in her rapidly clearing mind. She jerked upright on the sofa and scanned the library.

"You!" She pointed to Connor standing quietly with Lydia across the room. "It's you. You're the one. Bert said something about a man named Connor. I couldn't place it at the time but he was talking about you, wasn't he?" She glared at Connor, who appeared distinctly uncomfortable and more than a little guilty. "Why in the hell would you have me kidnapped?"

"Well actually, my dear . . ." Connor stammered.

"He didn't have you kidnapped, Maggie." Adam's cold, oddly harsh words drew Maggie's attention. His gaze met hers. "Lydia did."

"Lydia?" She gasped, her gaze jumping to the blonde. Lydia appeared a picture of complete control. Only her eyes revealed her remorse, eyes that pleaded for forgiveness.

Maggie threw the blanket off and leapt to her feet. "I thought you were my friend. How could you? And more to the point, why?"

"Maggie." Lydia approached, her hands held out before her in a beseeching gesture. "It was not expected to turn out this way. Connor was to provide me with men. And you were not to be harmed in any way. I did not think that—"

"No, you did not think at all, did you?" Adam's voice boomed behind Maggie. She glanced back. He stood close, a towering figure of icy golden rage. "You did not think she could have been killed, she could have been dishonored, she could even have been sold."

"Sold?" Maggie swallowed hard. "What do you mean I could have been sold? Like to a brothel or harem or something? Yuck!"

Adam ignored her outburst, his dangerous gaze still fastened on his sister. "She could have been harmed in other ways. Violated. Abused. We might never have known what happened to her. We might never have heard from her again."

Maggie frowned. Whatever Lydia had done, and it now appeared she'd done quite a bit, she didn't deserve this treatment from her brother. They were the only family each other had. Since Maggie's arrival, her influence had triggered more and more confrontations between the pair. She knew the importance of family because all she had left was her sister. She refused to come between this brother and sister. Maggie reached out and gripped Adam's arm. His gaze met hers and his rage softened.

Maggie turned back to Lydia, her voice quiet. "Why did you do it?"

Lydia sighed deeply. "I watched you and Adam. Each so miserable without the other. At first I merely wanted to get his mind off trying to force me into a marriage." Lydia shot Adam a quick glance, then returned to Maggie. "Soon it was apparent you obviously loved each other but neither would admit it. I thought if you were in danger, kidnapped, Adam would discover how much he cared. Saving your reputation would dictate he would have to marry you and the two of you would be together."

"That's what this was? Some kind of bizarre matchmaking scheme?" Maggie laughed, on the edge of hysterics. This revelation coupled with the events of the night was almost more than she could take. "You people are nuts. I thought you were all a little crazy when I first got here, but now that I've grown to know you . . ." She shook her head and wiped the tears from her eyes. "You just wanted us to get together? Jeez, Lydia. Adam and I have been sleeping together for days."

Only the sharp crack of thunder outside competed with the shocked silence that slammed into the room.

Lydia gasped.

Adam groaned.

Connor choked back something that sounded like a cross between a laugh and a snort.

Maggie stared at the stunned faces around her and grimaced. "Whoops."

Lydia turned an outraged expression toward her

brother. "You have bedded her? Seduced her? You with all your talk of propriety and your criticism of my behavior? You took advantage of a women who has little understanding of our lives and our entire world. She doesn't know the harsh rules the ton adheres to for unmarried women. Oh, Adam, how could you?"

"Lydia," Adam said sharply, "it's not like that. I love her. I want to marry her."

"What?" Maggie cried.

"Marry her?" Lydia snapped. "You'd bloody well better."

"I intend to," Adam said crossly. "And I didn't need your interference to reach that conclusion. I knew it days ago."

"Marry me?" Maggie whispered.

"Excuse me." Connor cleared his throat. "It appears to me this has become a distinctly family matter so I shall take my leave. Adam." Connor nodded, a barely suppressed grin on his face. "It has been, as always, an unforgettable experience."

He turned to Maggie. "My dear, I am truly sorry for any inadvertent role I played in this evening's fiasco and I wish you the heartiest congratulations. Be assured nothing I have heard this night will leave this room." He leaned toward her, a wicked sparkle in his eye. "But someday you must tell me who Bert is."

He threw Lydia a wry glance. "Lydia." He nodded once more and headed toward the door.

"I will see you out, Connor." She tossed a last withering glare at her brother and flounced out the door.

Connor's eyes rolled toward the heavens and, groaning, he followed her.

Maggie's shocked gaze turned to Adam. "Marry me?"

Adam shook his head, a gesture sheepish and endearing. "I had not planned on asking you this way. I wanted to ask for your hand with all the romance and beautiful words that would put even Shakespeare to shame."

Maggie was too stunned for words.

"Maggie." He strode toward her and wrapped his arms around her. "I love you. I cannot imagine life without you. I want you by my side always. I want you to bear my children and grow old with me. Maggie, marry me." The love in his eyes, the anticipation in his voice, the strength of his embrace nearly undid her.

"I . . ." Maggie's gaze locked with his. "I can't."

Shock slapped Adam and his face twisted in disbelief. "What do you mean, you can't?"

She pulled out of his arms and backed away, her gaze never leaving his. Maggie shook her head. "I'm not meant to be here, Adam. I'm not staying. We both know that."

"I know nothing of the sort." His voice grew sharp with the pain she read in his eyes.

"We've been through all this before." She turned away, no longer able to face his stunned hurt. "There is one person too many in this time. One person more than history says there should be. There's a definite imbalance. It's not right. Who knows what devastating changes my staying could bring? To the future. My future."

She whirled to face him, hoping to make him understand. "You talk about your responsibilities to your position and your family. I have responsibilities, too. To a future you know nothing about. I know the way things are supposed to happen. If I stay, it could cause some horrible ripple effect. It could change history. Maybe for the better, possibly for the worse."

"You cannot be positive of that."

"You're right. I'm not." She wrapped her arms around her chest in a protective gesture. "That's part of the problem. I just don't know. But I do know I can't take that chance. I can't take that responsibility."

His dark eyes flashed. "You have told me yourself there is nothing in the future for you. With the exception of your sister, you have no family. Your life, even the independence you flaunt so proudly, has not made you happy." The desperate note in his voice tore at Maggie's soul. "I am offering you a life, a future, here where you can be happy. We can be happy. You love me as much as I do you."

"Of course I love you," she said, her voice rising. "That's not the point. You think love alone will make this right?" A hysterical laugh punctuated her words. "You are a romantic. There's more than years that separate us. You love me now because of who I am, but it's my past, my history, that's made me what you love.

"Adam." She had to make him understand. "Remember the Elgin marbles? In the future the Greek government and the British government will go round and round over who should have possession of them."

"But we can care for them better," he said, puzzlement written on his face.

"You can today, but things change." She struggled to find the words. "For the Greeks, the marbles are a part of them, part of their history, part of their collective past, part of what makes them who they are. It's the same way with me. The nearly two centuries of history that separate us have shaped me as distinctly as any genetic influence. They've made me what I am. If I stayed, the woman you love might not exist because that history might not exist. Would you still love me then?"

"I will love you forever." His voice quietly rang with the truth of his words.

Pain seared her heart and she stared at his beloved face. She had no choice. When the carriage came it would take her back, her one chance for happiness lost.

"We don't have a forever." She shook her head slowly. "I'll love you, and cry for you, and mourn losing you for the rest of my life, but I can't stay here."

He grabbed her arm and pulled her roughly to him, his dark eyes flashing down at her. "Why do you refuse to understand? Refuse to believe this must be your destiny? To be here with me. Fate has brought us to each other and we belong together. Surely you feel that as strongly as I do?"

"Yes . . . no," she said. "I don't know. I only know I have to leave."

The room thickened with anger and pain. Long

moments passed. They stared silently, their eyes saying what words couldn't about love and loss.

Adam pushed her away and his expression changed abruptly, growing formal, remote, cold. His words were icy, as if a door to his heart had clanged shut, as if he no longer cared, as if anguish had frozen all emotions, destroyed all love.

"You say you love me. Yet you would relegate me to a yellowed, long-forgotten page in a history book. You would consign me to a dim memory in the dusty reaches of time. If this is your twentieth-century idea of love, then perhaps I am well off without it, well off without you."

His words pierced her soul with an almost physical pain and for a moment she didn't know if she could bear it. Adam pivoted sharply and strode from the room, leaving Maggie's cries behind him.

"Oh, Adam, no. I do love you." Tears welled in her eyes and streamed down her face. Her heart had never broken before, never known the kind of overwhelming despair that now coursed through her, never dreamed of grief this intense. How could anyone survive this kind of pain that ripped through her as sharply as a knife? How could she? Maggie collapsed slowly onto the sofa. She had just made the biggest decision of her life.

And she prayed it was right.

Chapter Sixteen

Maggie wandered through the next days in a haze of heartache and confusion. More than anything she wanted to be with Adam, wanted to make him understand, but he avoided her. He rose before dawn and left the house, returning, if he came home at all, well after she had fallen into restless, dream-plagued sleep. She listened for his footsteps in the hall, strained to hear movement in his room. Nothing.

Lydia seemed to avoid her as well. Two days after the kidnapping they ran into each other for the first time in the foyer. Lydia was no help.

"I do not understand, Maggie." Lydia shook her head in frustration. "You love Adam. He loves you. Why will you not marry him?"

Maggie sighed. She had explained over and over and was tired of repeating herself. Her explanations didn't change anything. "One more time, Lydia. I'm not supposed to be here, in this time, in this place.

There's one person too many here; there's an imbalance. I have to go back."

"And what about Adam?" Lydia said harshly. "What about him? Do you know in his entire life, I have never seen him the way he is with you. Not years ago when he was an impetuous, devil-may-care rake. And definitely not after Father died when he became so stiff, proper, and stuffy. These days with you, even when you are railing at each other, he has been alive as I have never before seen him. I've seen him laugh with you here." Her gaze locked with Maggie's. "You will destroy him if you leave."

"I don't have a choice," Maggie said. "Don't you get this at all?"

A shocked expression flashed across Lydia's face and she stared at Maggie. "You are scared."

"Of course I'm scared. Scared of messing up two hundred years of history."

"No, that's merely your excuse." Lydia's eyes widened and she nodded slowly, as if confirming her suspicions. "You are scared of what staying here would mean to you personally, not the coming centuries. Scared to throw your lot in with the man you love. Scared to build your own future with him. You would rather return to the safety of what you are familiar with, and I do not mean your horseless vehicles and your flying machines, but the comfort of not having a choice to make. You would rather go back to an empty existence than accept the challenge of a full, rich life here."

Lydia stared Maggie straight in the eyes and, shocked, Maggie read disdain and pity there.

"For all your talk of independence and freedom

and how you run your own life, you are as trapped as I. But my prison comes from my society and my times. Yours is of your own making. You have been offered all I want in life, a man who loves you and a future filled with happiness. You are willing to toss it all away because you lack the courage to follow your heart."

The icy expression on Lydia's face heightened her resemblance to her brother, and Maggie's heart wrenched at the recognition. "I used to envy you, Maggie, the life you led, the life you told me about. But with all your knowledge and inventions and freedom, it does you no good. At least I know what I am searching for. You do not even know that."

Lydia started to leave, then paused and pinned Maggie with a disappointed look. "I have the utmost sympathy for you, Maggie." She shook her head. "You are such a fool." Lydia turned and swept up the stairs.

Maggie gaped in painful astonishment. Lydia's accusations hurt. She couldn't possibly be right . . . could she? Maggie sank onto the stairs. Was she just making excuses? Was she scared of making a choice? Making a commitment? Her own sister had accused her of drifting through her life. Was she still drifting?

She desperately needed somebody to talk to, but Kiki wasn't here. Her friends weren't here. No one she knew would even be born for nearly 150 years. Other than Adam and Lydia, she had no one.

Except Edward.

She jumped on the thought like a flood victim to a rooftop and impulsively called for a carriage. If there was one rule she'd learned here it was that there was nothing more improper than visiting a man alone. But she was about fed up with the whole, primitive time period, the entire antique world and everyone in it. She was tired of feeling frustrated and helpless. Tired of hurting. Chances were Edward wouldn't be much help. She certainly couldn't explain everything to him. But he seemed like a nice guy, someone who might give her some support, who would be on her side. A friend. Right now having a friend wouldn't solve her problems, but it sure wouldn't hurt.

Maggie prowled the fringes of the room, absently picking up an item here and there. The parlor in Edward's house was charming, his home not as big as Adam's but just as opulent. What would have happened to her if she'd landed at the feet of some of the less desirable members of nineteenth-century London?

"Maggie." Edward strode into the room, smiling a welcome. He crossed to where she stood and took her two hands in his. "It is delightful to see you, but I must say I was surprised when I was told you were here."

She sighed and avoided his eyes. Now that she was here, she wasn't sure quite what to say. She drew a deep breath and gazed up into his concerned blue eyes. "I just wanted to get out of the house. I had to get away and I needed somebody to talk to."

Edward's brows drew together in a considering frown and his gaze searched her face. His words came quietly. "Has Ridgewood harmed you? Hurt you in some way?"

The unexpected question shocked her. She pulled her hands from his and turned away. "No. Of course not." The irony of his inquiry leapt at her and she laughed bitterly. "If anything, I've hurt him."

"How?"

Maggie wrapped her arms across her chest and stared unseeing at the Persian carpets beneath their feet. "He wants to marry me." Her gaze locked with his. "I said no."

In one sure step, Edward was beside her. He pulled her into his arms too swiftly for protest, crushing her against his chest.

"Then marry me, Maggie," Edward said, his voice rough with emotion. "You have intrigued me since the moment we met. Your air of fire, your manner of speech, all have enchanted me. I can make you happy as Ridgewood never could."

His lips descended on her startled reply, his mouth on hers in a kiss hungry and demanding. Too surprised to react, Maggie noticed only that while the pressure of his lips was pleasant enough, it wasn't what she wanted, who she wanted.

She flattened her hands against his chest and pushed him away. "Edward," she said indignantly. "Knock it off. I'm very flattered but I don't need a lover or, God knows, a husband right now. I need a friend. Don't you people make friends?" She glared at him. His expression changed from surprise to wry amusement.

"I don't think I want to be a mere friend to you,

Maggie." An odd but appealing smile twisted his face.

A weird sense of aprehension shivered through her. She pushed it aside and pulled a steadying breath. "Well, you don't have a choice. It's friendship or nothing. Take it or leave it."

His smile threatened to become a grin. "How could I possibly refuse such a gracious offer? Friendship it is then, although I must admit I have never been friends with a female before. This should prove quite interesting." He offered her his arm. "Now, my friend, if you'll allow me to escort you to a chair I will call for refreshments. Perhaps some tea?"

"Brandy would be better," she said, taking his arm.

He gave her a surprised look, then grinned. "Brandy it is then." Edward chuckled under his breath. "I will be your friend for now, Maggie, but I make no guarantees about the future."

"No problem." She sighed and sank into a chair. "I do."

Edward and Maggie spent the next few hours in companionable conversation. It was pleasant and relaxing to be able to take her mind off Adam, if only for a short time. The visit with Edward wasn't a mistake after all. The conversation did not return to her problems until she was nearly ready to leave.

"Maggie," Edward began, eyeing her over the edge of his glass. "Why will you not marry Ridgewood?"

She shook her head sadly. "I don't want to talk about it. Let's just say there are obstacles that make any long-term relationship between us impossible."

He gave her a disbelieving look. "From what I have

seen, Maggie, I do not believe you would let any obstacles stand in the path of something you wanted. I know no other Americans. Are you all so determined and outspoken?"

"No, and I'm afraid I'm not like that either. You give me way too much credit."

Edward peered sharply at her, then turned his gaze to the brandy in his glass. His hands swirled the amber liquid in a lazy, hypnotic wave. "Do you care for him?" he asked quietly, his gaze finding hers. "Do you love him?"

She stared into his eyes, reading concern and sympathy and, possibly . . . hope. Her voice was soft, the words nearly a whisper. "Yes, I do."

"And does he love you?"

She hesitated for a long moment and pulled her gaze from his. She stared unseeing across the room. "I believe so, yes."

Edward frowned thoughtfully. "Yet you will not marry him. You must both be very unhappy."

"That about says it, Edward." She laughed harshly. "Actually miserable, destroyed, devastated. All better words to describe what's going on."

"I know you are hurt . . . now." Edward paused as if considering his words. "However, it may very well be for the best."

Startled by his comment, Maggie's brows drew together in a questioning frown. "Why do you say that?"

Edward sighed. "I know he is a member of your family and I have hesitated to say anything, but at this point it may be ill-advised not to say something."

He paused, then plunged ahead. "The Earl of

Ridgewood you know today is a far cry from the man I first met years ago. Then he used people cruelly, particularly women, for his own purposes. Not just Cyprians and demireps, that is to be expected, but respectable, impressionable young women. Callously tossing them aside when his pleasure was satiated. For the last seven years, he has apparently abandoned that pastime, at least with honorable women, to concentrate on his business pursuits. But I do not believe he could have changed that much."

His words astonished her. It wasn't so much what Edward said. Maggie was familiar enough with Adam's past to be able to put Edward's comments in perspective. But the tone of his words seemed tinged with a vague bitterness.

He looked her straight in the eyes and issued a chilling warning. "Be careful of him, Maggie. He cannot be trusted with something as fragile as your heart. Do not change your mind. Do not give in."

Maggie left with Edward's admonition ringing in her ears. She knew Adam well enough to know whatever he had done in the past, he had never deliberately used or hurt anyone, especially women. His sense of honor was too strong. From what Lydia had told her it was highly developed even in his youth.

What bothered Maggie was how Edward had gotten this distorted picture. He admitted he barely knew Adam. She mulled it over in her mind on the way home and realized the culprit must be the vicious gossip Lydia claimed was the lifeblood of society here. What a shame it would still influence Edward's opinions of Adam even after all these years. This explained why Adam was always so concerned about Lydia's reputation and her own. Obviously whatever one did in nineteenth-century London might well be forgiven but never forgotten. A chill shivered through her as if a shadow passed over her heart. Even if the price was astronomical, maybe she was better off in the long run going back where she belonged.

For the afternoon, Maggie had managed to forget her heartache in Edward's pleasant company. But once she returned to the grand mansion, her very presence in the house, his house, triggered a wave of heart-stopping anguish. Edward provided a sympathetic ear but the man she really wanted to talk to was Adam.

On the way to her room she encountered him in the corridor where he could not escape.

"Adam, please." She turned pleading eyes toward him and laid her hand lightly on his arm. "We have to talk."

He glanced at her hand as if her touch somehow violated him and, trembling, she withdrew. His gaze met hers and she read icy disdain and hardened self-control. "I believe all has been said that needs to be said. By my calculations, you should be leaving in fifteen days. Please enjoy our hospitality during your remaining time here, but . . ."

His eyes narrowed and glinted dangerously. The line of his jaw tensed. He towered above her and for the first time in his presence a twinge of real fear rippled through her.

"Stay out of my way. I do not want to see you again." He turned and with determined steps strode down the hall. The vehemence of his words, the anger he could not disguise in his eyes, the rigid self-control guarding every line of his body all combined for an almost physical impact. Maggie staggered slightly as if she'd been struck. She sagged against the wall and those damn tears made an appearance again.

God, she had hurt him so much. How could he bear it?

How could she?

She hurt, too, after all. The realization hit her like a smack in the face.

Wait a minute. He wasn't the only one in pain. He wasn't the only one suffering. Sure, he felt like the world was ending but he only had to deal with his own grief. Maggie had her anguish plus the hurt and guilt of knowing her decision devastated the man she loved.

She swiped angrily at the tears drying on her face. He had a lot of nerve. Instead of each of them suffering they could be spending this time together. If this was all the time they had, it was just plain stupid to waste it.

The more she thought about it, the more anger replaced the sorrow in her heart. She'd be damned if she would continue to let him ignore her. This was her life, too, and she wasn't going to sacrifice these precious days because he was nursing wounded pride along with his broken heart. Her heart was just as broken.

Her world was just as shattered. Her misery was just as great, if not greater.

Her chin raised in defiance. Sure she planned on leaving, but she wasn't gone yet. Until she walked out of that door and stepped into that carriage and was tossed back to the twentieth century this relationship, or love affair, or whatever one wanted to call it wasn't over yet. Not by a long shot.

Regardless of what the high and mighty earl of whatever Adam Coleridge said, there was no way in hell she'd stay out of his sight. In fact, she was going to be in his sight so much he'd have to physically throw her in the street to get a moment's peace.

Maggie marched into her room and straight to the door to Adam's chamber. It wasn't locked. She cracked it open just a bit, enough to hear him come in but not enough for him to see her. She wanted to keep the element of surprise on her side. Maggie always was better in a fight when her opponent wasn't paying attention or thought she was unconscious or lulled into some kind of spiritless acceptance.

Ha! She'd show him. She'd never given up on anything in her life without a fight. She couldn't battle the forces of time but compared to that, Coleridge would be a walk in the park. Maggie loved him and he loved her and she wasn't about to let that go until the time came. No matter what he thought, this was not the time.

Maggie dragged a comfortable chair to the connecting door and settled in to wait. She would wait all night if necessary. After all, what was the loss of one night's sleep? She had to squeeze a lifetime of love into the next two weeks. One night wasn't too high a price to pay to get started.

If not for Richard Westbrook, Adam would have been embroiled in at least one, and possibly more duels in the few days since he'd taken up residence in a chair in front of the fireplace at White's. The illegality of dueling did not seem to appreciably diminish its frequency. Adam's surly, rude behavior had infuriated more than one patron of the exclusive establishment and only Richard's interference, including his subtle reminders of Adam's expert marksmanship, had averted disaster. Richard scanned the room and spotted his friend sitting virtually where he had left him hours before.

Richard sighed and strode toward him. It was fortunate Lydia had the presence of mind to send a message to Richard two days earlier about Adam's behavior. It seemed the years of proper living had abruptly vanished and Adam had reverted to the hellion days of his youth. Or perhaps residing in hell was a more accurate description.

Aside from his belligerent attitude toward all who came near, he seemed to want to do little more than drink himself into oblivion. For good or ill, he could never achieve that. Adam had the amazing ability to hold his liquor far better than an ordinary man. To Richard's keen eyes, the copious amounts Adam consumed had very little effect.

Richard sank into the empty chair next to his friend and signaled for a drink of his own. Something had to be done about Adam for his own sake and for Richard's. Amanda was quite understanding about the time spent with his friend in this sorry state but even her patience had limits. Richard had no desire to test them, and tonight he was determined to finally get Adam to talk about what happened. Lydia's note said only that there was trouble between Adam and Maggie.

"So, have you decided what you will do?" Richard quirked an eyebrow questioningly. "Or do you simply plan to remain here drowning in a vat of brandy for the rest of your life?"

"Go away, Richard," Adam said, his manner surly. "Leave me alone."

"I would dearly love to do just that but I feel an odd obligation to try to help one of the few people in the world I consider a friend." He lounged farther into the chair and chuckled. "I have no doubt you would do the same for me."

Adam ignored him and Richard sighed impatiently. He obviously needed to take a more direct approach. "Correct me if I am mistaken but I was under the distinct impression you planned on marrying Maggie. What has happened?"

Adam turned weary eyes toward him. "She won't have me, Richard." He turned his face back toward the fireplace and spoke so quietly Richard had to strain forward to hear him. "She says she can't stay here. Says she has to go home. She's not from here, you know."

"I know," Richard said, fighting the temptation to be amused. Perhaps the liquor had finally caught up with Adam. Neither of them was as young as they used to be. "She's from America, isn't she?"

"Not just America." Adam shook his head sorrowfully and leaned toward Richard as if confiding a great secret. "She's from the future. From 1995. Says if she stays, she'll muck up history for the next two hundred years, give or take a few years."

The liquor had definitely caught up with Adam.

Richard could no longer prevent the smile playing on his lips. "Well, that certainly is a dilemma. You say she can't stay?"

Adam shook his head somberly.

Richard was hard-pressed to keep from laughing. His friend looked so sincere and unhappy and was so obviously in his cups. Richard had never seen Adam in this condition and it indicated just how miserable he truly was, but even so, a woman from the future? The very idea was ridiculous, although Richard had to give Adam his due for imagination and originality.

Richard suppressed a grin. "Does she know precisely when she will be leaving?"

"About two weeks."

"Well then, it would seem to me that instead of wasting your time here, you should be spending every minute with Maggie. Attempting to convince her to give up the, um, future and stay with you."

"It wouldn't do any good." Adam shook his head in misery.

"Well, old man, I think you should bloody well give it a try. Now come on." Richard pushed himself out of the chair and stood over Adam. "We shall call for your carriage. It is past time we both retired to our respective homes."

Adam unfolded his body from the deep chair and rose beside his friend. Surprised, Richard noted Adam was far steadier on his feet than he expected.

"It won't work," Adam said sadly, shaking his head.

"Give it a try, Adam." Richard escorted his friend toward the door. "It seems to me that at this point

311

you have very little to lose. And possibly very much to gain."

Adam stalked into his room and shrugged his jacket off, tossing it on a nearby chair. He stole a quick glance at the door to Maggie's room. In recent days, that glance had become a habit. Startled, he looked again. From here it appeared the door to her chamber stood open. He moved cautiously closer. It was open. Gently he pushed and the door swung wide. Adam peered into the darkened room. There, curled up in a chair near the door, was Maggie, sound asleep.

Adam thought his heart would break anew at the sight. Her head rested on her arms; long, lush lashes swept her cheek; her lips parted slightly with each breath. Was it only two weeks ago he had watched her curiously as she slept? Wondering who this woman was? What she was like? A lifetime had passed since then.

Adam wanted to sweep her into his arms and steal her off to his bed. Wanted to keep her imprisoned there for tonight and always. His fists clenched by his side. No. If she would not stay with him willingly he would not force her. He would not beg.

He gently pulled the door back to where he had found it and headed toward his bed, pulling off his cravat and kicking off his shoes. The temptation of knowing Maggie was within his reach dictated he not remove his clothing. Adam turned down the lamp and fell into bed. Crossing his arms under his head he lay wide awake, staring at the canopy, asking questions he had no answers for.

Was Maggie right? Would it create a great imbalance in the fabric of time for her to stay with him? Could one mere person make a difference in the centuries to come, as Maggie believed? If she were correct, he had no right to expect her to stay. In fact, it would be as much his responsibility as hers to make sure she returned to her own time, but Adam could not dismiss the feeling that radiated from the pit of his stomach and filled every nook and cranny of his soul.

He and Maggie were destined, fated to be together.

In the meantime, should he follow Richard's advice? Spend every possible minute with her in hopes of changing her mind? Or was it better to acknowledge defeat and start getting over her now? Better to lose no time in returning to his well-ordered life? It seemed far less painful but somehow cowardly. How empty his life would be without her.

Eventually he would marry. It was his duty and responsibility to wed and produce an heir. But how could any woman compare to his outrageous, passionate Maggie?

Maggie. The only woman in a lifetime of searching he had found to love. The only woman he had ever admired for intelligence and courage and, God help him, independence. The only woman he had ever made love to whose body and soul soared with his own.

Would he ever escape the memories of their days together? Forget the sound of her laughter, the teasing lilt in her voice and gentle insistent demands of her touch? Would he compare every other woman to her? Search every face hoping against hope she had returned? Would he do that for the rest of his life?

And what of her? Surely she would marry someday and have children. Would she look at them and wonder what children she and he would have created? Or would her days spent with him simply become another adventure in a lifetime of adventures? Would their love and their passion fade to a dim memory somewhere in the distant past? Would she forget the fire and the frenzy and the way their souls forged together for all time?

Would she look for his grave?

The questions assaulted him, battering his mind, and he tossed and turned on the bed until he could take no more. He leapt up and strode to the chair, flinging his jacket to the floor. He positioned the chair in front of Maggie's door and pushed. The door swung open. She had not moved. Adam sank into the chair, propped his elbows on the sides and rested his chin on his steepled fingers.

Maybe Richard was right. Maybe not. At any rate, at this moment, he could at least be near her without her knowing. Without losing any of his masculine pride. He would commit every detail of her face, every line of her body to memory. And he would do it well.

It must last a lifetime.

Sunlight streamed into the room. Maggie's eyes flicked open. She jerked upright in the chair and winced, the crick in her neck a painful protest. Damn! She must have fallen asleep. Cautiously she leaned forward and peaked through the crack in the door. Nothing. She pulled the door wider and finally flung it open. Empty. Maggie moved to the bed and found the bedclothes disturbed. Adam had obviously been here and gone.

"Ha! If he thinks he can escape me that easily he's got another think coming." She stalked out the door, building up steam, heading for the breakfast room.

"Okay, where is he?" Maggie stormed in and scanned the room. Lydia sat serenely at the table behind a pile of correspondence. She glanced up casually. "Who?"

"You know who," Maggie snapped. "Your brother, that's who. Now where is he?"

Lydia peered around with an air of surprised innocence. "Well, I don't believe he is here."

"I can see that." Maggie clenched her teeth. "I have to find him. I have to talk to him. His days of avoiding me are over. And as for you . . ." Maggie paused to level Lydia a scathing glare. "You may be right. I may be scared about love and commitment and everything that goes with it. But if I had a choice . . ." She hesitated, then made up her mind and plunged ahead. "If I had a choice, I'd stay here with Adam. But I don't have a choice. And until I leave I want to spend every possible minute with your pigheaded, sexist, stuffy, annoying brother. Do you understand?"

An amused smile rested on Lydia's lips. "Bravo!"

"Bravo?"

"I was wondering when you'd stop behaving like a beaten puppy. It is not at all like you. I must say it took far longer for you to come to your senses than I'd anticipated."

Maggie narrowed her eyes in suspicion. "You expected this?"

"Oh, my, yes," Lydia said with a light laugh. "I assume you have concocted some sort of plan. Not a kidnapping, of course." Lydia had the grace to blush at the reminder. "But something equally as clever."

Maggie sighed and sank into a chair. At least she and Lydia seemed to be allies once again. One Coleridge down, one to go.

"I have to talk to him. I have to make him listen, try to make him understand. If, of course, I can find him."

"That's not at all difficult. I believe he is at his club, White's. It has become a second home."

"Great." Maggie leaned forward eagerly. "Where is this place?"

"It's on St. James Street, of course. Not far from here." Lydia's brows drew together in a delicate frown; then her eyes widened. Comprehension dawned on her face. "Oh no, Maggie. You wouldn't. You couldn't. It's not permitted for a respectable woman to even be on that street, let alone go into a club. Your reputation will be ruined."

"Oh, knock it off, Lydia. I don't have a reputation and I don't care what anybody thinks." She grinned. "If going into that hideout of his will make him listen to me, then anything is worth it." She stood and headed for the door. "I'll see you later."

"Wait," Lydia said. "If you are determined to do this, at least change your clothing. You look like— what is that quaint expression you use?—oh yes, pond scum. Your clothes have the appearance of having been slept in."

"Actually, I did sleep in them," Maggie said sheepishly. "Okay, I'll change and then I'll go."

Lydia sighed in resignation. "And when you are ready I shall accompany you."

"Oh, no, you won't." Maggie shook her head vehemently. "I don't have anything to lose here but you . . . This is your world. I don't see this as any big deal but I've been here long enough to know your society, the poundage or weight or whatever in the hell you call it—"

"Ton?" Lydia said helpfully.

"Yeah, the ton, they are not forgiving of people who break the rules. You've gotten away with a lot in the past, Lydia, but don't push it." Maggie shot her a firm glance. "You're not coming."

Lydia beamed. "That is so very thoughtful and kind but I'm afraid my mind is quite made up. I shan't allow you to go alone and the idea of missing out on an adventure of this magnitude, well, it really is worth the risk, don't you think?"

Lydia paused, abruptly serious. "Maggie, I am three and twenty, far past the time when most women wed. I have been out in society since shortly after my seventeenth birthday. To date, I have had numerous offers of marriage but none that I have been willing to settle for. It may well be that I will never find the love I desire, but I refuse to accept less. By accompanying you, my reputation shall very probably be destroyed."

A smile danced on Lydia's lips. "At the very least, after this Adam shall not find it at all easy to marry me off to some respectable but boring peer. The only men that will be willing to accept me will be

317

somewhat less than respectable." She shrugged sagely. "It's been my observation that men who are less than respectable are usually extremely interesting. Eventually, if I am forced to take a husband not of my own choosing, I prefer he be interesting." Lydia's eyes twinkled. "You do plan to go all the way inside, do you not?"

Maggie groaned, accepting the inevitable. "Oh yeah, all the way. We might as well leave no stones unturned, no conventions intact."

Lydia clapped her hands together. "Wonderful. This shall be exciting! Now hurry and change so we can be off."

Maggie sighed and stalked out the door. Bringing Lydia was a big mistake. Not only would Adam be irritated by her appearance at his precious club, he'd be angry that she'd dragged Lydia along with her. Oh, well. Maggie turned toward the stairs. Things could hardly be much worse. This might very well be her last chance with Adam.

Lydia's voice followed her up the stairs. "Oh, Maggie." Maggie paused to listen. "Do wear something pretty. Adventures always go so much better when one looks one's best."

Chapter Seventeen

"What do you think? Should we knock or just barge right in?" Maggie eyed the entry to Adam's club. Well aware of the startled male eyes peering at them from a nearby bow window, she and Lydia paused to consider their next step at the door of White's.

"Well," Lydia said brightly, "I should think if we knock, it would allow them the opportunity to refuse us entry. I believe barging in may well be our wisest choice."

"Good move." Maggie squared her shoulders and took a deep breath. While the idea of intruding on a hallowed men's club, a sacred shrine to testosterone, held a lot of appeal, now that she was actually here, the reality of what she and Lydia were about to do sent a flurry of winged creatures fluttering in her stomach. "The best defense is a good offense," she murmured. "Let's go."

Maggie gripped the doorknob and shoved, nearly

stumbling when the barrier to the masculine sanctuary opened smoothly. They stepped firmly across
the threshold. Maggie barely registered a vague impression of dark wood and dim lighting before the
apparent guardian of the male stronghold bore down
on them, sputtering and spewing like a masculine
avenging fury.

"I beg your pardon, miss, but women are not permitted to enter. This is a men's facility and we do
not—"

"Can it, pal," Maggie snapped. "Here's the deal. I'm
here to see Coleridge. Adam Coleridge. The big shot
earl of something or other—"

"Ridgewood," Lydia supplied helpfully.

"Yeah, thanks." Maggie nodded to Lydia then directed her best withering glare at the flustered, red-
faced protector of male virtue. "Ridgewood, that's
who I'm here to see. And I'm not moving one inch
until I do. So if you're really so threatened by having
two measly women in your bastian of male chauvinist pigdom, I suggest you get him out here right now.
Do I make myself perfectly, totally, and completely
clear?"

The sentinel was almost comical in his helpless
rage and Maggie wondered briefly if he would succumb to some kind of fit right here on the floor. He
drew himself up to his full height, not much taller
than she, and glared with righteous indignation.

"My responsibilities are to this club and to its
members and I shan't—"

"You shall. You will. You'd better," Maggie shot
back. "The way I see it, you have two choices. You
can stand here and let me make a scene so outra-

geous it will go down in history, and believe me, pal, I know what will go down in history, or you can haul Coleridge's butt out here. And you can do it now."

"I have no intention—"

"I'll handle this."

Maggie whirled at the sound of Adam's voice and her heart thudded in her chest at the sight of him. His figure, tense with controlled anger, filled a nearby doorway. His face, hardened with fury, was a fitting setting for eyes that blazed malevolently. Maggie's started at the sight of the man she loved giving every appearance of an intent to kill her, slowly and painfully. Only the somewhat haggard and weary look around his eyes that even rage could not disguise kept her courage up.

"Coleridge has, as you so colorfully put it, hauled his butt out here." In two long strides, he reached her, roughly grabbed her elbow and hauled her to a corner of the foyer. Not actually discreet, but the two of them no longer stood in the center of the room.

He glared down at her upturned face. "What in the name of all that's holy are you doing? Your presence is not only appalling but scandalous. There has never, I repeat never in the history of this club been a woman inside these doors. I know life is much different where you come from but I cannot believe even you have the audacity to totally fly in the face of the conventions of my world. Of my life."

His fury mesmerized her. For a moment, fascination with the sheer power of his anger overwhelmed her and she lost track of exactly what he said. Until he spit out the words guaranteed to catch her attention.

"Have you absolutely no sense of propriety? No understanding of a woman's place?"

She choked back a strangled gasp. "What a load of crock that is, Coleridge. I have every sense of a woman's place. It's in the house and in the senate!"

"What the bloody hell does that mean?" Confusion rang in his voice.

"Nevermind," she snapped. "It was an automatic response. It's from a bumper sticker. It doesn't—what? Lydia?"

"Signify?" Lydia suggested.

"Yeah, that's it, signify." Maggie sighed in exasperation and clenched her teeth. "You're getting me off track with your sexist, antique attitudes so shut up for a minute and let me talk." She glared at him and his smoldering eyes narrowed. "That's better."

"What do you want?" The words were clipped, slow and dangerous.

"I want you, you idiot." She stared into his rage darkened eyes. "I want you. I want to spend the rest of my time here with you. Every minute. Every day. Every night. I don't want to waste any more time yelling and screaming. I don't want to squander precious hours with both of us miserable. Being together now, when we can, has got to be worth something. Maybe it will hurt more when it's over, than if we stopped seeing each other right now. I don't know and I don't care. It's a risk I sure as hell am willing to take."

He raised a skeptical eyebrow.

"Don't you do that to me." She said, infuriated. "Don't you give me that superior little quirky thing you do with your eyebrow. It drives me crazy. I'm surprised you've managed to get through life without somebody trying to rip it off!"

Maggie drew a deep breath and threw down her final gauntlet. "Look, Adam. I know this is scary and maybe it's too much to ask. Maybe, you're all brave and macho when it comes to duels or whatever but when it comes to your heart, maybe you're just too much of a coward to take a chance."

Maggie tore her gaze from his and struggled to find the right words, fighting to gain control, willing herself to calm down. Her hands trembled. She raised her gaze again to his, hoping he could read all her emotions and mentally whispered a silent prayer to reach him.

"If I can't be with you for the rest of my life, I want to cram a lifetime of memories into the days we have left. We don't have forever and way too soon this will all be over, but I don't want to live without you. Not until I have to."

Adam stared at the fiery creature before him. His Incomparable. His Original. God, she was magnificent. Her green eyes flashed and glittered like living emeralds. Priceless. Color flushed her cheeks. Her attitude was stubborn and unyielding, her stance defiant. He read the challenge in her eyes and a glimmer of uncertainty as well.

How could he resist? How could he turn away? How could he tell her he had already decided a few days with her were well worth a lifetime with anyone else?

"I accept," he said calmly.

Her eyes widened with apparent surprise at the

ease of her victory and his surrender. "What do you mean, you accept?"

A smile tugged at his lips. "I mean, I accept your proposal, or challenge, or terms." He grabbed her and pulled her into his arms. Adam lowered his head until they stood nearly nose to nose. His gaze bore into hers and he noted with satisfaction the apprehension in the glowing depths of her eyes.

He gritted his teeth, his quiet words for her alone. "If you ever come here or any other place that is strictly out of bounds for women of my time and my world again, you will live to regret it." Maggie narrowed her eyes and opened her mouth. "Be quiet. I am not finished. I, in turn, will not use such a place to avoid dealing with you." Relief flared in her eyes and a smile teased the corners of her mouth. "Now," he growled. "Kiss me."

With a joyous cry she threw her arms around his neck and his lips crushed hers, seeking, devouring, breathing the life from her and returning it again, nourished and full. Maggie paid no attention to the faces staring from every foyer opening. She could have been anywhere and would not have noticed or cared. All she knew was the power and glory of Adam's plundering lips and her own impassioned response. All she wanted was to drown herself in the cascade of emotion and sensation rushing over her. All she needed was to be here, in his arms, where at least for now, she belonged.

Gently, Adam pulled back and Maggie stared up at him. "Wow," she breathed, and sagged against him, her knees too wobbly to support her. "We really do that well, don't we?"

He threw back his head and laughed with delight. "Yes, my darling Maggie, we do indeed." He gallantly offered her his arm and escorted her toward the door. "Now, shall we go home?"

"Lydia?" he tossed over his shoulder. "Your presence here has not gone unnoticed and we will discuss your actions at a later point." He sighed in surrender. "Right now, I will be happy to simply assume you are directly behind us."

"Of course, Adam, I'm coming."

Lydia trailed after Adam and Maggie, taking in as many of the details of White's as she could. This was an opportunity that came to a woman only once in a lifetime, if then. She peered around. It was all rather disappointing. She wasn't sure exactly what she had expected, but something . . . well . . . more. This was the epitome of the English men's club, the ultimate haven for the men of her world. A sanctuary where they pursued such manly pastimes as drinking and gaming. And it appeared dull and boring.

"What a shame," she murmured under her breath and swept through the hallowed portals of White's with a vaguely superior sense that even if men deemed it necessary to hide away from the world surrounded by their own kind, it was somehow pleasant to know the women who were forbidden entry weren't missing very much at all.

Edward Lindley lounged inconspicuously among the curious club members now dispersing from their positions in the doorways and entries surrounding the foyer. Many muttered in outrage at the feminine intrusion into their sanctuary. Still others chuckled in amusement and more than one wager was laid as to how soon there would be a Ridgewood heir.

Edward's casual attitude belied his intense scrutiny of the scene in the foyer. Judging by Ridgewood's miserable demeanor in recent days, Edward had been certain Maggie would have no more to do with the man. Now, however, it was obvious the pair had reconciled. Too bad. Edward actually liked the headstrong beauty. The idea of taking her for himself had entered his mind more than once. Still, perhaps it was not too late. Perhaps the seed he'd planted during their talk would eventually bear fruit.

If not, there were other ways to separate the American from Ridgewood. Other ways to destroy the earl's happiness.

Other ways to make him pay.

Maggie and Adam spent the next week alone together at his country home a few hours outside London. The house itself was a huge Palladian structure, enormous and elegant but somehow still a home. Adam's eyes glowed with pride as he showed her around. The better part of his childhood was spent here and Maggie envisioned hordes of happy children joyously careening through the halls. She ignored the pang in her heart at the thought. Those children would not be hers.

As lovely as the house was it could not compete with the beauty of its setting. The glorious English countryside blazed with a profusion of spring flowers, the rolling meadows and fields fresh and green and new with the promise of the season. This was how she had imagined it in visions conjured up by childhood tales of Alice in Wonderland and Peter Rabbit.

They filled long, lazy days discovering each other. Adam shared his love of horses and they rode nearly every morning. Maggie adamantly refused to ride sidesaddle and Adam grudgingly conceded. For one not used to it, the saddle could indeed be not only difficult but dangerous. Still, he drew the line at her desire to wear jeans, arguing that even if she did not care about her shattered reputation her actions reflected on his family. Maggie grumbled but compromised and directed a servant in fashioning a type of split skirt for riding that Adam reluctantly accepted.

The influence of the man she loved and the charm of the country reawakened the urge in Maggie to paint, an urge she thought had died long ago. Adam sent to London for supplies and Maggie applied paint to canvas with inspired abandon. Each brush stroke came stronger and surer and her canvases glowed with energy and light. With Adam lying on the grass by her side, she created works radiant with life, shimmering with color, ebullient with emotion. She alone recognized the influence of the impressionists yet to come. Maggie basked in Adam's enthusiastic admiration, warmed by the beacon of respect in his eyes.

It had been years since she'd picked up a brush for pleasure. Years since she'd had either the time or the desire to express herself on canvas for the sheer joy of creation. Instinct told her these were the best works of her life. The knowledge filled her heart. These paintings would stay with Adam, a part of her that would be with him always.

While she painted they talked about their lives and their worlds, their dreams and desires. Adam told her about his childhood and she pictured the tanned, golden-haired little boy running barefoot through the fields. He talked about his shimmering memories of a princesslike mother, beautiful and spirited and far too wonderful to grow old and Maggie saw the heartbroken 12-year-old coping with the death of a beloved parent and struggling to be a man. Eventually Adam told her of his wild youth, of his rebellious nature and scandalous actions. He spoke quietly of the father he had loved and fought and learned to understand only when it was too late, and Maggie glimpsed beyond the strong, confident adult at her side to the impulsive, headstrong young man, reckless and confused.

Maggie gave of herself as well. She shared with Adam her grief at the death of her parents and talked quite a bit about her sister, how Kiki had been both mother and father to her. She spoke with justifiable pride of her sister's successful career in a highly competitive field. She'd never told her sister of her feelings and a rush of shame swept through her at her selfish omission.

Maggie and Adam spoke of the future. His curiosity extended far beyond her abilities to explain. Some things he simply would not believe. He accepted the idea of airplanes but drew the line at space travel. When she told him men had walked on the moon he accused her of making it all up. But the concept of telephones and television and computers fascinated him. The gleam in his eye told Maggie he

328

would like nothing better than to get his hands on one of the cars he'd seen in her magazines. She'd laughed when he found the very thought of drive-through fast food, well . . . "highly distasteful and positively uncivilized."

Maggie refused to talk specifically about history yet to come. He had read her magazines. He knew her world was not perfect. But she could not bear to tell him of the horrible things man would do to man in the coming years. She could not tell him her own country would be ripped apart by civil war. Could not tell him his country would be threatened by conflicts so enormous they were called world wars. And she could not tell him about weapons that could wipe out entire cities.

The battle of the sexes was one war she eagerly leapt into. Maggie argued for hours on the topic of the intelligence and abilities of women. Adam acknowledged that she was indeed superior to women of his day but remained skeptical about women overall. Maggie grew more and more frustrated trying to convince him women shouldn't be treated like mere property, that they could, and should, take care of themselves. He would appear to give in and she would feel victory within her grasp, only to note the teasing glint in his eye and realize he was humoring her.

Their days were glorious, their nights . . . exquisite. Locked in each other's arms they explored the boundaries of desire, pushed the limits of their passion. Each time together was more magnificent than the time before. Maggie thought surely mere humans weren't meant to experience such ecstasy, surely mere mortals could not long survive such pleasure, surely only the gods themselves were allowed to slip the bonds of earth and soar to the heights where her soul and Adam's emerged as one. Even when time ripped them apart, a piece of their hearts would stay always with the other.

By mutual, unspoken agreement, neither mentioned the days rushing past, leading them inevitably to the end. Maggie couldn't help but keep a running countdown in her head. They returned to town a week before she was to leave, regretfully saying good-bye to perfect days and endless nights.

Maggie and Adam sampled all the delights Regency London had to offer. He seemed to want to show off his city and his century, seemed to want her to see everything in its best light. They returned to the British Museum and toured the Tower of London and Westminster Abbey. They attended a masquerade at Vauxhall Gardens and went once to the theater. Maggie was fascinated by everything and realized part of her pleasure came from the presence of the man at her side.

Now and then she'd catch Adam watching her speculatively and hoped he wasn't thinking about trying to change her mind about leaving. She'd brush the idea aside, refusing to dwell on the parting to come. But with every shared laugh, every tender moment, every passion-filled encounter came the unbidden thought. There were not many left.

For the most part, Lydia wisely left them alone, but two nights after their return to London, Adam and Maggie planned to go with her to another ball. Maggie didn't care how long she stayed, she'd never get over the passion with which these people threw themselves into entertaining and being entertained. Of course, they all seemed to have endless supplies of money and no real jobs to worry about.

Maggie dressed earlier than the others and wandered down to the library. She wore a rather simply cut, cream-colored gown and was no longer even mildly bothered by the revealing decolletage. She twirled experimentally around the room. Tonight, once again, Adam would take her in his arms and they would waltz, flying across the floor in a manner that was far too wonderful to be called a mere dance. Maggie would miss the waltz, miss the elegant clothes, and most especially miss this room.

The library would always be her favorite place. Here she and Adam fought and made up and made love. She ran her fingers lightly over the well-polished mahogany desk. Did this room, this house, still exist in her time? She firmly pushed the thought away. She wouldn't let such musings intrude on the precious little time left.

A discreet tap sounded at the door and Wilson entered quietly. "Miss, you have a visitor. Shall I show him in?"

"A visitor? Who would be visiting me? How strange. Well, thanks. I guess he can come on in."

Wilson withdrew and a moment later Edward Lindley stepped into the room.

"Edward!" Maggie beamed, genuinely pleased to see him. "How nice to see you again. But"—she gave him an apologetic glance—"I'm afraid it's kind of a bad time. We're just getting ready to go out."

"This shan't take long," Edward said somberly, and

331

Maggie frowned, puzzled by his serious tone.

"Okay, what's up?"

"Up?" Edward questioned, then shook his head as if to clear her unusual phrase from his mind. "Maggie, I know that you and Ridgewood have resolved your differences."

"How did you—" Maggie paused and the answer hit her. "Oh, the business at his club. Does everybody know about that?"

"Only most of London, I should think," Edward responded wryly. "You have created quite a sensation."

"And quite a lot of gossip, too, I bet." Maggie laughed and shrugged. "That's the way it goes. By the way, I haven't thanked you for listening to me when I needed a friend. I really appreciate it."

"I told you then I did not merely want to be your friend." His blue eyes glittered strangely. "I want much more than that."

"Edward." She gave him a teasing smile to hide her growing unease, increasingly aware of the odd way he stared at her.

"Come away with me, Maggie. Marry me. We can be in Gretna Green before morning."

Speechless, Maggie stared. "Edward. Haven't we been all through this? I appreciate the offer. It's nice to be asked but I don't want to marry you. Adam and I are, well, involved. So thanks, but no thanks."

Edward's eyes darkened, his features hardened. He appeared different, frightening somehow.

"Edward, don't take it so hard. I can't imagine you honestly thought I'd accept."

"It would be for the best, Maggie." His voice was

332

soft and persuasive and he slowly approached her. The narrowing distance between them unnerved her but Maggie stood her ground. "Ridgewood is no good for you, Maggie. He will only destroy you."

"That's okay, I'll take my chances." This was getting really weird. Maggie didn't think Edward would actually hurt her but the look in his eyes was definitely spooky. Adam should be down any minute. Stalling Edward seemed her best bet. "What's Gretna Green anyway? Sounds like a golf course."

"It's a village just over the Scottish border." He had crossed the room. Only the desk stood between them. "Eager lovers go there to be wed."

"Well then, we can't go there, can we?" She inched backward. "I'm definitely not eager. And we're friends, remember, not lovers."

"Not yet," he growled, circling the desk.

She matched her movements to his, keeping the desk between them. This guy was definitely nuts. Maybe she needed to be firmer. "Edward, there's no way I'm going to marry you, so you can knock this nonsense off."

"Maggie, you will accompany me. Willingly." He paused and pulled a wicked-looking dagger from beneath his coat. "Or not." He shrugged as if he didn't care one way or the other. "It is up to you."

"Edward, don't you think you're being overly dramatic?" Again they circled the desk in a bizarre dance. "You have a real problem with rejection, don't you?"

The gleam in his eye seemed sharper, his look crueler. "It is your decision."

"I don't think you've given this enough thought."

Maggie kept her gaze on Edward on the opposite side of the desk, watching out of the corner of her eye for the door to the library to open. Surely Adam would walk through any time now. "I'd make a lousy wife. I'm stubborn and impulsive. I have absolutely no regard for propriety. I mean look, I've already created a major scandal."

"It adds to the excitement, Maggie."

Her mind raced; surely there were other reasons why she'd be a bad choice for a wife. "You're in line for a title, right?"

"I will be a baron when my grandfather dies." His eyes narrowed suspiciously. "Why?"

"Well . . ." *Why, Maggie? Think!* "Then I'd be like, what, a baronette? It sounds like something you'd get at a movie. I'd like a soft drink and a box of baronettes. See, I don't even know the right words and I am completely irreverent. I'd only embarrass you. And besides . . ." It hit her. "I'm an American. You guys don't think too highly of Americans. We're crude, we're boisterous, we're big mouths. And none of us have titles. All your friends would think you'd married beneath you."

"I do not care," he muttered through clenched teeth.

They kept their measured pace, Maggie not letting him get any closer, keeping the desk between them.

"Edward, I don't get it. Why are you so hot and bothered to marry me anyway? Basically we've just shared a couple of drinks together. Even where I'm from, that's no basis for a long-term commitment." The dagger in his hand matched the daggers in his eyes and it finally dawned on Maggie. This time she

334

was in real danger. Even the Rocky Mountain School of Karate and Martial Arts self-defense course for women never covered how to defend yourself against a knife-wielding, nineteenth-century lunatic while wearing an elaborate, formal gown.

"Ridgewood wants you. That is enough for me."

"Adam? No, you've got it all wrong." Where the hell was Adam? "You were right all along. He was just toying with me, using me. He's going to dump me anytime now. So if that's what this is all about, you can forget it. It's all a mistake." She smiled and shrugged, hoping he would buy the lie.

"I do not believe you." He spit the words at her and the two stared at each other.

"Maggie, are you in here?" Adam strode into the room, apparently unaware of their guest.

"Adam!" Maggie lunged toward him. In a flash, Edward grabbed her arm and crushed her against him, pulling her behind the desk, the dagger poised at her throat.

"Maggie!" Adam leapt forward then pulled up short. The meaning of the scene in front of him clear. "Good God."

"Adam," Maggie squeaked. "I believe you know Edward Lindley, don't you?"

"Lindley, what is the meaning of all this?" Adam appeared calm but Maggie sensed the tension in every line of his body.

Edward's voice rang cold. "I have waited a very long time for this, Ridgewood."

Edward stood slightly to Maggie's side and she could get a twisted glimpse of his features. She did not like the look of sheer hatred on his face.

"Adam, he says he wants to marry me. I keep trying to tell him he doesn't want me for a wife. I can be a real bitch. Tell him, Adam."

Adam shrugged. "I vow, she can be most exceedingly difficult."

Maggie gave him a scathing glare. His agreement was a little too enthusiastic. "And I have a nasty temper and a vulgar vocabulary."

"Bloody hell, Lindley, she sounds like a street urchin half the time, the other half like a seasoned sailor."

Adam was trying to help, but he didn't have to enjoy it quite so much. After all, she did have a knife at her throat.

"See, Edward. You really don't want to marry me."

"Perhaps," he said quietly, "I shall kill you instead."

"Oh, great." Maggie groaned. Suddenly marriage didn't seem so bad.

Adam was obviously taking Edward's suggestion seriously. It wasn't anything he did overtly, but his voice hardened, his stance tightened. His gaze captured Lindley's. "Why?"

Edward laughed, an eerie, definitely crazy sound. "Why, Ridgewood? I cannot possibly expect you to remember someone who obviously played such a tiny part in your extremely full life."

"Remember who? You?" Adam stared, puzzled.

"Not me." Edward scoffed. "Eleanor Chatterton."

A wave of emotion swept quickly over Adam's face, vanishing as abruptly as it appeared.

"She had position and wealth," Edward said. "But that meant nothing to me. I loved her. I loved her for years and was living for the day I could make her mine. But she had eyes only for you. Even when you rejected her and I offered my suit, she disregarded me." Edward paused as if remembering the scene, then continued bitterly. "She said if she could not have you she would not settle for me. That night she took her own life."

The room fell silent.

"Oh, Edward, I'm so sorry," Maggie said softly.

Her words seemed to drag him back from the past and he raised blazing eyes to Adam. "You did that to me, Ridgewood. Now I shall do it to you. I shall have the woman you love. She will belong to me."

Adam gave him a look of disgust. "She will not belong to you and does not belong to me. Women are not property to be passed around like cattle."

"Adam!" Maggie cried with delight. "You've finally got it. I am really proud of you." In her surprised pleasure Maggie instinctively took a step toward him, only to be jerked back hard against Edward's chest.

"Quiet!" Edward shouted. "Listen to me closely. She will marry me or I shall kill her. Either way, Ridgewood, you lose and will finally know the same pain I did."

"Wait a minute," Maggie tossed in. "You're going to kill me to make him miserable? Don't you see a problem here? I mean, yeah, he'll mourn and grieve for a while but then life goes on. I'll be dead and buried and he'll be alive and well. Do you really think this is the best way to get even?"

"Does she always talk so much?" Edward said impatiently.

Adam shrugged in resignation. "Always."

"Okay, guys, let me make sure I have this straight. It's marriage to Edward or death, right?"

"Precisely," Edward said.

"Well then." Maggie paused and took a deep breath. "I guess it's marriage. Okay Edward, I'll marry you."

"Excellent," Edward sneered.

"Bloody hell," Adam said.

"Well, Adam, it's not like I have much of a choice here." An idea flashed through her mind. One that might work. If she could get Adam to understand. Right now he looked so flabbergasted she wasn't sure if anything could penetrate. Still, she sure didn't have much to lose. "So, let's toast our engagement. Brandy sounds good to me. And Edward, you could probably let go of me now, you know, put the knife down."

"I am not a fool," Edward growled, but he did relax his grip.

"Now, Adam." Maggie's gaze locked with his and she prayed he'd understand. "Remember the first time we met, the very first time? In this very room? You told me how great that brandy was?" She glanced at the heavy crystal decanter on the table and his gaze followed hers. "Remember how I offered it to you that day?"

A puzzled frown knit his brow. "You offered it to me?"

"Yeah, remember?" *Please remember.* "But you pointed out how fine it was and suggested I have something else instead?"

"I suggested . . ." Comprehension finally dawned on his face. "Of course, yes, certainly I remember."

Adam strode to the table and grabbed the decanter. He approached Edward and Maggie cautiously.

"Don't come any closer," Edward barked.

Adam stopped in his tracks. "I was simply going to offer the brandy."

"And I really need it, Edward." Maggie words bubbled out fast and furiously. "All this excitement, I really think I'm going to pass out or something." She willed herself to go limp and sagged in his arms, forcing him to pay more attention to the arm supporting her and less to the hand with the knife. "Oh, yeah, I'm going to faint. Right here. Any minute."

Her eyes met Adam's. Surely he understood. "Probably going to keel over right here on this desk. Yeah, I can feel it coming . . . right . . . now!" She lunged forward, flinging herself over the desk. Maggie caught a fast glimpse of Adam hurling the decanter like a major-league pitcher. A sharp pain pricked her neck. A thud sounded inches behind her. Brandy rained over her head and the decanter hit the floor with a resounding crash. She jerked up from the desk and whirled around. Edward lay unconscious on the floor.

She stared at Adam with open admiration. "Good shot!" She glanced at Edward. "Jeez, I hope you didn't kill him."

Adam was at her side in a second, crushing her to him. "He deserves it, but I doubt if he's dead." He tipped her chin up and stared into her eyes. "Bloody hell, Maggie, I don't even know what to say to you anymore. Every time I turn around you're in some kind of trouble and you always seem to be able to get yourself out of it."

Maggie pulled back and gazed into his face in amazement. "Adam, you're the one who did it. You saved my life."

"No, my love. It was your idea." He shook his head slowly. "You are indeed well able to take care of yourself. You don't need me."

His statement hung in the air between them and Maggie didn't know what to say. She stared up at him and read fresh pain in his eyes. She wanted to reassure him. Of course she needed him. Didn't she? The thought shook her, and at this moment she wasn't sure if she knew the answer.

"Adam, don't be silly." She laughed nervously, dismissing his comment. It was an unsatisfactory response. She knew it and sensed he did, too. Maggie hurried to change the subject.

She stepped away and gestured to her clothes. "What a mess. I'm a disaster. I've got brandy just about everywhere." She reached a hand up and swiped at her neck. "Look at this." She held out a hand covered with brandy and . . . blood.

"Blood!" she cried. "I'm bleeding! He cut me!"

Adam leaned forward and examined her neck. "Maggie, it's barely a scratch."

The room swayed around her. "Adam, you don't understand." The lights grew dim. "It's blood, it's my blood." Her knees buckled slowly. "I'm not very good with blood," she murmured and crashed face-forward onto the desk once more, this time for real.

Adam stared blankly for just a moment, then chuckled. He swept her into his arms and carried her to the sofa, the chuckle growing to a full-fledged laugh. The woman who stood up to him without a second thought, handled kidnappers with apparent ease, and unflinchingly dealt with a knife-wielding lunatic, his courageous, spirited Maggie . . . couldn't bear the sight of her own blood.

Chapter Eighteen

Maggie's eyes fluttered open and Adam's amused face filled her line of sight. "Adam." She struggled to sit up. "What happened?"

He sat on the sofa beside her reclining figure and chuckled. "You fainted. I never would have imagined"—he shook his head wryly—"you, of all people, overset by a little blood."

She clapped her hand to her neck and fingered a bandage there. "It's not that I'm afraid, actually," she said defensively. "It's just that when it's mine, I find it, well, unnerving." She glared up at him. "Does this make you happy?"

He took her hand and raised it to his lips. His gaze never left hers. "Ecstatic."

The touch of his lips sent a thrill of electricity racing through her and she wanted nothing more than to be crushed in his arms, lost in his embrace.

"Hey!" She sat upright abruptly and stared toward

the desk. "Where's Edward?"

"The servants are watching him. He is still unconscious. I have sent for the authorities."

She searched his face anxiously. "What was that
all about? Was there any truth in what Edward
said?"

Adam pulled his gaze from hers and stared unseeing across the room. "Eleanor was the woman I told
you about. The woman gossip linked me with right
before my father died. I paid perhaps more attention
to her than I should have, but I never believed she
considered it was more than a mild flirtation."

He sighed heavily and continued. "She died about
a week after my father did." His shoulders sagged. "I
did not know for nearly two months. Her family let
the world believe it was a carriage accident, but they
wanted me to know the truth."

"That she killed herself?" Maggie said gently.

"God, no." Adam raised startled eyes. "Eleanor and
I liked each other, enjoyed each other's company,
but we were never in love. She had no reason to take
her own life." He reached forward and grasped her
hands. His eyes gazed deeply into hers and she read
concern there, as if Adam worried about her reaction
to his words. An icy hand of apprehension gripped
her heart.

"Maggie," he said slowly, "Eleanor's family
thought she had another suitor, one she spurned in
favor of me. She did not kill herself. She was mur-
dered." He gripped her hands tightly. "I believe the
suitor and the murderer was Edward."

"What?" She snatched her hands from his. "You're
saying he's done this before? That's really hard to

343

believe." Could she have been that wrong about the man? She shook her head. "Edward was my friend."

"Maggie." Adam spoke calmly and retrieved her hands. His gaze was tender, his words firm. "He tried to kill you. He has apparently been watching me for years, waiting for me to find love. His friendship with you was a sham, a pretense." He reached forward and brushed the hair away from her face, then cupped her chin in his hand and stared into her eyes. "He would have killed you, Maggie, have no doubt. He is insane with his need for revenge and has already killed one woman."

She stared at him, shocked. Her voice was barely a whisper. "He really would have killed me, wouldn't he?" Adam nodded somberly and she shook her head in amazement. "Jeez, this is turning out to be one hell of a vacation."

Abruptly shivers shuddered through her and she couldn't seem to control herself. "Adam, hold me."

He pulled her swiftly into his arms and held her tight against his chest. Maggie let his comfort and strength surround her. Lethargy crept over her and without warning exhaustion gripped her. Maggie wondered dimly if this was some sort of delayed re-action of shock to the events in the library and the revelations afterward. Edward. A murderer. She snuggled deeper in Adam's embrace, sighed heavily, and closed her eyes.

There was something she needed to tell him but her mind was too fuzzy to concentrate. Something he said earlier that she had let slip by. Something he had wrong. What was it? She seemed almost drugged with fatigue and weariness. Whatever it was, she could tell him later.

She still had time.

Even the encounter with Edward did not take Maggie's mind off the days relentlessly racing past. She and Adam spent every minute together, neither mentioning her impending departure. Still, it colored every thought, every action, every moment.

Maggie insisted she and Adam take the pictures remaining in her camera. They drove around London surreptitiously taking photos. Adam commented that they probably looked like a pair of cutpurses plotting break-ins with their secretive behavior. But Maggie snapped that it was easier to deal with a few suspicious looks than to try to explain a device that hadn't been invented yet. The pictures were important to her. They would be the only tangible evidence she'd have of her time here with Adam.

Maggie was able to introduce Adam to a genuine thief when Bert showed up at the house. Adam accepted Maggie's request for passage for Bert and his family without question and graciously thanked the young housebreak for bringing Maggie home. Adam quirked his eyebrow at her when he heard Bert's last name but he never confronted her with the questions the man's presence brought up. Questions Maggie had avoided facing. Questions about changing history or being a part of it, about coincidence versus destiny. When Adam stared speculatively at Bert, Maggie could tell the same questions ran through his mind. She wondered why he never asked them out loud but was grateful for the omission. She didn't know the answers.

She'd catch Adam staring at her but his look was different than it had been before the incident with Edward. In the country, his glances were curious, considering. Now they appeared infinitely sadder, and somehow resigned and accepting. Even without words, Maggie sensed he'd given up any hope of her remaining in his world. It was better this way, though the realization left her vaguely disappointed.

All too soon, May twelfth dawned. Maggie and Adam stayed together in his room for much of the day talking quietly about nothing of importance. All they had to say to each other had either already been said or would never be spoken aloud. Each knew the other's feelings about love and loss. Maggie's conviction that she had to leave remained firm. Yet with each hour that passed she knew it would be harder and harder to say good-bye.

They made love for the last time. Slowly, almost reverently, their usual joy in each other now poignant, bittersweet.

At the end, he gathered her in his embrace and she wept in his arms. For the life they would never build, and the children they would never raise and the golden twilight years they would never share. He held her close and they promised quietly that no matter what happened in their separate futures, they would cherish this time spent together always.

And vowed they would never forget.

After dusk, Lydia joined Maggie and Adam in the front salon, the beautiful green-and-gold room Maggie admired so much when she first arrived. The air lay sluggish around them, thick and heavy with tension and apprehension.

Maggie leaned against the fireplace, dressed once again in the clothes she wore when she dropped into their lives. She had abandoned the fashionable and extremely becoming dresses she had worn for the last month and instead donned the odd, heavy blue trousers, scandalously thin yellow shirt, the leather jacket that looked far more appropriate for a man than a woman, and the bizarre shoes that so fascinated Adam.

The bag full of wonders from another time was looped over one shoulder. Maggie insisted Adam keep the mathematical item she called a calculator, he was so taken by it. Her arms folded across her chest, only her gaze shifted, fixed on Adam pacing in front of the fireplace. Now and then their eyes met. Adam's glowed dark, forbidding, and anguished; Maggie's mirrored acceptance, heartache, and despair.

Lydia watched them silently. They were obviously deeply in love and just as obviously in pain. Her throat ached with tears she refused to spill. This was, after all, their sorrow. She was scarcely more than an observer, but one filled with helplessness and frustration. Lydia was not used to such feelings and she raged inside at the tragedy of it all and her own sense of futility.

She alone still held out a single thread of hope. Lydia had never really believed Maggie would be taken away on this night. Never truly imagined that Maggie and Adam were not destined to stay together always. Maggie's leaving was as farfetched as the whole idea of her arrival from the future in the first place. But Lydia had seen the proof of that. This return trip so far was simply a theory. Lydia stood by the window, periodically pulling back the heavy brocade drapes to peer into the empty street.

Nothing.

Lydia prayed Maggie was wrong. Prayed her theory was flawed. Prayed her carriage would not come.

She noted the time on the mantel clock. Good, it was growing late. Surely it would soon be too late and Maggie's belief that she would return to her own time on this night would be shattered. Lydia nervously checked the street again. Where mere moments ago it was clear, a mist now grew noticeably thicker.

Her heart sank. She glanced at Adam and Maggie, too deep in their own thoughts to notice. The tiny spark of hope within Lydia died A fog-filled night brought Maggie and it appeared one would now take her away.

Lydia turned again to the window and drew back sharply as if stung by what she saw. For a moment she toyed with the idea of not saying anything, of pretending there was nothing outside. She shook her head sadly. It would be no use.

"Bloody hell," she murmured quietly and turned toward the lovers. "I am so sorry." She could hardly bear to say the words. "It appears your carriage has arrived, Maggie."

The color swept from Maggie's face and her anguished gaze caught Adam's. Lydia discreetly left the room. Maggie and Adam stared for a long, silent moment.

"I guess this is it then," Maggie said quietly.

Adam nodded. "It would appear so."

"I don't want to go," she whispered.

Adam just shook his head sadly. It had all been said over and over. Now that it was time, Maggie didn't know how she could bear to leave him.

"Oh, Adam." She sobbed and threw herself into his arms.

"Maggie. Maggie, my love." Adam rained desperate kisses on her as if devouring her would keep her by his side. Waves of despair washed over them and they clung to each other, drowning in their desperate sorrow.

"Oh God, Maggie," Adam whispered hoarsely. "How can I live without you?"

"I can't stay, Adam, I can't. This isn't where I belong." She wrenched herself out of his grasp, knowing if she didn't leave now she never would. Everything told her she had to leave. There was no choice. She started toward the door, then turned back to him. Reaching her hand up to his cheek, she touched his beloved face one last time.

"Forever, Adam. Through all time. Through eternity itself, know . . . I will always love you."

He caught her hand in his and kissed her palm. She gazed into his endless, dark eyes for the last time. A sob choked her throat. She pulled away and ran out of the room, through the grand foyer, and out the front doors. Lydia stood on the steps, staring at the horse and carriage.

She grabbed Maggie's arm. "Maggie, I beg of you,

don't go. Don't do this." Her amber eyes flashed and she caught Maggie's gaze. "It will kill him."

Maggie shook her off. "I have to. You know that and you know why." Maggie swatted impatiently at the tears on her face. "I was right about this damn carriage coming back, wasn't I? I'd say it's a good bet I'm right about the rest of it, too. About one person too many here. About an imbalance." She shook her head and took a deep, steadying breath. "Once I leave, everything will be right again. In history. In time. It will all be back to normal."

"Normal?" Lydia laughed hysterically. "Nothing will ever be normal here again. Adam will die a little each day without you. Oh, he'll do his duty and take care of his responsibilities, but you take with you his heart. Normal, Maggie?" Lydia shook her head. "Look at what you've done to me. You've shown me there will be a time when women will not have to hide their intelligence. When women will be able to stand up for themselves without apology. When marriage will not be their only future. I will not see it, but knowing it will come has changed how I look at myself and everything around me."

Maggie stared, horrified by Lydia's words. "Oh, Lydia, I'm so sorry."

"Do not be sorry." Lydia shook her head and smiled wryly. "It was a wonderful adventure."

Maggie threw her arms around Lydia and embraced her desperately, tears choked with laughter.

"Take care of your brother for me, Lydia," Maggie whispered. "Help him to go on. I love him so much." She released Lydia and stepped toward the carriage.

"Ready, miss?" It was her gnome. Any lingering

doubts vanished. He had returned for her. She nodded silently and he helped her into the carriage.

Maggie turned. Lydia stood on the steps, tears streaming down her face. In the open doorway, Adam stood alone, fists clenched at his sides. She raised a hand in silent farewell but let it fall to her lap. It was too late for good-byes. The carriage moved forward sedately, in no apparent hurry. Adam's figure blurred, obscured by the swirling fog and the tears in her eyes.

Chances and choices, her driver had said on her first ride. *Destiny is a matter of choice, not chance . . . a little bit of both . . . take a chance . . . just mebee . . . that is destiny.*

But she never had a choice, never got to decide whether to take a chance. Maggie had always believed there were no options here, that she had to go back.

A startling thought lanced through her with a physical jolt. Adam didn't know that. She never told him what choice she'd make if she could. How could she leave him forever without letting him know? It was the least she could do for the man she would always love.

"Wait! Stop!" she screamed. "I can't go yet." Maggie stumbled from the rolling carriage. Adam raced toward her and she tumbled into his waiting arms.

"Oh God, Maggie, I thought you were gone forever," Adam cried.

"Adam." She pulled back and stared directly into his eyes. "I couldn't leave without telling you. If I had a choice, if I had to make the decision, nothing could

351

tear me away from you. Do you understand? Nothing."

The glimmer of hope died in his eyes and he shook his head sorrowfully. "No, my love. I fear you are mistaken. I learned the night with Lindley, you do not need me."

"Not need you? What an idiot you are, Coleridge. You've never been so wrong." She shook her head slowly. "I may not need you to protect me or defend me, but without you I don't know how I'll go on or survive. I don't know what will keep my heart beating, how I'll take a breath without you. Need you? Oh, Adam, you're all I've ever needed, ever wanted, ever dreamed of." She shrugged sadly. "Without you, my life won't be worth living."

"Then stay with me, Maggie." His dark gaze searched hers. "Surely one mere person will not make that much of a difference to the next two hundred years."

Maggie shook her head. "I can't take that chance. One person just might throw everything off. I have to—"

"I'll go."

Astonished, Adam and Maggie whirled to find Lydia smiling serenely behind them.

"No," Adam said.

"Yes," Maggie whispered.

"Adam," Lydia said gently, "it would seem the perfect solution."

Adam stared at his sister. "I cannot permit you to go off to God knows where, to remain for the rest of your life."

Lydia sighed. "Adam, my love, we both know I

have not found my proper place in this world. My recent actions have fairly guaranteed an acceptable offer of marriage will be not be forthcoming. Here my age is already a hindrance, but Maggie assures me," she said, her eyes twinkling at her brother, "in her time three and twenty is considered extremely young."

"No, Lydia." Adam shook his head firmly. "In her world you would be alone and helpless with no one to guide you, no one you could turn to."

"Yes, there is." Maggie spoke up thoughtfully. "There's my sister, Kiki. She could and would be more than happy to take Lydia in hand."

Adam frowned. "I daresay I am hard-pressed to trust my sister's fate to someone named Kiki."

"Her real name is Katherine," Maggie said. "Most people call her Kat. Better?"

"Hardly."

"My sister's a wonderful person, Adam. Kiki would take good care of Lydia." She caught Adam's gaze. "Especially if she knew I wasn't coming back."

"And what of you, Maggie?" Adam pulled her to him and searched her eyes. "You said if you had a choice, you would choose to stay with me. You appear to have it now. Will you give up all you know, all you have ever known? Your sister? Your comforts? Your history?"

Maggie stared up into his deep, smoldering eyes, eyes she could gaze at for the rest of her life and consider herself lucky. She nodded slowly. "In a flash, Coleridge."

He crushed her to his chest, and joy swept through her. A question sparked in her mind and she pulled back. "If I can." Maggie turned to the gnome still seated in the carriage. "Can I? Can I stay? Can Lydia take my place?"

The wizened old man seemed to consider the question. He studied each of them in turn, each waiting expectantly. "Gots to have me a fare."

Disappointment ripped through her. The gnome's bright blue eyes peeked out from his wrinkled face and caught her gaze. "But sometimes, miss, a fare is only one way."

The meaning of his words hit her and she reeled with the impact. "One way? You mean I'm not supposed to go back? I'm supposed to stay?" She glared in irritation. "Why didn't you tell me?"

Her driver shrugged his ancient shoulders. " 'Tweren't my place."

"It's settled then," Lydia said with satisfaction. "Shall we go?"

"I am still not certain . . ." A frown furrowed Adam's brow.

"Adam." Lydia laid a gentle hand on his arm. "I fear this is not your decision and I have made mine. Do not make this parting more difficult."

Adam pinned her with a steady stare, his words heavy with emotion. "You realize this is more than likely permanent. You shall never return." His dark eyes gleamed. "We shall never see one another again."

A wistful smile touched Lydia's lips. "I know."

For a long moment, sister and brother gazed quietly at each other, one with the sorrow of a final good-bye, the other with the barely suppressed anticipation of a new life.

"Okay," Maggie interrupted, "I hate to break this up but if you're going to take off we've got to get going." Her mind raced. "I have to write you a note for my sister to explain all this. She's never going to believe it. There has to be something to convince her." She snapped her fingers. "Adam, is there a Bank of England yet?"

"Most certainly," he responded in a somewhat haughty tone.

"Don't be such a snob," she said, "not now. We can set up an account for Lydia and Kiki; that will take care of money. I can put my things, things Kiki will recognize, in a safety-deposit box or something. If we're right, you'll be getting back on the same day I left. And here." She pulled off one of her filigree earrings. "These are one of a kind. Kiki had them made for me, so she'll recognize them. I'll give the other to the bank to use for identification."

Maggie rummaged in her purse and pulled out her sketch pad and a pen. Quickly she scribbled a note to her sister, folded it, and handed it to Lydia. She pawed through her purse again, this time coming up with her hotel key and a fistful of pound notes.

"Here's the key to our hotel room. The address is on the key chain here. And you'll need this money for a cab to get there." Maggie grimaced with concern. "I just wish I could be sure you'll get there okay."

"Beggin' your pardon, miss," the gnome interrupted. "She'll be just fine. I ain't never lost a fare yet." Maggie wasn't sure why, but a profound sense that everything would indeed be all right flooded through her at his words. Lydia would be well taken care of.

"What about my clothes?" Lydia frowned, glancing down at her lovely rose-colored gown. "Won't I look extremely odd in your time?"

Maggie laughed. "Lydia, trust me. In London in the 1990s nothing is extremely odd. Wait, one more thing." Again Maggie dove into the bottomless purse and pulled out her camera. "Give this to Kiki and tell her to have the pictures developed right away. It might just be the one thing that really convinces her."

Maggie glanced from Lydia to Adam and back again. This might not be the perfect, totally correct choice, but it seemed more right than anything ever had in her life.

"Time's awasting, miss." The gnome's voice signaled their time was indeed up.

Maggie and Lydia embraced. Maggie whispered into her ear, "Tell Kiki not to worry. Tell her I'm happy and I've found what I was looking for." She pulled back and her gaze met Lydia's. "And thank you."

"No." Lydia laughed lightly, her gaze still linked with Maggie's. "Thank you."

The women broke apart and Lydia turned to Adam. He pulled her into his arms. "Take care, little sister. I will miss your laugh and your extravagances and your exasperating adventures. I am still not fully convinced of this."

"My dear, darling brother, of course you aren't. You have spent far too long looking after me." She drew back and excitement sparkled in her eyes.

356

"Don't you see how right this is? I want so much more than I can ever have here. Since I first met Maggie I have suspected her world was much more suited to me than my own. Much more forgiving." She grinned. "This will be the adventure of, well, a lifetime."

She kissed him lightly, squeezed his hand, and turned to the carriage. "Sir, if you will?" Lydia presented her hand to the gnome. He helped her into the carriage and took his place on the seat in front. Lydia twisted around and waved gaily, then eagerly settled in. The carriage slowly moved off.

Adam wrapped his arms around Maggie and they watched the retreating carriage.

"Will she be all right, do you think?" A worried note sounded in Adam's voice.

Maggie snuggled deeper in his arms. "Oh, I think she'll do just fine. It's the twentieth century that needs to worry."

"And what of you?" He nuzzled her ear. "Are you happy with your choice?"

She sighed and leaned her head back against his chest, her gaze never leaving the carriage. All she would never see or do again flashed through her mind. She would miss her sister fiercely, but Kiki would understand.

Her commitment was to more than just Adam. She was now a permanent part of his time. A time that had always been remote and unreal for her. A time she'd never given much thought to. A time she would spend the rest of her life in. Maggie would now have to at least try to become a proper nineteenth-century woman, with all the annoying restrictions that entailed. There was time enough for that. There was all the time in the world.

It was a trade-off. She wasn't giving up so very much compared to all she was getting. A chance to live a new life by the side of the man she loved. The man who loved her. Was she happy with her choice? She murmured quietly, "Ask me again in about thirty years."

Adam chuckled softly. He and Maggie stood watch until the carriage disappeared into the mist and the future. Together they turned and stepped into a future of their own.

Epilogue

May 13, 1995

Kiki Masterson sat in a small, private room at the
Bank of England staring at an old-fashioned trunk
and a large, flat parcel wrapped in brown paper. She
clutched an envelope of freshly developed photos.
Kiki had toyed with the idea of developing them herself but she was almost afraid to look. She'd been in
a state somewhere between disbelief, curiosity, and
sheer panic ever since that ditzy blonde had shown
up at her hotel room last night.

The blonde said her name was Lydia Coleridge,
and carried a note from Maggie, one of Maggie's favorite earrings, and her camera. The message was
short, to the point, and made no sense at all. It simply told her to present the earring at the Bank of
England with identification. It asked her to take care
of Lydia and not to panic and call the police. The

note closed by saying Maggie loved her and hoped one day she'd understand. Kiki prided herself on being a calm and rational person who took life's unexpected turns in stride. She could handle anything.

Except, perhaps, this.

She'd questioned Lydia most of the night and the story the young woman told was unbelievable. Kiki would not have bought it at all except for a couple of odd things that didn't add up. Lydia was either the best actress ever or had lived all her life in some remote, uncivilized part of the world, or . . . in another time. She was genuinely fascinated with literally everything from the light switches to the television to virtually every item in the bathroom. And her English was far too perfect, far too pure. Classic.

Lydia's clothes were hand-sewn and she needed help getting in and out of them. They were possibly the best historical reproductions Kat had ever seen or . . .

They were real.

And Lydia had called her Kiki in a completely natural manner. Almost as if Lydia had spent a great deal of time with someone who talked about her a lot. On her passport, her name was Katherine. Professionally she was Kat. Only one person in her life ever called her Kiki.

Maggie.

Kiki would have dismissed it all as some kind of con, would have called the police but for an instinctive gut feeling. A feeling that had saved her life more than once. A feeling that, as weird as it sounded, told her the blonde was indeed telling the truth.

The evidence mounted. Kiki brought the earring

to the bank and learned there really was an account in her name. The bank referred to it as a legacy and the bank officer who explained said there was a single stipulation. She was to administer the account but it was to be shared with one Lydia Coleridge. The account was opened approximately 176 years ago. With interest and compound interest and specific, confidential instructions for investments it amounted to what the bank officer said with no little pride could be considered one of the largest private fortunes in the country, perhaps even in the world.

Kat knew the answers to all of her questions were probably in that trunk. Still, she hesitated. What if it was true? What if it wasn't? Maggie could still be in trouble. Kat set the packet of pictures aside and took a deep breath. Standing, she leaned over the chest and with a determined tug, yanked on the lid. It stuck for a moment, then gave way with a moan.

Kat peered inside. Most of it was filled with antique leather-bound books. Packed in one corner she found her sister's oversize, leather purse. Kat would have known it anywhere. She carefully pulled it from the trunk, the leather now cracked and weathered with age. Inside, Kat discovered Maggie's wallet and gently opened it. It creaked with the movement and Kat worked carefully, prying out credit cards and a driver's license. All the dates were current, all the cards curiously discolored. Old. Antique.

She pulled out the packet of pictures, drew a deep breath, and checked inside. These were the pictures Maggie had developed just two days ago, now yellowed and fragile, and Kat stared in fascination. She reached for two magazines still in the bag. Current issues of *Time* and *Cosmo* crumbled with age. Finally, she pulled out a digital watch and a plastic calculator, both in remarkably good condition although obviously old and worn.

Maggie must have simply used up the other things she typically kept in her purse, like pens and makeup. The thought nearly passed unchallenged, then hit Kat with an impact that left her breathless.

Oh, dear God, it's true!

Kat gripped the edge of the desk to support herself against the swirling maelstrom of emotion threatening to engulf her. Lydia. The account. The purse. It all added up. Her sister was really gone.

Dazed by the revelation, Kat stared into the trunk. Abrupt anger washed over her. She needed more than bits and pieces. She needed to talk to Maggie, needed to hear this from her. She reached for the closest book when her eyes caught sight of a folded paper that had slipped beneath the purse. With a trembling hand, Kat slowly pulled it toward her. She knew before she opened it that this was the message she hoped for. Kat unfolded the paper and read the faded words in her sister's familiar hand.

September 16, 1870

My dearest Kiki,

I can scarce believe it has been 52 years since I left your world, although, if all went well, I suspect for you it has been but a day. I have rewritten this particular letter every year. In this trunk, you will find my journals with the entries addressed to you. One for every day of my life. It was my only way of sharing those days, and my thoughts, with you.

Lydia has by now explained what happened, how I came to travel through time, and why I chose to stay. Please watch over her as you watched over me. Treat her as a sister. She will need you as I did. The accounts should enable you both to live free of financial concern.

We have prospered here as well, helped by the history lessons I fought so hard against as a student. I wish now I had paid more attention. My family accepts my unique ability to know what will happen before it does and, I say with satisfaction, I have used the knowledge wisely. Yet I do not feel I have tampered with history. Looking back, I firmly believe it was always my destiny to be here.

It is odd to think by the time you read this I will be long dead and buried. I see you in my mind as vividly as if I had never left. My beloved Adam died three months ago. He lived to be far older than most do in this day and age. I anticipate I will soon follow and the notion does not displease me. I do not fear death. Adam and I will be together again and this time nothing will tear us apart.

Do not grieve for me. I have led a wonderful life full of love and laughter and miracles. I made the right choice.

I have no regrets.

Your loving sister,
Maggie

Tears blurred Kat's eyes and she blindly groped for the envelope of pictures, spilling them on the table. She fanned the photos out and recognized scenes of London. But a different London. Somehow more sedate and gracious. She picked up a picture of a handsome blond man in a book-lined room. Adam. Then she spotted one of Maggie, apparently in the same room. Her eyes twinkled at the camera and the photographer and she seemed to be wearing some kind of robe. Kat laughed through her tears. Maggie would show them. She'd set Regency England on its ear.

Kat scooped the pictures up and set them aside, reaching now for the package. Her fingers shook slightly and she fumbled at the knot in the twine around the brown paper–wrapped parcel. She managed to get it untied and the paper fell away. Kat gasped in astonishment and delight. There were two paintings, back to back. The first was a portrait of four young children at play, three girls and a boy. It was clearly Maggie's work, free in spirit and slightly impressionistic. Their hair color varied from blond to dark red and Kat could clearly see glimpses of Maggie and the man in the picture in their faces. She choked at the recognition.

Maggie's children.

She propped the painting against the trunk and turned over the second. Her heart caught in her throat. It was of Maggie and the man she now realized was Adam. Maggie was a little older but beautiful, serene, obviously happy. Maggie did not paint this one and whoever the artist was had talent, managing to capture the love shared by these two people. It radiated in their eyes.

The second painting joined the first and Kat sank down in the chair at her back. Here was her proof, here were her answers, her sister's way of letting her know she was all right. Tears slipped down her cheeks. She would miss Maggie terribly even though it appeared Lydia would keep her more than busy in the sister department. She laughed out loud. Leave it to her sister to hand her a project like that.

Her gaze drifted back and forth between the happy couple in one painting and the laughing children in the other. It would be hard not to grieve but she had the paintings and the journals to keep her close to Maggie. A sense of calm and peace sifted through Kat. Her sister had finally stopped her drifting.

Finally found the place she belonged.

Finally found her happiness somewhere in yester-day . . . and forever.

Don't miss these tempestuous romances about modern-day heroines who journey to different eras to find the men who fulfill their hearts' desires.

Enchanted Time by Amy Elizabeth Saunders. With an antique store to run, Ivy Raymond is too busy to look at men from her own century. Then a kooky old lady sells her a book of spells, and before Ivy knows it, she is living in a castle with a handsome knight and ready to steal a love that is either treason or magic.

_52049-4 • $5.99 US/$7.99 CAN

A Tryst In Time by Eugenia Riley. Devastated by her brother's death in Vietnam, Sarah Jennings retreats to a crumbling Civil War plantation house, where a dark-eyed lover calls to her from across the years. Damien too has lost a brother to war—the War Between the States—yet in Sarah's embrace he finds a sweet ecstasy that makes life worth living. But if Sarah and Damien cannot unravel the secret of her mysterious arrival at Belle Fountaine, their brief tryst in time will end forever.

_52052-4 $5.50 US/$7.50 CAN

Dorchester Publishing Co., Inc.
65 Commerce Road
Stamford, CT 06902

Please add $1.75 for shipping and handling for the first book and $.50 for each book thereafter. NY, NYC, PA and CT residents, please add appropriate sales tax. No cash, stamps, or C.O.D.s. All orders shipped within 6 weeks via postal service book rate. Canadian orders require $2.00 extra postage and must be paid in U.S. dollars through a U.S. banking facility.

Name _____

Address _____

City _____ State _____ Zip _____

I have enclosed $_____ in payment for the checked book(s). Payment <u>must</u> accompany all orders.☐ Please send a free catalog.